CAPITAL GAMES

AUDACITY SAGA BOOK 2

R. K. THORNE

IRON ANTLER BOOKS

Edited by Elizabeth Nover, Razor Sharp Editing

Cover art by Julie Dillon

Cover design by R.K. Thorne

Version 1.2

❀ Created with Vellum

To my grama, for always supporting me, and for all the Columbo. Just one more thing…

PROLOGUE

LORD REGENT JUN IL LI straightened as the broad, white silk drapes parted, revealing his hosts. He had settled himself as comfortably as he could on one of the low white ottomans that surrounded a glass table laden with decadent-looking food, little of which he recognized. The older woman ushered in the younger, a kind and gentle hand guiding by the waist a blond girl in a stunning blue gown. The girl's eyes stared off as if into nothingness, as if she saw neither him nor the room. Nor any of it. She was perhaps eighteen or nineteen, but young by comparison.

"Dr. Arakovic," he said, standing. Standing was not strictly necessary, as his rank was far above a civilian, but she had been an excellent client for his labs. And hopefully would continue to be.

"Welcome, honored Lord Regent," the woman said smoothly. She guided the girl to another ottoman, where the shining gown flowed gracefully around her as she sat, like a fairy settling down on a cloud. "We're so happy to have you join us. Have you met my daughter Cassandra?"

"I have not." He bowed deeply to her, and the girl, still not looking at him or meeting his eyes, gave a muted bow of her own. Perhaps her mental faculties were not quite functional at the moment. "A pleasure to meet you, Cassandra. Unless she is a doctor like yourself?" He smiled warmly.

Arakovic smiled warmly back. "No. Her pursuits have always been of a more… interpersonal than scientific nature."

The doctor gestured for him to sit, and the two of them sank to the ottomans in near unison, the doctor beside her daughter and Jun across from them. The daughter had a certain beauty and likely could have been a candidate for complete Enhancement had she so chosen. Or had she been selected. Hair color was easy to change. But she did not seem to have acquired these features from her mother, whose hair was tucked in a bun of silky auburn and whose eyes glittered with intelligence that somewhat made up for their flawed brown color. She was much too far from the standard template, and of course too old, but he was surprised that he found himself liking something about her that he couldn't quite name. Nearly treasonous, but it was what it was. He needn't speak of it to anyone.

He of all people would certainly never question the perfection of the template.

"This is a fine room," he said, rather than sharing any of these thoughts. "I didn't know this hotel had such pleasant arrangements. What brings you to Desori?"

Arakovic smoothed the soft grass green of her skirt with a palm. Surely she couldn't be nervous. He was a scientist of plenty renown, but she was at the very least his equal, and privately he thought her work to be far superior in many ways. If only she could be convinced to contribute to the template, to perfection, to Enhancement. But such efforts had been tried and failed long ago.

And of course, whatever renown *he* had achieved in the past was no longer relevant now. He'd been relegated to—of all things—a fate almost too awful to imagine.

A salesman.

"Well, you know there aren't many places one can pursue one's scientific interests without interference anymore." She shrugged. "And we've been reviewing the work of your labs. Excellent progress."

"I'm glad you are pleased. Do you think the research shall continue?"

"Yes, I think so. There are many variables I have yet to isolate. I—"

Even the mention of variables made his thoughts fuzz. Curse it all. Chaos would have been kinder than this embarrassment. "Sadly, Dr. Arakovic, I must admit I cannot contribute to your work, as my work —and my ability to do it—has been stolen from me."

Her brow furrowed. "By whom?"

"Of that, we are not sure, but we are doing our best to find out."

"What happened?"

"My personal lab on Helikai was attacked, and although I survived, my brain was permanently altered to avoid all thoughts of my former work. Or science at all. We have been working on a cure." Privately, he held no hope. His scientists Enhanced the human genome. They weren't practiced at examining injuries or flaws on this level.

And part of him also knew they were entirely unmotivated to do so. In secret, he had probably been deemed much too far from perfection now to be worthy of such resources. And he couldn't say he disagreed with that assessment.

"I'm so sorry to hear that," said Arakovic, folding her hands in her lap. Her nails were neat, trim, unpainted. "I don't know how I'd live without my work."

He didn't know how he would either. He didn't entirely intend to continue doing so. But he kept himself from saying that.

She reached down and picked up a delicate white cup. "Would you care for some tea? Sushi?"

"Certainly."

Arakovic poured three cups. She handed the first to him, took one for herself, and handed the third to her daughter. Strangely, the girl perked up at this. Until that point, she'd only stared out the wide windows at the skyscrapers. But now she took the tea, her eyes clearing.

She glanced at him for the first time, but the coldness, almost black in her eyes, made him catch his breath. Had they been so dark when she entered the room? He could have sworn they hadn't been.

Perhaps not a candidate for Enhancement after all.

The girl let out a nonsensical giggle.

"My dear Lord Regent. If you would do us the honors of starting the meal."

Arakovic held up a small plate of delicacies, including a small cookie, something pureed on a cracker with a vegetable-looking garnish, and a pat of rice with something like a white frill of tentacles on top of it. An octopus of sorts?

"Of course." An odd tradition, the starting of the meal, and he'd never lived in a culture that subscribed to it. But there was no reason not to oblige. He wouldn't be much of a salesman to offend over such a small matter.

He stared at the offerings. None looked appetizing. He ought to start with the riskiest first. He took the rice tentacle and in one fell swoop popped it in his mouth and bit down.

The tentacle moved.

He started, bumping the ottoman back a bit, then froze. How embarrassing. It surely must be his imagination. Only absolute barbarians ate *live* food—

It moved again.

The girl's black eyes were boring into him, and he met her gaze, almost involuntarily. She was grinning.

He screamed.

Or he tried to. He covered his mouth with his hand and tried to spit, wretched, gagged. But the tentacles seemed to be latching on. Expanding. His mouth filled with liquid. To his horror, black liquid dribbled from his mouth, across his robes, and onto the white, immaculately carpeted floor.

"What—what is the meaning of this?" he tried to say.

The words were unintelligible. Liquid, black as ink, dribbled everywhere. Perhaps it *was* ink.

Arakovic smiled now too. Calm. Unalarmed by his display. "The meaning for you, Lord Regent, is over. The meaning for *us* is just beginning."

He sputtered and tried yet again to spit out the vileness to no avail.

Again, again. He was retching, but nothing came out but darkness.

Without warning, the creature slithered down his throat like a mole digging a tunnel, and then the sensation was gone. He sat still, frozen, staring. Was it over? He clutched at his throat—or tried to. His arm didn't respond.

The girl's head tilted a little to one side.

Of its own volition, his head tilted with her.

Her head tilted the other way. To his horror, his own followed. She smiled brightly, the movement a touch mechanical. Like a doll trying to look happy.

"Good work, dear," said the doctor, patting her daughter on the shoulder.

"Where is the empress?" the girl said, directing her words at him.

Now she spoke? She had a sweet, girlish voice that didn't match her eyes; he imagined she could be very persuasive. What was happening? What girl or demon was this?

"My *name* is Cassandra." She pursed her lips. "Learn it. Or our use for you could very quickly run thin."

A chill ran through him. A Natural. She was a telepath, wasn't she? And Degora had always lectured him to take precautions...

"Tell us, dear Lord Regent," said Arakovic, her voice as polite and sweet as it had always been. "Before we grow bored. Where is the empress?"

Never. He wouldn't tell them anything. Couldn't.

"I-I can't tell you," he sputtered instead. He couldn't remember even thinking of speaking.

"You have her," said the girl—said Cassandra. A sudden savage rage bubbled underneath her words. "Where? Tell us."

"I don't have her." It came out entirely undignified—a plea, a cry, a wail. "I thought I was going to die."

"How did you lose her?" Arakovic's voice was harder now, the kind of voice he'd use on an idiot.

"In the raid. When I lost my work. When they damaged my brain."

"Who took it?"

"No one."

"He gave it to someone," Cassandra snapped.

"Tell us. Who did you give it to?"

He gritted his teeth. "A... a Theroki."

"His name. Now."

"I-I don't remember."

"Try harder, Lord Regent."

"I never used his name. I'm sorry, I—"

Cassandra's eyes narrowed. *Try harder, Lord Regent.* The words echoed viciously, sending shooting bursts of pain through his skull.

"I will—I will! Uh, it was something—something of the Faros cluster type. It was Tridelphi..."

"That's a rank, not a name."

"K! It was something starting with a *k*," he shouted, an unaccountably huge wave of relief flooding him.

"Hmm. I don't know if that's enough to let him live." Arakovic looked down at what had seemed her marionette a bare few minutes ago. "What do you think, Cassandra?"

"We need a name. A full name," Cassandra said coldly. "And you'll find who's the marionette in this show soon enough."

He dredged every memory, his brow furrowed. Sweat beaded across it, and his body shook. Then at last the memory sprang forward, clear as crystal, and he shouted it out, relief sweeping his lungs with the words.

"Sidassian! Kael Sidassian!"

CHAPTER ONE

ELLEN DUCKED down into a crouch behind the shipping crate as laser fire slammed the cliffside above her. Melting bits of stone rained down.

She let her back fall against the crate's metal casing, still crouched. The crate would have been hot, even blazing in the noonday twin suns, if not for her armor. Instead, she had the familiar smell of battle —clear, filtered, and exactly sixty-eight degrees.

Smoke from a destroyed pirate's lander wafted past her visor and obscured her view for a moment. The display still showed three hostiles highlighted and waiting behind her, their red-gold squiggles swimming at the edges. It also showed Levereaux and Zhia and the others glowing aqua at her sides. The display was a new invention of Xi's to try. So far it had only made Ellen dizzy twice.

They hadn't counted on a serious altercation on this mission, or she wouldn't have had the new mode on. It was just a supply drop-off. A quick drug donation to a fairly well-staffed but under-supplied state hospital had seemed so—

Laser fire sliced at a bizarre angle into the rock before her. "Hey! Whatcha, scared?" a pirate shouted from behind a rotted-out shed, another burning lander parked beside it. "Come out, come out, wherever you are!"

Two targets down, three to go. Especially that one.

She shifted forward onto the balls of her feet and twisted back toward the enemy, preparing to reengage.

"Howdy, Commander." Simmons's voice suddenly cut in over the comm.

She stilled, brushed some of the dust from her visor. "Little busy here, Doug."

"Too busy for details on your next mission?"

She rolled her eyes, raising her head just enough to get a look at their attackers. "I haven't even finished *this* one yet."

A combination of pirate laser and ballistic fire peppered the crates, as if to reinforce her point.

"I thought you were just delivering medical supplies," he shouted over the din.

"Medical supplies—a.k.a. drugs!" Levereaux shouted beside her. Ah, apparently the doctors were on the line as well. Ellen ignored the two of them and lined up her next shot.

"A.k.a. chems. A.k.a. things people like to steal, Doug," Ellen muttered. "I know this may come as news to you, but painkillers can be used for recreational purposes." Wait for it…

"Oh, okay—I mean I patched through ten different star systems to get this connection, but I can just try again tomorrow—"

Boom. Her ballistic hit one pirate in the eye. He crumpled.

"Fine, fine. Shoot." She needed a fresh ballistic magazine anyway.

"Literally or figuratively?"

She could hear the silly grin on his face as she ducked back down. "Don't test me, Simmons. As if you've ever held a gun." She smacked the magazine in and locked it. Battery was getting low too.

"Do water guns count?"

"I'm giving you ten seconds to get to the point." She rose carefully and lined up her next shot.

"All right, all right. I'll give you a hint—"

Boom. Another pirate went down.

"Ten. Nine. Eight—" She took a quick breather, twisting to a seat as she checked the status of Levereaux and the others.

"Josana's gonna like it."

"Oh, no," Levereaux groaned.

"Oh, hell," muttered Dremer, back on the ship.

"Not Capital. Really, Doug?" Ellen turned back, rose to a crouch, and aimed with fresh malice.

"You guessed it! You ladies are good. I need you to get there pronto."

Boom. Another down.

Three down to her, Nova had taken another two, and Zhia had gotten the far one in heavy cover. Looked all clear.

"Zhia—give me a readout. Any remaining hostiles? Our patron has me a little… distracted."

Doug snickered. "Oh, I think it takes a lot more than my mumbling to distract you. But I'm sending more mission details to your desk. You can think of it as a little vacation! I know the last few missions have been hard on you all."

"A vacation, huh? Yeah, right." Ellen sighed. "Well, at least maybe the little minx will cause less trouble on her own, bigger hunting grounds."

Levereaux shook her head. "Not likely. We'll be lucky if she only gets into trouble we don't have to deal with."

"You read my mind," said Ellen.

Zhia cleared her throat. "All clear, Commander."

Ellen nodded. "Let's get these supplies to the hospital. Search these hostiles for idents and affiliation. Kael and the others have to be waiting for us already, so get moving. Talk to you back on the ship, Doug."

She straightened cautiously, scanning the gory scene. Could never be too careful. Computers and sensors were great. Then other computers learned how to outsmart them over time. The cycle continued.

"Cheerio, Commander! Or what is it that you all say?"

She frowned. "I have no idea what you're talking about."

"I know! It's roger, right?"

Suddenly Jenny's voice cut into their line, sending Ellen's adrenaline pumping. That only happened on the urgent channel. "Team A, we're taking heavy artillery fire here at the hospital. Estimate three, maybe four heavy guns. Mortars, maybe? They ain't fancy, but they still hurt. Front entrance is buried. We have one injury, requesting urgent backup."

Simmons swore. "I'll go. Roger, over and out."

"On our way, Jenny," Ellen said, her heart pounding as she lurched toward their flyers to get them restarted. There was only one reason Jenny would be comming and not Kael. "What's the status on the injury?"

"I'm stabilizing him, and I'll be able to do it better and faster when you're here and I'm off the line."

She shoved down her irritation. "You're in a hospital. Make use of it."

"I'd call it that in name only, ma'am."

She sighed as she hit the lander into gear, leaving Zhia to finish the ident checks.

Xi painted three mortars on the helmet overlay. "I cannot locate a fourth target, Commander. They are unfortified from your direction." A small inlay photo jumped up—a shot of two of the guns from Mo's top of ship surveillance.

"Mo—take target one."

"Got it, Commander."

She set the flyer to auto, which was risky since it didn't have road maps to follow here. She just aimed it for the grid of the second gun and crossed her fingers. Because she was busy configuring the multi's laser for range, standing, and aiming it over the windshield. They didn't have enclosed flyers—or fully automatic ones—for just this purpose.

Between her and Mo, they had exceptional aim, and the second group of pirates or whoever they were went down without any further fight. But the damage had been done.

The hospital looked like all hell had broken loose. Ellen's heart sank. How had these assholes gotten word that a new shipment was coming in? Had the only thing protecting this hospital been its poverty?

She groaned inwardly as she leapt out of the flyer. A man in a doctor's white coat, two Teredarks, and six Ursas in similar white coats were emerging from the hospital, headed toward the rubble.

The Teredark stopped, bent its head slightly in her direction, then clicked some at the man. The Ursas were shaking their furry heads. The man clicked back once or twice in the pale human imitation of Teredark native. The Teredark—who seemed to be the leader—made a dismissive gesture in Ellen's direction and slithered toward the rocks.

The man approached her, his face pained but not with hurt or sympathy. More like anger. "He says to you people to leave from this place. Your medicine is not worth the cost."

"They're free," Ellen grunted, even though she knew what he meant.

"No. They are not." Pressing his lips together and raising his chin, the man turned and followed the others toward the rubble.

"Jenny, Kael, do you read? We've cleared out the artillery, and—"

She stopped short when Kael appeared, leaning heavily on Jenny with one arm around her and the other around Merith. Something about the sight made her blood run cold.

"We read you, Commander," Kael said. "Thanks for the pest control."

"Yeah, Xi patched us in on Mo's cam," Jenny said.

"That was kicking," Kael agreed.

"She is a master," Ellen said, relief easing into her veins. It was really just one bit of bad damage to the knee and thigh of the armor. Nothing an armor case and a lot of skin glue couldn't fix, from the look of it.

"Pretty sure he meant you, Commander. Mo's too efficient. We never get in in time to see her come to the rescue."

Ellen didn't know what to say to that. She slapped the crate behind her instead. "Get the pirate in the flyer and then you two help me unload this stuff. They said they want us out of here."

"Really?" Jenny grunted.

"In not so many words."

"I will insist again that I am not nor was I ever a pirate," Kael grumbled as they let go of him next to the flyer. He thunked down without much ceremony and a clank loud enough to make several Ursas flinch.

"You've only got one leg right now, don't you?" Ellen shot back, smiling to herself.

Jenny snickered. "I'm all out of wooden pegs, so I guess I'll just have to heal him."

———

KAEL SLAMMED the lid shut on his armor case. The nanos and the case went to work on their repairs with a little hum and a whirr. They'd have a little more work to do than normal this time. He ran his fingers over the cool, shining, gray steel shell for just a moment. Two months in, not having to pull out his repair kit after every single mission still felt like a massive luxury.

He rose and limped over to the desk. *His* desk, although he was still getting used to the idea. All this space after a decade of life hot bunking in Theroki filth... well, it was one of many things that was taking some getting used to. Also the easy accessibility of skin glue, nanos, and a brace that would have him healed up before the day was over.

Cabin 6A looked largely unchanged from two months before. The vid screen on the wall held a changing montage of nature videos that Dr. Taylor had said would help with stabilizing some of his biochemical processes. The new chip no longer messed with him directly, and Dremer had declared his prefrontal cortex "mostly fine" and "perfectly adequate," whatever that meant. Eventually, his body would get the message, but it would take time and practice as his brain had had years of training in letting acid build and build in his veins. Metaphorically speaking. And, of course, the nature videos couldn't hurt. Unless they drove him crazy. But unlike Taylor's meditation exercises, the bird-filled forest and the wind over the sand dunes actually did make him feel better.

Right now, a small tropical waterfall trickled over shining black stones. That, combined with the exertion of the hospital delivery mission, left him with a calm, mellow buzz. His team had had plenty of cleanup work to do, scaring away bandits near the hospital before Ellen and Zhia ever got there.

The holodisplay on the desk patiently pulsed amber with a message from Doug. He tapped the base, and the holo sprang to life.

About time. The final details of his new identity danced before him. He read it over quickly. Still born on Faros IV, in a similar but different region; that seemed smart. His new persona hadn't ever been a Theroki though. He'd worked security on the water farms prevalent in the Ramadd region for two decades before taking to the stars. A simple life, now with a little more adventure.

Guess he had better read up on water farms.

His eyes flicked over the new name Doug had assigned, and he chuckled. He sent a quick reply back. *Kael... Asidian? Very creative, Doug.*

Doug must have been working at the same time, wherever he was, because it was barely five minutes before he replied. *What? I like the sound of it. Unless you have a better suggestion... ?*

Kael shook his head. He did not. That was why he'd been glad to let Doug pick. That didn't mean he wasn't going to tease the man over it. He answered one more time before shutting down the holo screen. *Not everyone can have a name as versatile and impressive as Douglas Oliver Simmons. It'll do.*

He hit the shower and retired to his room with water, a stolen meat-stuffed pita, and a handful of dried figs, waving off an invitation to join Nova and Fern at the mess table. It wasn't really stolen, of course, but it still sort of felt that way. Taylor had said to give it time.

The meat and figs were insanely delicious. While he'd only run into the gifted Amaya actually cooking one time, he'd been sure to thank her profusely and wasn't surprised to find she'd hailed from Faros VII.

Picked up as part of the same passenger program that had drawn him in.

He hadn't run into her beyond that one time. She was somewhat reclusive, cooking in large batches at odd hours, but then again so was he. Being part of the crew hadn't drawn him out much more over the last few weeks than it had when he'd been trying to keep his Theroki head low and out of trouble. He wasn't entirely sure why he was keeping to himself. Perhaps it was the same reason—this was a good gig, and he didn't need trouble. Maybe old habits died hard. Maybe he was just too tired; they worked hard.

Maybe it was Ellen.

He wasn't avoiding her exactly. But he might have more interaction with Simmons than half the crew, although he and Nova had—cautiously and with Zhia's somewhat absent supervision—taken to sparring regularly at least three times a week. One way to get over someone trying to kill you was to fight them again, he supposed. And again and again. And every fight where he didn't utterly lose it reinforced for him that things had really changed. They were really different. There was no oath programming, no bloodlust. None artificially manufactured by a microchip, anyway.

He had really done it. Escaped.

Hard to believe, but they'd done the impossible.

One thing hadn't changed though. Ellen was still his commanding officer, and nothing more.

He alternated between spending the day trying to accept that and plotting wild ways to change her mind. He regretted both sorts of days.

He didn't act on any of it. He'd made his thoughts on the matter known. She could come to him if she changed her mind.

She hadn't.

And it hurt like hell. He'd been right to think that working with her would be torture. But all in all, he came out ahead. Pain, but also purpose. He owed them every freedom he had. The least he could do was carry a rifle and obey orders. While he got paid for it, no less.

Finishing his dinner, he flopped down on the bunk and watched the wall display shift from prairie grass waving in the wind to a sunset over the ocean. He sucked in a big breath and exhaled it out slowly. That one was his favorite.

He wasn't happy. But this was as close as he'd maybe ever been.

After a while, he started to feel that itch of being watched. He'd shut his eyes, listening to the waves and thinking. Without looking up at the maintenance crawl space above him, he smiled.

"Isa. Cut it out. Don't you have something better to do?"

"But you're so relaxed," she said shamelessly from the ceiling—her observation superhighway. They were all creatures in a human zoo for her to study. He wasn't clear on exactly how many of them knew it. "It's so calming, even when it hurts."

She knew of his struggles to come to terms with everything, of course. He hadn't much tried to hide them, and Ellen was too often in his thoughts to conceal anything anyway. "Humans are complicated, kiddo. But you can get calm watching these too. Just try it."

"I don't feel calm. I feel bored. And antsy. I tried."

"Ah. Maybe you should try meditation then."

She snickered. Every time *he* tried meditation, he ended up throwing something. Once he'd hit one of Xi's cleaning bots, and Xi had made him repair it even though he knew she could do it herself. Faster.

"That was funny," Isa agreed. "You didn't have to repair it."

"If you are speaking of the damage to my robots," Xi put in, "the work was easy for Kael. There's no need to worry on his behalf."

His turn to snicker. "I think Xi just wanted the company."

"I have the constant company of the whole crew," Xi said placidly. "I do not need to manufacture tasks to interact with humans. And the two of you should be preparing for your sleep cycles. Especially you, Ms. Isa."

"Don't tell her, Xi—just one more minute." Isa shifted in the tiny metal tube above his cabin. "Her" being Bri, her mother, of course.

"Sixty seconds, and no more."

They all lapsed into silence. Hmm. Perhaps he didn't *need* to leave his cabin to have a conversation or two.

"If it wasn't for the company, then why'd you make me do it?" he asked.

"I believe you would call it... a challenge."

"A challenge?"

"A challenge to myself. I wanted to see if you would do it if I prodded. I won two credits from Nova."

He snorted. Well, he had. Mission accomplished, Xi. "You bet on me? Don't spend that all in one place, lady." He had long ago given up resisting anthropomorphizing her.

"I have not done so. Since I have no corporeal needs, I cannot decide what to spend it on. And indeed I am not a human entity or citizen of any country, nor do I have a bank account to hold the credits. One of my robots is holding the hard currency for me while I decide."

"I'm sure you'll figure it out." Or start asking him for suggestions. He had better get thinking. Was there *anything* you could buy with only two credits?

"Sixty seconds have elapsed."

"Good night, Kael," Isa said placidly. The sound of her shifting away up the crawl space was almost imperceptible.

"Good night, Isa. Good night, Xi."

Xi lowered the lights and dimmed the wall display, and he shut his eyes.

———

BEFORE ELLEN HAD EVEN FINISHED STOWING her armor, Simmons's face popped up on the holodisplay above her desk, and he'd launched into the details. His mug was emblazoned with a cartoon cat wearing a grass skirt today, and he shrugged as he took a sip of coffee. "Anyway, it's not as bad as it sounds. Should be nice and easy. Not filled with—whatever it was you encountered on those last few missions. Aliens? Mutants? The white spider tentacle monsters."

She, too, shrugged from her spot kneeling on the floor as she checked that her shoulder pauldron was fitted correctly into its repair case. They hadn't gotten adequate samples to figure out what the monsters were. Far from her only regret from those missions.

"Well, anyway. I doubt they're on Capital." He adjusted his wire-rimmed glasses.

"Is that a promise?" She hammered the bicep piece home harder than she needed to. The suit could do this all automatically, but she preferred reviewing each piece herself.

"Uh… no. But from an after-action perspective, you have to admit the telepaths were a big problem."

She pursed her lips as she moved to check the top femoral plate. "True. So. What can we do about it? Train Isa to fight them? She's too young, Doug."

"I found something better. Although we should consider training Isa too."

She stopped and leveled a glare at him. "She's fourteen."

He held up his palms. "For her own protection! You really think ferrying her around the galaxy into active war zones is conducive to her safety? What if one of those things had somehow followed you back to the ship? You wouldn't have been the only one at risk, I think."

"I'm not a telepath."

"Tell that to the monster-aliens. I saw the recordings."

Good thing he couldn't see inside her head too. She just pressed her lips together and focused on the shin plate. But he was right. Those creatures *had* talked to her, and Isa *would* be safer with training. Finding someone to teach her while they spun around the galaxy would be nigh on impossible, though.

Doug's spoon tinkled in his mug as he stirred. "So this ties right back to the mission. A friend of a friend on Capital is doing some cutting-edge research into telepathic blocking. But she's run into some kind of personal issues. I don't know the details, but we all think she'd be a good candidate to bring into a cell, particularly on your ship. Obviously she's a she, so nothing to worry about there. And if we can help her with whatever her predicament is, we'll do some good too." He grinned and rubbed his hands together in front of his face.

She lifted an eyebrow. "You don't know what her problem is?"

"No. She's afraid to discuss it. Although I'd guess it has to do with getting access to her research."

"And all we have to do is get her to give up her whole life and join us on an unknown, anonymous spaceship, huh? That should be easy." She narrowed her eyes at him.

He grinned behind another sip of coffee, the spoon still in the cat mug poking him in the cheek. "Especially with your natural charisma."

She snorted. "Does she know anything about the Foundation?"

"Yes! So you have that going for you. She's working in a facility we fund. So you can bring her tools and equipment along, no need to replace it or really upset her work."

"Aside from taking it off planet and into space? And dragging it all over hell and back? I doubt that will be... calming."

"Well, with what I know of her work, she can do it anywhere. But you'll have to see what she thinks of the idea."

"All right. Don't forget, I still need that intel officer too."

"I know, I'm working on it."

"Are we planning to take everyone on your little voyage into city life?" Ugh. She always felt so out of place on these inner worlds. Few of them were like where she'd grown up in the SHR. Many of the worlds in the Pacific Alliance Systems had maintained cultural identities connected to their mother nations on Earth, the Saeloun Hanguk Region included although the Union influence had been strong in the last few decades. But very few inner worlds bore any resemblance at all to the cultures that had founded them.

Even fewer resembled the insides of battleships. And that was the real problem, wasn't it? Her home planet was a montage of Union ships and military bases.

Doug's shrug brought her back to the present moment. "Look over the rest of the mission details and see what you think. We're going to need people that are good, in armor but also without. You may not be able to wear armor everywhere you'll need to go to convince this woman."

"And what part of Capital are we touching down on?"

"Appellate 481. To Josana's great luck. Your target's name is Dr. Chayana Persad."

Ellen took a deep breath, surveying her armor. She almost wished she weren't done stowing it away. She much preferred that to facing down Simmons at the moment—or the next topic she needed to bring up.

She was too tired for this.

But she steeled herself to keep going anyway. "What about Arakovic? Did you find anything in the lab files?" For the better part of two months, Simmons had been digging through the data they'd stolen from Vala's lab connection after rescuing Kael.

"Yes—and no. We were logged in past one layer of security, so we got some information for free, but there's a lot more security levels further down. Tough stuff. I've cracked some but not all. But I did find that she had a formal connection to the Enhancer labs we hit."

"Formal? You mean, she didn't just infiltrate them?"

"Nope. She's not their enemy. She's their *client*."

"Their client?" Ellen thumped the armor case shut and snapped its tabs. "I didn't think the Enhancers took on clients."

"They don't like to advertise it. And they're very selective. They only offer their services to like-minded souls. We think it may be a means of recruiting new scientists, if they can convert them fully to their ideology. Beyond that, the Union and the Puritans are both putting the squeeze on the Enhancers pretty heavily. Someone's gotta bankroll their creepy experiments." He grinned and shrugged boyishly. "Especially with a piece of prized research vanished into the ether. That can't be helping matters."

Ellen scowled, thinking of the fetus now floating in an orb of green goo in their lab downstairs. The Enhancers' empress, now in Foundation hands.

Audacity's hands.

"She's not research. She's a person. Or she's going to be a person. I think."

He nodded solemnly. "Which is why it's good that we've got her and not them. I also hope to find more about… what she is, for lack of a better phrase, in their files."

"Back to Arakovic."

"Right. I've established she had them doing work for her. It doesn't take a genius to guess that it was related to the aliens-monsters-animals-whatevers you encountered. But I haven't been able to crack the security around the deeper files yet."

"I'm shocked."

"Arakovic clearly means business, and the Enhancers have never been stingy on security around their research files. If we hadn't infiltrated them with so many nukes on other systems, I wouldn't even be this far. Fortunately, they're not half as good at physical security."

"So you're still working on it?"

"Computers are chugging away. Some things just take time." But he didn't look happy about it.

"Does this have anything to do with this Persad or Capital?"

"I suspect Arakovic may be connected to the blackmail, or whatever her problem is, but with so few details, that's real conjecture. But I have a hunch. This trouble smells like her."

"Why do you say that?"

He shrugged. "Well, what is Arakovic's goal? What's the goal of her research?"

Ellen frowned. "I'm not sure I want to think about that."

"You better."

She ducked her head, knowing he was right. Know thy enemy as one would know thyself. Or better. "Well, it's something to do with telepathy add-ons. But not normal telepathy. The Songbird project connected multiple minds. Blurred people. Maybe with the goal of making them connected permanently?"

"And the Starbird project also essentially connected minds to other minds—or at least the written works of other minds in the network. It connected living minds to the vast information stores of both the living and the dead."

Ellen rose from the floor and strode to her chair, hardly paying attention to what she was doing as she sank into the soft cushion of the bolted seat. "What is she building—a hive mind? Why would anyone want that?"

"I haven't exactly found her diary. But if a certain scientist had drugs that could neutralize the power of telepaths... or something like that... that certainly seems like an opposing vector of research to me."

She rubbed her chin. "It would—could, at least—make this Persad very dangerous to Arakovic's plans. Whatever they are."

"Again, it's a hunch. Maybe Arakovic just wants to pursue knowledge, understand telepathy in a certain context. Then Persad wouldn't be in her way."

"Maybe." Ellen scowled.

"I know. It just doesn't feel right. I think Arakovic has her finger in this pie. The question is where and how—and why."

She nodded. "We'll do our best to find out."

"One more thing. While I was poking around in the Theroki databases on Kael's behalf, I found they've got Arakovic in there. Recently added in the last two weeks. After Kael joined us."

She sat forward. "Really?"

"Yep. Listed as *persona non grata*."

"What?"

"Someone to shoot on sight. Apparently they don't know about the Enhancer connection, cause they're still staffing half the labs she's hired out. But at some point she hired a ship of theirs for some kind of outsystem mission."

"And?"

"And the entire vessel and its men never came back."

She pursed her lips, tapping her fingers on the desk. "Outsystem, huh? Is that a clue, or just random?"

"No other outsystem connections yet. But we'll see."

"Just what is she up to, Simmons?"

"Doug."

"Whatever. So many Theroki. They'd come complete with ports, upgrades, and defiance repression built in, you know. How does that fit in? Enhancer labs? Kidnapping kids in gangs? Starved telepaths? Whatever those... things were?"

"I don't know. I don't know."

Unfortunately, she was starting to have a feeling that she did.

———

SICK BAY WAS NEARLY SILENT, or at least so Ellen thought at first. As she stood and gazed at the little fetus hovering in the glowing purple goo, sounds started to prick at her ears. The whirring of soft, cold fans, nearly silent beeps along with one flashing green light—the heartbeat? —the occasional liquid splash.

How strange that that little metal cylinder had turned into this. How strange that this purple mass of an artificial uterus and fetus would turn into a person eventually. Right now it looked more like a mutant shrimp.

And how strange that this capsule-shrimp-human had been the catalyst, the cause that would bring Kael into her path and change her life forever.

Of course, externally it hadn't changed much at all, except that she had one more, very reliable lieutenant.

Internally, well… she'd never been so frustrated with herself.

She'd made a real mess of things. And for a supposed genius, she was having a hard time finding a way to fix them.

She'd had two months of Kael on her team, a few cabins away most hours, and she hadn't figured out one damn thing. She'd spent some days puzzling through a solution and others grinding her teeth at fate. A part of her still felt the risk was too great. If it came down to it and lives were on the line, what if she played favorites? How could she ever forgive herself if she did? Worse, how would she live with herself if she *didn't*?

The other half of her, perhaps the more practical half, had to admit that it was already too late. Whether Kael knew her feelings and regrets or not, they were still in there, guiding her attention, twisting at her gut. They would already influence her choice, whether she liked it or not.

This was the part of her that had sprung to life as he'd led Jenny and Merith up the ramp to the ship after that last disappointing mission. Things had gone all fubar, and he'd still acted like he was on a pleasure cruise. Eh, for him, perhaps he was. He'd limped past her with that usual glint in his dark eyes and that smile that seemed just for her, and she'd just nodded back and felt like a fool.

She had so much more to say than a nod but no words for any of it. Turned out growing up in the military didn't teach you how to talk about your feelings.

More and more, she'd found herself here in this sick bay, back at the start. Staring at this creature. Trying to figure out how to untangle everything.

A snick announced the opening of the sick-bay hatch. Light footsteps approached behind her.

"Beautiful, isn't it?" Dremer stepped up to Ellen's side. Lavender light played across the lines of her skin. Dremer might love cybernetics, but she was no Enhancer, and her skin showed the delicate beauty of age.

Ellen could only nod and turn her eyes back to the child. The girl.

"Hard to believe she's supposedly an empress, eh?" Dremer checked over a readout on the machine before them.

"Yes."

"Not an empress of much. They've got fewer Enhancer outposts all the time. But still. Why would someone want an infant—less than an infant—as their ruler?"

"Who recruits children to play war games?" Ellen twisted her lips. "Genetic perfection—or genius—above all?"

"Hmm. Perhaps."

"Children are more easily molded and manipulated?"

"More likely. I wonder what powers they've given her." Dremer leaned both hands against the railing around the chamber, her face thoughtful. "Do you ever think about having children, Commander?" Dremer said softly.

"I think that'd be putting the ship after the rocket. I can't even figure out how to talk to—" Ellen stopped short.

Dremer's eyes lit up with sparkling laughter. "I meant in the general sense rather than the specific, but you know, if you'd like to discuss that too…"

"I'd rather not."

"Well if the time ever comes…"

"Do *you* ever think about having them?" There, let her answer the tough question first.

Dremer smiled, to her surprise. "I did, once. Back at university, there was a fellow I was taken with for quite a while."

"What happened?"

"Bastard turned out to be a Puritan at heart."

Ellen snorted. "Ain't that how it always is."

Dremer raised an eyebrow. "They all turn out to be Puritans?"

"They turn out to be… not what you need."

"Oh, I don't know." Dremer straightened, folding her arms across her chest as she leaned back. "Most of us don't know what we need, especially not at the time. I do have a few eggs frozen, tucked away."

Ellen pursed her lips. "Is that regret I hear?"

Dremer's smile was only in one corner of her mouth now. "Perhaps not regret. I couldn't have done anything differently than I did. I'm a lover of cybernetics. It's my work, my passion, my everything. But if I knew then what I knew now…" She shrugged. "Maybe we weren't as incompatible as it seemed. But quit dodging the question. Your turn."

"I'm still a kid myself."

Dremer let out a bark of laughter. "Says the highly decorated war veteran in command of over twenty soldiers and civilians and her own ship. And this is hardly your first rodeo. You weren't even a kid when I first met you."

Ellen waved her hand. "Well, thank you. But you know I was."

"If childhood is about innocence, I'm not sure you ever had time for that."

"War will do that. Besides, I chose the wrong path for a family years ago." If she'd chosen it at all. There hadn't exactly been alternatives. Try to save your planet—or die on it? Let me think.

"No such thing as the wrong path for a family with today's tech."

"My profession is killing things. Not growing them."

"Your profession is *far* more than that." The harsh edge to Dremer's voice caught Ellen off guard.

"Maybe. But I don't need to leave an orphan behind." She knew that very well, too. Her parents hadn't left her much but the two tattoos she'd gotten to remember them by.

"Hmm. So that's a no to babies of your own?"

"It's not a no exactly. It just feels far away, I guess."

"You've got time."

Yes, she thought, feeling a wave of relief. She came in here when she'd worked herself into a froth. But there really was time, wasn't there? Not to think about children—that was futuristic nonsense. But she had a minimum of four more months to figure out what to do about the whole... situation. And probably much longer than that.

There was so much time. She let out a breath she hadn't realized she'd been holding.

Dremer cleared her throat, and Ellen blushed, realizing she'd just been standing there, silent. "You've just been in here a lot, looking so lost in thought, staring at our little friend. So I wondered what you were thinking so hard about."

"I'm—" Ellen groped for an excuse. Marveling at how this bundle of genetic material could have caused such chaos in her life? "I'm wondering what she'll be like, what will happen to her," she lied.

"The computer's still running her DNA Enhancements. Some are easy to recognize, especially when we compare them to Levereaux's and other standard edits the Enhancers always employ, especially in women. But of course, this was the culmination of a great deal of unique and cutting-edge research. Some of these seem like garbage edits to me. Levereaux will hopefully know better. There's work around the telepathy mutation for sure. Her rate of growth seems to be advanced, even if we account for the benefits of the artificial devices. I'd estimate her at around ten or twelve weeks traditional gestation, but she's progressing much more rapidly than that."

"Are there any downsides to that? Will she be okay?"

"No downsides we can detect so far. She handled the move from the capsule to the chamber well. I'm guessing they didn't want their child empress to be a child for very long. Either way, we'll have a maturity date soon."

"What then?"

Dremer smiled, eyes twinkling. "Then the fun begins, and I guess I'll have a child after all."

CHAPTER TWO

JENNY TOWELED off her hair roughly and wrestled her red-orange tangle into as near-perfect a bun as possible, stopping short as she caught her reflection in the small, silver-framed mirror over her desk. She stared for one long moment, then the next.

What mattered was that Adan was happy, she lectured herself. If she truly cared about him, she'd stop overanalyzing what Josana had that she didn't have—and just try to be happy for him.

Granted, that'd be a lot easier if Josana weren't so awful.

Maybe he just didn't like redheads? She flinched and darted away from the mirror, toward her locker. No, she was *not* going to do this. Stark naked and freezing her ass off were not ideal conditions for pity parties or self-analysis.

She grabbed her shorts and shoved a leg in, quick as she could. Her hot shower had been great to rinse the battle off, but the ship air was damn *cold* around her now. She kept her quarters a bit frigid intentionally; it was a more optimal temperature for sleeping. Her friends used to joke that Jenny had only started climbing mountainsides to reach a temperature that was more tolerable than the steamy temperatures back home on Capital. Space had been the logical next step.

But seriously, what kind of idiot doesn't like redheads? Who were also galactic-class athletes?

Her kind of idiot, apparently.

Growling at herself, she shrugged into her bra. The air swirled the scent of orange blossoms and peaches—the scent of home. Cold, humid, stirring something melancholy in her chest. Her mother's Capital apartment had always smelled like this—but from real trees, not these synthetic compounds. Those trees had been one of the few real, authentic things about home—and about her mother. Even the royalty of the athletic augmentation world had their Puritanical indulgences.

She yanked a black jumpsuit from the top locker drawer. Xi's cleaning robots were doing a much better job with the laundry than Jenny had expected. Each was perfectly folded and sorted by color as she'd always done—olive, navy, black, orange. The drawer shut itself as she risked another glimpse in the mirror and smoothed back a few stray strands that had escaped.

Maybe it was the white hair. Maybe she should dye hers. Or get a gene mod. Neon orange worked well for Nova. Of course, that would require shaving her head so it'd all grow in the same color.

Yeah, right. Because the reason Adan was obsessed with Josana and not with Jenny all came down to hair color.

Either way, it didn't matter. Oh, Josana was certainly pretty, in that holier-than-thou, unnatural sort of way, like a neon sign pointing at a poetry reading. And she certainly had the cultured bourgeois act down, if Jenny wanted to be polite—or the snotty rich kid, if she wanted to be less so. That elegant veneer had to be what drew him in. Right? Because he was smart, and sweet, and funny—and quick on the wing, too. He seemed way too smart to fall for such a superficial ice queen.

Either Adan was very mistaken about Josana—or Jenny was mistaken about him. And she wasn't sure she really wanted to know which.

She heaved a disgusted sigh, plucked a zeefruit from the yellow bowl on her desk and sank down on her bunk in defeat.

The comm chime sounded—the tone she'd set for Ryu. Oh, good. A welcome distraction. "Yes, Commander?"

"I've got some details on the upcoming mission I'd like to go over with you. Can I stop by?"

"Of course, ma'am."

"Be there in five."

The channel clicked off. Ryu never wasted words. A blessing in a boss. No bullshit. Just the way Jenny preferred it.

The door slid open, and Jenny sprang to her feet. Ryu waved her back to her seat on the bunk. "Did I interrupt anything?"

"No, ma'am. Just snacking." And wallowing in my personal problems.

Ryu leaned against the wall inside the door, ignoring the desk chair. "Well, I've got some good news and some bad news."

"Yes?" Jenny's gut twisted. Ryu didn't usually have bad news, and what little she did never resulted in the commander coming to visit *her*.

Folding her arms across her chest, the commander eyed her for a moment before speaking. "Next mission's on Capital."

The knot in her gut twisted tighter. Jenny winced. "What's the good news?"

Ryu shrugged. "I thought that was kind of both."

Jenny groaned. "Formally requesting ship-guarding duty, ma'am."

"I'm afraid that's not an option this time. Patron Simmons has concocted a cover plan for the mission that puts you at the center of it."

She hung her head, but only for a second. Straightening, she forced herself into a curt nod.

"I just want to run the plan by you before I brief the team. In case you see any holes in it. You're the Capital native, after all."

"And I've done so well not publicizing that embarrassing fact."

"You can also tell me if you don't want to go along with it."

Jenny frowned. "Hey, now. Have I ever not followed orders? Shirked responsibility?"

Ryu smiled slightly, a rare glimmer of emotion. "You have an exemplary record, Corporal Utlis. But maybe there are alternatives that might be less personally painful for you. Let me walk you through it and see what you think."

"Of course, Commander."

"We're seeking to recruit another scientist to join our team. Dr. Chayana Persad. Designs telepathic resistance drugs. We think."

Jenny couldn't help but raise an eyebrow. "Didn't think such a thing was possible."

"Neither did I. Perhaps she's found a way."

"Or she's a con artist."

Ryu raised an eyebrow.

"There're more than a few of them on Capital, you know."

"More than on any other established world?"

"Yes. Trust me, the fancy clothes make it easier to hide, not harder."

"Noted. But here's the real rub. The cover story he's concocted is that we want to commission her to design you some performance boosters."

Jenny choked, even though she'd swallowed the last bit of fruit minutes ago. *"What?"*

"Does that sound like a plausible request?"

"I don't do performance-enhancing substances, Commander. And everyone knows that. It was highly publicized. I'm a poster child for the anti-augmentation community." To her parents' chagrin.

"I never saw you on any Puritan posters. They're really missing a wonderful promotional opportunity."

"I'm not a *Puritan*." She spat the word out with a bit too much disdain, but Capital was a neutral planet. Neither Union nor Puritan. That was one rare piece of her home planet she wasn't ashamed of. "Look, it's just a sports thing. The anti-aug community doesn't turn down therapeutic or life-saving treatments. Or even cosmetic ones."

"Well, we don't have to publicize it. We may not even need to say why we're trying to meet with her to anyone but her. We just need an excuse ready. You can deny it all as vicious rumor. Is it plausible? Vaguely?"

She fidgeted. "Sure, it's plausible... I guess. They'll say I *am* getting older and all that shit. It's excellent tabloid fodder. But I worked for *years* to prove I wasn't like—" She stopped short.

"Like what?" Ryu asked gently.

"Like… my parents. My mother's damn near an android by now. And my father… Well, let's just say it's not something we agree on." Jenny ran a hand over her face. "Oh, this is going to be a circus, isn't it? What if we can't convince her to join us? What if she jumps right on the net and tells everyone this bullshit story?"

"Commander, if I may?" Xi's voice chimed in from above.

"Yes, what is it, Xi?"

"I can furnish you with a Capital-appropriate legal secrecy agreement you can have the doctor sign before disclosing this. We may not wish to enforce it in Capital courts, but it might be enough to keep her and others from contacting news services before we can divulge our true intent."

"Good idea, Xi. Would that ease your mind, Jen? We want to use your reputation; the rest of us will play the part of your security team."

The urge to groan returned. "My… security team?"

"Simmons is hoping we can justify carrying around more than your average muscle and firepower by capitalizing on your celebrity on Capital."

That was fairly smart. And sounded like it would work. But… Jenny swallowed. "My 'celebrity,' huh?"

"Does *that* part seem plausible?" The slight lift of Ryu's eyebrows told Jenny her commander knew the answer as well as she did.

Reluctantly, she nodded. "Not my usual style, but it is very plausible." Jenny had always preferred to lay low, keep a low profile. Blending in when she could and knowing how to defend herself were better security strategies than strutting around like a peacock. And it kept the cameras away—and the god-awful pressure. But lesser-known athletes from lesser-known families kept entourages in the dozens. Jenny's preference to lay low had been more bizarre than standard behavior on Capital. In fact at times, it had backfired, as her lack of bodyguards, assistants, and trainers had served as its own fascination to the wealthy masses. "He didn't sign me up for a competition again, did he?"

"Nope. Sounds like a security nightmare, so thank God. His suggestion is that beyond the commission, we're vacationing on the side."

She snorted. "As if we'd pick Capital for that."

"We're in the minority there. Lots of people love Capital vacations." Ryu's eyes twinkled.

"His plans are improving. He needs to work vacation into all of them."

"So you'll do it?"

Ryu's words pulled the knot in her stomach to near snapping and sent a little jolt of familiar anxiety into Jenny's veins. "You don't understand, Commander. I'm getting older. I've stopped competing. Even visiting some brain scientist might be construed as something if the press gets word of it." She sighed, running a hand over her face.

Ryu came over and sank down beside her on the bunk, putting a hand on her shoulder. "Does it matter what they think?"

Jenny looked up and met Ryu's intense, dark gaze. Her eyes were soft now, softer than usual anyway.

"Did it *ever* matter?"

Jenny smiled and blew out a breath. "No. You're right. It never did."

"It takes a long time and a lot of wisdom to learn that lesson." Ryu took her hand away.

"Thanks." Jenny stood and straightened, turning to face her commander. "All right, I'm in. A little Capital bullshit is not going to scare me."

Ryu nodded curtly, and a glimmer of a smile flashed across her lips. "Great. I'll have more details at the briefing later." She stood, patted Jenny on the shoulder once more, and strode out through the hatch.

Jenny sank back onto the bunk, lying down this time, and tried to let the tension drain out of her.

It only half worked. Headlines were flashing through her head. How many times had they questioned her purity, her augmentation?

How many fanatical Puritans had become huge fans just because of her stubborn insistence alone?

Jenny was no Puritan. But drugs, augmentation… it was a slippery slope. It was all about money. Who could afford something better. Who could pay to win.

Everything on Capital was like that.

If she'd been pushed into competing in the first place, at least she had always competed on her own terms.

Those days are over, she reminded herself. You have a new mission now. A better one. A life that means more than record times and gear sponsorships. A life you chose for yourself.

Still. The tightness remained in her stomach. Maybe it was time to head to the mess, get something more than a little fruit to eat.

Ryu was right. It didn't matter what they thought. And it never really had.

———

"ADAN, WE NEED TO TALK."

Adan spun his pilot's chair around. Josana stood in the hatch, wearing her short red velvet robe, her high leather boots, and her sternest expression.

Uh-oh. This couldn't be good. That outfit meant business.

" 'Bout what?" He laughed nervously. As if he didn't know. And things had been going so well.

"Surely you heard about our next stop before I did." She folded her arms as her lips twisted into a crooked smile. Her eyes laughed at him. "Aren't you the first one to hear about our next destination?"

He dodged answering that. She had an uncanny knack for picking at operational details he didn't care for anyone to know. It wasn't that he was paranoid, but…

Well, no. He was definitely paranoid. He wouldn't have survived outsystem without a fair amount of paranoia to watch his back. But he also wasn't stupid. He was realistic. Josana might have finally warmed to his longtime flirtations a few weeks ago, but he hadn't stopped looking for her ulterior motive. She was wealthy, connected, gorgeous, young.

And he was... also young?

He wasn't turning her away. But he certainly hadn't stopped pinching himself.

"Capital, I hear," he said as he swiveled back toward the controls. He might not tell her if he were the first to hear their next destination —he wasn't—but she was definitely one of the last, so there was no harm in discussing that.

She clapped her hands. "I know, isn't it wonderful!"

He pursed his lips and tried not to scowl.

She must have caught his expression reflected in the view screen. "Oh, can't you be happy for me? You know how long I've wanted off this dump."

He rolled his eyes. "The *Audacity* is not a dump. But of course I'm happy for you." It was self-pity he was drowning in. "What am I going to do without you, though?"

She strode over and dug her fingers into his shoulders, massaging hard. "Well, that's just what I wanted to talk about."

Adrenaline flew through him. He ought to be excited at words like that combined with physical affections—unless she was breaking up with him—but that wasn't what coursed through him now.

It was fear.

Why? He had no idea.

That same nervous laugh escaped from him again. "Whaddaya mean, Jos?"

She bent so her lips brushed his ear. "I'm staying. Why don't you stay with me?"

"On Capital?"

"Obviously."

He winced. This was a discussion he didn't want to have. "It won't work."

"Sure it will." Her fingers dug in harder, deliciously. Determinedly. She didn't like taking no for an answer. "We can play *Red Dwarf Commander*—on the beach."

"I don't know if the holos work when sand gets blown into them."

"One way to find out, eh? So you'll stay?"

He sighed even as his cheeks warmed. He'd tried to avoid talking about this with her. But there was no avoiding it now. "I can't. I'm from the outsystem, Josana. I don't have any citizenship. It won't work."

"So?"

"Nada. You get me? None at all, let alone a compatible one. No visa. No permission to work. Or live."

She waved that off. "Tell me. Do you *want* to stay with me? If so, there are... ways to work out the details."

He rolled his eyes again. Sometimes he forgot she was so young—and the naïveté that came with that. "You can't just work out *that* detail."

"Assuming we could."

He sighed, then shook his head at her. "Spoken like one untested by the cruelties of the world."

She laughed and bent down close again, catching his eye in the reflection of the darkened view screen. Her eyes were twinkling like the stars shown in the space beyond. "I *am* the cruelties of the world, my dear."

His eyes widened. What the...

No. She was a seventeen-year-old who wanted to go home to her friends and go to classes and prep for tests for med school.

Wasn't she?

Her grin broadened, a cat hunting its prey. "Leave this ship and its pathetic notions of grandeur. Come with me," she whispered. Her breath sent a shiver through him. "All the machismo and the optimism and the starry-eyed ideals? It's all nonsense."

"No, it's not. You don't know what you're asking." Leave *Audacity*? Ryu and Xi? Flying?

The stars?

"Sure, I do." Was her grin a touch wicked? Was it his imagination?

"And what would I do while you're off in classes?" he said, immediately regretting it. He shouldn't lead her on.

"Do whatever you like," she said, laughing. "Lie around my apartment and wait for me to come home."

"Sounds so..." Boring as hell? Domesticated? He settled for sarcasm. ". . . intellectually stimulating."

"You name it. Play *Red Dwarf Commander*, for all I care. I know people, just like you do."

He frowned at that. He couldn't imagine who she thought he knew. He was a nobody from a dust ball that was lucky it had a name and a single hospital and police station. Ryu was the most influential person he knew. Or maybe Patron Simmons.

"Look, we can find something 'intellectually stimulating' for you to do. Promise me you'll think about it?"

He nodded. Apparently finished with her massage—and her request—she patted his shoulders, squeezed one last time, and turned to go.

He listened to the thudding of her boots down the hall until he lost the sound. Then he let out the breath he'd been holding and loosened his shoulders.

He couldn't really leave the stars... or any of it.

But Capital. Many considered it the cultural and financial center of the galaxy.

His mother would laugh if she could see him slumped in his chair now. Oh, big problems, kid—the pretty girl you're in love with wants you to stay on her fancy home planet with her. And not work. You could just play *Red Dwarf Commander* all day. Sometimes, with her, because she likes it too. Of course, it'd mean you'd have to give up flying your swanky space ship. She'd be happy he had better problems these days, even if she'd laugh. He'd grown up with his bare feet in the dry, red dirt of Bantilla, and never would he have imagined he'd have a chance to see Capital, let alone live there. Island after island, all water and sunshine.

It was impossible, of course. But it was a nice dream.

———

A DROP of sweat slid down Kael's forehead and dropped through the cargo bay grating below his feet. The gravity bar was already set nearly as high as he could manage it, but he jerked the settings a notch higher and heaved again. He managed the lift just barely, then sent it crashing down with more force than the gravity bar alone was exerting.

Well, he might not be a Theroki anymore, but tossing heavy things around still felt good. Old habits died hard.

Ryu's voice came from the catwalk behind him. "I'm sure the repair bots will be glad to have something to do, but what did the *Audacity* do to deserve such treatment?"

"Sorry, Commander." He winced. "She's the only home I've ever known. You don't think she'll take it personally, do you?"

"I know I won't," Xi chimed in.

Kael snickered.

Ellen slipped down the ladder behind him, quiet as a cat. "Something bothering you, Kael? I got your message."

If her eyes lingered at all, he didn't spot it.

And that was fine. Completely fine. He didn't care. Not anymore. He took a deep breath, the musk and oil of the cargo hold mixing with sweat. Okay, that was a lie. But he was working on it.

He tried to center himself like Dr. Taylor had been coaching him. The chip modifications Dremer had made had eased some of the ebb and flow of wild emotion inside him, but not all of it. He hadn't dealt with any of it for so long. Taylor had him doing meditation.

Mostly that just made him more frustrated. And more eager to throw things. But, you know. He was working on it.

Just like he was working on accepting his new very platonic and unromantic working relationship with Ellen. And her reasons and all. Praise the Almighty, he'd escaped the Theroki. A lifetime conscription and basically a death sentence. He *should* be counting his blessings. It was a work in progress.

He turned and faced her, leaning against the nearby wall. "Just a couple questions about the upcoming mission. Ma'am."

"All right. Shoot." She had stopped at the bottom of the ladder. The dim cargo bay lights cast velvety highlights across the curves of her black armor.

He might as well have out with it. "Have I done something to jeopardize your trust?"

Her eyebrows shot up. "Excuse me?"

"Have I slipped up somewhere and I didn't realize it? I assume if I had you would tell me, but—"

She folded her arms across her chest. "Without a second thought. What's this all about, Kael?"

"Staying on the ship, Commander? Really?"

"That's not a question."

"What did I do to get benched?" She hadn't stationed him on ship-guarding duty on any of the missions since he'd signed his contract.

Until this one.

She tilted her head and propped a hand on one hip. "What, you want to see Capital? It's not going to be a fragging vacation."

"You said you needed the best unarmored combatants. But you're sending Zhia instead of me."

"So?"

He couldn't take standing still anymore. He started pacing, staring at the floor as he spoke. "Look, I would be perfectly happy to guard a potted plant of your choosing if you so desire. Your wish is my command. But I stayed alive as a Theroki by trying to understand orders, asking questions. And you told me yourself asking questions is critical to mission success."

"Figures you'd be paying attention."

"And it's... well..."

"Spit it out, Kael."

"You've never left me on guard duty before."

Her gaze pinned him to the wall, unreadable for a long moment. "Everybody does guard duty sometimes."

"Is that it? Or..." He stopped his pacing and took a step closer. Then he took another, until they were barely a foot apart, so she could hear his quiet words. "What is it you're not telling me?"

Surprise flickered over her features and then vanished, and he couldn't tell if that had been exactly the right thing to say or exactly the wrong one. "I should have known," she muttered. She continued louder, but still hushed. "Let's discuss this further in my cabin. Get cleaned up and meet me there?"

"I can go now." Not like she cared how he looked, she'd made that clear enough. He snatched a towel off the railing to mop his brow. "I'm good."

One eyebrow raised, she ran her gaze over his sweaty form. Hmm, perhaps he should have taken the hint. Just because she wasn't interested in him didn't mean she wanted him dripping sweat all over the floor of her cabin.

"Fine." She climbed back up the ladder. "Let's go."

He followed her, throwing the towel over his shoulder and feeling more like an overeager puppy than a professional soldier. Her cabin was on the opposite end of the ship. She stopped by the door as he stepped past her, keying in a code to the lockpad as the door slid shut behind them. "Xi, mute this box for me, please."

"Yes, Commander," came Xi's smooth voice from overhead.

"What does that mean?" He frowned, glancing around him. Ryu's room was sparse and neat as always. The desk, the bunk, the holochess, the bookshelf of what appeared to be actual paper books. Someday he'd get a closer look at the titles. The punching bag was stored away today, somewhere in the floor or ceiling.

Ellen strode to the holodesk, not looking at him. "It means she's turning off recording to the ship's databanks for this room. Cut this part out too, please, and delete it."

"If you're going to beat the shit out of me, Commander, at least let me put my armor on."

She let out a bark of laughter. "Yeah, right. As if I'd have a fair shot if I gave you any warning."

"Is that supposed to ease my worry about an imminent beating?"

"No." Face blank, she started punching commands into the desk. Always as old-school as possible in her tech, it seemed.

"Mute complete," said Xi placidly.

Ellen strode closer, stopping just inches before him and eying him a

long moment before shaking her head. "What I have to say doesn't
leave this room. Got it?"

"Of course."

"We have a traitor on board." Anger glinted in the corner of her
eyes, and her jaw tightened.

"A *what*?"

"A traitor. A spy. A leak. Something. Someone is deleting data from
our missions. Armor cam footage. Confiscated data. And they're also
deleting evidence of their activity in the system, even surpassing Xi
and her alarms at times."

"Shit."

"Yes. Shit is right."

"What does this have to do with me playing your guard dog?"

She glared at him. "You'd prefer to be my attack dog?"

He couldn't hold back a smirk. "Definitely."

She shook her head. "Preferences noted, but this is serious, Kael.
Three days ago, someone bypassed one of Xi's safeguards and
accessed Adan's medical records—all of them—allowing them to
discover he has a serious allergy to philopraxis. Luckily, Xi caught the
record of access and the time before they could edit it to cover their
tracks. But unluckily, *who* accessed the file had already been erased.
But we know they are on board."

"So you think someone is trying to hurt Adan?" he said slowly.

"I think someone is trying to *kill* him. I didn't assign you here to
guard the bridge. I want you guarding him."

Eyebrows raised, he just stared at her for a moment. That was
certainly not what he'd expected to hear.

"We checked sick bay. The usual store of philopraxis is suddenly
and conveniently missing. Records show no one has accessed it in
months."

"How is it administered?"

"Injector. Could have been a coincidence. We use a lot of sedatives
for anesthesia, and when the landings are particularly bloody, we do
run out of even the less commonly used ones sometimes. Things get

messy, or there may have been a species that required philopraxis's unique properties. Recording isn't perfect."

"But you don't think that's what's going on."

"No."

"So you weren't trying to bench me."

"No. I assigned you this because I *trust* you." She folded her arms across her chest, eyes narrowing.

"And you were going to tell me that... when?"

She sighed, the tension in her face easing. "Eventually."

"Eventually?"

"I hadn't decided."

He snorted, then ran a hand through his hair, which was still too long and needed utterly shaved off at this point.

"When we landed, at the very latest. I've told Adan the basics. But this doesn't make sense. Why would anyone want to kill Adan?"

"Because he's the pilot?"

"Possible," chimed in Xi. "But Fern is a reliable backup pilot for most scenarios, as am I. What does the loss of Adan alone do?"

Kael rubbed his chin. "Maybe they aren't planning to stop with Adan."

"Also possible," Xi agreed.

Ellen scowled. "Even worse. We have to figure out who it is. And stop them."

He rubbed his chin. "Do you have any theories on who could be behind all this?"

"Well, Adan has the skills to edit the files, but why would he want to poison himself? The files we're talking about are not open access. Only comms officers and the doctors have access. And me."

"So, Zhia, Merith, Levereaux, Dremer, and Taylor?"

"Yep."

"Oh," he said, dots connecting. "That's why you're taking Zhia."

"Yes. But we don't have an excuse to get Merith or the others off ship. Yet. I'm working on it. Well, except for Dremer, who's always willing to go. Taylor may go down with Josana to help her get settled, but I can't count on it. But she's the least likely to be able to hack those files."

"Well, why not take us both with you instead? And leave all the suspects here."

She frowned at him.

"We'll be sitting ducks just hanging around on the bridge, bored. Zhia can guard the ship. The others would naturally stay here anyway, right?"

"They have the right to leave. Run errands. But mostly, yes."

"Even if they leave, I should be able to keep Adan away from them more easily."

"You *do* just want to see Capital, don't you?" she said, eyes twinkling.

Xi's voice chimed in. "Commander, I cannot control environments off the ship as thoroughly as those onboard. I may be able to detect a philopraxis injector when it enters the bridge or other locations. However..."

"Yes?"

"However some of my sensors were clearly thwarted when the drug was taken from sick bay." There was a pause. Was it his imagination or could an AI sigh? "Ordinarily, I would suggest my observation would be the most effective and thorough security. Human senses cannot easily surpass mine."

Ryu raised an eyebrow. "But... ?"

"But considering the deft hacking taking place, I suppose there may be more security in unplanned locations. Much as I might hate to admit it, Kael's suggestion is an excellent tactical option. According to my calculations—"

"C'mon, Xi. You have to make him work for it. You can't let new recruits go around thinking they run the place."

"But *Commander*—" Xi started.

"Don't worry, Xi. Good idea, Kael. There is one complication to the matter. Adan, as an outsystemer, doesn't have citizenship on a core planet. Doug offered to get him one, or a new identity, but he doesn't want it. It shouldn't be a problem as long as we stay on the right side of Capital law. We can get him a travel doc. But if for some reason he were to break the law—or even be accused of breaking it—things could get very bad very quick. Noncitizens are supposed to be afforded a trial on Capital, but sometimes those trials take suspiciously long to be scheduled."

Sounded better than Faros. "How long are we talking?"

"A decade is not unheard of," Xi said placidly.

Kael winced. Maybe not better than Faros then. "Well, we'll be on the right side of the law, won't we?"

Ellen leveled a stare at him. "Because you've known me to be a very law-abiding galactic citizen?"

"Good point." Breaking into and blowing up or stealing from Enhancer outposts was probably not legal. And that was just one of many missions. That he knew about. Right and just were not always the same as legal.

"We may not all be on the right side all the time. Just make sure the two of you are."

"Got it."

"He doesn't usually go on missions either. We'll need some explanation for why he's necessary to the team."

"Is there something he can do or acquire here that he can't other places?"

"Yes," said Xi. "But not legally."

"Like what?" asked Ellen.

"Scripts. Hacking utilities from experts. Even some drone hardware upgrades. A few of those *might* be legal. All would likely be useful."

Ellen tapped her chin thoughtfully. "Well, we don't have to actually *acquire* them for a cover story to work. I'll brief the others on the changes. Good work, Lieutenant. Anything else?"

"No." He started to turn to go. "Oh, uh—the capsule. How is… she doing?"

"I just checked with Dremer. She's doing well. Growing fast," she said slowly. "Nothing to worry about."

"Good."

"I'm sure you could stop by and ask yourself."

"No thanks, ma'am. I'm ready to go hunt down my charge and start this mission."

"I'm sure it can wait till after dinner. But look, I care about Adan. He's a good kid."

"Isn't he older than you?"

"Only by a little. But he's had a tough life and deserves better. I wouldn't like to see him buy the farm so soon. Watch him like a hawk for me, okay? I wish I could do it myself."

As if he hadn't already been determined as hell since the moment she'd said she trusted him. "Of course, Commander. Like a hawk on a rabbit."

The door slid shut quietly behind him as he strode away.

He'd meant to form plans as he walked back, think about how he was going to stick to Adan like glue without it seeming suspicious. But his thoughts just hung in a haze, ignoring the practical.

She trusted him. She'd given him a mission she couldn't give to the women she'd served with for ages.

Maybe a chance to prove himself. Worthy of trust.

Maybe worthy of more than that.

He whisked down the ladder and around the last corner. He was so lost in his thoughts he almost ran into Zhia, who was perched low on a stool right outside his hatch.

"Shit—sorry, didn't see you there."

"No problem." She barely looked up, finishing a curve of thick forest green against the metal.

He eyed the painting, seeing nothing but splotches of color yet. "What... are you doing?"

"Oh, I'm throwing a party. What does it look like?"

"Did the commander approve that one?" And what did it mean if she did?

Zhia grinned, only a little sheepishly. "Not *yet*."

"Bet you'll be disappointed to give this up while you're out on the mission," he said casually, sidling around her toward his hatch.

She groaned. "If it'd keep me away from Capital, I'd paint you whatever you wanted."

"If that's the case, I'll take an ocean view. But it can't be that bad, can it? I mean, I know Capital types, but—"

"It's that bad. Now quit talking about it. You're ruining my groove."

Laughing and shaking his head, he headed into his cabin and shut the hatch behind him.

CHAPTER THREE

"HEY! I hear you're coming with us!"

Adan barely had time to set down his coffee mug before Jenny plopped down in his lap, her arm flopping across his shoulders. He glanced at the door. He knew she meant it only in a friendly, brotherly way, but it still made him nervous Josana would walk in and not be a fan.

"So I heard." He shook his head and pretended to be very interested in the view screen, even as the sweet scent of citrus and springtime flooded his senses. Usual Jenny. He shoved aside memories of the orange groves his mother had kept once upon a time. That time, bittersweet as it was, was long gone.

Feeds of readings from the nearby systems streamed past. Xi was watching them; he didn't need to. But Jenny didn't need to know that.

"You excited?" Her hand squeezed his shoulder.

"I guess," he muttered, shrugging. He *was* excited, but that was another thing he wasn't sharing.

"Liar." Her stare was boring into him, but he held on to the view screen a little longer before he met her shining green eyes. When he did, her smile lifted. He strove to ignore it, just as he strove to ignore her curves pressed against him. And the slight sprinkle of freckles on her nose. Or how she seemed sized just right for just this spot. Eyes, keep focused on her eyes. No, the view screen.

"I don't mind hanging out on the ship with Xi." He glanced up to indicate his invisible flying companion and copilot. "But it'll be a nice change."

"Sure, whatever you say. Does Xi make a good *Red Dwarf Commander* opponent?"

He snorted. "No."

"You haven't asked," Xi said coolly.

"I prefer fair, even match-ups."

"Do you really? Or do you just prefer winning?" Jenny's eyes twinkled.

He dodged the question, mostly because she had him pinned. He *did* prefer winning. But he wasn't terribly proud of it. "I don't need to play to know Xi can beat me senseless."

Jenny let out a chuckle, throwing her head back. "Oh, certainly getting beaten senseless only happens in the *field*."

"Brainless?" Xi offered. "Witless? Adan, I am offended you do not believe me capable of modulating my abilities to your skill level."

"Offended? That's a new one," Jenny muttered.

"Sorry, Xi. Noted. But surely on the ship I'm safe to not get beaten beyond, say, a mild depression," said Adan.

Jenny snapped her fingers. "That reminds me why I stopped by. Do you have something to wear other than this?" She plucked at his jacket collar.

He frowned, looking down. He loved that damn jacket, even if it was getting too old and wearing thin in spots. Ones like it were hard to come by. Tan canvas and covered with pockets and pouches of every kind, it held immense utility, even if it wasn't the most fashionable choice. "What's wrong with this?"

"It doesn't deflect lead."

"Oh. The commander said we were wearing civvies."

"Well, yeah, but you never know when shit goes sideways." She wiggled in illustration, and he swallowed. Might be time to ask her to get off him. Enough wiggling from anyone in her position could wake the dragon, and he didn't want her to get the wrong idea. He shifted. His hand slipped off the armrest and came dangerously close to brushing her thigh.

He gripped the armrest with renewed vigor and cleared his throat. "Must you always invade my space to have a conversation? And do *you* have anything to wear? I've never seen you wear anything but naval jumpsuits and climbing gear, none of which look like civvies to me." Not like the robes and dresses some of the other women wore. Like Josana wore, except those delectable corsets she had... This was definitely the wrong time to think about *that*.

Jenny sprung away and into the copilot seat, seemingly unfazed by his comment and as effervescent as ever. "I have lots of things to wear. My adoring public awaits."

"Your what?"

"Point is, do you have armor to take as backup?"

"No." He narrowed his eyes at her. "I didn't ask you to protect me, Jen. And I'm willing to bet I've survived plenty worse than anything we'll encounter on Capital." Now if someone on board were truly out to drug him to death, that might be a different story. And he might be paranoid, but he wasn't paranoid enough to believe *that*.

"Maybe you have. That doesn't mean you won't buy it tomorrow." Jenny waved him off. "You should have a case of armor in the unlikely event that everything goes to hell. Right now, *Audacity* is your armor, right? I have an old one you can borrow. I'll let the commander know."

"I'm sure that won't be necessary."

She stood up and jabbed a finger at him. "Tell you what, hotshot. I would rather not pull a bullet out of your shoulder, so we're taking it anyway. You said you're willing to bet, right?"

"I'm always willing to bet."

"Then if it *is* necessary, you owe me a cigar."

A crooked grin stole onto his face in spite of himself. "All right. And if it's not necessary, *you* owe me one."

"Deal. But it better be a good one. Not those cheap ones you picked up at Molyarch." How did she know he'd picked up any at Molyarch Station? They were cheap, she was right. It was all they'd had.

She held out a hand, and he shook it, her grip firm and skin rough.

"It's almost like you hope I'm going to get shot at," he said before letting go.

"I like cigars, what can I say. And winning bets. And especially cigars I smoke after I win bets."

He lowered his chin and gazed at her over the top of his flight glasses, smiling broader now. "Prepare yourself to be disappointed."

She only beamed back at him, a beat longer than perhaps she should have, and then she bounded off, presumably to do as she'd said and chat with the commander.

———

KAEL BOUNCED HIS BOOT, tapping it erratically against the metal floor grating. His arms folded across his chest, he'd been leaning against the wall and waiting outside the bridge for at least fifteen minutes. His Foundation-issued flight suit was black and conspicuously inconspicuous, but it was also just the right temperature, and its pockets had pockets. Too bad he couldn't fit anything in there that would help him find Adan. And make the pilot talk.

"You're sure he's coming, Xi?"

There was a pause before the AI answered. "Yes, Kael. He has stopped for coffee."

"Better be damned good coffee to be fifteen minutes late for his shift." Fern's blond head leaned out the door, looked in both directions, gave Kael a friendly nod, and then disappeared back into the bridge.

"Better be bringing me some," Kael grumbled.

"I took the liberty of suggesting that," Xi said. "But he did not seem to appreciate the suggestion."

Kael snorted. Yeah, this mission was going great already. "Well, I do, Xi. You sweetie, you're always looking out for me."

"I look out for everyone on the ship equally, Kael."

"And I am one of everyone." He gave the ceiling a wink. "And happily so."

"I… do not think I understand. Technically this is true, but I sense more is meant. My models cannot interpret your expression."

"My expression."

"This… wink."

"Ah, don't worry about it, Xi. Just bein' myself."

"There, again, this expression is most—well. Let us discuss it later."

A set of footsteps finally rounded the corner, and Kael shifted forward quickly, ready to follow his quarry onto the bridge. Adan approached, coffee indeed in hand. Two cups, actually. The pilot had his own navy flight suit, tousled brown hair, and a clear chip on his shoulder.

Kael propped his hands on his hips. "Aw, you shouldn't have."

"I didn't," said Adan with a smile. "This is for Fern."

"See ya, losers." Fern swirled past, pivoting to grab the coffee and disappearing down the hallway. "Better not be late tomorrow, Adan! Ship's yours."

Adan only pursed his lips after her, glanced at Kael in annoyance, and shuffled onto the bridge. "What do you want, Theroki?"

"Where have you been? I've been looking for you everywhere."

"Cabin." Adan plopped down into the pilot's seat, deposited his coffee in the cupholder, pulled up the last shift notes, and hit several keys that began reconfiguring the workstation.

"Well, that's what Xi said. I checked there. You didn't answer."

"Musta been asleep—"

"Sure you were. Do you know how loud I can knock?"

Adan narrowed his eyes in a way that made it clear he *did* know just how loud Kael could knock. "What's this about, Theroki?"

Kael didn't bother to hide his scowl this time. "Did you get the mission update from the commander?"

"Hmm, yeah. About that." Adan swiveled his chair to face him and knitted his hands behind his head. "Look, I'm happy to come along and see Capital. Would be nice to see things not as a drone for once. But I don't really need a babysitter, okay?"

Kael gestured at his chest, easily twice the size of the pilot's. "Do I look like a babysitter to you?"

"I could see you tending babies."

Kael's turn to narrow his eyes. "Most childcare workers have less muscle mass."

"What I'm saying is I can take care of myself."

"Sure you can."

"Hey, the outsystem was way tougher than a civilized place like Capital."

Kael pursed his lips. "You know this isn't about that."

"Yeah, yeah." Adan spun his chair around and enlarged the report, ready to drop the subject. Except that he kept talking. "Look, just because some drug went missing doesn't mean I need some overzealous rookie stuck to me like dreck on my shoe just to impress the pretty commander."

Kael grabbed the back of the pilot seat and swung a shocked Adan around, catching the spinning chair by the far armrest. Praise the Almighty for zero-g rated coffee mug lids that kept the hot black stuff inside. Kael leaned in, face inches from Adan's.

"I am *not* an overzealous rookie."

"This right here?" Adan held up a forefinger and wiggled it in the space between them. "Not exactly proving your point, hotshot."

"I'm not the one making light of a death threat." He didn't back off. Not yet.

"I'm noticing you didn't correct me on the 'impress the pretty commander' part."

Kael forced himself to take a deep breath rather than crush the armrest into a twisted memory of its former shape. Dr. Taylor would be so proud. "I'm going to do my job. Whether you like it or not. It means more to me than your annoyance."

Something flickered in Adan's eyes. A bit of doubt? Bravado quickly covered it. "I'm sure between me and Xi we can handle it. Right, Xi?"

"Actually, I will appreciate an additional set of eyes, especially if you are not within the confines of the ship."

Adan shook a playful fist at the ceiling. "Traitor. Look—I'm telling you, Theroki. I. Don't. Need. Your. Help."

"I'm not a Theroki anymore." Kael's voice was quieter now and hard as steel.

Adan smirked. "Just cause she trusts you doesn't mean I have to."

Just when he knew Adan wouldn't expect it, Kael straightened and folded his arms across his chest. "What is it you object to? Receiving help from a former 'pirate,' or the fact that someone thinks you need help at all?"

Adan's lips twisted. "Can it be a bit of both?"

A huff of bitter laughter escaped Kael. "Well, last I checked, you weren't the one giving the orders around here."

"So?"

"So you got a babysitter whether you like it or not."

Smirking to himself, Kael turned on his heel and headed off the bridge. He'd clearly have to plan ways to protect Adan *without* the pilot's help. Maybe this mission wouldn't be such a cakewalk after all.

He was going to need his own cup of coffee. Or something stronger.

———

EVERYTHING WAS A SEA AROUND HER, midnight blue and deep. Some part of Ellen's mind clenched in fear, but another part—the part of her out front, in command—leapt with excitement. Her fingers flexed in her sleep, searching, reaching, stretching.

Hungry.

Points of light sprang to life like stars, glorious and golden. Thin tendrils connected them, so fragile and tiny one could barely see them. But she knew they were there.

Oh, she knew.

Beyond seeing them, she could *feel* them. Like blood in her veins. Like her own heart beating. Like breath.

Once a Starbird, always a Starbird.

Her mind flew along the connections, soaring above the data, digging. Not even for anything in particular, just hungry. More information. More knowledge. The more she knew the more she might protect her world, her team...

Herself.

At the idea, something cracked. Some part of her mind screamed—but which? The sea around her shattered, panes of blue falling into a night deeper and darker, black and cold.

No, it couldn't go. Not yet. Not so soon. She needed it, she needed it. Not yet, not so soon.

She *needed* it.

She woke with a gasp, reaching out into the dark, empty cabin. She froze. Tiny lights blinked green on the holodesk, not golden, and faint white stripes indicated the way to the bathroom. The darkness around her was now dotted with pale mint, orange, twinkling blue.

The golden connections, the midnight sea. All gone.

The silence, too, was gone, replaced by a constant, familiar hum that she couldn't quite name.

She scrambled out of the bed, almost falling, stumbling to the port-hole. The stars sparkled back at her, placid and timeless. Dispassionate and cold. The starscape was no comfort.

The cabin overheads flickered on, the bright lights scaring her back against the wall, eyes darting around in fear.

"Commander Ryu," said a quiet voice.

Xi, she realized belatedly. And the hum—her ship. *Audacity.* She pressed the pads of her fingers to its cold metal walls, searching for balance.

"How many stars in the Andromeda Galaxy?"

"At last estimate, one trillion."

"What is the temperature on Faros at—"

"It varies on average from a comfortable fifteen degrees Celsius to twenty-seven degrees Celsius."

"What about—"

"Commander, may I suggest these?"

The rest of the lights dimmed, leaving only her punching bag and gloves lit. She hadn't realized the lights could even *do* that.

Weakly, shaking, she straightened, her eyes fixed on the gloves. Some of the tension drained out of her.

Yes.

She staggered over, slipped her hand inside the first. Tightened her fist.

One day, Arakovic. One day.

She slipped on the second. Yes.

All the information she needed was right here.

———

JENNY WAS the first to arrive in the quiet, echoing cargo hold. She scanned the room before taking a deep, bracing breath and hitting the cargo hatch button.

Warm, humid air filtered through the contaminant field, hit her like a wet towel in the face, and wrapped around her as the ramp lowered. She failed to suppress a groan. Blasted, horrible place. And this was nothing compared to the heat on the ground. Thank God for armor cooling units.

Except she wasn't going to be wearing one today. Her armor was packed in its case near her feet, along with extra armor for Adan. She tucked another stray red strand back and frowned down at her Utlis Sportswear–brand gear in annoyance—an aubergine soccer jersey and a charcoal tennis skirt, plus a simple silver breather. The air on Capital was usually very safe, or so they wanted you to believe, but it wasn't worth taking any chances. Few did.

The clothes were of her mother's more stylish tastes, not her personal choice. But since they planned on walking, they were likely to run into some fans, who'd be weirded out if they saw her in her armor. Or wouldn't have noticed her. It would have been really, *really* nice to have hidden inside her hard metal shell, but that didn't play into Patron Simmons's plan.

People were supposed to know she was here. So she had to play her part. Her old part. Her old self. Like riding a bicycle, right?

A bicycle you hated.

"Happy to be home?" Josana tilted her head up on the catwalk that overlooked the hold. "I thought I'd be the one most eager to get off." Her eyes narrowed and nose scrunched in a sneer.

"Kiss off, Josana." She focused on ignoring Josana and walked back to the ladder on the far side where her pack waited. Capital was annoying enough without having to deal with Josana's nonsense.

She must have been grumbling to herself as she checked the pack was secure, because she didn't hear the footsteps approaching. She didn't notice anything really except that awful warm air invading, stealing away the crisp coolness of space.

"You okay?"

Jenny's head snapped up. Adan was standing at the base of the ladder, one hand still on the railing, one eyebrow raised over those gorgeous, intelligent eyes crinkled with laughter. If only it wasn't at her consternation. "Uh… yeah. Just checking my pack."

"You seem pretty agitated for just checking your pack. Did I hear something about 'blasted warm weather'?" Adan sidestepped to make room for Kael clomping down the ladder after him. Great—double the audience.

She ducked her head, blushing. Checked another strap. "Just not looking forward to this," she muttered.

"The heat's really not that bad. You get used to it." He sidestepped again to the other side of her, eying her ministrations.

Her cheeks only grew hotter. As if it weren't already warm enough in here. Yep, he doesn't know. She had kept this secret a little too well.

"Although I grew up on a desert planet. Maybe I'm biased." He shrugged.

Kael stopped at the base of the ladder, gazing out the cargo hatch with a whistle. You could just see the tops of the skyscrapers. "Me too. This seems like a wetter heat, though, don't you think?"

"Capital is a tropical climate," she said numbly. "At least here at the epicenter. But most of the population is settled on one of the many equatorial archipelagos." Only at the very end of her ramble did she notice Adan glaring daggers at Kael. Kael, for his part, was ignoring the pilot. What the hell?

"Oh, yeah?" Adan finally glanced out the hatch now too, before resting his gaze on Jenny again. "You doing some reading on the mission?"

She wished she could have reveled in the fact that he was actually making small talk. If only the topic were more palatable. "I've, uh, been here before."

"Really?" said Kael. "Climbing competitions?"

"You could say that," she muttered.

"Corporal Utlis grew up here." All three of them looked up to see Commander Ryu stopped on the catwalk above them. She leaned on the railing with both hands, eyes gazing out over the city skyline. "As I believe she's told you, she's a legend. Here and elsewhere."

Jenny blushed harder. Her usual bravado had fled with the tropical wind. Capital always took her down a notch. Horrid place. She resumed fussing over her pack.

Ryu started down the ladder. "But especially here."

Jenny finally risked raising her eyes. A mistake. Both men were staring at her. She swore, hefted it over her shoulder, and headed for the hatch.

"Did you know she was from Capital?" Kael was saying behind her.

"No."

"Guess you never can tell, can ya?"

"I heard that," she snapped, glaring back over her shoulder at them. Then she continued out through the barrier and into the heat. She ought to be glad they were surprised, she supposed.

But it was hard to be cheery on this stupid rock.

"Uncharacteristically pissed, too," Kael observed.

"Agreed."

Adan and Kael gradually caught up to her, their own packs over their shoulders, joining her on the platform just outside the cargo hatch. Kael stopped beside her, and Adan scooted over to the other. Was it her imagination, or was Adan trying to distance himself from Kael? Odd.

"Now you don't see that in the outsystem." Adan sucked in a huge breath, then let it out slowly.

The glorious splendor of Capital stretched before them. Begrudgingly, Jenny reminded herself to take a moment, to *try* to appreciate it, to see it through their eyes if she could.

Even if the core was rotten, the shell was sort of pretty to behold.

Sort of.

Their landing platform was several hundred feet in the air. Stretching before the *Audacity* were buildings as far as the eye could see, packed together in pillars of white, silver, ivory, and sky blue. Rich, grassy parks were the only breaks in the porcelain expanse. Palm-lined pools and canals glimmered turquoise as peacock feathers, winding from parks toward the ocean to the east, not a one of them naturally occurring. All of it a lesson in artifice. Skyscrapers dominated the skyline, stretching into low clouds that hung not much higher than their dock, maybe a hundred feet more above them. Lush plant life adorned levels and rooftops, breaking up the alabaster with strips of verdant jungle. Above them, the ship docks continued until the clouds obscured them.

"Faros has more concrete than sand at this point," Kael breathed, "but I've never seen anything like *this*."

"A nice facade," she admitted grudgingly. "Don't let it fool you."

Adan waved a hand at the view. "What could you possibly have against a place like *this*? Paradise."

Her lips thinned. See if he thought the same thing as a noncitizen in a court of law. She dodged his gaze. "Paradise only for some."

Josana strode up beside them breezily. "Don't listen to her. It *is* paradise, and not just of the tropical kind. The mind rules here. Science, art, intelligence—all held in the highest regard."

"Sounds pretty good to me." Adan's eyes had a dreamy light to them as he gazed out at the city.

"Only for some," Jenny repeated again, more insistently this time.

Josana waved her off.

"What do you mean, only for some?" Kael leaned one arm on the railing, turning toward her.

Before she could answer, Josana cut in. "That's nonsense. Our judi-
cial system is *beyond* fair."

Jenny rolled her eyes as she turned toward Kael. It was probably
best if she just pretended Josana didn't exist for the duration of this
mission. Otherwise, she might have an aneurysm. Or murder the bitch.
She held up her hand and rubbed two fingers against her thumb, as
though rubbing old-fashioned bills of currency together.

The former Theroki frowned and mouthed the word *money* silently,
one eyebrow raised.

She nodded and turned back, only to notice in the corner of her eye
that Adan had slipped his hand around Josana's waist. Jenny tried not
to glower at them.

"I'm just *so* happy to be home." Josana heaved an exaggerated deep
breath of the tropical air. "Can you smell the coconut? And the plays,
the productions, the installations—I have so much to catch up on! And
the architecture. I can do nothing but bask in the beauty of human
achievement for a while—"

Jenny couldn't take it anymore. "Oh, just kill me now," she
muttered, slapping a hand to her face.

"Now just because my status is so far above yours—"

"Your status as more fake than counterfeit dahkmas?"

Josana stopped and narrowed her eyes. "Envy is really not
becoming on you. You should really work on that."

"If you were any more full of it, you'd bubble over with bullshit.
How about you work on *that*?" The words popped out before Jenny
could stop them. Hmm, maybe glowering would have been better.

Kael chuckled. "Now *there's* a mental image I didn't need." He
glanced back at the ship. Looking for someone? Jenny almost
snickered.

"It was either that or me vomiting over the side," she said, cupping
her hand to direct her voice only at the Theroki.

"In that case, I approve of your choice."

Josana couldn't simply drop her gushing without protest, however.
"You athletic types can be so rude. No respect for the finer aspects of
society."

Jenny rolled her eyes again and forced her anger down. "Thanks for reminding me so perfectly why I left. Kael, any idea where the commander wandered off to? I'm ready to get started. Are we missing anyone else?"

Kael's eyes widened slightly. "Why are you asking me?"

She grinned at him. Because she knew he paid better attention to where Ryu was than anyone else. But she didn't say that. "Cause you're the ranking officer out here—and on this away mission. Didn't you realize?" Of course, by ship seniority alone he would have never made lieutenant right off the bat. He did have the advantage of his prior Theroki experience, which was more military than her own training had been. But truth be told, she and Zhia had just been fairly sure they'd never get the poor bastard hooked up with the commander without an officer's rank of some sort.

And it also gave someone competent for Zhia to shirk off her duties onto in the meantime. That seemed to be working quite well at the current moment. Besides, seniority and resumes were bullshit. They knew he could do the job.

Kael only continued to stare for a split second—and was rescued by the appearance of Ryu in the hatchway down, armored up and pack in hand. "Looks like she's incoming. With her, this is everybody."

"Ready to go, Commander?" Jenny called.

Ryu spared a crisp nod and started down the ramp.

"C'mon." Jenny shifted her pack higher on her shoulder. "Let's get this shitshow over with."

She headed toward the ramp, but Kael didn't follow, to her surprise. But of course—he hung back, waiting for the commander. Jenny twisted her lips, only a little bitter.

A few moments later, boots trotted up behind her. Even more surprising, they belonged to Adan, who was glancing over his shoulder as he caught up with her. Jenny spared a glance back too—to see Josana falling in beside Kael, who'd fallen in beside the commander.

Again with the distance. She was not going to believe that he was walking beside her so much as avoiding Kael for some reason. Why?

They walked in silence for a flight or two. He stared out over the city, not watching where he was going. Poor wide-eyed tourist.

"So you want a tour guide or something?" she said.

"What?" He hadn't been paying attention.

"You got questions about this place, Adan?"

"Well… yeah."

"Good. It'll give me something to do."

"Uh, okay. Why's it called Capital, when it's not the capital of anything?"

"Some of the Movers who founded this place were very ambitious. And egotistical. The rest were Buddhist monks. Makes for a weird combination. You'll see. Next question."

"Um. What's the deal with these docks?" He waved a hand up and behind him.

"This is the Edern Docking Port."

"Why's it go so high up in the air?"

"For efficiency. And because horizontal space is at a premium on Capital. Land itself is the greatest luxury. If we wanted to have a patch of land just for our ship, I imagine the cost would be astronomical."

He frowned. "But those parks…"

"Some of them are government-controlled land. No better way for them to invest, i.e., hog valuable assets. Most of them are not open to the public, though."

He raised an eyebrow. "Really?"

"Land is the greatest luxury. That includes trees. Why do you think so many of the buildings are brimming with them? Everything is made into a symbol of status here—or of your lack thereof."

"Do those championships pay well, for all that travel?"

"Huh? Oh, not exactly, but the sponsors pay decently. Climbing is a pretty popular sport here on Capital. Guess it helps to have vertical exercise options with all the tall buildings, I don't know. The trips usually paid for themselves and a little more to live on for later."

They rounded a third flight of stairs, and suddenly it seemed to dawn on Adan that this was only going to keep going.

And going. And going.

"Wait a minute," Adan said. "Is it stairs all the way down? This *entire* way? No elevator or tube or anything?"

"Only if you have a medical reason to need it." Jenny smiled. "Or sufficient credits."

"Why do you think I'm carrying our luggage?" Ryu called from behind them. Jenny winced a little. Hadn't realized the commander was listening.

"Because we don't have sufficient credits?" Adan grinned.

Jenny laughed in spite of herself. As if. The Foundation most certainly had the credits. But there were much better things to spend them on.

"Well, it's not because I'm the newbie."

At that, Kael grabbed the tractor out of her hand. Jenny thought she caught a trace of a smile behind a partially darkened visor. "Let me take that," he said. "I *am* the newbie."

"Do you even need that?"

"No. But no sense wasting energy."

Jenny tore her eyes away. God, she'd give a hundred climbing trophies to see him "accidentally" ram that floating pile of armor cases and bags into Josana's knee.

Jenny and Adan slowly pulled ahead, as maneuvering the tractor was not entirely simple in the narrow grated stairwells, and Adan seemed to be in a hurry.

"So… I didn't hear your answer. What did you mean, only for some?"

Jenny shrugged. She was tired of bickering about this place, and she especially didn't want to do it with him. "Josana has her opinions. I have mine. Maybe you should ask her."

"I heard hers. I'm asking you."

"This is paradise if you have the money, the status. The right paperwork."

His eyebrows rose at that last one. "Ah. Yes."

"But much more often it's about status."

"Well, where isn't it about status? Isn't that what military rank is all about? Everyone cares about that."

"That's different." Neither she nor Adan had served in the military outside of this outfit, but he chose the oddest times to remind her of that. He'd been a commercial pilot, sort of. For bandits, basically. As a pilot, he was more isolated from the rest of the team on the *Audacity*, especially when it came to day-to-day duties. "Rank is about the chain of command. It's about working your way up, about coordination and responsibility on the team. Duty. Here status is about what favors you can pull. Who you know. How much money you can plunk down. Look, I'm not saying that doesn't happen in the armed forces. But it makes me sick how much it happens here."

"So you're saying you don't care about status?"

"I don't. Definitely not the way they do here."

"Why did you compete, then, if not for status?" He smiled.

She took a deep breath, trying to let the venom drain away before answering. "Wanting to win is not necessarily the same thing as wanting status. Sometimes it's personal. I like bettering my record. I'm competitive. But not just so somebody will like me. It's for me. But I don't expect Josana would understand that."

"Ah," he said slowly. What the hell did that mean? He seemed lost in thought.

"And I didn't have a lot of choice about it," she added hastily into the silence. What if he never asked her about this—or anything—again? "My parents required it. Mostly my father. My family is full of acclaimed athletes."

"Really?"

"Really. Look, see?" She pointed at the white insignia on the sleeve of her shirt, *UTLIS* in clean, heavy letters.

"Is that… your name?"

"Yes. Well, my parents' name. They have a whole clothing and accessory brand. And don't even get me started on sporting goods. Jewelry. Holo training programs. The works."

He raised his eyebrows. "I had no idea."

"My father even froze himself in order to travel back to Earth to compete in the Olympics. The real Earth ones. Or, at least that's his plan."

"Are you serious?"

"As a heart attack. It's a stupid scheme. Even if he survives, even *if* they allow someone with his level of augmentation to compete in the future—and they don't today—there'll still have been two hundred years of technological advancement. Those future athletes are going to leave him in the dust. Er, powder. He's primarily a competitive skier. Assuming they still have snow on Earth then." There hadn't been much when the first Mover ships had begun to leave Earth, but propaganda said it was better there now. Hard to say if what news they received over the light-years was really true or heavily edited.

"A skier. And he raised you *here*?"

"Oh, yes. There are plenty of indoor and underground mountains for skiing. It's a common pastime, nice break from the heat."

Now both his eyebrows just stayed raised. "That's... extravagant."

"Yep."

"Wait—you said he froze himself. Does that mean you're never going to see him again?"

She drooped a little in spite of herself. Telling herself she didn't care was harder than convincing herself not to. "You are correct."

"That's awful. Didn't you want to go with him?"

"What, on that fool-brained scheme? No way. I have every intention of living my life right now. The right way. On my terms."

"But... won't you miss him?"

She said nothing for a long moment. The truth seemed too callous to admit. Finally she let out a long sigh. "Rub it in, why don't you, Adan?"

"Shit. Sorry."

"Want to throw a little salt on the wound? Lemon? Season the treat while you're at it."

He said nothing for a long moment. His voice was softer when he spoke again. "I lost my mother in the civil wars back on Bantilla. If I could have a chance to see her again, or to have stayed by her side..."

Her anger melted. "I'm sorry to hear that." She glanced out at the city, groping for words. Only a dozen or so more flights to the bottom.

"I… my relationship with my father wasn't like that. It was complicated. I never wanted to compete."

"And yet—you're a legend."

"Exactly. What I wanted didn't matter to him. I was a walking sack
of genes. He even told me once how he'd wanted to engineer me to be
a boy, but my mother drew the line and wouldn't let him. Wanted to
conceive the usual way."

"Old-fashioned?"

"Lazy, I think? I don't know. She only carried me for a few months
before she got bored and annoyed with how it was getting in the way
of her career. Then it was off to the uterine chamber for me."

"Wow. Evicted early." He ran a hand over his face, as if trying to
wipe the perpetual amazement off of it. "This place is… different than
I thought."

"It takes time for your eyes to adjust to see the shadows," she said
softly, staring at her boots. She forced her head up, straightened. She
needed to keep an eye out for hostiles, not be gazing at her navel, even
in places like Capital. Even she who knew better could be lulled by its
illusion of peace and safety. "So my father and I were never on good
terms, and it got worse once I left and joined Commander Ryu on the
Audacity."

"Why?"

"He said I was abandoning my career. He was right about that. But
I was at a point where I could win all the nonaugmented competitions
I bothered to enter. He'd reached that point too. Many do, and then
they enter the next arena, redesigning their bodies for better and
better performance, employing their own engineers and scientists to
develop tech no one else has, to put them at the absolute top of their
game."

"You didn't want to go there?"

She shrugged. "Seems more like car racing than athletics at that
point to me. Who's got the most tricked-out chassis? Who can *afford* it,
if we're being honest? But also it was never really *my* career. It was his
career, continued."

Silence for a long moment. Only their boots on the metal grating, the screeching of wary birds from a nearby nest as they reached the highest treetops.

"I can see why you didn't go to Earth then."

"I *do* miss him." She gritted her teeth, hating to admit it. "I would have liked to have convinced him that this—my real career, my first career—was better. More meaningful. At least to me. As long as he was here, there was a chance I could have changed his mind."

"And now…"

"And now there's not. Unless I live to be three hundred." She shrugged helplessly.

"Hey, you never know." He gave her a crooked smile.

She wanted to debate that point, but he was right. She was young. She couldn't know how time would change how she felt about some things, like if it'd be worth trying harder to live to three hundred. Or freezing herself. Or hiring a mercenary ship to chase down her dad's frozen corpse and blow it up.

They'd reached the bottom, and she led the way across the bridge to Appellate 481 as they talked. The delicate white arms of the bridge arched over their heads like the rib bones of some giant dead animal.

Loud speakers blared at them above huge industrial filters three stories high. "Welcome to Capital. The air quality today is level turquoise. No contaminants, viruses, or other foreign agents are detected. Pollen management is active. Filters are active. Remember, Capital air is extremely safe to breathe. Breathers are not necessary. Genoterrorists will be prosecuted to the fullest extent of the law. Welcome to Capital! The air quality today is turquoise…"

They'd barely gone two blocks into the city before she heard a cry.

"I know that face! Well, the Movers be damned. Aliandaranda—get over here." A little of the pep in Jenny's step returned as a group of girls just about her age rushed at them from the corner. "This way. *Now*. I need a picture!" The leader—the one who'd spoken—wore a shocking orange plasticky dress that cut off surprisingly high up her thighs and had very tiny orange fish swimming through the fabric. The blond with the trendy name as long as a jungle snake was arm in arm with the leader and wore something more akin to traditional Capital robes, although with a belt of glowing silver. The third was black haired, black lipped, and black eyed, without even the whites of her eyes showing—and significantly less enthusiastic than the other two. Was that a mod or an augmentation or just contacts or—no, on second thought, Jenny didn't want to know.

And she didn't have much more time to analyze anyway, as the leader with her brunette bob and orange dress was quickly in Jenny's face. Orange lips, too. Matchy-matchy must be on trend this week. "I saw you in that three-hundred-meter free climb—the one where you broke the record—"

"Well, I saw you twice—" The blond cut in, nudging the leader aside.

"Hey, you there." Orange Dress wiggled and then snapped her fingers in Adan's face. His eyes widened. "Let's go. Picture. We don't want to waste Ms. Utlis's time."

Amused, Adan took the tablet that was shoved vigorously into his hands. He backed away a few feet and snapped some pictures.

"Amazing work, boyo," said the blond, swiping through his results to check.

"Well if I can take video with a drone, I sure as hell should be able to—"

"You what?" Blondie tilted her head and frowned.

Adan looked like he was struggling not to roll his eyes. Well at least Jenny had no competition in that department.

"And now," Orange Dress declared, "we owe you a mangabrew."

"A what?" said Adan.

Now Blondie looked like she wanted to roll her eyes. "You haven't had? Well, then you *definitely* need a mangabrew."

Orange Dress had never really let go of Jenny, which was somewhat starting to freak her out, and now Blondie deigned to grab Adan by the arm and shuffle the group of them up the street. Hmm, maybe she shouldn't count the girl out so soon. A call sounded in the distance behind them, likely just street noise. A lander screeched past them, leaving clouds of steam in its wake, and then they all crossed to the next block.

"Is there anywhere that just serves coffee?" Jenny eyed the mangabrew shop warily as they approached. The sign illustrated a squid shooting ink into a red bowl.

"Oh, you don't want that." Orange Dress shook her head, her perfect bob barely moving. "Mangabrew is the absolute zenith, Utlis. You've got to try it."

Jenny tried not to laugh at the odd mix of presumed friendliness and formality. The woman didn't call her Jenny, oh no, but she had to make it seem like they were at least a little friendly somehow. "Oh, we definitely *will* try it. But my friend just flew us here, and we're a bit worn out."

"Oh…" The blond one squeezed Adan's arm closer to her side and smiled up at him. "You didn't mention your friend was a *pilot*."

Her companion leaned in and cupped a hand toward Jenny's ear. "Think she's looking for a pilot to take *her* to the zenith, if you know what I mean."

Something in Jenny's face must have given her true feelings away, some small zing of hurt or jealousy in the eyes, because Orange Dress's eyes widened. "Silieantrana, I think Utlis's *friend* needs some coffee. Come *on*."

With Jenny blushing and searching for words to correct the mistake, Orange Dress dragged her farther down the street, Adan and the other two in her wake.

Fortunately, Orange Dress had the good sense to take off after the coffees were acquired. Jenny was still eying the biological readout on the coffee on the public meter and checking it hadn't been tampered with. It at least *seemed* safe to take a sip… God, she would have preferred armor. There was no telling if this "coffee" was the usual decaf stuff or some other concoction masquerading as the good stuff. Whatever.

The three of them were already fluttering down the next street before she'd even managed a sip, Orange Dress burbling happiness all the way. "Wait until we tell Sarlano that the queen of climbing is in town. And *we* had coffee with her. And he didn't."

Adan stared after them, then took a sip as if he hoped it would help him recover. "But... we didn't have coffee with them."

Jenny snorted. "Things are different here. By their rules, we did."

"They didn't even buy anything for themselves. Or say anything. Or even *ask* you anything."

"They plunked down the money to get the bragging rights. We're too far apart in status and acquaintance for them to also ask for the time. Polite girls, really."

"Seriously?"

"Yes. Smart not to push it. This way I might actually give them the time if I ever run into them again."

"But you... I... you, uh..."

"Hardly know them? Yeah."

"So why would you bother to talk to them now or next time? It's like they're buying access."

"Yeah, sorta. I might bother because they've shown social dexterity. Respect. An astute knowledge of hierarchy and status." She let her voice lilt on the last words, in imitation of the girl's slangy intonations —and Josana's to some extent. "Personally I prefer to make friends with people who seem authentic or clever. But this is the way the system works here. You know, giving you a tour of your new prospective homeland."

Adan opened his mouth as if he were going to ask something more, but they'd delayed long enough that the other three caught up.

"Done being legendary, Corporal?" Ryu stopped and lightened her visor.

"Yes, ma'am. Sorry, ma'am." Jenny raised the coffee in an informal salute.

"If anyone's sorry, it's me." Ryu's eyes twinkled. "Stay closer, will ya? We were worried we were about to lose you. Let's move out."

"Coffee?" Josana asked as they began walking. "How passé."

"There was a mangabrew shop a block that way," Adan offered.

"Is that what those girls were drinking?"

He nodded. "Yep. Add it to your to-do list."

More blocks passed in silence as the whole group eyed the buildings and shops around them now. And the crowd. They passed food stores hawking all manner of foods, both familiar and exotic. A new trend toward crunchy and nutty appeared to be taking off. The fashion boutiques were in another district, but there were some odd fabric shops, as well as tea and spice shops too. Some were styled to look ancient and traditional, like steps leading up to an old monastery of red mud with wind chimes hanging. Those sat right next to glowing feats of technology with spinning displays selling the latest improvements to the apple.

She did manage to gawk alongside Adan as they passed the Mover temple. Models of the colony ships, replicated in sheer iridescent plex, floated above the vast grassy park with only fleeting holograms moving through the space in a ghostly array of pastels. They were like some bizarre daytime *aurora borealis*. A temple where no one worshiped had always seemed strange to her, and few truly worshipped their ancestor Movers anyway. Which had always seemed ironic to her. If there was anyone worth worshiping, the people who had brought them here seemed fair. A two hundred year journey facing possible death must have drawn brave souls. Or desperate ones.

The streets were just as clogged with people as she remembered. Maybe eighty percent humans, but there were many Ursas too. Any Ursa who had a taste for fashion eventually made their way here. Several notable Teredarks had made careers as models for designs too large and outlandish for human bodies, but few actually wandered the streets or the shops. Nothing was built for their size or their mandibles here. No, the humans were strange enough, a vast array of clothing shapes, sizes, colors, luminosities, and textures. A recent trend seemed to be incorporating live animals, as she saw several more trapped fish and one monkey hanging around a woman's neck and shuddered.

She and Adan gradually pulled ahead again. The district grew less commercial and more industrial as they neared Persad's research complex. Their first stop.

"Is that—are those—" Adan stopped short.

Jenny followed his gaze to a large tiered building with open sides, each floor shining with artificial sun and waving grasses. Pounding across artificial low hills were herds of white horses, extinct rhino horns genetically engineered to grow from their foreheads in a gorgeous iridescent sheen.

"Oh. Yeah. Those. Unicorns. Neat, huh? All three levels of this structure have pastured herds under reflected sun."

"Wow. That's... a lot of unicorns. Are they just genetically altered horses?"

"Pretty much. Oh, and this farm is on the small side. Probably cause it's close to the docks here. They likely have crops further up."

"Wait. Farm?"

"Oh yeah. People love 'em."

"People love... what? I don't see anyone riding them."

"Yeah, these aren't for riding. Those ones have more colorful manes." She cleared her throat. "Uh, how to put this... Unicorn is a delicacy on Capital."

"Delicacy?" Had his face just turned slightly greener? "You mean they *eat* them?"

"Yeah. Brutal, isn't it?" She shrugged as she tucked a windswept bit of hair back behind her ear. "Think of that when your Josana spouts off about fine art and culture. Food is part of culture, you know."

He was frowning at her. "She's not *my* Josana. Or she won't be after this liftoff."

She raised her eyebrows and jerked a thumb back toward the dock. "You two seemed cozy enough back there."

"Yeah, I guess." He rubbed the back of his neck, a little embarrassed. "She wants me to stay. With her. Here."

"Ah." Probably why he'd weaseled his way onto this mission, for more time with Her Awfulness. Jenny didn't see how that could work with his citizenship. Maybe Simmons had offered to fabricate something. Adan had always been stubbornly against that in the past.

A long, awkward silence stretched out.

"So do it," she said finally.

"I can't." He was still rubbing the back of his neck. "And leave the stars? Flying? The *Audacity*? Ryu and Xi?"

"Well, that's more than a few reasons." Her voice was mild, much milder than she felt. Couldn't *she* be one of those reasons? "So don't do it."

"It's not that simple."

She turned a steady gaze on him. "Sure it is. If you love her, some things are worth the risk."

His eyes met hers and locked, staring for a long moment, long past anything comfortable, but she couldn't look away.

Thank the heavens, Kael trotted up, breaking the moment. "Quit getting so far ahead, you two. Did you see those unicorns, Adan? Crazy!"

"She says they eat them."

"What?" Kael pinned her with his gaze. "Wait—have you?"

"Once. But I try not to eat species that are nicer or smarter than me, as a general rule. Or ones that are mystical symbols of goodness and purity. Let alone all of the above."

He blinked, looking back as the herd thundered past them again. "They eat... Wow."

"But do they have dragon steaks? Phoenix wings?" Adan grinned.

Jenny smacked him on the arm.

"Kidding."

"There *are* fairy wings. Do *not* ask about that. If you do, I warned you." Jenny clapped Adan on the shoulder as she smiled at Kael. "That's just Capital for ya. Beautiful as a porcelain statue on the outside. Rotten as a corpse underneath."

She turned away and kept on walking, leaving the two of them standing there, staring.

They had a mission to do.

CHAPTER FOUR

THE TEAM ARRIVED at Persad's building, floating cloud of gear and all, about thirty minutes after they'd started. Ellen wanted to size up the situation, see how receptive Persad was, before they figured out where they'd stash their stuff. Maybe if they got lucky, they'd be heading straight back to the ship.

The five of them reached Derad Tower and paused, gazing up at the creamy white tower that seemed to sway slightly in the wind. Five of them, because Ellen had insisted on getting the mission started before escorting Josana to her apartment. Or her parents' apartment, or whatever it was. No one was there waiting for them, so it didn't much matter.

As Doug had instructed, she approached the east service entrance and held up her gauntlet for her credentials. The door dinged and slid open with a puff.

"Well, that was easy," Jenny muttered as they filed in.

"Too easy?" asked Adan. The first door snicked shut behind him, and the decon scan swept over them. They should be clean, especially after a short walk in a place like Capital, but one never could be too careful.

"The Foundation owns this building," Ellen reminded them. "If not on paper, then in practice. Dozens of research labs here. It shouldn't be that surprising Doug can get us into our own building."

The decon computer must have been satisfied, because it popped open the next door and allowed them inside.

Following the briefing plan—and the map of it overlaid on her helmet visor—she led them from the service corridors to the main halls through several flights of stairs and one elevator. They conveniently bypassed any kind of main reception or security.

Then again, they actually had a legitimate key for once.

They reached their final elevator, which took them the last thirty-six floors to their destination. The eerily silent hallway was painted a pale baby blue. Shining gray floors made it clinical, sterile, and stylish all at the same time. Their footsteps echoed. A black plate lettered in crisp white on the left side read *Dr. Crispin Ostrov*, on the right *Totaku and Associates*, and farther down *Dr. Alemeda Rosenberg*.

The elevator doors dinged behind them as Kael arrived with the gear. They hadn't all fit in one trip. She shuffled down the hallway more earnestly now. Eight doors down, in accordance with the mission plan, the plate read *Dr. Chayana Persad*.

The door stood open an inch, unlatched. All the others had been closed. The mission plan did *not* include that.

She caught Kael's attention. He lowered the gear and darted to the other side of the door as Ellen readied her multi.

She nudged the door open another two inches. A tiny tinkle of bells.

"Dr. Persad?" she called.

No answer. Walls the orange of the boldest sunset caught her eye, along with a glass table littered with tiny bits of electronics.

"I smell—is that cardamom? Anise?" Jenny whispered. "Coming out of there like there's a window open or something."

"On the thirty-fourth floor?" Kael leaned a little closer, trying to see inside.

Ellen nudged the door open a foot now, accompanied by the

jangling of the bells. "Hard to sneak in without making a noise, isn't it." She nodded toward Kael.

"Because she was worried someone would be sneaking?" He pivoted into the doorway and scanned the far corner they could see best.

"My thoughts exactly." She raised her voice. "Are you in here, ma'am? Dr. Persad?"

Still no answer.

"Okay, go."

He thrust the door the rest of the way open, and the two of them swept in, heading for the far office room. The place was tiny, and half the space was taken up by the flood of glittering, disassembled components, so they cleared the place in no time.

Kael straightened in the doorway to the second room. "No one's here, Commander."

She waved for the others to come in. "This was her office address, right?"

Adan jerked a thumb behind him. "Her name plate is on the door."

"Maybe she keeps irregular hours?" Jenny shrugged, hands spread.

"Then why was the door open? And—look." Kael pointed at a nearby coffee pot. "Still brewing. Someone was just here."

Ellen pursed her lips. "Either they left in a hurry, or... they're still here."

Her eyes traced the walls, but the orange went on seamlessly, almost like plastic molded just to this space. Strange. She turned her eyes to the ceiling, looking for any unusual crease that might indicate a hiding place.

"Can I help you?"

A man with short, curling black hair stood in the doorway, eyebrows raised. He wore a high-collared, charcoal coat that fell to his knees—one that could conceal all manner of weapons—and a silver stud winked at her from his right ear. A dark wooden cane was clutched in one hand, and although he leaned on it, her gut screamed that he didn't need it. His every detail was controlled; shoes shined, hair styled just on the border between traditional and edgy, salt-and-pepper beard. He was handsome—and he knew it.

She was glad he couldn't see her eyes narrowing behind her visor. But it would be impolite to leave her visor dark on any inner world. Sometimes civilization was so fragging annoying. She smoothed her features and lightened the visor in greeting. But she didn't retract the helmet. "We're looking for Dr. Persad. We have a commission. Do you happen to know where she is?"

He spread his hands, palms up. "Isn't she here? She just got in for the morning a few minutes ago. I said hello to her in the hallway."

"The morning?" Adan muttered behind her.

Ellen pretended not to hear. "Does she usually start the day after 1200 hours, Mister... ?"

"Ostrov." He gave her a bright, winning smile as he took a step forward and held out a hand to shake. "Crispin Ostrov, and it's Doctor, actually." He glanced at her hand, seemed to realize shaking hands in armor was awkward bordering on dangerous, and straightened, wiping the palm along his coat. "I'm not Chayana's keeper, but many of us work at whatever hours suit us."

"I see." Ellen ignored additional grumbling from Adan and hoped this Ostrov didn't notice. "Makes it a bit hard for potential clients."

He raised just one eyebrow now. Huh, his eyes were green, like Technicolor emerald green. An unusual color, probably engineered. "Well, you *could* make an appointment..."

Hell, she hadn't meant to give away something like that through banter. Time to end this discussion. "Ah, yes. We will. Are you one of her fellow scientists, then, Dr. Ostrov?"

"Fellow researcher and friend. My lab is three doors down." He waved his cane in the general direction.

"Well, thank you for stopping by. We'll just have to check back later."

He took another step forward. Damn it, why were her shoulders clenching up? This man—physically at least—was harmless. "Do you have a comm address at which she, or I, could reach you? I could let her know that you were here. When she gets back."

Ellen hesitated. Did she want Persad to know they'd stopped by? Or anyone for that matter? The words were a little off, her gut screaming that he wanted the comm info for some other reason.

He wasn't the polite, helpful sort. She could just tell.

"How about you give me yours instead?" she said.

He raised his eyebrows again, and she could have sworn Kael stiffened in her peripheral vision. Ostrov reached into his pocket and smoothly handed her a printed paper card. It was a practiced move, quite comfortable for him. "It would be my pleasure," he said. "I'd love to get more acquainted. It's not every day lovely armored women come strolling through a high-security office building on a casual business call."

She stared at him flatly. Lovely? It was all she could do not to snort.

He smiled, undisturbed by her gaze. "But you know my name. You won't leave me wanting, will you?" His eyes twinkled again. "Do share your own."

Bastard. "Ryu," she said. "Chief of security for Ms. Jenny Utlis. But please keep that to yourself." Even if it was their cover story, it'd only feel more real if she acted secretive about it.

"A delight to meet you, Chief Ryu. Good day to you all."

She pocketed the card as he waved goodbye and headed back toward the lab.

She switched on the thermal readout to see if he *really* went where he said he was going to. The room held its breath.

She nodded to the others when he did. For now. She turned back to the team. "All right, look around one more time and then let's get out of here."

"Should we leave a note or something?" Jenny peered into a second room at the back of the office.

Ellen scanned the shelves and hooks by the door, looking for some clue as to where and how far Persad had gone. "Hmm. No, I don't think so. I don't have a good feeling about this."

Kael bent down and examined the bells on the back of the door. "Did she know we were coming and want to avoid us? Or did she think someone *else* was coming?"

"Someone dangerous?" Ellen tilted her head pointedly toward Ostrov's office.

Josana pursed her lips. "Or did she simply have to pee? All of you have such a flair for the dramatic."

Ellen wished she'd already darkened her visor so she could roll her eyes in private. "All right, we'll find a base of operations close by, and we'll come back."

"Wait," Adan said. He stood beside Jenny, peering back into the second room. "There's a holodisplay back here. Far from new." He strode into the room, and the others followed. Rounding the desk, he held out his hands as if he were scanning the cluttered work surface with them—a sea of papers and pens and mugs and cups. "Old school. No biometrics I can see on the workstation. You want me to try… ?" He inclined his head and raised an eyebrow.

She pursed her lips. Not even on Capital for a day, and they were already having him break the law. But considering the computer and the research almost certainly belonged to Capital… presumably that meant Doug could get them out of any trouble they got themselves into. "All right, do it. It's on me if we get caught. I'll watch the door. Josana stays with me. Jenny—that back exit. Kael, stay with Adan."

Josana folded her arms across her chest, rolled her eyes, and followed Ellen out to the main entryway.

———

ADAN PULLED on his gloves and surveyed Persad's desk, letting his instincts work. He could start with the machine, as time was of the essence. But he had a feeling a physical shortcut was close by—if he only looked for it.

"What you're doing… Is that a felony?" Jenny asked softly.

"Like breaking into an office isn't?" Adan didn't look up from the desk as he rummaged through the many crumpled and scattered papers. How people worked in such chaos he did not understand. A clue had to be here somewhere, he just knew it.

"Technically, breaking and entering is a misdemeanor here," Kael informed them. Trust the Theroki to know the penal code. Adan bit back a comment. "And the door was unlocked, so…"

"So we're safe on that count?" Jenny said, smiling.

"Yes. We were concerned passersby."

"You notice he dodged my question, though."

"Yes. I did. He's good at dodging things, in my experience."

"Aha!" Adan held up a crumpled pink square of paper in triumph, ignoring the dig. A list of a dozen common account usernames—and their passwords. "She should really upgrade this to biometrics. This is ridiculously ancient."

"What is that?" Jenny said, stepping toward him and squinting. "What did you find?"

"This, my dear, is the key to our locked door."

He jabbed at the laptop, and it came to life. He quickly entered the combination that looked most likely to him. No, not that one. Perhaps that was mail. That was the one people usually held most dear. Perhaps the third…

Yes. The screen unlocked. Jenny peered over his shoulder and Kael shifted in return, feigning interest, but the tension in the air was suddenly thick.

She bent to read what was on the screen, her face so close her cheek almost brushed his ear. The memory of orange groves and summertime stirred in him, less bizarre now with the warm wind blowing in from a tiny window that was indeed open.

Still, he tensed. What if this was her plan? Jam him in the back of the neck and let him seize up? They were probably far from medical help here, if the Capital types would even give it to an unregistered outsystemer like him.

His fingers flew through the displays, looking for something of use. "Aren't you supposed to be watching the exit?" He tried to make it sound casual.

She jumped. "Oh, sorry. I'm being annoying, aren't I? I hate it when people read over my shoulder." She scampered back, and Kael eased back a little in response.

Hmm. Maybe he shouldn't be giving the Theroki such a hard time.

Xi wasn't all-powerful, and if Jenny had wanted to kill him here... maybe she could have.

Adan shook his head, trying to shake off the fear. Focus, man, focus. The mail application was open, as were two spreadsheets in the background that didn't hold anything interesting. Many, many unopened—or at least marked unread—messages awaited Persad, but one had been opened, presumably being read just before they'd arrived.

We want the schematics of the new design. No more dalliance. Stay where you are, and we won't need to do anything drastic. We're sending coordinates on where to deliver the information.

"Commander!" Adan snapped. "You're gonna want to see this."

Ellen stalked in and leaned over his shoulder. "Damn it, so... she either left to try to get away. Or they were already here? Do you see any coordinates?" She stepped back, propping a gauntleted hand on her hip.

"Hello?" called a voice from the outer room.

"Shit." Adan quickly locked the machine and tried to replace the passwords back into their seemingly random location, hoping the chaos worked in his favor just this once. He jumped up and pulled off the gloves, shuffling toward Jenny and then regretting it.

While he'd covered his tracks, the commander had calmly waltzed back out to the main room. "Dr. Persad? Good day, ma'am."

A long silence followed. How were they going to explain their presence in her office? The outer room, maybe, but there was no way this wasn't an intrusion.

"What do you people want?" the woman said, her voice cold.

"Pardon our intrusion, ma'am. I'm Ellen Ryu, security chief for the athlete Jennifer Ryan Utlis. You've heard of her?"

"Oh, my. Well, yes, of course," the woman said. Her voice relaxed slightly. Adan couldn't see the doctor from this angle, only the commander's back. "Who hasn't?"

Adan made a face. Jenny had not been kidding about her fame here on Capital. She elbowed him.

"Forgive the intrusion, but my team wanted to be sure the premises were secure, as Ms. Utlis is with us."

"Oh. It's quite all right. Pardon my manners. And… did you find it adequately secure?" There seemed to be genuine curiosity in the statement.

"Yes, no interlopers so far. Although we were concerned you weren't here."

"I had to take a quick trip to the, uh, bathroom facilities."

"Ah, yes, of course."

"What can I do for you, Ms. Ryu? Can I offer you all some coffee? Are there… more of you?"

"Come on out, Ms. Utlis, team."

Adan followed Jenny and Kael back out into the main room, stopping just inside the interior office doorway with Jenny. The dark-haired doctor eyed them curiously, beautiful and painted brown eyes exaggerated by the enhanced magnifying monocle. A small yellow light twinkled near her temple. Unlike the slick gentleman that had interrupted them earlier, she wore peacock-blue cargo overalls that were completely covered in pockets. His sort of fashion—practical. No breather. He supposed that made sense, inside this facility, especially one run by the Foundation.

"Ms. Utlis," Dr. Persad said, extending her hand. "It's a true, true pleasure to meet you. My son is a huge fan." Did her voice falter a little at the word son? "We saw you compete at the Ranunculus Towers competition. Impressive as always. I hear you never lose."

Never? Adan risked a glance at her.

Jenny smiled and bowed a few centimeters. "Thank you, Dr. Persad. I always strive to do my best. That's all any of us can do." She was perfectly at ease with such praise.

"And these others? Who are you, young man?"

Persad's monocled eye pinned him to the wall. Adan froze. Damn. No cover story for *him*.

"Pardon my boyfriend." Jenny smiled and casually slipped an arm around his waist as if it were the most natural thing in the world.

Adan choked on a cough. His blood pressure had just doubled, he was sure of it. He glanced at Josana, whose jaw had tightened but she wasn't yet glaring.

Jenny's smile widened. "He's a bit of a science buff himself and has long admired your work. So he's a bit tongue-tied."

"It's an honor to meet you," he blurted. That much was true. "You've done some amazing small electronics research."

Persad smiled, amused. "I know. Thanks."

"Which is why we've come, Doctor," the commander chimed in. "Is there anywhere else we could talk?"

"No," said Persad, smile vanishing. "This is a perfectly fine place to speak."

"Well, this is a particularly sensitive issue, and—"

"My office is very secure, I assure you, Ms. Ryu."

"I am sure that it is," Ryu said, even though clearly before neither of them had seemed very sure of that point. "But Ms. Utlis has struggled with the press in the past. We must be sure even her inquiries remain confidential. Would you be willing to guarantee that?"

"Of course—"

"In writing?" Ellen gestured to Adan, who pulled the contract up off his wrist holo.

Persad squinted at it, then held up her own wrist holo. Very nice. Maybe she'd spent her budget for upgrading that ancient machine in there on her wearables. "Send it to my AI, please?"

He nodded, flicking his finger toward her. The contract flew toward her, then disappeared, only to be reborn out of her holo. Persad flipped through it but couldn't have read much. Her AI chirped its approval, having compared the contract to her pre-approved standards.

"Very well, I've signed it. Here you go. Now what is this all about?"

Ryu nodded. "You've done some cutting-edge research recently on new… augmentations, let's say. Could you tell us about them?"

A brick wall came down over Persad's features. "No. I couldn't. That's not how this works. You tell me what you need, I tell you if I can make it for you. That's it. You want to hear research, read the journals."

Jenny smiled sweetly, inclining her head. "We were hoping to adapt some technology *before* it reaches the journals."

Persad's lips pressed together, her chin jutting up slightly. "I can't tell you my latest research, and—"

"Can't or won't?" Ryu cut in. Adan almost snickered. Way to win her over, Commander. Maybe Patron should have put someone a little more charismatic in charge of that duty.

Glowering, Persad folded her arms. "Both. And I can't think of how any of it could be adapted to sports anyway."

Jenny still had an arm wrapped around him, he realized, as she withdrew it to take a step closer to Persad and bow slightly. Persad immediately eased, but not completely. Then Jen took it a step further and took one of the doctor's hands in her own. "Madam, a mutual friend said you might have something brilliant we could use, but he couldn't divulge the nature just yet. And he said that you also might have a problem we could solve in exchange for your services."

Persad's eyes widened. "A… problem?"

"But—" Jenny never got to finish her convincing.

Glass cracked sharply in the other office room, then shattered. Kael dashed toward the doorway, and Ellen had already drawn her rifle and was blocking Persad, pushing her toward the three of them.

"Over here," Jenny hissed, dragging their shoulders down as shots rang out. "Get down. You three, back in that corner."

Damn. Looked like he was going to owe Jenny that cigar sooner rather than later.

Persad dropped to a crouch beside him behind a steel cabinet topped with multicolored building blocks.

Kael took the other side of the door beside Ellen as the fire suddenly stopped. Jenny was checking her rifle in a crouch between Persad and the doorway.

"You're… well-armed, for an athlete," Persad said. "Is that legal?"

Jenny looked up and grinned, but held a finger to her lips for quiet.

A man dressed entirely in black rounded the doorway, firing into their corner. Adan should have ducked, but he froze. Josana let out a screech, throwing her arms around him.

Kael raised his rifle and slammed the butt of it into the assailant's jaw just as a second attacker rounded the corner. Ellen fired, sizzling bolts arching into the man's body, leaving him on the ground twitching. Hmm, set on stun? Did she hope to capture them?

Recovering slightly, Adan shrugged Josana off, groped for the pistol on his hip, and at last had the presence of mind to ready it. At this rate, he wouldn't need it though.

Kael assaulted two more incoming while Ellen's rifle took three others down. Hell, that had been no small number. Were those the men from the message?

Silence descended around them. Not even so much as a groan filled the void.

"That's all of them, Commander." Kael's voice carried from the far room. "This place is pretty busted up, though."

Adan glanced at Persad. Her face was grim, mouth set in a thin line, black eyes worried.

But not at all surprised.

"Are you going to call the police?" Josana straightened beside him, staring wide-eyed at the carnage. Feeling silly still crouching, he straightened too. Jenny and Persad did too, but with more of a natural ease.

"No," Persad said quickly. "Uh, no need."

Josana scowled, incredulous. "No need? At the very *least* you need a very diligent cleaning service."

Persad's eyelids were hooded, as if she wished an annoying pest would fly away. "I'll call building security."

"Good idea," the commander said. "How about we get out of here? I think we have some… things to talk about, Dr. Persad."

Eyes wide again, Persad's gaze darted to each of them in turn, and he had a feeling she was wondering if she had a choice in the matter.

"Any idea who these people are, Doctor?" the commander asked, casual as brushing the dust off her armor pauldron.

Persad frowned. "Not at all." The lie was plain in her voice; she didn't seem to be trying much to hide it.

"Perhaps you have somewhere else safe we could go to talk?" Jenny gave her another friendly smile as she swung her rifle onto her back. Good thing she'd carried at least that much.

Maybe it was the celebrity, or maybe it was the sweetness inherent in those green eyes, but Persad's resistance melted just enough.

"We can retire to my home. I'll just get my computer."

"Yes, of course, Doctor." Ellen gestured graciously through the door. The woman headed back. Ellen watched her while she held up a hand and whispered loudly toward Kael, "Yours has a stun setting too, you know. I thought you completed that training ages ago."

He grinned. "Yeah, but what's the fun in that? Attacking an unarmed scientist—they deserved it. I want them to remember it in the morning."

"They'll feel the stun in the morning too, especially after I stun them again on the way out the door."

"But it's just so clinical. You're classier than I am, Commander." His voice took on an ironic, Capital-esque lilt at the end of it.

She snorted. "Fine, fine. As long as we're under ten hostiles."

"Yes, ma'am."

Persad joined them, and from the look on her face, she may have heard some of those final words. The engineer clutched her laptop *and* the scrap of passwords to her chest. "Got it. Let's go."

———

DR. PERSAD'S APARTMENT—BECAUSE it didn't appear that houses as Kael knew them existed on Capital—was only two buildings away, but they still made a rather obvious parade moving from the Derad Tower to the residential complex. His neck itched. He found himself trying to glance at the rooftops, always feeling like someone was watching—but the rooftops weren't there. Half these buildings went up far above the low, puffy cloud system that had moved in.

Still. Someone was watching them.

They made it into the building and the elevator shaft unmolested, though.

"Come on inside. Let me just disarm the alarm system." Persad shooed them further into an elegant cream-walled foyer. Leafy green plants stood in rectangular gray pots over rich wood flooring the color of coffee. She shooed them again. "Go on. Farther. It needs everyone out of this area."

Since when did security systems act like air locks? He frowned but followed Adan further inside. Maybe it was specific to this apartment building. Or Capital. Or something Persad had custom built, for all he knew.

A familiar hissing sound pricked at his ears. He spun toward Persad, but it was too late. Adan swore behind him as he bumped into the invisible wall. Blue light ricocheted out like a coin dropped into a fountain.

The pale glow of a force field surrounded them.

Kael glanced up and froze. Outside the barrier, Persad held a tiny laser pistol to Jenny's neck.

"Impressive, Doctor." Ellen calmly folded her arms across her chest, looking supremely unperturbed. "I take it this isn't a health quarantine."

"Where is he? Who sent you?" Persad's voice was harder than granite, eyes grim, determined.

"The Foundation," Ryu replied. "Where is who?"

"Don't act like you don't know."

"It's true." Jenny sounded admirably calm for having a bullet less than a foot from her jugular. "The mutual friend I mentioned, remember? We're Foundation, we just want to help."

"The Foundation doesn't exist."

Ellen retracted her helmet—a serious gesture of goodwill. Kael followed. The biochem readout had been clean seconds ago. "You know very well it does," Ellen said, "since you work in one of its facilities. Our patron—"

"I'm supposed to just believe you? Just take you at your word for it?" She glowered.

"Last I checked our secret organization didn't wear uniforms."

"Nice try, but I don't think so. You saw those men back there."

"And what would have happened if we hadn't been there, Doctor?" Kael tilted his head at her. "You clearly need more firepower than just that little flashlight."

Persad scowled at him. "Proof. Or I'm calling in the inspectors."

"Hold on, maybe I can get some." Ellen held up a palm and drew the comm unit from the chest of her suit. She stabbed a finger at the screen and swore at it several times. For a genius, she sure could get pissed at technology.

A rainbow of color swirled on-screen as the call sought its other half for the better part of a minute. Adan cleared his throat behind Kael. Ellen tapped her foot. Persad's narrowed eyes darted around, no doubt seeking any sign of trick.

"Y-ello?" Doug's cheerful grin abruptly filled the little device screen. Sunshine slanted at dramatic angles across a messy desk and glinted on the gold wire of his glasses.

"Simmons, we're here with Dr. Persad. But she appears to need some convincing of... well, who the hell we are, to be frank."

"Simmons?" Persad said, as if she recognized the name. The gun at Jenny's neck drooped, and Jenny relaxed a fraction but didn't make a move to disarm Persad. Maybe that was why she was so relaxed. She probably had no doubt she could snatch that weapon if she needed to. But an elbow to the solar plexus wasn't winning anyone over.

"Ah, yes. Convincing. Hold on one minute." Doug rose and disappeared to the right of the screen. "Mom!"

Jenny snorted. Kael caught her eye.

"Mo-om!" Doug shouted off-screen again.

Kael raised his eyebrows. "Does... does Patron Simmons live with his mother?"

Laughter burst out of Jenny in spite of the sheer danger of the situation, and Kael twisted back to see Adan smiling. Josana had a bored look on her face. They were terrible captives—hardly taking their imprisonment seriously at all.

A woman's sun-weathered face appeared on the screen, her chin-length wavy hair the exact shade of Doug's. "Oh, hello there, Ellen. I've heard *so* much about you, darling. Would you be a dear and put Chayana on the line?"

Lips pursed, Ellen held up the comm so Persad could see it and shrugged.

"Catherine?" Persad blinked in confusion.

"Chaya! Yes, hello dear. I told you I was sending some help, didn't I?"

"Yes, well. You could've been a little more descriptive. Specific. Maybe said, 'darling, they're on their way.' "

Kael stifled a snicker as the engineer's regular down-to-earth tone shifted to mimic Doug's mother's more refined lilt.

"I apologize. I should clearly have given them a secret password. Now, be a dear and put down the weapon."

Persad sighed, returned the safety, and slipped the tiny pistol back into one of her many pockets. Note to self: there could be all kinds of dreck in there. She reached over and palmed off the force field, arms and shoulders drooping. The force field shimmered out of existence.

"Thanks so much, Chaya."

"You're lucky I even talked to them." She blew out a breath.

"It wasn't safe to say anything sooner than now. But these people are my son's friends. You can definitely trust them."

"Friends?" Persad squinted at Ellen.

Ellen brushed a stray hair back with gauntleted fingers. "More like we work for him, ma'am. Do you believe us now? I'd like to escort you back to our ship. If a Foundation laboratory isn't safe, I doubt this apartment is any more secure."

"No." Persad shook her head, jaw set tight. "I can't. I'm not going anywhere."

"Another attack is likely. For your safety, Doctor—"

"No." The power of the word, hard as granite, seemed to echo in the foyer.

Ellen propped a hand on her hip. "Well, why the hell not?"

"I can't tell you. Even if you *are* part of the Foundation."

"Do you want our help or not?"

"Chaya, darling," Doug's mom cut in. "Just tell them what you told me. It's too important. You're going to have to trust us."

Persad's mouth pressed into a thin line, her forehead creased. After a moment he realized her lower lip was quivering. Finally, after a long pause, she spoke, although her words barely reached him over the hum of the ventilation.

"They have my son."

CHAPTER FIVE

"WHAT DID SHE SAY HE DID?" Kael asked again. "Something about communications infrastructure?"

"Nothing official. He's on break from school. Indefinitely." Jenny shook her head at the wrist holo they'd hacked into. "From the look of this, he didn't do much of anything, if you ask me. Nothing productive, anyway. Lots of rides to fancy nightclubs, rich celebrity's houses. Not much on here other than travel details. Odd."

"Oh, he did something all right." Adan cleared his throat, then glanced over Jenny's shoulder at the door to make sure Persad wasn't too close. "Take a look at this."

The desk screen had its holo off; images splayed across the glass surface almost like real images on an actual table. Over a dozen images of beautiful young women smiled up at them, accompanied by a few short sticky notes.

"They're... all very pretty." Jenny groaned. "God, just who I want to go hunt all over this hell hole for, some playboy. From the looks of this list, we'll probably find him in a two-week-long orgy or something."

"What does that note say?" Kael pointed at the nearest yellow square tucked under a photo of a brunette wearing a gold and silver breather whose metallic tubing evoked delicate butterfly wings.

Adan leaned closer rather than blowing it up, likely to preserve the placement. "Dipeli Tsao. Missing since 04-032-738. Last seen: Elder-flower Club."

Jenny's eyes were wide. "Playboy or psychopath?"

Kael elbowed her and glanced at the door. "It's her *son*, remember? Ease up. Where else does it mention? Are those locations on the wrist holo? And while we're at it, where was the last place he went?"

Adan was already on it. "Another says the Elderflower. This one says the home of Reordan Esomo. And... the Chartreuse Poppy?"

"All of those are in here," Jenny added. "He at least visited them all. The last place he went isn't that helpful, because it was here. For whatever reason he didn't take this with him wherever he went after that."

"Intentionally?" Adan scratched his sideburn.

"Unless someone picked him up here without leaving a trace."

"There's one more here. Anaka Cho. Last seen: home of Crispin Ostrov."

Kael groaned. "Great. *That* guy."

"I know." Jenny nodded. "Seemed like a well-pedigreed creep."

Adan smiled crookedly at them. "Maybe you've found your multiday orgy then."

Just at that moment, Persad appeared in the doorway, eyebrows shooting up. "Uh... excuse me?"

"Oh, that's nothing!" Adan's laugh was thin and nervous.

"Need any help finding anything?" Persad looked unconvinced.

Kael smirked. Adan elbowed him hard. Not that it mattered through the armor.

"No, we're almost done," Jenny said, her face beet red. She held up the wrist holo with an overdramatic flourish. "Got some info off here. Have you tried any of these places he went to yet?"

Persad pursed her lips. "I tried to get the police to, but I don't think they believe me that anything's wrong. I visited a few, but there are back rooms I can't get into." She massaged her furrowed brow. "If he's just living there, he doesn't want to be found. But it's... it's not like him."

"Did your son have a girlfriend or any women he dated?" Jenny asked.

Persad shook her head. "No. He went out many nights. Said he was always working. Never brought any girls home. He was a hard worker, a momma's boy, really. We told each other everything. Said he wanted to find a good Hindu woman, but they are so hard to find these days." Her voice faltered, and she stopped. "Sorry, I'm rambling."

They all nodded. Her pain was suddenly palpable, thickening the air.

She shook her head. "Listen, I'm making some coffee. Come on out when you are done and I'll fix you some."

Kael listened carefully as her footsteps trailed off down the hall. Then he met Adan's eye. "Think she's right?"

Adan scratched his temple. "I think she believes what she says." He unlocked the screen now. "But I'm not sure they were as close as she thought they were."

"Wait." Jenny held up a forefinger, paging through the wrist holo. "These trips *do* have him returning home nearly every night. Sometimes as early as midnight."

"So?" Adan asked.

"So if he had relationships with any or all of these girls, don't you think he would have stayed over once in a while? I don't see any signs they're part of a celibate sect..." Her eyes darted around the room with new purpose. "If there even are any. I know shit about religion."

"What's the date on his trip to the Elderwhatever Club?" Kael said, leaning over the holo now too. "Before or after the date under Ms. Palmer here?"

Jenny read the numbers off. "Only a single trip."

"It's over a week later!" Adan's eyes lit up. "He went there *after* she went missing."

Karl nodded crisply. "He wasn't dating them. He was looking for them."

Jenny frowned. "The question is, why?"

"And what did he find out?"

————

"HERE. THIS IS HIM." The kitchen wall display shifted to show a young man perhaps Ellen's age.

He had a wide smile, his arm thrown around his mother, the same bronzed skin and black hair, although his was short and neat. He had a tablet on his lap and a stack of actual paper books beside him. He looked just as he described him—studious, industrious. A boyish charm, a small mole over the cheekbone. Nothing really much out of the ordinary, although the jacket he wore in a similar style to Ostrov's seemed a bit high fashion to Ellen. Everything here seemed high fashion to her. But she wouldn't have even made him for a Capital type if she'd run into him on a space station or something. She didn't think.

She sat in Dr. Persad's kitchen, hunched over a glorious white marble bar. Persad was keeping busy on shiny white counters, pulling out all sorts of things in some kind of stress-induced frenzy.

"Coffee, we need coffee," she muttered.

Ellen couldn't argue with coffee. The smell of it alone had her mouth watering, and the calming cream tiles and white marble of the elegantly appointed kitchen were definitely more different than the *Audacity*'s mess. Maybe it should have been more homey, but Ellen had always felt more at home in the industrial corridors of spaceships. The others had been shown to the young man's room to look for some clue about where to get started.

Ellen zeroed in further on the tablet in front of her, pretending to read for the first time the message Adan had hacked into.

"I see. All right. This will help. Tell me about your son, Dr. Persad. Do you know who this 'they' is?"

"Not beyond that email."

"Do you have any suspicions?"

"I doubt there's anything you can do." Persad ran her fingers through her hair, removing the delicate monocle for a moment and setting it on the counter. "I only know that someone sent me that message. But I can't even trace it back—nothing. They're not amateurs, whoever they are."

She turned back away, angrily punching commands into the food generator, churning out cup after cup of coffee. Apparently not *everyone* drank manga-whatever-it-was.

She slid the second cup over to Josana, who had the good sense to only sneer slightly once Persad's back was turned. She muttered a mild thank-you. The girl lounged in a chair Ellen would have looked like a toy soldier in, shapely legs crossed and one arm slung over the back like the thing was a chaise lounge.

Ellen accepted the next cup with a grateful nod.

"Coffee is sort of... illicit in Capital, you know," Josana said mildly. "The doctor honors us."

Ellen frowned down at her cup. "This is illegal?"

Persad nodded. "All stimulants and depressants are. A holdover from the original colonists."

"No alcohol either? But didn't we *buy* coffee or something on the way here?"

"It's all decaf," Josana said, frowning down at her cup as she took a sip. "Supposedly. They don't even bother to label it, just assume you know."

Persad nodded and waved a hand in the air. "It just means the real stuff costs a ton on the black market—and you better be prepared if an inspector shows up at the door."

"An inspector? Like the ones that won't listen to you about Vivaan?"

Her gaze dropped to the floor. "Yes. And I tried bribes, trust me. Not for caffeine. For my son."

Josana frowned harder now.

"So... someone else is bribing them with more?" Ellen said slowly.

Persad nodded. Josana had the decency to look a little sad while she frowned.

Ellen cleared her throat and took a sip. "When did you see him last?"

"Two weeks ago."

She hissed in a breath and hoped Persad didn't notice. Two weeks was a long time to be missing. That kind of time could mean no one was finding her son alive again. "And did he say anything about where he was going? Can you tell me more about that day?"

"Just to the library to do some research. I asked at the library several times, but no one can remember seeing him that day. So it must have happened between here and there."

Ellen rubbed her chin. Or that was a lie, and the library wasn't where he'd been headed.

"There's not much else to say. I got up to go to work, made coffee. We had some together, talked. He never came home." Persad stared down at the mug in her hands now, a lost look in her eyes. Like she was waiting for everything to make sense.

"I understand. Did he often visit the library?" Most research could be done at home, especially on well-connected, high-tech worlds like Capital. What could he have needed from a library specifically? "And which one was it?"

"Lotus River Archives. And no, I remember it because it seemed odd for him." Muffled laughter drifted from across the apartment where the others were reviewing the son's room. Persad frowned. "Let me go check on... if they need anything. Be right back." She shuffled out.

"Why there?" she muttered.

To her surprise, Josana answered. "Public law enforcement records are stored there. Not freely accessible on the net here."

Ellen frowned. Since when did Josana care about anything, let alone a tidbit like that? "How do you know—"

A soft chime at the door cut her off. She started from her seat as she seized the rifle from her lap.

Josana snorted. "Do you really think whoever's trying to kill her will just politely knock?"

"You never know."

"They seemed like bust-through-the-windows types to me. Literally."

"But look how well that worked."

Their glaring contest almost distracted her from Persad rounding the corner, heading for the door.

"Wait!" Ellen scurried in front of her as she hit the helmet raise button. "Let me do it."

Persad nodded. "We do have the finest security in this building."

"Security that's probably easy to case if you just ask for a prospective customer tour. So let me. Unless you've got armor you want to put on?"

"No, no, by all means." Persad stopped at the door console and hit a button.

Ellen stifled a groan. Not *him* again.

"Ostrov," Persad grumbled, not sounding particularly thrilled either. She looked to Ellen. "Ready?"

Stepping between the woman and the door, she held her multi low but ready. "Go ahead."

With a beautiful answering chime sequence, the door slid open. Ostrov practically fell inside on a stream of words before it opened. "Chayana—are you all right—I heard gunshots. But when it seemed clear—oh." He stopped short. "You again. Well, hello."

"You've met?" Ellen didn't miss the tinge of anger and suspicion returning to Persad's voice.

"He so helpfully stopped by while we were waiting for you to return," Ellen said, her tone dry.

"I see you met your objective, then."

"I always meet my objectives, Dr. Ostrov." His long, angular coat had plenty of room to hide weapons, but she couldn't see any obvious ones, nor did he seem to be going for the pockets, so she stepped aside to reveal the doctor behind her.

He raised his eyebrows, an intrigued glint in his eye as he leaned in her direction. "Please, call me Crispin."

She thinned her lips. Yeah. Right.

The door slid shut behind Ostrov as he took the hint and shifted his focus to his colleague. "As I was saying, Chaya—I rushed over when the chaos had settled, but then you weren't there. And then security showed up. What happened? Are you all right?"

"You could have called," Ellen heard herself say. Damn—now she had his attention again.

"So could you." He smiled, eyes glittering. "Sometimes visiting in the flesh is just… so much better, don't you think?"

Something about his words made her want to shudder. She ignored him instead, which seemed far crueler. He just wanted the attention.

Persad was sighing, folding her arms across her chest. "I don't know what it was all about. We had some rather unfriendly visitors."

"After your research, perhaps?"

She shrugged. "That would be the obvious thing. I have no idea."

He shook his head. "You would think, given the, ah, high security of the building, that wouldn't be a problem."

"Foolish me, to have windows on the thirty-fourth floor of a skyscraper."

"Indeed." He glanced from the doctor to Ellen and back again. "Is it just the two of you then? Perhaps I could take you both to dinner tonight to recuperate?"

Persad timed it so that he missed her eye roll.

"I believe we will be busy discussing business matters, Doctor, but thank you for the invitation."

Ostrov was unswayed, flashing a larger grin. "Please, I beg you to humor me. You know it's not every day we have a war hero among us humble scientists."

She stilled. He dropped it casually, that he knew who she was, but she could read the edge of threat in his voice, the feral tinge to his smile, all carefully mingled with fake admiration. Or perhaps it was real admiration, hard to tell. She'd never been good with admiration.

"War hero?" Persad said, frowning.

Ellen grunted, not a trace of a smile on her face. "Hero or villain. Just depends on which side of the war you're on."

Ostrov laughed. "We're neutral here, remember?"

"I remember." Her own voice was gaining an edge now, from more than annoyance.

"Chaya, you seriously recognized Jenny Utlis but not the architect of the SHR defense? The galactically renowned strategist?"

Persad's eyebrows shot up. "Uh. Yes, I suppose that's exactly what I did."

"He's cheating. I gave him my name. He didn't recognize anything."

"You gave me part of a name, and I recognized that." He shifted closer again now. "Please, I must admit to being a bit of a strategy game buff. It would be heaven to play you at *Peaks and Valleys*. Or Go, perhaps?"

She pinched the bridge of her nose, forgetting she was still in her armor. "I, uh, can't leave my command."

"I'll bring dinner to you both then. Let us demonstrate feats of strategic brilliance. I'll pour wine and feed you sushi."

She narrowed her eyes at him. In spite of the horror show that sounded like, he was sticking to Persad like flame on rocket burners. He asked too many questions. He could have something to do with the son's disappearance—or the attack—or both. She should accept his offer, try to wheedle information out of him.

If only she could do it without wincing.

"I assure you, Dr. Ostrov, that the same brilliance that allowed me to defend my planet and avoid certain death also allows me to navigate food from a plate to my face."

He straightened, his face falling. He opened his mouth, looking ready to back off. Yeah, no one had ever accused her of being excessively charming.

"But I suppose I could crush you at *Peaks and Valleys* if you really want," she ground out. "You can work your way up to Go."

Someone stiffened in her peripheral vision. She turned her head minutely. Kael had stopped in the doorway. Shit. When the hell had he gotten here? She couldn't look at him or she'd give it all away.

"Excellent, it's a date then." Ostrov grinned and slid smiling eyes over in Kael's direction, pausing briefly, his grin widening.

She glanced more directly at Kael now but couldn't read anything. Apparently Ostrov was better at this than she was. She opened her mouth to say dinner should include everyone, but then she would have to tell him exactly how many of her team were here on the ground. And who knew who *he* would share that information with. Damn this man. She shut her mouth again.

He patted Persad on the shoulder congenially, looking pleased with himself. "I'll be back at seven then? Be safe, friends."

No one said a word as Ostrov turned and left. She scowled at nothing, and everything, and she could have cut the air with a knife.

She looked balefully at Kael, searching for words to explain, but his eyes were fixed on the door. There was something strange and new in them—shut down, closed off.

Fragging meddling Ostrov.

"We've got some ideas, Commander. Whenever you're ready."

She gritted her teeth. Sure. Just go back to work like it's nothing. That's what she did every time. Why would this moment be any different?

It clearly *was* different, though, because Persad was looking from her to Kael and back again, confusion growing.

"Fine," she spat out. "Everybody in here."

He jerked his thumb over his shoulder. "There's something in there you should see." His eyes flicked up and met hers now, guarded.

Their gazes locked. What did he see—or hope to see—that kept him from looking away?

"You found something in the holos?" Persad continued glancing between them, but apparently whatever weird vibes they were giving off weren't enough to keep her from asking the important questions.

"We did." Kael broke away first, meeting Persad's gaze with a curt nod. "Adan did. This way."

"Having your own personal hacker comes in handy, I guess," Persad muttered as she followed.

"You have no idea." Ellen had to smile a little at that. If Persad thought one was good, she should try two.

They crowded into the bedroom as Kael ran them through a quick recap of all they'd found. Josana even hung in the doorway, although Ellen suspected it was more out of boredom with the kitchen than interest in the young man's welfare.

"Why would Vivaan be searching for these people?" Persad was shaking her head.

"You know as much as we do." Adan shrugged.

"He never spoke of this to you?" Ellen bent closer, trying to study their faces.

"Never. I'm... I never expected anything like this."

"What did you expect?" said Kael from beside her.

"Something to do with my research. Some kind of extortion or something. I don't even know what to make of this. Is he... stalking them?"

Jenny sat one hip on the edge of the desk. "Looks more like he was trying to help. We don't even know if he ever met any of them."

"But then, how did he get this information?"

Adan was glaring at a tablet in one hand and stabbing it with a finger with the other. "I'm trying to figure that out, ma'am, but that may take a while."

"What exactly are you researching, Doctor?" Ellen said softly. "Something worth kidnapping your son for, I take it?"

Persad pressed her lips together in annoyance. "I'd rather not say, but we're likely far beyond secrecy at this point." She sighed. "It might be considered dangerous to some. It didn't start out that way for me."

"We're going to need a few more details than that." Ellen gave her a moment before urging her on. "Patron Simmons already told me it has something to do with telepathy. A drug, he thought."

"Fine, fine." She glanced at Jenny. "Ah. So you're not really looking for anything from me."

"No." Jenny crossed her arms. "Well, not for my climbing career anyway."

Persad raised her eyebrows.

Way to let the cat out of the bag, Jen. Ellen's turn to sigh. "We are hoping your research might help us."

"Is that so."

"But we're going to help you either way," she hastened to add.

A tight silence stretched on for a few seconds, then more.

"We can help you find Vivaan," Kael said. "That's what matters right now. But we need to know everything we can."

Persad gave him a long, hard look. "Implants."

"What—" Kael looked a little freaked out.

"Telepathy-blocking implants," she amended, keeping her eyes locked on Kael. "Chips are the prototypes actually, although I may have to expand to larger subdermal units. That's my area of research. Not drugs. I couldn't find a way to do it biochemically, noninvasively, although I tried. You need more of an electrical field than that. But they can interoperate with power armor and some popular existing implantation network infrastructures like yours."

Kael slowly raised his eyebrows. "Didn't think it was that obvious."

"This whole ordeal has... heightened my powers of observation, let's say. Can't be too careful."

"No, indeed you can't." Kael frowned, thoughtful.

"So—who would object to telepathy-blocking augmentation?" Jenny asked.

"Enhancers, for one," Ellen said quickly. And her good old friend Arakovic.

Persad nodded. "That'd be the biggest group. There're also a few Puritan fringe groups who are so dogmatic they believe Naturals should be given free rein to do what they will. Most of them are cults, dominating domes and moons in the outsystems, but they do exist. But beyond that, it would be useful for any group to get an advantage over another. Both Union and Puritan military officials have come courting in the past. They each have their own—failed—research programs."

"They've approached you in a Foundation building?" Adan didn't look up from his work on the tablet.

"Well, it's not like we advertise that's who owns it. But no. It was before I met Catherine Simmons and accepted Foundation funding. And site security."

"So they definitely are aware of your work," Ellen said.

"Well, yes. But many of them didn't think I could do it."

"And have you?" Adan smiled slightly, without looking up.

"Three weeks ago I completed my third successful test, this time with a powerful Natural. It works." Excitement in her eyes flashed for a moment before falling into worry again. "Hence my panic over Vivaan. But I hadn't heard anything until this morning, except for the message I showed you. And they didn't mention him and they still haven't sent any coordinates. Unless it was just some kind of tactic to distract me before they smashed in the windows?"

Ellen shrugged. "It's possible. This Natural—who was it? Someone you can trust?"

"A friend of Ostrov's. Etrianala Kentt. Runs a local wine garden, what's it called..." She snapped her fingers.

"The Elderflower Club?" Kael said slowly.

"That's it! How did you know?"

Ellen ran a hand over her face. "I think I know where we're headed first."

"Do we really want to walk in there with our heads full of secrets to face a powerful telepath?" Adan looked up from the tablet for the first time.

Ellen looked at Persad. "No, you're right, we don't. Interested in a few more guinea pigs, Doctor?"

Persad raised one brow. "I am. But you can't just waltz in there in power armor."

Jenny nodded. "It's prestigious. You'll need an invite. And before you ask, no—I never ran in those circles."

All eyes slowly turned to Josana.

She tilted her head. A smile slowly grew on her face like a cat who'd just caught some very nice prey. "Well, well. I did."

Persad stepped closer, all five feet of her suddenly threatening. "You will help. Won't you."

The corner of Josana's mouth ticked up. "I've got a price."

"What?" Ellen's voice was all but a growl.

"I get to decide what you wear."

Ellen rolled her eyes.

"It's that or no deal. You go on my reputation, I won't have you ruining it."

"No, we can ruin it from up close just fine," Kael muttered.

"Fine." Ellen waved it off. "We'll go tonight. After we get rid of Ostrov."

Persad looked distressed. "What if I can't get you outfitted that fast? They're prototypes. If they don't work reliably—"

"Go get started. We have to pursue every lead we have as soon as we can. See how far you get. If you can't get done—then tomorrow." And she stared hard at Josana. "And you—go get whatever you need to."

"Got credits?"

"Take Jenny."

"Commander!" They both simultaneously objected.

Ellen rolled her eyes. "Can't you order on the holo or something? So you don't have to be seen together, heaven forbid?"

Josana sighed. "I suppose that will work. I need the two of you out of that power armor though."

Kael balked. "Why the hell do you need that?" Ellen stifled a smirk at Kael's alarmed tone.

"Sizes. Obviously."

"Get it from Xi," Ellen said quickly. "Jenny can get her on the comm. Xi knows better than any measurement you'd do."

"Fine." The girl had the gall to look disappointed. "What time is your hot date, Commander?" Her eyes twinkled with malice.

"Seven." She preferred to think of it as an interrogation.

"All right. I'll be ready by eight then."

———

"SO... YOU LIVE WITH YOUR MOTHER?" Ellen quirked an eyebrow at the view screen.

Doug chuckled, but he didn't even have the decency to be embarrassed. Today in questionable fashion choices was a green shirt festooned with fancy cocktail glasses in gold, orange, and red, umbrellas tilting out the sides and all. "I'd have told you if you asked, Commander. My dad too, in fact."

"Where exactly?"

"Not over the net. But it's in the ship's databanks, if you ever need to know. You know, in an emergency."

She raised an eyebrow. "Is there a reason I should be worried about that, Simmons?"

"Nah." He smiled, but she caught an edge of nerves in his tone.

"Are your parents Foundation people too?"

"Foundation council. Founder sort."

"Well, look at you, following in their footsteps."

He shrugged. "Not really. Mom's a chemist. Dad's a zoologist. They were horrified I wasn't into physical sciences."

"Well, at least you have parents to disapprove." She smiled, said it cheerfully, but his eyes widened in horror.

"Oh my God, sorry."

"I didn't mean it like that." She shook her head. "See? This is what happens when I try to chat."

"It's fine, really. Awkwardness is fine. You're a child prodigy, I'm a computer geek. The fact that we have moments that *aren't* awkward is what's amazing."

"Thanks for that little reminder. While we're getting all personal— do you live on the beach or something? Are you here on Capital, actually? Cause I have to go on this date with Ostrov to try to get information out of him and I can't take Kael because he'll stare daggers the whole time, and Adan's busy with the mission, and Jenny has to help Josana buy us new outfits, and it'd *really* be nice to have someone to deflect that asshole right now." Her eyes widened at the deluge that had just come out. "Um… maybe I should stop chatting for a bit."

It was his turn to chuckle. "Sorry, yes to the beach, but no to Capital. Do I look like a Capital type to you?"

"Hardly." His shirts were basically the antithesis of culture and fine fashion.

"I'll take that as a compliment." He raised his mug in a toast. The cat in a hula skirt greeted her today. "But what's this about a date?"

"Oh, yeah." She sighed. "I called to brief you. I haven't approached Persad specifically about joining us yet, but she has told us about her work and agreed to share. You see, Persad's trouble is a certain... loved one has gone missing, so we're going to do some asking around."

"Loved one?"

"She has a son."

"Great, more men for my all-female ship."

"That's counting your chickens before we can even find them at this point. She hasn't been friendly so I'm not extremely optimistic she'll come along. But I'm doing my best."

"Is that who the date is with?"

"Uh... no. Getting to it. So to look for the son, Josana is trying to get us into a nightclub that was one of the last places her son is recorded as visiting."

"Sounds like you're plenty busy. You should swing by that Enhancer High Command address too while you're on Capital, take a look."

"Will do, once we know more about the kid." Or they hit a dead end. "Another thing. So this date. One of her colleagues, a certain Crispin Ostrov, keeps hanging around. He recognized me. Or looked me up and wouldn't admit it. He's suspicious as hell, trying to get me to play strategy games with him. I'm going to extract some information while I cream him." She widened her eyes. She didn't usually get this open or honest—or confident—with people. But well, she kind of hoped that someone like Doug would understand. Or at least not judge her.

And indeed he chuckled. "Wish I could see that."

"Well, I'll be wearing my armor, so there's always the cam footage."

"I'll stay tuned. If it doesn't get deleted." He rolled his eyes. "No closer to any clues on my end on that, by the way."

She almost pointed out that her gut was beginning to zero in on one person—Merith—but then what if she broke into this video too? She needed harder proof before she could act.

"I notice you're not claiming 'I wouldn't spy on you.' "

"I'm not going to lie. You're too smart for that. I'd totally spy on you. But only benevolently. And maybe out of boredom."

"Doug!"

"And if there are no movies on the vid screen?"

"You have no shame."

He snorted. "Kidding. I do live on a beach. I have other things to do."

"Like hot bikini-clad women?"

His eyes widened now. "What's gotten into you, Commander?"

"If I'm supposed to call you Doug, you should probably call me Ellen. And I don't know. I'm trying here."

"But 'Commander' has such a ring to it. And no, I don't wear swimsuits made of money, so bikini-clad women don't give me the time of day."

That truly did surprise her, though. Aside from his taste in kitsch, he was plenty handsome. And funny too. And kind. He had to check a lot of boxes for a lot of women. "Did you offer them a spaceship? That got my attention."

He giggled. "No. Good idea, I'll try that. Are you flirting with me, *Ellen*? I thought your heart belonged to a certain former Theroki."

Her face fell, and his mirrored hers in a millisecond, instantly painted with regret.

"What? Sorry. Did something go wrong?"

"No, not exactly." Was she really going to talk about this with *Simmons*? "I, uh, it does. Still belong to him, that is." He just doesn't know it. "But it's a little more complicated and messy than that."

"Well, if anyone can solve that puzzle, it's you."

"I wish I had your confidence in me on that problem."

"Maybe confidence *is* your problem?" He tilted his head, a strange, sympathetic expression she'd never seen before on his face.

"Maybe." She gazed at him for a long moment, then shook her head, shaking off the moment. "That's not the mission. I'll figure it out. When this is all over." She'd find some way to make all this nonsense up to Kael. Could she justify more than one set of astronomically expensive armor?

"I'm certain that you will. But if you're off on dates with this Ostrov, I hope he's ugly, or you know…" He raised an eyebrow.

She hung her head. "He's tragically not. Just an asshole."

"Then you may have to deal with it sooner rather than later."

Her jaw tightened. "Good point."

"All right—keep me updated. Okay?"

"Okay."

"Over and out." With a grin, he hit the button and his face disappeared.

Next she dialed up Nova. Her orange bob was bright enough to burn the screen as she appeared.

"What's up, Commander?" She smiled, lolling back in a chair. Fern's chair, actually. A jungle of ferns and shiny leafed plants filled the room behind her, with two red-suited legs sticking out from a bunk. Presumably Fern.

"Mission is evolving. I'm going to need a little backup down here from you and Mo, okay?"

"Of course, Commander."

"Sorry to tear you away from your R&R."

"I already learned two new songs and cleaned my weapons three times over. Got nothing else to do." Although she did glance over her shoulder at the bunk.

"About that. We've got to visit some bar tonight or something."

Nova cracked her gum as she propped her hands on her hips. "If you're looking for advice on what to wear, *jagiya*, you're asking the wrong person."

"Oh I know. But no. Josana's getting us into the place and demanded full creative control."

Nova's mouth fell open, and even Fern sat forward on the bunk.

"And you *gave* it to her?" Nova exclaimed.

Ellen shrugged. "Didn't have much choice."

Fern looked at Nova. "If you're going down there, I want pictures."

Ellen snorted. "Well, you *are* coming down here. And you're bringing me some weapons that I can conceal under… whatever Josana picks out. So imagine your basic worst case scenario."

Fern covered her mouth, trying to conceal a laugh.

Nova jawed her gum and grinned. "Like a bikini or something?"

"Oh my God." Ellen slapped a hand to her face.

"You want firearms or just blades or… ?"

"Grab an assortment. I have my laserblade but that's it."

"Sure, I'll take care of it. And I'll get Mo. Give us an hour or two."

"Xi has our location. Oh, and bring some weapons for Kael too."

Nova's eyes widened as she nodded. Fern's eyes glowed with amusement, more delighted by the second. Ellen shook her head.

"It should only be for a day or two. I hope."

Nova leaned forward, ready to hit the sign-off button and go. "Anything else?"

"Nope."

"See you soon."

Now to the next item on her list. Dremer's face appeared on-screen, her lab full of silvery clutter behind her. Ellen didn't waste any time beating around the bush.

"I'm getting a temporary chip over here."

Dremer raised her eyebrows. "I assume I don't have to tell you I'm concerned."

"Trust me, so am I. Pretty sure Persad doesn't trust us enough yet to send you all her work so far though. But the tech is useful."

Dremer's eyebrows raised as she processed what Ellen was implying. "Ah. I see. But you'll be connecting to your suit?"

"Not most of the time, actually. But I think there will be a window."

"Xi, can we transmit an encrypted copy of the basic chip programming if she can connect to the suit?"

"This depends on how long she is able to connect via suit to the ship and the size of the chip software, but most likely yes. We have excellent encryption."

Dremer tilted her head. "You get it here, I'll take a look for anything dangerous."

"Will do."

Dremer grinned. "Don't do anything I wouldn't do."

"No promises, Doc."

Dremer turned to the side at some sound. "Oh, hello, Merith. No, it's okay, come on in. Good luck, Commander."

"Thanks. Over and out."

She'd just leaned back in the chair, hoping to relax for a few before Ostrov showed up, when the screen fluttered to life again with a request.

Ostrov. Why was he calling instead of showing up? She waved acceptance at the thing like dismissing an annoying bug.

Ostrov's face filled the view screen. It was all she could do not to groan.

"Ryu! Something has just occurred to me," he said before she could open her mouth. "I have a brand-new, state-of-the-art *Peaks and Valleys* gaming table. And Chaya sadly does not. I simply must insist the two of you come up here to play."

Oh, for heaven's sake. What could she say to that? She groped for an excuse, but his smile grew smug as the silence stretched on. Eh. Whatever—she could handle the fool. "Fine. I'll check with Dr. Persad."

"Or come without her." That smile widened, clearly indicating his preference.

"See you shortly," she said curtly. She slapped the button to cut him off. His smug smile vanished.

Well, frag. She hit the space for Persad's comm. Lazy, perhaps, as she could just walk a room over, but what the hell.

"Here." Persad raised her head from tinkering to face the screen, her hugely monocled eye rearing up. The equipment she was hunched over likely magnified the work on top of what her monocle could do, or perhaps it was an electronics printer. Or maybe she just liked the dramatic effect. Some fashion statement.

"Do you do all that work by hand?" Ellen asked absently.

"Nah, there's a printer that does the finest electronics. State of the art. But it's the connections. And a few other things that are much too hard to explain. I could program nanos but then I still have to verify they did the work correctly, and..." She looked up, the giant eye blinking. "Am I rambling?"

"No. Just answering my question. But it's really beside the point. Sorry for distracting you. Ostrov just called and said he wants us to go up there."

Her face fell into a frown of disgust. "Oh, that man."

"Yes. But he seems keen on me going by myself, so I think I will."

"Really? Excellent! That would give me more time to work on the chips. I'm surprised you can take one, by the way." Her head bent down even as she was talking, unable to resist continuing her work.

"Long story."

"Your augmentation is better hidden than the Theroki's."

"Former Theroki. And don't call him that, he's not especially fond of the reminder."

"I wouldn't be either."

"It has a certain brutish charm."

"He does, doesn't he?"

Ellen opened her mouth, starting to say that wasn't what she'd meant. But what the hell *had* she meant, then?

Persad continued. "I guess I can't be surprised that their work isn't as delicate. I presume yours was Union?"

"Technically, yes. Sort of. As I said, a long story for another time. Going to this thing with Ostrov alone will also mean I don't have to both guard you and try to get information out of him at the same time, so it's easier for me too. And perhaps then the chips will be ready when I get back?"

"I've got his almost done, so I think so. Yours should be more straightforward."

"Got it."

"I've made some assumptions on standard Theroki hardware ports. Do you have any info on yours?"

"Sending it over now. And Kael's too."

"Fantastic."

"Off to greet Ostrov."

"Wear your power armor and bug repellent."

Ellen couldn't help but grin. "Already planning on it."

———

OSTROV OPENED the door and his eyes flew up. "Armor. Really."

She looked down at her form and back up at him. She'd set the lean Foundation armor to a sleek black.

"Oops." She blinked, voice dry.

"I suppose I should be flattered. Ah… come on in." He grinned and held the door as if it were truly in danger of sliding closed, and she stepped inside. An expanse of brutally modern, richly furnished apartment stretched out behind him. A charcoal sofa floated above orange carpet, a large holodisplay took up one wall and part of the floor, and a sleek bar curved around the far edge of the room. Three doors led to other parts of the apartment. He shrugged. "You shan't be the first awkwardly dressed genius to enter here."

It was all she could do not to roll her eyes. As if she'd show up here, with him, unarmed or unarmored. Especially with one of the women downstairs having last been seen at his place. She was tempted to pounce right on it, ask him when he'd seen her last to get revenge for that comment. But that didn't seem like something charismatic people did.

He leaned out into the hallway.

"Persad bowed out," she grunted.

He grinned even wider. "She never was one for strategy games, although she's quite good."

"Some work came up suddenly."

"I'll bet it did. Can't say I'm disappointed, though."

She steeled herself not to react. He suspected something, that she and her friends were up to something here on Capital, something more than accompanying Jenny. The question was—what was he guessing they were doing here?

"I'd offer to take your coat but… clearly that isn't necessary."

She shrugged. "At least I left off the helmet."

"Indeed, you're sure letting your hair down now."

"I can raise it if you like."

"No need to get feisty."

"I'm always feisty."

"Can I get you a drink?"

Hell, she probably couldn't turn down every single thing, but consuming anything was a bad idea. "Trying to dim my wits to buy you some time?" She gave him a slight smile. A predatory one.

"Never. I want you to know I beat you fair and square."

"I don't see how that will happen, since you won't win." She glanced quickly around the bar; vacuum packs and bottles lined one ledge at the back. She pointed. "Is that zeefruit juice?"

He nodded. "Want to get hopped up?"

"On sugar?"

"Of course. Everything I have is illegal here, and I'd never *dream* of being anything but a law-abiding citizen." He leaned against the back wall, hands folded behind the small of his back, and she did have to admit he knew how to show off the strong lines of his form. Surprisingly masculine for a scientist. His smile was smaller now, more friendly. Designed to look humble and draw her in.

"It'll do."

He handed her a pack. "Let me get you a glass."

"I'm fine." Not happening. "So where is this table of yours?"

He pointed into the next room. "My, my, you aren't much for foreplay."

Actually, with the right man, foreplay seemed to be all she knew how to do.

Where the hell had *that* thought come from? Shit—and now she was blushing. Fortunately he seemed to attribute it to her "awkward genius" as he closed in on her, looking a little flattered. Small graces.

He was still closing in, looking as if he'd come up behind her.

She turned to meet him head-on. "I thought eagerness was a desirable quality in a woman."

His eyebrows flew up, and he slowed his approach. "I can't disagree with that." He grabbed a glass off the bar and pointed toward the other room, clearly suggesting she go first.

Great.

Juice unopened, senses on high alert, she spun and headed for the indicated room.

Xi, you watching? Through the suit's connection to the ship, and her arm port's connection to the suit, she'd asked Xi to explicitly tag along. Not that all recordings didn't go to Xi eventually, but it made her feel a little better about handling Ostrov.

I'm present, Commander. No warning indicators that my presence might be interrupted either.

Good to hear it.

As she stepped into the room, a low blue light came up, the source somewhere near the floor. Windows surrounded the curved room, providing a magnificent view of the Capital skyline, the sky purple with sunset and the moons hanging like ornaments to match the delicate towers.

"Pretty," she murmured.

"Thank you."

In the center of the room was a round table, the top of it flat black glass, surrounded by six plush white chairs in a swooping, rounded design.

The hair on the back of her neck was standing up as Ostrov slowed to a stop behind her, rather than beside her. Without moving, she tensed, readied herself. If he didn't truly want to play, this was an elaborate ploy to get her alone. She'd assumed his motives were amorous, but now that she was here... it felt different. Dangerous. Or maybe those two things were the same for him. She repressed a shudder.

"There she is," he said, his breath whispering against her hair and the skin of her nape.

She drew another careful breath, in the nose, out the mouth. An elbow to the solar plexus really wasn't justified yet, as rewarding as it would be.

"State of the art." He eased beside her, finally, a remote in his hand. His thumb punched the button dramatically, and the table sprang to life, holos in a variety of colors dancing through the space above the table until they settled into elegant blue dots and lines, pools and valleys, summits and cliffs. A beautiful, geometric game, if not the most challenging. *"Peaks and Valleys.* Room for as many as ten, but I prefer one-on-one." He smiled crookedly at her. "Don't you?"

"I'm not much for sharing. And more players just increase the chance that luck influences the gameplay. It's purer with two."

He raised his eyebrows. "Ah, indeed. Now, the map is set. And I promised you dinner. You take a look at it, plan a move or two. I'll be right back."

Hell. She sank into one of the velvety chairs as he swaggered out. Now how was she going to handle this? She was showing plenty of trust by being in here without a breather or helmet. Wasn't that enough? People who hadn't spent as much time in the deep going from atmo to atmo tended not to value that trust as much, she supposed. She withdrew the needle from the gauntlet and slid it into the top of the juice box as she groped for a plan to deal with the food.

Clean, Xi murmured a few moments later. *Matches factory specifications.*

Ellen pressed the button to pop out the thigh compartment to discard the needle and slowed. Maybe… Her suit was going to have to clean overtime if she filled it with whatever dinner he'd cooked up, and there still probably wouldn't be enough room. But she could feign nerves. Or travel sickness or something.

As footsteps approached, she hastily let the compartment retract. It slipped silently shut. It'd be open again soon, wouldn't it?

He sat a plate down before her, gesturing like a maître d'. "Sushi, red curry, dim sum, red bean mochi."

"Wow. Covering all the bases, aren't you? Did you pick something from every major Old Earth Asian culture?" Because he wasn't sure which one she belonged to… ? She hid a wince. If he'd looked her up, it couldn't be that hard with a bare minimum of effort. Sure, her father's father had been descended from Australians, but the planet *name* was pretty clear.

"I did. I thought Vietnamese might be overdoing it. But if you stick around for a second date…" He winked as he sat down directly across the table from her.

She should try to be more polite. "Well, uh, thank you. This looks great." For me to slowly smuggle off the plate and into my leg compartment.

"Did you get a chance to study the map?"

"Hmm?" She picked up a piece of sushi and waved a hand. His eyes tracked her hand earnestly. "Oh, I don't need to study it. I'm ready. You can go first." It was a standard starting map, one of two hundred and change that were part of the game package. She might have played it fifty times or so. Some of her favorites she'd played a hundred times or more in the first few months of trying to get the chip out of her system.

He shook his head. "No, no—you. I insist. You're the guest. I have home-field advantage."

She set the sushi back down as if annoyed and not simply stalling. "Let's flip for it then." She took a sip of the juice, hoping she wasn't emphasizing it too unnaturally. She wanted to make sure he saw her consuming *something*, since most of that curry was going into her pants.

He grabbed a nearby coaster. "Heads or tails?"

"Heads. Of course."

He laughed lightly, one of the more sincere expressions she'd seen on his face. "So cerebral, and yet so rough. I must admit I like you, Ellen Ryu."

The sound of her name on his lips gave her a chill—the creepy kind. She kept her eyes on the coaster.

"Heads will be the stars, then, and tails the blank side." He tossed it up and let it land in the middle of the table with a soft flop. The elegant star pattern stared up. "And it's heads! Your move."

She rolled her eyes. Now he'd wonder if that was how she'd beat him. She stood and stabbed a finger at an orb high on one peak, claiming it as her own. It glowed a sudden gold, like the sun, and she smiled at that, inadvertently letting a real grin slip out. She drew the orb to her desired spot in a valley and ended her turn with a smack on the table.

His eyes bored into her, curious, as he studied the map to take his turn as well.

She reclined back in the chair as far as it would go—which wasn't far—and knitted her hands behind her neck. "Did you know that the name Ellen means the sun? Like a sunbeam, a ray of light," she explained. "The gold. It's fitting."

"Indeed it is." He rested his cheekbone against his fist, leaning on the table casually. In that pose, he looked more like a magazine model than a scientist. The shadow of a beard was even more dramatic in this darker room.

"What did you say you researched again?" she muttered.

"I didn't say anything about it, actually."

She waited. But he said nothing. She frowned. "Top secret?"

He lifted the shoulder he wasn't leaning on. "I'm not supposed to talk about it."

Of course. She hadn't identified herself as Foundation to him. So he ought not to mention it. She nodded, accepting that. He didn't need to know, although he ought to suspect. "We all have our secrets. I'll just imagine you're designing a better gerbil and leave it at that."

He barked out a laugh, and she regretted the flippant comment. It was like she was flirting with him. Frag. "I truly wish I could share it with you, I'm sure you'd appreciate it. But I am obligated to move on to other, less interesting matters... Let's see."

"Like your turn?"

"I suppose." He gripped his own point of light, and it flooded a vibrant red. That also seemed fitting, but she wasn't sure why. He moved to capture a small peak, an aggressive tactic. "How long are you planning to stay on Capital?"

"It's not clear yet. But I don't expect more than a week. We're acquiring some new things for Ms. Utlis's career. Depends on how long it takes for them to be fabricated."

His eyes twinkled. He wasn't buying it. "That's a shame. You're so straightforward. Down to earth, as the silly saying goes. You don't fit in here, but I wish you did. I rather like it. Refreshing."

She raised an eyebrow, but said nothing. She simply took her turn, a seemingly lateral move.

On his next turn, she took the opportunity to smuggle one piece of some kind of white meat and one bamboo into the hip compartment. Next she went for the first piece of sushi, a small, white delicate fish on top of carefully shaped rice. Maybe octopus?

He looked up just at the last moment, and she fumbled it. The sushi fell silently to the floor.

She buried her consternation in a frown and a blush, faking pondering the game. He had a clever edge to his strategy, but it wasn't going to work. She moved her next two captures to block not his next move, but the ones he was clearly planning beyond that.

He outright scowled now, and it was all she could do not to smirk at him.

She glanced down, hoping to still sneak the piece she'd dropped somewhere hidden.

That was odd. All she saw was shiny wood floor. She hadn't heard any cleaning robots. Where had it gone?

She blew it off and refocused on the game. Her move had gotten his attention. He was concentrating on the game now, and she was concentrating on dramatic juice sipping. One fermented veggie made it into her compartment. Who served that on a date anyway? Good thing she was armored.

He took his turn. She'd left him with two options: follow his original plan, or try to respond with the optimal moves for the new situation. None of them were great, but she didn't think he'd thought that far ahead yet. He went for the current optimal move, marginally better than the original route she'd messed with.

So he favored adapting, rather than sticking to the plan. She made a mental note as she rose and seized another orb.

His eyes tracked her move, and he sat back in his chair when she slapped her turn over. "My, my. You are… unexpected."

She narrowed her eyes a bit as she sat back down. When was the last time he'd spent significant time training in military strategy? She didn't see why he should be at all surprised.

He pondered a little longer this time before hastily taking a turn. She timed the disappearance of part of the dessert with his jerky movements.

"There! Let's see how your fancy IQ manages that!" He sat down, looking satisfied. "We plebeians might surprise you."

She snorted. "If you make your living as a scientific researcher, I'm sure you're not too shabby yourself."

"I suppose my IQ has paid a few bills. Saved me from a few stupid decisions in my day."

She shook her head, absently beginning her next, more complicated turn. "People with high IQs still do stupid things." As she knew too well.

"Really. Ellen. Don't you think that's a little blunt?" He frowned as he watched her hands move. "You just said I wasn't *too* stupid."

"I was referring to myself."

"Oh." He stood, started his move, and captured a piece she'd moved into a bait position.

She swore. All part of the act. Maybe she'd let him think he'd almost pulled it off, not mention she'd set a deliberate trap.

"My, my. I didn't know Union officers were so prone to profanity." He grinned. The edge to his voice was back, too. Strange timing. Now that he thought he was winning, he wanted to threaten her? Or was his ego starting to form some hairline cracks?

She cleared her throat. "*Former* Union officer. Have you met many? I shouldn't think there'd be many on Capital."

"There aren't. But there may be enough to find out the standard reward for calling in deserters." He leaned forward, relishing what her reaction would be.

She smirked, and a little puff of laughter escaped in spite of herself. It was far from a *standard* award. "Now, now. Was it my move or what I said that made you turn to threats?" She completed her next move, an innocuous one, so as to keep him talking. She couldn't win just yet.

"Threats? No, no, you misunderstand me. Sorry, I know the Capital ways of etiquette can be hard to grasp to outsiders. I was simply curious."

She snorted. "So was I."

They sat in silent tension for a moment.

"For the record," she added, "Union officers are typically clean-cut.

I wasn't a typical Union officer." Special teams were… a little rougher, but it came out sounding arrogant as hell. Oh, whatever. What did it matter what this jackass thought?

His smile perked up in a way that made her want to swear again. Ugh. That was the problem. He *liked* arrogant. Time to change tactics.

Time to end the game.

She shoveled the biggest scoop of curry she dared while he took his next turn. There. Her plate looked at least half eaten. He leaned back with his own version of her gesture, hands folded behind his neck and grinning.

She stood, moved one piece, which set off the chain reaction he'd missed. The mountain range he'd been pinning his victory on disintegrated under him, the red orbs falling into the virtual water with an admittedly beautiful splash. And her turn wasn't done.

She let out a low whistle, pretending not to notice his shock. "This *is* quite a beautiful table you've got here. Maybe this is your area of research. Better gaming tables. If so, bravo, well done." It was a salve, a bit of butter in the coffee to toss his disintegrating ego off her trail.

But she wasn't done. Three more moves cascaded her way as she captured major objectives. Five, and it was over.

He blinked. "Well then."

"Great table. Probably time for me to head back to my team now." She was still standing from her turn.

He held up a palm. "Wait. Are you always all business?"

"Yes." She said it without a hint of a smile.

"All right then. Let's get down to business."

"I thought this *was* the business."

"This was the first step in the qualification process. I have information."

"And? Who doesn't."

"Information I am certain you will want." He leaned forward, elbows on the table, and knitted his fingers together in front of his mouth.

She shifted slightly, eager to make for the door. What fresh hell was this? He hadn't just been hitting on her? "Name it."

"First—a harder game. I want you to prove you're the genius you say you are. I can't trust my information to just any hooligan."

She scowled. "Hooligan? Is that what I look like? I just beat you, I'll remind you."

"You did indeed. But you still look like you're better with a gun than a puzzle."

She blinked as the silence stretched out for a long moment. Something in her flinched at the comment, the part of her that knew she wasn't like other women, that maybe she ought not to crush men at strategy games or tell them to slag off like she wanted to right now. It was a stupid part of her, but it suddenly stung. No matter. She wouldn't let it win. She physically shook herself, pushing the feeling away.

"Name the puzzle," she said instead.

He smiled, a wicked twinkle in the corner of his eye. "I shall. I'll send it to your contacts. Persad has them, yes? It will take a few weeks to complete."

"Weeks? I don't *have* weeks. I'll be long gone in weeks."

He shrugged. "Not my problem."

"How do I know your information won't be stale by then?"

"Trust me, this tidbit is evergreen."

CHAPTER SIX

"SO WHEN DO I get my cigar?"

That was all the warning he had before Jenny had dropped herself into the mustard-colored armchair he was sitting in. Surely his lap also being there was just a coincidence.

"You don't. They weren't shooting at me, they were shooting at Persad."

Jenny scowled, lips pouting. "You're not going to go all technical on me, are you, pilot? I shoulda outlined clearer rules for this bet."

He glanced at the door, not wanting to think about what Josana's reaction would be to this scene. "Too late. No bullets bounced off me yet."

"Well, you weren't *wearing* it. So it would have gone *in*." She jabbed a finger into his shoulder, hard. "That's my point."

He rolled his eyes. "Point taken. I'll wear it next time. Someone had to make you not look like a freak while you greeted your adoring public." His eyes darted to the door again.

"You could have pretended to be *my* security for once!" She followed his gaze, then sighed. "You know Persad still thinks we're dating, so..." She shrugged. "Nothing to worry about there."

"You know that's not what I was worrying about. Why must

you... ?" He groped for words, trying to shove down the leap of suspicion that rose up. The one that said Jenny would know that Josana's wrath wasn't worth a silly hug. That she must have some ulterior motive. Possibly a dangerous one.

"Must I what?" Jenny wasn't playing along.

He sighed. "Always sit like this."

She raised an eyebrow. "I don't know what you could possibly mean."

"I haven't noticed you sitting in Kael's lap lately. Or Dremer's, for that matter."

"Oh, I just miss the smell of your cologne," she said, grinning again. "And your cigars." She inhaled deeply, leaning closer to him, her chest pressing softly against his to dramatic effect. He couldn't tell if she was mocking him. Especially since her own warmth and the scent of apricots and peaches had taken over his senses. "And I'm anticipating my victory," she whispered into his ear, sending a shiver through him.

"Anticipate or not, you're not gonna win." He kept his voice hard and glanced at the door. Josana was due here anytime now. She wanted to talk, the kind of talk that should be written with a capital T.

She pointedly sighed in the door's direction. "Fine, I'll extricate myself." She dropped into the armchair beside him, once again humming to herself.

His lap felt colder than usual, her absence more obvious. Strange. He felt an odd sense of regret now, that he'd been unkind and needed to make amends. He opened his mouth, maybe to apologize. But what could he say that made any sense?

He shut it as someone approached up the hall. Too late. The boots were too heavy to be Josana's, though. Adan still tensed a little, but then relaxed as Kael came stalking around the corner, scowling.

"*Peaks and Valleys*. Stupid games," he was muttering to himself as he plunked down on a nearby chaise that was completely at odds with him. His eyes caught on Adan's. "Do you know how to play that?"

Adan frowned. "Yeah, I guess. Why? I mean, I'm not great at it."

"Teach me."

Adan shrugged. "Sure. Okay. Get your tablet or comm or something for your end, I'll install it."

Kael nodded. "Be right back. Gotta hit the head too."

Adan had it loaded on his comm and was working on showing it
on the coffee holotable when Josana swept in, a wrecking ball about to
make waves.

"C'mon." She waved to Adan as she brushed by. "We're leaving."

"Hey, no!" Jenny shot up from her chair. "But Kael said—and the
commander—" She waved down the hallway in the direction Kael had
gone.

Josana rolled her eyes and threaded her hand in Adan's. He didn't
miss Jen's eyes fixing on the motion. "We have things to talk about.
Let's go."

"I'll be back, Jen. See ya." He let himself be led. Sure, Kael was
going to be pissed when he got back, but if he waited for the brute to
return and tried to argue it, he'd never get this chance. In spite of
trying to keep his distance from the Theroki, though, Adan did feel a
little bad as they hit the elevator tube and he realized he had in fact
given Kael the slip. The guy *was* just doing his job, after all.

Maybe he could play *Peaks and Valleys* while he waited.

If Josana had wanted to kill him, though, she'd had ample opportunity. At this point, she was the only person he felt reasonably sure
wasn't out to kill him. And once in a great while, a guy just wanted to
go out with his girl for a date without a babysitter. Especially before he
left her on her home planet forever. Was that so much to ask?

He didn't think so.

She led him to a flyer that took them to what she called the bakery
district. Stepping out, he was a little too aware of the kaleidoscope of
shifting color around him, of all the crazy fashions, or the viciously
sleek ones. Most people were not wearing khaki with pockets.

Maybe he'd start a trend.

Laughing to himself, Josana led him to, of course, a mangabrew
cafe. The outside of the place was shining red enamel punctuated a
grid of by circular windows. Inside, the entire back wall held an
aquarium filled with black, squid-like creatures. Little shiny white

tables studded most of the floor. Carefully manicured, bored-looking women similar to Jenny's fans lounged back in semi-recliners of some kind of plush gray fabric. He caught a dozen glances in his direction, most of them vaguely put out.

Josana led him to a curvy chair of his own. He sat sideways on the edge. No way he could relax with what *they* needed to talk about. Josana, however, did not have the same problem. After setting a tiny ceramic cup of viciously bubbling black liquid in front of him, she draped herself across the chair like it was made to showcase her. And she subtly took a sip. The drink left a thick black coat across her upper lip, and she swiped it away with her tongue.

He was simultaneously horrified and very excited.

"Go on, take a drink." She pointed.

"Uh—working on it," he replied.

"Okay… So what do you think? Let's talk about my offer. Now that you're here."

He glanced around. He was here all right. Where was this—*what* was this place, exactly?

She set down the cup. "Stay."

Like it was that simple. "Don't you see I don't belong here?"

"I don't see why."

"I'm a pilot."

"You could drive luxury flyers if you want. Although you certainly wouldn't need to. I think you're better than that."

He blinked, unsure of what to say to that.

"Or there's even racing. It's about an hour flyer away, but they do love it in Appellate 629."

That sounded mildly interesting, but not if he had a spaceship as the alternative, one that flew around not just to make faster times, but to change things. Permanently. He shrugged. "I don't think so, Jos. I don't think this is going to work. Much as I wish it could."

"What about programming? I'm sure there's lots you can do anywhere."

"Even if there is, I don't have a work permit."

"Don't worry about that."

"I have to worry about that, what do you mean? It's a no go."

"Let's say I could take care of that for you."

"But you can't."

She rolled her eyes. "But I *can*. That's what I've been trying to tell you. So much for subtlety."

He blinked. "What?"

"Just pretend that's not a problem. Would you stay?"

He frowned harder at her. It just didn't add up. It had *never* added up. "Let's be honest with each other, Josana. We've been together for three weeks. You're way out of my league—"

"Now, that's not true," she said earnestly.

"Why are you so serious about this?"

"You haven't even had a drink."

"Neither have you had a second one."

"That's because it's terrible."

"I figured. Don't dodge."

"Fine! Fine, fine." She shook her head, looking off into the distance. "It'd have to be said sooner or later anyway." She met his gaze squarely now, eyes serious. "I run a business here. A *very* lucrative business. I'm not coming back to go to medical school, except maybe as a cover."

He frowned. "What kind of crazy cover is that?"

"An expensive but useful one."

"What *kind* of business that you haven't mentioned it before?"

She smiled sweetly. "I provide a host of sensible and exotic recreations to some of Capital's finest—and most wealthy—citizens."

He stopped short. "Are you serious?"

"As a heart attack."

He was shaking his head. This couldn't be real. Innocent, naive Josana was... what was she? An underworld maven of some kind? He wanted that idea not to make any sense, but that would be lying to himself. The idea fit her perfectly.

"Chems or sex?"

She scowled and hushed him.

"So both?"

"I hate you right now. Look, have some class. You can't talk about it directly like that."

He collapsed back into the recliner, not even caring now. "I *told* you I don't belong here."

She pouted at him. "Don't be like that. Look, my offerings are primarily chemical. I'm not some madam or companion or something. That is entirely too tiring, and how the hell would I have done that from the ship?"

"You ran an illegal business from our *ship*?" He spread his palms flat on the table. "Does your sister know about this?"

"I suspect yes. I doubt Xi missed it, and she would certainly have told my sister. At the very least, Xi knows I make regular shipments from time to time."

"You were picking up *chems* at our stops? And sending them off for money? Holy hell. I can't believe you're a—"

"Damn it, Adan. Subtlety. Please. Give it a try." She flicked a packet at him, eyes flashing with laughter. A tiny square of blue powder mixed with black and silver tablets shaped like hearts landed on the table almost silently. "There, see for yourself."

He froze. "Don't do that, hell." He knew what that was. Osiris. Even that tiny square could be worth hundreds of credits in the outsystem, where supply was fairly common. Here it'd be worth more. Way more. He had no idea how much. "Put that away."

"Nobody cares about that here. Or I wouldn't have come here. You think I'm stupid?"

"Put the fragging thing away. You *do* realize I'm unregistered, right?"

She rolled her eyes again and took a sip of her drink, glancing over at the bar. She didn't move to touch the packet.

He glowered at her and then pocketed it himself when he couldn't stand it any longer. "Wait. What the hell does that have to do with us?"

"Well, if you stayed, in addition to the pleasure of your company, I think we could make a lot of money together. I need network protection, and there're lots of other... lucrative endeavors we could tackle that I'm not equipped for on my own."

"How many of them are *legal* endeavors?"

"Now come on. Jenny grossly overstated the—"

"That many, huh?"

"When you know the right people, it's not a problem. 'Legal' has a more flexible meaning here."

That phrase. *Know the right people.* It made his stomach turn. And worse—was all this just her trying to hook him in to work for her? To just... be her computer guy? He groaned aloud without entirely meaning to. "You're barking up the wrong tree, Jos. You shoulda told me at the beginning and I'd have told you it would never happen. I swore leaving the outsystem I'd leave that life behind. I don't do illegal."

"It's not *exactly* illegal."

"I don't do questionable either."

She stabbed a finger at him. "Every single thing you do on the *Audacity* is questionable, if not illegal. How dare you judge me."

Well. She had him there. "But it's for a noble purpose. It's helping people."

"Do you really know that?"

He gritted his teeth, hating the way the comment niggled at him. "Yeah."

"Isn't it noble to help relieve people of pain, of suffering? Is there a real difference between chemicals taken for recreation and chemicals taken as medicine? Both of them are helping people. Coping with life's struggles and tragedies, bringing relaxation when it's impossible— those aren't meaningless. Or unethical."

"It is when those chemicals are also poisoning them. And addicting them to have to come back to *you* for more, so their problems just get worse."

"Not every chem is like that."

He pointed at his pocket. "This one is."

"Why do you have to be such a fragging white knight? C'mon. I make people happy. Bring out their true selves and throw off their inhibitions."

He shook his head.

She sighed. "Fine."

"Sorry you wasted your time." He didn't try to hide the hurt in his voice.

She shrugged. "I didn't. You're a really loyal guy I would have liked to have on my side. You're smart, and you rarely bore me. That can't be said for most people. And you're even a decent lay."

He snorted, a weird mixture of warmth and hurt swirling at the words. "Wow. Glowing testimonial. Decent if you're alone in the deep with no other options?" He had loved her. Or he'd thought he did. Perhaps it was just the idea of her, more than who she really was. The status, much as he hated to admit it. The bitter taste in his mouth wasn't the mangabrew, which remained untouched and still bubbling. Why the hell was it bubbling?

"C'mon, like you said, it's been three weeks. It's been fun but it's not like we've been serious or anything."

He went completely still.

"Oh. I…"

He held up a palm. "Don't worry about it." He rose to get up.

She sat forward on the edge now. "If you feel that much, then why won't you stay? You can have a good life here, we can build something—"

A good life, perhaps. But not one he could have laughed with his mother about. He had to be able to look himself in the eye in the mirror at the end of the day. "No. Like I said, I don't belong here. I should have never even entertained the idea. That was just leading you on. But I guess I wasn't the only one."

She blinked. "That's it then, I guess."

"Yeah, I guess. Goodbye, Jos."

And he turned and started to walk away.

"Wait!"

He turned. She was wincing as she downed what was left of her mangabrew.

"I have to go back to Persad's too. And I have the flyer waiting."

"Oh." He ran a hand over his face, feeling suddenly exhausted. "Well, c'mon then."

———

KAEL WAS SITTING on a chair in Persad's son's room, trying to read an obtuse article on *Peaks and Valleys* but mostly fuming, when he saw them return. He had one of the remote monitors pitched on the side of Vivaan's desk. Persad opened the door to her suite, and Adan strode in, face looking grim. Kael almost thought Josana wasn't with him, but she followed a moment later.

But Kael's business wasn't with her. He rose and strode to the door. If he timed this just right...

Just as Adan came into view, Kael reached out and grabbed him by his collar, hauling him into the room. He slammed the door control and waited a split second to slam Adan into it once it'd slid home. Hopefully Persad wouldn't notice and this fancy high-rise had some sound dampening.

"You've got a death wish," he growled.

Adan rolled his eyes. "I was fine. I was with Josana. She's had ample chance to kill me before you came along."

"No, I mean from *me*. I'm going to kill you personally if you do that again."

"I thought you were trying to impress the commander, not get kicked out."

"Is that your problem with me? Cause last I checked she's off having dinner with that smartass scientist."

Adan frowned. "She is?"

"I don't care about any of that. I care about doing my job. And you're keeping me from doing it."

Adan sighed and removed Kael's hands from his collar. Kael let him. For now. "Ostrov's an ass. That doesn't mean anything. She's just talking to him because his name's in Persad's data." Adan gestured at the young man's desk as he sank into Kael's former seat. "She's just using him. Just like Josana was using me."

"Pardon me?" Maybe this could give them a clue as to who was after him. Doubtful, since Adan seemed completely uninvested in figuring out who was trying to kill him. But Kael could hope.

Adan waved him off. "She's... not as young and innocent as she seems."

Kael kept his face a frozen mask. She hadn't seemed terribly innocent coming on to him in the mess, or any of another half dozen times, but that seemed unhelpful to mention now. After she'd hooked up with Adan, Kael had just assumed the girl was in permanent heat. Or bored as an ice miner on a desert planet.

"She wasn't after me. She probably just wanted me to hack her out of... difficult situations. Or something."

Kael frowned. "Illegal situations?"

Adan mimed a firing gun with one hand. "Yep. And you thought Ostrov was the smart one."

He scowled now. "He is."

Adan shook his head. "No, he's not. If he were smart, he wouldn't think he could beat her."

A bark of laughter escaped him.

Adan continued, seeming to relax a little at the topic change, the light returning to his eyes. "Imagine that as a first date. You invite a girl over for dinner and arm wrestling and just destroy her five or ten times. Is that your idea of showing her a good time?"

Kael blinked. Well, actually... He had no idea what his idea of showing a girl a good time would be. Back on Faros... well, there'd been no money then, and that had been a different life, but with Asha there had been sunsets on the roof, sandstorms spent curled up in cozy tents, listening to street musicians, walking through the vibrant hum of the districts around them hand in hand.

Glory be, how strange that it could sneak up and stab him in the heart again just in the middle of a conversation. Eleven years of feeling nothing ought to have dulled the pain, but it seemed to have only delayed it.

"Kael, you okay?"

"Just... bad memories, that's all."

"Of a girl?" Adan said slowly.

Kael hesitated. Did he really want to go there? "Yeah. A girl. When we were teens."

"Before the whole Theroki thing."

"Yeah. It's complicated."

"Is she still out there? The one that got away?" Adan glanced at the door. At Josana? "Or the one that didn't really love you anyway?"

"She's not. Not still out there."

Adan shook his head. "Married."

"Dead." Because of him.

His face must have been truly dark, because Adan rose and put a hand on either shoulder. "Whoa, whoa. I'm sorry I brought it up."

"It's fine. It's been a long time. I just… you said your idea of a good time. It's been a long time since that was an option for me."

Adan's eyes widened slightly as that sank in. "Right. Well. I'm sure you'd do a better job than that fool any day."

Kael wasn't so sure. What *had* he done? Saved her life a few times until she relented and bought him a beer? Traded war stories? The life-saving ought to count for something, but that was hardly romantic.

Maybe she wanted romantic. In the grand sense.

But no. She'd said no. She didn't want anything from him. Besides, asking her out for some nonsense thing like dinner and strategy games seemed… disrespectful? Disingenuous? Certainly anticlimactic. How could dinner be exciting when you were used to being shot at together? Who needed games when you had actual strategy? What was he supposed to do?

But of course, he wasn't supposed to *do* anything. He was a convicted criminal, a kid living under bridges and in caves who'd barely gotten a third grade education, even if he'd fixed some of that in later years. It didn't matter. He'd been an outcast from the day he'd been born, and no change of name or job was going to change that—to him, to her, or to anyone else.

Before he could think the better of it, his fist lashed out and slammed into the wall beside him. Adan jerked back.

Kael shook the pain out of his knuckles and stared at the dent he'd left behind. Great. The missing guy was definitely going to appreciate the new hole in the wall over his bed. And he'd been doing so well with his anger management.

Adan stuck his face right in front of Kael's, waved his hand up and down. "Hey. Everything on in there?"

"Slag off, asshole. You didn't have a chip messing with your head for a decade, so I don't expect you to understand."

Adan frowned hard. "I didn't say I *blame* you. He's an ass. But he's not her type. Quit worrying."

"I'm not worrying about anything."

Adan looked pointedly at the dent. Kael just grunted in form of reply. It wasn't exactly a growl, but… Was he supposed to be counting to ten or something?

"Right." Adan drew out the word, then pursed his lips. "Look, sorry I snuck away. That was an asshole thing to do. Guess Josana brings that out in me."

"That's hardly surprising. She's a total—"

"Can you at least wait until I'm over her to tell me that?"

"No guarantees. But you completely broke it off?"

"Yeah. Listen, I won't take off again. I swear. I'll stick with you, we'll find Vivaan, and we can get back to the ship and off this stupid rock."

Kael took a slow breath, studying Adan's face and trying to cool down. The pilot seemed sincere. "All right, fine. I guess. Truce?"

"Truce."

"But I swear I'll break your legs if you're lying to me right now." Yeah, really had a grip on the anger now. He sounded like he was back in the Gray Dragons. He shook himself, tried to throw it off. Both the anger and the past.

"I've had enough lies for today. I'm not."

Kael held out a hand to shake, and Adan grasped it. "Praise the Almighty for that," Kael muttered. He was proud to not overly crush the pilot's hand. Presumably he needed it unbroken.

"I, too, am pleased with your decision to stay," came a voice from Vivaan's desk.

They both jumped, Adan clutching his chest. "Frag—don't scare me like that, Xi."

"My apologies. I did not anticipate a fear response. I am not used to operating in this fragmentary environment."

Kael shook his head. "We didn't expect you to be talking out of this random desk, that's all. You haven't before."

"Noted in the fragmentary behavioral profile. I appreciate your continued assistance with detailing my reaction models, Kael. My speech from this unit is not entirely random, as Adan has requested I take a thorough look through Mr. Vivaan Persad's files to check for anything that may have been missed."

"How's that going?" Adan ran a hand through his hair. He looked exhausted.

"I have not found anything else I would consider suspicious. In fact, the suspicious thing might be the overall lack of data. Either he was very uninterested in technology or he had not operated this unit for very long."

"Maybe he has another computer somewhere," Adan said.

"Maybe the doctor is holding out on us." Kael raised an eyebrow.

Adan frowned. "Has she given us any reason not to trust her?"

"Not exactly. But if you get the chance to poke around while we're gone…" Kael raised his eyebrows suggestively.

Adan rubbed his chin. "Hmm. I'll keep that in mind."

———

ELLEN WAS STILL FUMING when she marched back into Persad's apartment. How that man could piss her off when she'd beaten him so soundly—and so *gently*. Jesus, she could have rubbed his face in it if she'd wanted to.

She hadn't. And she hadn't even gotten any useful information out of him.

And now that idiot wanted her to waste her time on another stupid game. She'd crush him.

Before she could find someone to take out her exasperation on, Persad stepped out of the workshop room, her monocle blinking in surprise. "Ms. Ryu! Just in time. I have both chips ready. If you'd like, I can get your lieutenant and we can begin…"

Shoving down the lashing anger, she nodded bluntly. "Of course. Where do you need me?"

"Just in there. Be right in."

No one was in the foyer or the main seating area. They must have all returned to their rooms to rest and recharge. Smart. Unlike her, wasting her time with that idiot. Now she had no real new information, except that he was playing some kind of elaborate game, and she was pissed as hell.

The workshop was lined with high tables covered with tiny bits of electronics parts, tools, and what were probably the fine-electronics printers Persad had mentioned before. She sank into a generic, uncomfortable looking chair against the wall.

In the middle of the room, Persad had a very different chair, presumably for the chip installations. It was more like a table really, with just a slight angle to sit on, foot rests and arm rests.

And restraints. Ellen eyed those uncomfortably, but they looked unused. They'd probably just come with the chair.

The main body of it was heavily padded, almost like a sofa, except for the opening down the middle. Something like a masseuse's table, except instead of leaving room in a round circle for a face, it left a whole strip down the back.

For the neck and spine and the bits and bobs the cybernetics researchers loved to tuck along them. She was alone now, so she did shudder this time. But it was only a moment or two before Kael and Persad entered.

His expression was uncharacteristically dark, and it didn't lighten when he saw the chair. Or even when he met her eyes, which surprised her a little. Whether she liked to admit it or not, his eyes usually lit up when they rested on her.

"You first, Lieutenant."

He headed straight for the chair, no hesitation, stepped onto the footrest, spun, and lay back into the thing. Ellen stood and came closer.

"You don't need a clean room for all this, Persad? I didn't feel a buzz on the way in."

"I have some scrubbers in my work area, but no. Nanos do the trick in here. Just like the ones in your interfaces, I'm sure."

"Did you get some rest, like the others?" she murmured to him, as Persad got situated. She shouldn't be distracting Persad at the moment.

He shook his head. "Not as much as I'd like."

Persad held out a comm for him to see the specs Ellen had sent earlier. "Can you verify these are your upgrades?"

His eyes widened. "Where did you get those?"

"I sent them," Ellen put in. "Dremer wrote them down when she updated your chip."

He let out a low whistle. "I guess it's right. That's more detail than I've ever seen." He shrugged and flopped back in the chair. "Does it really matter?"

"Of course it matters. Timeframe of installation?"

"About eleven years ago."

"Hmm. How did you become a Theroki, anyway?"

"I don't like talking about it."

Persad frowned, but at the computer monitor to her side. "I can see that. That was quite the heart rate and adrenaline spike."

He blew out a dejected breath and closed his eyes. "Yeah. I'm working on that."

"And you, Ms. Ryu. I didn't expect you to have a chip interface as well."

"Wasn't my choice."

"They didn't exactly ask either of us," Kael muttered.

Ellen wasn't sure Persad even heard him. Ellen stepped closer and leaned one arm against the chair arm while keeping her eyes on the doctor. She'd promised she'd watch his back—literally—if this ever happened, so she wasn't going to let him down. She meant it in a friendly way, but her forearm brushed his, only the smooth black fabric between his arm and hers. She could feel the heat of him, and suddenly the brush didn't seem so benign.

She shifted her arm away, not wanting to distract him, keeping a watchful eye on Persad. "The universe sure has a way of teaching us we don't always get what we want, doesn't it?"

She felt the pressure of his eyes boring into her but didn't turn her head. She tried to keep her eyes on Persad, but finally she relented and met his gaze. He was frowning.

"What?" she said.

"You can be brutal sometimes, you know that?"

She stared back, wide-eyed, and opened her mouth. What could she say to that? What did he even mean? The silence stretched on.

Oblivious, Persad spoke first. "Okay, I've got a handle on these. Take off your shirt."

He sighed, leaning forward and pulling the thin black fabric over his head.

A ripple of muscle, skin, and ink. Scars. She averted her eyes a split second too late. Hopefully he didn't notice. Still, her attention was pinned on him in her peripheral vision as he dropped back into the chair, the way he twitched when Persad found the panel. Several panels, actually, from the series of clicks and puffs that came from his back.

"Okay, we are cooking now. Oh, this is convenient. This should only take a slight modification, hold on. I made this for a newer model of multiple-chip interface, so it's a little too small, but that's an easy enough fix... Not too bad back here, for eleven years of..." She turned back to the table behind her, bent over the magnifying glass. She trailed off, lost in her tinkering.

Ellen glanced back at Kael and found him watching her, his head cocked to one side.

"There we go!" Persad held up the tiny device triumphantly. "Now brace yourself, I'll just slide this in. Let me know if anything goes haywire!"

"That's reassuring." Ellen frowned around at Persad but thought better of distracting her at the last moment. She leaned back to study his face for any sign of a problem instead.

Kael was ignoring the doctor with a long-suffering air. His eyes were still trained on Ellen.

"What?" she said again.

"Sometimes I can't figure you out, Commander."

She swallowed. "I'm not that complicated."

"Aren't you?"

Something must have slid home, because he winced, his head jerking back suddenly. And then the expression was gone.

"There." Persad straightened. "How do you feel? Now this piece goes on the scalp…" She slipped something that looked like a pebble under his hair. "Also interferes with communicators too. They won't work near your head or inside armor. You keep it at arm's distance and on speaker mode, and it should be fine though."

"Great," Ellen muttered.

"Let me just take some quick diagnostics."

He blinked. "I feel… fine. No different, actually."

"Excellent. All your readouts are normal. Looking good. Closing you back up." She futzed around for a few more minutes and then straightened. "Done. You're free to go, Mr. Asidian. All right, Ryu, your turn. I'll go get your chip. Take a seat."

Persad shuffled out, and Kael stood and stepped away to let her in. She tried to focus on the chair and not the fact that he was only now putting his shirt back on.

She flopped back. Good thing she'd had the foresight to wear a tank top.

He turned back toward her, the tattoos and scars vanishing. "Think she'll be able to find the panel buttons in one shot? That schematic you sent me was crazy complicated."

"If I hadn't been being tortured, I'd have been super impressed you executed it from a distance while we were all losing our minds. It's not easy. I can't really hit all six pressure points by myself, although I don't know why I'd want to."

"Well, you know, it was life or death." He shrugged. "That changes things. Doesn't it."

She took a deep breath, trying to relax and train her eyes on the ceiling.

"It makes you nervous," he said softly.

"Very."

"The chip part in general, or this whole… ?" He gestured vaguely at the chair.

"Both. But being… worked on, that's the worst of the two."

He frowned. "I think I remember where the pressure points are. Would it help if I…" He gestured vaguely at her neck. "So she doesn't have to struggle? If I don't get it right away, we can leave it to her."

Strangely, it did sound less scary to have him do it. Especially since she could see him, and it wasn't just someone clinking and tinkering at the base of her brain. "Sure, go ahead."

"Really? You sure?"

"Yeah, it will save time." The words felt like a lie. It *would* save her time, but Ellen didn't really care about that. She took a deep breath and closed her eyes.

"Let me see," he muttered.

A warm spot came to rest gently below her jaw, and a wave of shock rocketed through her. Somehow she'd thought he meant he'd use telekinesis, just like he'd done back on Upsilon.

But no.

One fingertip pressed behind her ear, whisper soft against her ear lobe, and it took a herculean effort to conceal the shiver. Another found the correct spot at the base of her neck. The six points were a little odd, but not that hard to reach if you had two hands, approaching from the front. At her own angle, that was another matter.

He found the two spots just behind her jaw on the other side. How were his hands rough even when all they did was wear power armor? The points of warmth of his fingers touching her, sent ripples of energy across her skin, and she felt her lips part, unintentionally.

Her eyes snapped open, suddenly afraid. Not at what he was doing, but at what it revealed.

She couldn't tell if his eyes were trained on her neck or her lips, but he frowned in concentration as he pressed into the last spot. Some mechanism connected and slid home.

She winced, her body tensing as the tiny compartments opened. One at her neck, the other more secret compartment farther down her back. It was still hidden by the shirt. And it'd been redacted from the specs she'd sent Persad. An emergency chip rested inside, in case someone could hijack her via the primary opening. If they missed the slightly more hidden one, allies could activate the fall-back remotely, and it would reclaim control. Well, mostly only Dremer or Simmons could do that. They had to know it was there to activate it.

Funny how she wanted to tell Kael about it now. Not because she didn't trust Persad, but more because it seemed like he ought to be one of the ones who knew.

Damn it. It'd only been two months. She trusted him too much. Far, far too much.

He must have seen the expression in her eyes change. "You okay?" His fingertips still rested on her skin. He probably didn't know it had worked, since it had opened nearly soundlessly.

"Yeah, yeah," she said quickly. She was being stupid, trying to draw the moment out. If she wanted him to touch her, she should tell him that. Like a normal person. "Thanks. It worked. Glad that's done now." She forced out a laugh that sounded nervous and a little crazed.

He hesitated, eyes searching her face as if he'd thought he'd seen something and then lost it. She saw that expression of searching her features often enough on him.

Slowly, he lifted his hands and started to draw away. But at the last second, he brushed the back of his knuckles against the edge of her jaw.

It was such a brief moment to send such a thrill of lightning through her. She knew what'd come next. He'd pretend it was an accident, and she'd pretend to believe him. Like they always did.

They didn't make it that far. The door opened, and Persad waltzed in, muttering to herself. She stopped abruptly, head cocking to one side and eyes doing their dance between the two of them again.

Kael snatched his hands away and sank into the nearby seat, eyes dark and turned toward the floor.

Ellen jerked a thumb at her shoulder and back. "Got the panel open for you, Doctor. We thought we'd save you the time."

"How very… considerate of you. Okay, let me go over your vitals, and we should be ready to get this started."

Ellen took another deep breath, desperately trying to steady herself against two whirlwinds now. She let her eyes drift up to the ceiling, conveniently avoiding him, and she could feel he was still looking away. Brooding.

"You got any cookies in this place, Persad?" she said. She couldn't even muster a frown at the wobble in her voice.

"Didn't Ostrov feed you adequately?"

That wasn't helping. "You think I'd eat anything he offered? I'm starving."

"You're anxious as hell, by these readouts. Do you want a sedative?"

"No," she snapped. She took a deep breath. "I'll breathe through it." She closed her eyes.

"Hmm. Yes… maybe. That's better. Oh? Oh, yes. Third cabinet on the right."

Ellen didn't even register that last bit until the door opened and shut, but there wasn't much time for processing. The hot searing twinge slammed into her neck, a pinch like a needle sliding into a vein, then ice. Fingers in her hair, gentle ones. Pins and needles starting between her shoulder blades and shooting out to her fingers and toes. Frag.

Deep breaths, deep breaths.

"Almost done. Closing you up. Take it easy, it's okay. Almost done. There. It's all right."

She was panting, cold sweat beaded on her brow, when the door reopened again.

"We're good. All done. You can get up."

She lowered her eyes from the ceiling tile. He was back in the chair, a plate balanced on one knee. A half dozen perfectly round, pale cookies topped with little bits of pistachio sat prettily on the dish. She staggered out of the chair. The pebble was cool, a light pressure on the top part of her skull.

Persad patted her on the shoulder. "Good job. Let me go put this away." She wandered out the door, eyes still on the devices and read-outs in her hand.

They were alone.

He lifted up the plate. "You look like you need one of these."

She grabbed one and took a bite. "I've been better."

"And you've been worse."

The words hit her like a fresh spring wind over the hills. Relief. It was true. She smiled at him now, wide and sunny, and didn't bother to try to hide it. He looked a little startled.

"You're right about that." She bit into the cookie and chewed with gusto. "So right. Let's go find our quarry, shall we?"

He rose. "It would be my pleasure, Commander."

She picked up a cookie and put it in his hand. "Pretty sure we're drinking tonight, so..." She took the plate and headed for the door.

"On duty? Always breaking the rules." His eyes twinkled as he followed her out into the hall and headed for his room.

"Well, we have to fit in, right?"

"I doubt you'll ever do that, Elle."

She ducked her head as she hurried into her room. She had armor to put on, Persad's hard work to secretly download to make sure it wasn't going to drive her insane or take over her mind, Josana to deal with, and a long night to get ready for. But that damn smile just wouldn't go away.

CHAPTER SEVEN

ELLEN HADN'T YET FINISHED REMOVING her armor when the chime sounded. She tried not to groan. She hadn't been procrastinating; she just wanted to make sure Xi had plenty of time to finish the download of the data and get it to Dremer. Even if it had finished ten minutes ago. The fact that she was still armored aside from her head and her hands had nothing to do with the fact that Josana was now standing in her doorway, with the biggest, most sincere grin Ellen had ever seen the girl attempt.

"Welcome home, Ryu. Ready for date night part two?" The door slid shut as Josana bustled in with her packages. "Really getting out there these days in your retirement. Good for you. How was the lover boy—what was his name? Ostrov?"

Ellen narrowed her eyes. "Arrogant."

"Arrogant can be fun." Josana gently set her burden on the room's small guest bunk.

"Not on him, it's not."

"Are you ready for contestant number two?"

"We're trying to find a kidnapped," and now she lowered her voice, "and possibly dead young man. This is not a game show."

Josana rolled her eyes, lifting one longer package—no, a black garment bag—and hanging it on a hook by the door. "Even in suffering, we must take amusement where we can find it. You don't find it amusing to have them all posturing for you? And ignoring me, too. The indignity." She shook her head.

Ellen couldn't tell if that was sarcastic, teasing, or sincere. "You have Adan."

"Actually, no, I don't." Although still smiling, Josana gave her a withering glare. "Even *he* picked you over me."

"Me?"

"You and his job."

"You shouldn't take that personally. Pilots don't like to leave the stars. Or ships they have all to themselves. Once they get a taste…"

"And do marines like to leave their power armor?" Josana glanced pointedly at the armor she was still wearing.

"No. They don't." Ellen blew out a breath, reluctantly freeing the forearm piece and the elbow. Heaven forbid she just automatically release it all and get it over with.

"I know." Josana's grin was absolutely murderous. "So much black," she purred, running graceful, long fingers down Ellen's newly unearthed forearm. Ellen took a step back before she even realized she was doing so, and Josana's grin widened. "You need to live a little. Your outfit is here. Call me if you can't figure out how to clothe yourself. I'll be with your date number two." Then chuckling a little to herself, she palmed open the door and disappeared before Ellen could think of a clever retort.

She was torn between a desire to do whatever it took to block Josana from being alone in a room with Kael and dutifully revealing what horror Josana had conjured up. Would it even be recognizable as clothing? Who knew, considering fashion around here?

She gripped the elegant black garment bag with one hand, seized the zipper with the other, and took a deep breath.

Please be a boring robe please be a boring—

She yanked down the zipper like ripping off a dirty bandage. Bright fragging blue shown out from between the two zippered halves, soft blue but bold too, vibrant like the color of the shallowest water on the Capital beaches. She caught her breath, then forced herself to slide the bag away to reveal the form of what was inside.

It *was* a robe, actually. A really, really short one.

Sashes of ice blue, peacock, and fuchsia belted it at the waist, the fabric shimmering. It didn't look long enough to cover her ass.

Only one way to find out.

She unceremoniously yanked the thing out of its packaging and turned it this way and that. Hell. She was reaching for the comm to call Jenny when there was another knock at the door.

"What?" she snapped.

Josana leaned in, her eyes dancing with glee. "Forgot the shoes." She held out a box.

"You're a sadist, you know that?" She snatched the box from her hands.

"I do." Josana only grinned wider. "I own it."

"Get out."

"Don't you want to see what's inside?"

Ellen propped a hand on her hip. "I am equally capable of violence without my armor, Josana."

She rolled her eyes. "Back to the boy toy then."

"You—" she started. "He is not—"

The door shut in her face.

She dropped the box on the bed and stared at it for a long second, maybe two. She reached closer, hesitated... But there was nothing for it. Sound-muffling boots and power-armor boots were her only other options. In other words, they *weren't* options. She'd never get in with them on.

She forced herself to flip open the lid, tossing it sharply aside and jerking back like she expected a grenade.

But inside was something far, far worse.

High heels.

———

JENNY WASN'T USUALLY one to sulk. But between this odd

mission, Adan traipsing off with Josana like Capital was an amuse-ment park fairyland for their budding romance, and just being on this stupid rock in the first place, she found herself sitting alone in Persad's tiny solarium, brooding, when Ellen's call came in on the comm.

She punched the button to audio only and raised it to her ear.

It had been a long time since she'd heard her commander swear like that. Maybe never.

"I know, I know." Jen rubbed a hand across her forehead.

"She's a sadist, Jenny. I'd hate to see the psychological workup Taylor has on her."

"You mean you haven't seen it?"

"I'm afraid to look. It's not like she's mission critical. Until now anyway. This is awful."

"I know. I'm sorry I couldn't stop it. I couldn't decide whether to say something or not say something. She started poking me. Do I say you don't usually wear high heels? Would that discourage her or encourage her? I dodged the question, but she could smell blood. Like a fashion-police bloodhound."

Jenny of course couldn't blame Ryu for her lack in that particular, somewhat useless skill. At twenty-two, with a life exclusively in the military and with little or no family, it wasn't *that* hard to have avoided the damn things. Union dress uniforms didn't use them. Jenny had to secretly admit she envied Ellen a little bit, having made it to this age before someone twisted her arm into the things. Jen was pretty sure she'd gotten her own first pair at four, to be shown off at her mother's cocktail parties.

"She's a cruel, cruel woman." Something thunked loudly on Ryu's end of the comm.

Jenny winced. This focus on Josana wasn't helping her brooding. "Are you going to be okay? I mean, isn't that dangerous?" Stilts would probably have been a safer choice for a mission.

"I'll deal. Maybe I'll just go barefoot."

Rubbing her forehead, Jenny leaned back on the soft white solarium couch. "How's the dress?"

"You can't see my ass. I think. Barely. Maybe it depends on the angle."

"That's a low bar you've got there."

There was a slight pause, and the voice that came through eventually was less irreverent, more vulnerable, shaking slightly. "This is going to be so embarrassing."

Jenny took a deep breath, let the silence ride for a while, before she said, "Does it matter what they think?"

Ryu let out a crazed bark of laughter. "Good point. It doesn't." She cleared her throat. "You're completely right."

"It doesn't, *but*... I hear a 'but.' "

"Maybe there might be an opinion or two that *does* matter to me, and I don't want to look like a fool, in front of..." she grumbled.

Jenny grinned. "Gosh, Commander, it's sweet of you to worry about me, but I'm not judging you. Actually, I kinda envy that you've avoided those contraptions this long." Obviously, it was not her that her commanding officer was concerned about, but Jenny played along.

Ryu snorted. "How will the ship ever fly again? I'll lose everyone's respect. It'll be mutiny. Zhia will don higher heels and take command. Chaos!"

"We all are left to Chaos in the end," Jenny said mildly. "Look, tell me what these shoes look like."

"Expensive. Very expensive. Black leather. Classic, actually. Josana could have chosen a lot worse. The only problem is the heel."

"How high?"

"Eight, maybe ten centimeters?"

"Oh my God."

"I know. I'm going to kill her. Murder her slowly in her sleep. Should I use a pillow or just my hands, you think?"

"Just so you don't have to wear the shoes? Cause I'm pretty sure you would still have to wear them, even if she's dead, but then we'll have a body to dispose of. That's not making our lives easier. And I doubt her sister and therefore Dr. Taylor would approve."

Ellen sighed.

Jenny rubbed her chin. "I tell you what. Here's my suggestion.

Wear them out of the building. Gives you a good excuse to hang on a certain beefy arm. Then—"

"Why would I want an excuse to—" Ellen started.

Jenny pretended she hadn't heard that. "—when you get downstairs, have Xi find a store nearby and get you a new more practical pair."

"Oh. Wow. That's a good idea. Will do."

"You're welcome."

"Sorry. Thanks. I'm a little distracted over here."

"Go ahead, finish getting ready. I'll be there to see you off."

"I wish you wouldn't."

"And miss sight of the heels?"

"And possibly my butt cheek. You've been warned."

"I've seen that already, remember? But I've got some climbing shorts. That oughta cover ya. I'll be right there."

"Jen, you're a life saver."

The call ended, and just as Jen was about to switch off the comm, a different name started up. A name she didn't recognize. A shot of fear went through her. She hit audio only and accepted the call. "Hello?"

"Is this Ms. Jennifer Utlis, renowned climbing champion and brilliant progeny of the Utlis clan?" The man's voice was formal, stilted. Fancy. Fit for on-air broadcasts. She went very still.

"How did you get this number?"

"Ms. Utlis, I am Sarlano Crane, lead anchor of the Dailyglow Network. You ran into one of my assistants and got a lovely... coffee together. She mentioned how gracious you were and that perhaps you might deign to do an interview. Your adoring public would love to know—are you in town for a competition? What are you doing on Capital, Ms. Utlis? Can fans catch a glimpse?"

She was shaking her head, habitually, manically, without intending to. Which one of those girls had been a reporter? Or was it all of them? No wonder they followed the protocol. "No competitions at this time," she managed. "Just... visiting my mother." She winced. She had no intention of visiting her mother, and her mother wasn't even *on* Capital currently anyway, conveniently enough. It was a bad lie that wouldn't hold up. But now they'd try to stake out her mother's apartment.

"Please, Ms. Utlis, can I call you Jennifer? Such a beautiful, old-fashioned name. Jennifer, we'd love to interview you. Perhaps talk about how your parents picked such a gem."

Jenny blinked until she finally snapped out of it. "Sorry... who are you again?"

"Sarlano Crane, lead anchor, Dailyglow." His voice burst with pride. If she turned on video, he would probably be in full on-air regalia over there.

"Listen, Sarloto—"

"Sarlano."

"Sorry. Anyway, I'm not here to make an appearance. I don't have anything to say."

"We can think of some easy questions, it'll boost ticket sales and sponsorships, and—"

"I'm sorry, but not at this time." The words came out in a rush, and before she could muck this up further—or worse, get pressured into agreeing—she hung up.

———

KAEL'S NECK was still itching where the chip had gone in when Josana appeared in the doorway, a devilish grin on her face and a gleam in her eye. The itch of course was all in his head; the chip wouldn't itch, and if something were wrong, he'd be more likely to get a vicious zap or lose all feeling in his neck. Neither were fun experiences.

From the look on Josana's face, this wouldn't be either. He'd retired to Persad's study as a temporary room to get ready for this little mission of theirs after the chip removal. It seemed safer than Vivaan's if any additional wall-punching urges were to spring to mind.

"Let's get this over with," he growled. He was definitely feeling punchy already.

She draped a black garment bag over Persad's holodesk and took a bag off her shoulder. From inside she withdrew three boxes. "First, we're going to do something about that hair."

"Glory be, about time." Her glee seemed to dim a little at his relief.

"This goes on your head and does all the work." She indicated a nondescript black box.

"Wow, that's terrifying."

She rolled her eyes. "The big Theroki scared of a little autohaircut? That explains a few things."

"Like *what*?"

She just shook her head. "Suit's in here. Put it on, and come out where I can check you did it correctly."

"There's a correct way?" He raised his eyebrows.

"Yes. You'll see. I'll shine you up like a new ship hull."

"I thought you hated space."

"I do. It's just an expression." Her eyes were rolling heavenward as she shut the door and left him alone with the insanity.

The box... could have been worse. It presented him with a number of options, rejected his request to buzz everything off, and offered a choice of three pre-approved haircuts, which he felt was starting to really overstep the bounds. They were short and more "officer material" than he might have ever considered, but perhaps it was fitting now that he'd somehow ended up an officer. The box was quick and efficient and cleaned up its own mess. The suit was far more complicated. Men really put up with this shit here? He shook his head. Of course, if you compared it to armor that assembled itself, perhaps that wasn't really fair. But even his old Theroki armor did that.

One haircut and one puzzle in fabric later, he emerged.

"I have *no* idea if—"

Her eyes widened in horror. "You're helpless." She rushed over to him and began making adjustments. "Hopeless. Helpless and hopeless."

"I tried to tell you we're not cut from the same cloth," he muttered. "But you didn't believe me." He pointed at the rather high popped collar and the thin silver chains that looped around the shoulder. "This is absolute nonsense. People actually wear this stuff?"

"Yes. Maybe it wasn't the fashion on Faros—"

"It's been a decade since I've been to Faros anyway."

"—but there was a time on Earth when these styles were popular. Don't ask me who decides when to recycle them." She tightened a strip of fabric around his neck almost vindictively, then banished her annoyed expression as she appraised him head to toe. "Not that I'm complaining, because this is just zenith." She turned him to face the mirror, hands on his biceps. "I don't know how your date will fair, but you'll do wonders for my reputation."

He shifted away from her slightly, but she held him in a death grip. Her fingers tightened once, and then she let go and walked away.

"Offer's still on the table, Theroki," she said, walking away.

He pretended to ignore her and stared at the person in the mirror. Funny how a haircut could change the face. But it wasn't just that. His eyes looked... different. Less hard edged. It had to be the chip's changes sinking in. Or maybe all the fragging meditation.

Nah, couldn't be that.

Of course, having his own cabin and a lot more sleep and colleagues he could trust and a commander he could... And a great commanding officer. Well, all that couldn't hurt. He looked like a younger version of himself. A happier one, as hard as that was to believe.

How strange.

That was how he came to be standing silent and alone in the hallway when a clatter rose up behind him in the hallway and he turned.

And saw legs. Miles and miles of legs.

Before he could take in the entire scene, his brain caught on those legs. And that skin. He'd seen her in fitted armor suits plenty of times, but this was the real deal. Bare. Impractical. Nothing between his body and hers but the air.

Looked like he'd have something new to fuel his totally inappropriate fantasies about his boss. Guilt would be sure to come along for the ride.

The silence seemed to stretch on forever. The hallway, the whole apartment, was empty and silent, just the hum of ventilation and their breathing over the sandy hallway tile, the fancy wood paneled walls.

"You think this will help find her son?" he said after forever had come and gone.

She inhaled sharply, then breathed it out. "Don't know. But we've got to try, right?"

"Right." He nodded.

"You…" She hesitated. "You look distinguished. Like an admiral."

"That's a first." He snorted. "Are you sure? Cause I feel like an idiot. Who wears this ridiculous side cape thing?" He flounced it out to the side, jangling the decorative silver chains.

"Admirals. Union ones, anyway."

"Oh." They did sort of look like epaulets, now that she mentioned it. He swung his left shoulder back and forth. The right one was thankfully just a normal shoulder.

She snorted one short laugh. "Also other fancy rich people. Some military dress uniforms."

"Ah. Well, you…" He started before he had formulated what exactly he was going to say, and he had to stop himself before the words "look practically naked below the waist" tumbled out. Smooth, Kael, real smooth. He should probably say something professional and not too complimentary, given all their history together, but as he scrambled, nothing came to mind.

Her eyes widened slightly. And now it was just getting more awkward by the second.

"You leave me speechless," he said quietly, shrugging and giving himself over to the compliment.

Except the slight furrow of her brow told him perhaps she wasn't so sure that speechless was a good thing.

Oh, but it was. Beyond her own lithe athleticism so effectively on display—perhaps Josana really did know what she was doing—the color was striking. Blue satin, the color of a clear summer sky, fell in a fairly simple kimono that cut off at the earliest possible moment. Other than the sexy shoes, there wasn't much else to it. She'd probably taken half the time to dress that he had, if that.

She was leaning with one arm on the wall for balance, and as she took a step toward him, he realized why. Her ankle wobbled, and she ducked her head.

He pretended he didn't notice her adorable blush. "Speaking of ridiculous, she's really outfitted you for fighting, hasn't she."

"Mm-hmm. This outfit is a death trap."

"It really is. Lucky for you, my ability to carry you doesn't depend on my armor."

"Sorry I can't say the same thing."

"We all have our strengths." He grinned.

She sighed, stepped out of the shoes, and picked them up, one finger hooked in each heel. Bare feet grazed expertly, athletically across the cold tiles. He swallowed.

"For me, these shoes are not one of them." She glared at the things as she held them up in front of her face. "But worst-case scenario, you have my full permission to toss me over your shoulder. C'mon. Let's find Josana, Nova, and the others and get this over with. I sure hope he's at that club. Or we find *something*."

"Did you say Nova?"

"I sent for more weapons. Ones I can hide in this... scarf I'm wearing."

He snickered. "Wise choice. More weapons, always good."

———

ADAN DRIFTED out of the cabin Persad had suggested he could use. The apartment smelled warm and homey, of curry and garlic, and it was far warmer than any spaceship he'd lived on. A commotion in the living area had drawn him, but he stopped pretty quickly at the edge of the hallway. Josana was looking over her victims—the commander and Kael—and Adan wanted to keep his distance. He didn't even want to look at Josana, but the spectacle was too great not to stare. Jenny stood nearby, leaning against the wall and messing around with a tablet while she watched, eyes twinkling. He paused beside her, hands in his pockets.

He met her gaze with a smile, remembering his earlier sense of regret and the cigar comment. "Wow, they sure shine up right, huh?"

She shrugged. "Yeah. It's not that hard really, if you know what to do. What to buy. Who to buy it from."

"Pretty hard if you don't though. Or don't have the credits."

"True. Unfortunately, I'm no stranger to fancy parties." She squinted at something on the tablet, lips pursed in thought.

"Unfortunately?"

"Yeah." She shifted slightly from leaning on her bicep to leaning on her back, facing him. "God, they're so boring. Parents always dragged me. I mean, I can do it, but it's not me."

"Me neither. Obviously."

"Hmm." Her face was a bit cold as she watched them, and if he didn't know better, he would have thought he saw a touch of anger around her eyes. "But is it who you *want* to be?" Her green eyes pinned him now, ruthlessly.

"I don't think I'm invited. So the point is probably moot."

"Ah. So that's it." Her soft smile was sad.

His brow furrowed. "What's 'it'?"

"Nothing like something you can't have to make you want it." She jutted her chin at the fancy couple—or maybe Josana.

He scoffed, gestured vaguely at them. "I don't want *that*." And it felt kind of good, especially in Josana's direction. To say aloud that he didn't want her. It felt true, surprisingly enough. But Jenny didn't just mean Josana, or nice clothes, did she? She meant the lifestyle, and a cold feeling settled in his gut, a thought that he might be exactly that stupid.

"Aren't you thinking of staying here?"

He looked down at his feet, trying to think of a way to say that he'd rejected the offer already, that things were over. That he'd been a fool, an easily manipulated fool. An easy way to say that didn't come. He shifted his weight and retrained his frown on their comrades.

Jenny was probably right. It wasn't parties, per se. But Josana's offer had drawn him in, even when he knew it was impossible, stupid. But sneaking around on a fancy paramilitary vessel no one knew about didn't do much to help him figure out what he *was*, if he wasn't that poor, red-dirt-covered kid. He was something else now, but what? A pilot? Somebody's potential computer guy?

"Adan?" she said softly, and he realized he hadn't answered her.

He opened his mouth but came up with nothing.

"Are you okay?"

He tried for another moment to speak, then shook his head, turned, and retreated back into the cabin.

———

NOVA DID NOT DISAPPOINT. One laserblade the size of her pinky finger, a mini Red Death the size of a lipstick tube, and a garrote for absolute emergencies, and Ellen was ready to go. Kael had a lot more potential hiding places and strapped himself up with a scanner-defying boot knife, among other goodies.

"All right, enough. We're leaving," she grunted. She padded toward the door. At least the cool marble felt good on her feet. She'd have to wear the dang shoes once they neared the street, she was fairly sure. But if she delayed any longer, she was sure Josana would try something with the cosmetic box she'd been fiddling with in her hand.

"Oh, you can't *walk*." Josana jumped forward, one palm raised to stop her. "You can't show up on foot! And definitely not *barefoot*. Movers be damned, you'll ruin me forever."

"Does everyone drive because they are all wearing these insane shoes?" She strode back and shook the things in Josana's face.

"Well, yeah. Probably." Josana stared, clearly not seeing a problem with that.

"Oh." Ellen let her hand holding the shoes fall to her hip. "Oh."

"Listen, there's a flyer waiting downstairs. I've taken care of it." She rolled her eyes again. "You think I'd leave a detail like that up to you? Besides, it's on the 140th floor, and the entrance is on the outside of the building. You actually can't get in from inside."

Ellen doubted that very much. There was some way food and drinks and employees probably got into that place, not to mention emergency exit tubes. But this wasn't that kind of mission. They didn't need to sneak in in spite of Kentt. They needed to just walk up and talk to her. "Fine, fine. Anything else?"

"You two look great," Jenny said, practically beaming.

Nova, grinning too, snapped a picture. "This is going to make Fern's day."

Ellen considered seizing Nova's comm and running, but Xi probably had this all on video. Nova and Mo were still armored. Mo, for what it was worth, seemed only mildly curious.

"Don't embarrass me," Josana said, pursing her lips.

"God, you really know how to win 'em over, Josana," Jenny mumbled.

"If I cared about your opinion—" she started before Ellen cut her off.

"No guarantees." Ellen turned and headed for the door, and Kael followed.

Stepping into the elevator tube, she was relieved to see no one trailing after them. "Xi," she said into her comm. That and the fake lipstick tube had been permitted to go into a pocket in the belt along with her few other necessities. "Can you find me some nearby shoe stores between here and the Elderflower place?"

"Yes, Commander."

She sighed. "Call me... call me Ellen tonight, Xi." It was probably long overdue that she dialed back the formality with the AI. Everyone else already had. And she didn't want anyone tonight overhearing the title.

"Exception created for this evening, expiring at sunrise tomorrow. Will this timeframe do, Ellen?"

"Yes," she muttered, feeling too awkward and guilty floating barefoot in an elevator carrying her shoes worrying about how she instructed an AI to address her. The scorchingly handsome former Theroki beside her—that looked nothing like one—certainly had nothing to do with the awkwardness. Nor did his seeming inability to look at her beyond that first open-mouthed, stunned stare.

They floated to the ground floor and regained gravity, heading through the lobby toward where a bank of flyers waited to service the building. Coming up beside her, he laughed softly to himself, those eyes still trained on the mosaic glass floor.

"What is it?"

He hesitated for a second, than glanced briefly her way. His eyes seemed to sparkle, brilliantly alive. "Back when we visited Molyarch, I had this thought then that we'd definitely never be in that position walking together on Capital."

The corner of her mouth crooked up. "And yet here we are. Just goes to show you, you never know."

"I'm not sure if I should be pleased or terrified."

"Ellen?" Xi's voice spoke up, wisely discreet.

"Yes?"

"I regret to inform you that there are several shops, but none of them are open. I contacted each by comm to see if I could arrange them to open specifically for you for a price, but none have responded. Apparently today is some kind of holiday. There are many on Capital."

She groaned, stopping just short of the doors outside.

"Also, something else. There has been unusual access activity around the calls you made earlier back to the ship. And elsewhere."

"To Doug?" she murmured.

"Yes. The call records were not altered or deleted, only accessed, though there was an attempt to remove the record of access. Only because of the redundancy we set up did I find the discrepancy."

"Hmm. Is there anything we need to do?"

"Not at this time. I can find no further action to take. But consider any information discussed on those calls at risk."

Tonight's weapons, the new chip, her tortured heart... Doug's location hidden somewhere in the *Audacity*'s memory banks. "That is not good."

"We'll deal with it when we get back," Kael reassured her.

She nodded, pulled herself straighter. Right. First one problem, then the next. One step at a time. She dropped the shoes to the floor and began wiggling one foot in. "All right. Sorry, Kael, but you're going to have to help me with this. I just can't walk in these things."

She hesitated, glaring. He held out the crook of his arm, and she only paused once before she took it, clutching him for balance as she slipped the shoes on. And then to simply walk.

Outside, it was raining. Or at least, it felt like it at first. After a moment or two, she realized it was just the heavy mist of a very thick fog, basically a dense cloud on the ground. It all seemed odd given the tropical-island setting, but she shrugged it off and made the fastest beeline she could through the mist toward the flyer. For all she knew maybe the fog was human generated.

She waved him in first, frowning at how the hell she was going to do this. One leg first? Butt first? How did anyone… ? There were no answers to be had in her analysis. She didn't *know* the answers. She hadn't lived a life where people walked around in fancy clothes and took flyers to parties. And thank God. But there was nothing to draw on. She just went for it.

She made it the last few steps toward the flyer surprisingly well, even if the shoes were starting to rub above her big right toe, but that was it. Ducking to get inside was a bridge too far. She wobbled and basically fell inside, landing nearly on top of him.

Hand gripping his knee for balance, she righted herself enough to rip off a shoe and glower at it. "Oh, these are done for. I never thought I could hate a shoe. Not this much."

She eyed the spot where the heel joined the base, waiting for his response. None came. She twisted to meet his gaze.

Or actually no… His eyes were locked on her hand clutching his knee.

Right. Most COs didn't get so familiar. Her hip was also pressed to his outer thigh. She hadn't really moved away after she'd fallen against him. She didn't want to.

He wasn't asking.

She pretended not to notice his lack of response. "Thank God for pocket laserblades." She reached into the wide belt where it was tucked in the single smartly sewn and padded satin pocket.

He jumped, suddenly remembering her stare. He cleared his throat as he met her eyes. "I have one too if you need one."

Only then did she release his knee, and only because she needed one hand to hold the shoe and one hand to mutilate it. She was still perched a bit precariously on the seat edge, her hip still touching his leg, but she didn't care. The flyer started to move, apparently not needing instructions that they weren't bothering to give anyway. She remembered herself. "Can you check its destination?"

He glanced at a wall panel, then hit a different one on a ceiling readout. "Elderflower it is. Our fate is sealed now."

"Thanks." She sighed, turning the shoe this way and that, studying its construction. If she just lopped off the giant heel, would she still be able to walk on it? Probably it wouldn't be easy, but maybe it'd be an improvement. "It's embarrassing to admit, but I've never really learned to walk in high heels." Her cheeks were permanently made of fire. They should build space ports out of her. Fusion power plants. She twisted to face forward, as much to avoid his reaction as to better attack the shoe, and relished his warmth still against her hip.

She fired the blade up. Now where to try exactly...

"May I help you, madam?" An indignant male voice suddenly erupted from the shoe, its accent haughty. If the shoe had a nose, it'd be looking down it at her.

She blinked. Was she losing it?

"Madam, please put down the knife," the shoe said again.

"What the—"

"I am your shoe soul, madam. There is no need for violence."

"I can see that but—"

"No, ma'am. I am the soul of your shoe."

"What kind of nut programmed the sole of a shoe to talk?"

The shoe actually made a clearing its throat sound through the tinny speaker. "A very rich designer nut, whose creations are highly sought after. How did you come to possess one of these highly coveted artworks without knowing that?"

"Art or not, I need to be able to walk, damn it."

"Plebeians! Help! Someone, help! I'm in the hands of plebeians!"

"Hush." She looked over her shoulder at Kael. "Maybe I should just go barefoot. Maybe I can pass it off as some kind of hot new trend?"

"Works for me." He shrugged.

The shoe, however, scoffed. "How dare you. I am a fine shoe concierge. I simply objected to your bladed brutality."

"My what?"

"I am an incredibly sophisticated artificial intelligence, state of the art and highly dedicated to managing your footwear. And this is how you treat me? How dare you."

"Frag."

"Can we please get down to the truly critical matter—the subject of why you feel the need to wield such a weapon in my direction? Hmm?"

She waved the shoe at Kael. "This just gets worse and worse. What do I do with *this*?"

"Have Xi talk to it?" he suggested.

The shoe nearly growled as she refocused on it. "I am detecting some deep customer dissatisfaction with these shoes in their extra high heel form. Is that interpretation correct?"

"How'd you figure that out, genius?"

"Your uncivilized desire for violence gave me a clue. Would you prefer a shorter heel, madam?"

"Uh... well, yes."

"Loquacious, aren't you. You're a dear."

"Why do I always get the weird AIs?" she grumbled.

Kael snickered. "It's probably your charming personality."

"This shoe can take on a variety of forms, including eight, six, four, and two centimeters and flat. Would one of those latter options be more to your taste?"

She narrowed her eyes. "Let's try the two centimeter."

"Excellent choice. Much more your speed."

"You're rude. For a shoe."

"You try waiting in a box for an eternity only to be brought out, tossed around, and walked on by an idiot who doesn't appreciate fine art. And *then* having a sword swung at you."

"It was hardly a sword."

"Given its relative proportion to my size, I disagree."

"Look, sorry I offended you, shoe. No one told me you were there, all right? Someone bought me the shoes. She's also kind of rude, so you might like her. She didn't tell me you were there." Oh, Josana would probably be enjoying this if she were here.

The shoe made another *hmph* noise, and she almost couldn't believe it, but it shrank the heel to less than half its size and went silent. It felt incredibly awkward now, but she stuck the thing back on.

"Better?" Kael asked mildly.

"Much. Do you have a name, shoe sole?"

"Well, most just call me that. But yes, I do." He stopped, not deigning to share it.

"And it is?" She'd win this shoe over if it was the last thing she did.

"My name is Richard 87437."

"Of course it is. Okay, Richard, Kael, we're off to quite a start on this mission. Can I call you Dick, Richard?"

"No, you may not."

"Rich?"

"That's tolerable, I suppose."

"Excellent." She flopped back off her perch finally, trying to relax for a moment, now that the shoe matter was settled.

Beside her, Kael stilled. She realized his arm had been braced over the back of the seat, and now she'd fallen back into his range. Almost like he had his arm around her. She could even feel the warmth of his arm through the coffee brown of that insane great coat that perfectly matched his eyes. Frag. If he'd just drop his arm an inch more…

He did the opposite, swinging it back toward him and scooting across on the seat toward the far door. Away from her. And he kept his eyes on the window now. Mist—or was it clouds now, as they rose into the air traffic lanes?—drew slashing lines of water across the windows and obscured the towers of Capital.

Her shoes were shorter, her thigh was starkly cold where his leg had been, and she was tired already.

CHAPTER EIGHT

THE FLYER PULLED up outside the Elderflower Club and glided smoothly to a stop. She opened the door and stepped out. If the shoes hadn't staggered her, the transparent blue petroglic under her feet most certainly did.

"First time?" A smiling woman approached with an ID scanner.

"Whoa." Kael emerged from the vehicle and found his footing beside her.

"Yeah," she muttered to the attendant. "That obvious?"

"No, no way." The woman shrugged a shoulder. "There're new people here every night. You sort of train yourself to see it."

"Any advice?" She wasn't usually one for woman-to-woman confidences, and it probably showed, but the woman gave her a sympathetic smile.

"Try to have fun?" Still smiling as she scanned their idents, one eyebrow lifted in amusement.

"Isn't that the point?" Kael was scanning around them, certainly getting the lay of the land just as she had. But he didn't look nearly as military as his usual self. He looked... bored. Like a bored rich guy.

Weird. Appearances could be so deceiving.

Which of their new acquaintances were deceiving them, and which weren't? Which of her crew, for that matter? Her fingers tensed slightly at the thought of the leak, but she held off further emotion, lest the attendant think it was directed at her.

"Yes, that is the point, Mr. Asidian. That doesn't keep some people —many people—from failing at it. Ms. Ryu, Mr. Asidian, you two are all clear. Have a good time. Here's a drink from me on the house." She awarded it, smile sparkling, with a dramatic press of a button on her scanner. "Tell Josana I said hello."

"Thanks," Ellen murmured, "we will."

She kept her eyes focused up on the shining bars of lavender around the Elderflower's entrance, and not down on the unimpeded view of a dozen layers of air traffic below her.

"Well, that was nice of her." He glanced back over his shoulder.

"You play this part well."

"Me? What part?"

"Rich Capital type. Didn't think you had it in you."

He laughed outright. "Yeah, right. I don't."

"What other reason does she have for comping us? It can't be because Josana's so likable."

He nearly giggled as they approached the main door. "All I know is that it wasn't *my* ass she was looking at when I looked back."

She ignored the blush on her cheeks. "That's because your fancy cape is in the way."

"Slag off, Ellen." His tone was playful as he swaggered beside her toward the club. "I thought you said it was distinguished."

"It is."

"I thought you liked it."

"I didn't say I didn't."

"That is such a you thing to say."

Not knowing how to respond to that, she didn't reply.

Smooth graphics whirled on a wall display by the door, elegant, thin, white lines and bars and numbers spinning: the air composition inside, as well as confirmation of the absence of the most common contaminants and pathogens. She still wasn't removing her breather. Josana had dug up some fancy, expensive ones that were nearly invisible if you were okay with putting them way up your nose and having to keep your mouth and possibly eyes shut if the thing alarmed. And then of course, decon showers. Hers looked like little more than a silver nose ring, and Kael's was barely a stud. Not the most comfortable, but discreet. And it sure fit the crowd.

The man at the door raised an eyebrow, looking Ellen and Kael up and down. "Are you two here for the... special events?"

"We're friends of Josana Viliant," she said, although she damn near had to grit her teeth to say it. She had no idea what special events, so she dodged. "We need to see Etrianala."

He nodded as if that had been a yes. "Don't they all. Good luck in the competition." He glanced back at the attendant who'd cleared them, then stepped aside and waved them through. Apparently they had fallback checks.

She eased past him and into a dark hallway. She couldn't see anything but black.

"The competition?" Kael raised an eyebrow.

She shrugged. "I guess we'll find out."

Inside, the music was smothering. Bass beats pounded at her rib cage, the notes wild and dangerous. Her heart sped up. So many people. So many potential hostiles. A nightmare, if anything got out of hand. The club itself was a strange combination of a sea of frothy revelers, a bar full of holier-than-thou types—her classic Capital stereotype —and an environment so incredible, it actually made her pause to appreciate it. The ceiling was a latticework of tiny white flowers that moved and shifted as if swept up on rolling ocean waves or stirred by a finger trailing idly through a pond. Columns dotted the place, breaking up the view, but their shapes were like the tall trunks of trees, organic and winding, and yet they glowed from a deep black within to a pale blue at the edges, almost like they were encased in a force field. Except that was impossible, as force fields were always flat planes. The floors glittered black, and the purple of a nebula and a thousand stars swam underneath dark feet. It had to be digital. Or something. Her bet was that it would shift to something else as time passed or the music changed. On top of it all, fountains filled corners and sprayed water that caught the flashing lights from the dance floor in a myriad of hues. And all the while the white flowers swirled and swayed.

She bent close to his ear and yelled. "Some wine bar, huh?"

"Wine *garden*. But you should never trust what you read on the net."

"Shoulda brought an ear piece to talk. This sound is enough to fry my circuits."

It was an expression, but his eyes twinkled with laughter. He smiled, a slight edge to it, then bent to her ear himself. "Does this make you uncomfortable, Ellen?"

"No," she shot back, stubborn as a mule kick. What a lie. Of course it did. The shoes were uncomfortable enough, without the dress, without him looking like a younger and cooler Ostrov, without his breath tickling her ear lobe.

Damn this whole stupid plan.

"Let's do a lap and see if we see either of them!" she shouted.

He followed, scanning.

Their initial pass turned up nothing. No sign of Vivaan or Kentt or even any of the women he'd been searching for.

She decided to take a break and took a place at the bar with a sigh. No need to look more vulture than human.

"See anything?" she shouted as quietly as she could.

He shook his head. Still scanning. The incessant scanning, the always turned away gaze—they were starting to bother her, but she couldn't quite put her finger on why.

A live bartender, not even a fancy droid, wiped the bar behind them, and she turned. Funny how only the richest and poorest places had real people. Droids were middle class—and could listen to your woes for hours. Not this guy. He wasn't listening to anything over the music. He had a house breather on that a delicate sign behind him suggested you could rent for a nominal fee. Its tubes were white and silver and blue, and he had the wide-sleeved, flouncy shirts she'd seen on the streets when they arrived. The latest fashion? That he could afford?

"Wine? Or even better, beer?" she asked him.

He shook his head. "House drink is an elderflower 'wine.' "

"Uh, okay?"

"It contains no alcohol, of course."

She sighed. "Fine, whatever."

"And you, sir?"

"Whatever she's having."

The bartender lifted his eyebrows slightly but complied.

"When in Rome." Ellen pursed her lips as she leaned on the bar. "Josana said alcohol is illegal here."

"Does that mean I need to stop calling you Ellen? If we're not drinking?"

She snorted. "Nah. Don't stop."

He grinned, glanced at her before back to the crowd. "So what does that really mean? Do we need to slip him a twenty-credit card to get beer?"

"I don't need beer. I'd rather keep the credits. But yeah, that'd be my guess."

"Odd."

A girl from beside Kael seemed to have been listening and took her opening. Her dress was a wall of purple sparkle that shifted as she moved. Whatever gave the dress its pigment was somehow suspended within liquid inside. "It's a Buddhist thing, a holdover from the old founders' traditions." She draped herself across Kael's shoulder and looked deep into his eyes, smiling slyly as an amethyst the size of an eye twinkled in a bracelet lounging around her wrist. Lips and nails glittered in coordinating shades, and Ellen tried not to openly scowl.

"Uh..." Kael grunted. "I don't see much Buddhism going on in here."

"No, you don't, do you?" she said, laughing. "They battled it out with the Hindus, the Americans. The spirit of asceticism didn't really last—"

"I hadn't noticed," Kael murmured.

"—but for some reason we kept substance limits and a park or two." She shrugged and leaned even closer. "Are you Buddhist? Or here to visit the Movers' temples? They're so beautiful. You look like you're definitely on vacation. The pilgrimage type?"

"Does he look like the pilgrimage type?" Ellen grumbled. But in truth—she didn't know *what* type he looked like just at the moment. Josana had been stunningly successful at polishing off a lot of rough edges.

"Hmm." The girl tapped a finger to her lips, parting them slightly, brazenly appraising.

"He's not *your* type, whatever that is," Ellen snapped, hooking a finger in the girl's fancy bracelet and removing her hand from Kael's chest.

The girl gave her a death glare, the augmented lavender color of her eyes flashing. "And you *are*?"

Kael chuckled softly.

"I'm his boss. And we're working."

The girl rolled her eyes, then looked at Kael. "Call me when you're off. I'll be at it all night." She winked and turned away, throwing in one last long, meaningful look back for good measure. Kael didn't turn his eyes away. Ellen gritted her teeth. He resumed scanning the club.

The "wine" arrived, and she pinned the bartender with a glare he hadn't earned. "How do people talk over this racket?" she shouted at him.

He pointed at the dozens of small arches lining the walls. "Sound buffer over there if you got deals to make."

"Thanks."

"Don't sweat it, lovely. You want company in one, or anywhere else, you just say the word."

She was too surprised to even glare at him over that. She grabbed her drink and pointed an index finger in that direction, right in front of Kael's face so he'd finally look at her. "That way. Come on!" She strode away, hoping to God he would follow, and snagged one of the few open ones. It had a high seat rounded in a U shape and a dark wood table, and it barely fit the two of them. Delicate violet flowers with long unfurling petals hung above their heads and around the arch in exquisite cascades. As she slipped through the electronic barrier, all the sound muffled. Praise heaven. As if to rub in the effect, a fountain trickled water down carefully placed rocks on the wall behind them, ending comfortably above the seating area. Like a fragging spa.

He slid in beside her and let out a sigh of relief. "Oh, this is good. Still got a good view. None of the jackhammer in the ear."

She nodded, said nothing, pretended to be as interested in scanning as he was.

"What do you think that platform is for?" He indicated the raised area in the center with his chin. It glowed silver and bright, like moonlight shown on it, however impossible that was.

She scanned the area around it. "Dancers? Some kind of show?"

"Maybe."

"But then why is there a railing? And no dancers?" And tough-looking guys manning the stairs leading up to it.

"This doesn't look like a rough crowd. Why is nothing happening there? You know, it kind of looks like…" He hesitated.

"A fighting ring?"

"Yeah. But I don't see any fighters. You think that could be what he meant by competitions?"

"Could be. I don't see anything else to compete at around here, other than who can look the most bored."

"Ah, you gotta look harder. Those two over there are competing for who is prettier and gets more attention. That group is competing for who can slip the bartender the most bucks so that maybe one of them can actually feel a buzz. Those two are competing over the same woman. And, you're right, there're at least ten boredom competitions going on." He grinned at her, eyes meeting hers for a split second. "So what now?"

She snorted. "Let's just wait for a bit. Get the lay of the land. See if we can spot either of our targets."

He leaned back. "Sit and watch is something I can do. Better than stand and watch."

"And you thought you got out of the Theroki so you could quit standing around on guard duty."

He smiled. "Hush, now."

"I *want* their attention."

"You want accurate attention, though. Let's not have them thinking I'm something I'm not. To your point, this feels more like attack dog than guard dog to me. And this is guard duty I *chose*. That makes a world of difference."

"Point taken."

"And no one's shooting at me."

"Yet." Now that they were in the alcove, she held her comm over the wine as it did its little scan dance and took a sample, came back green. She took a sip while she checked his too. Surprisingly good. "So we got time to kill. While we're on the subject of your former establishment—you have any old colleagues you miss?"

"Nah. My next up—my commanding officer—was fine. Do you have any old squad mates you miss?"

Her eyes darkened. "None of them are left."

He frowned. "You went back for them already? Tried to get in touch?"

"Yes."

"Maybe I should be trying harder to reach out," he muttered. "Especially those ones I knew who didn't join up on their own. Not that we had a lot of heart-to-heart talks. So what happened to them?"

"Who?"

"The members of your squad. Your teammates."

"The ones I was networked to? I... don't know exactly. It was over a year before I could function again, and by the time we could look for them, the unit had been broken up. Most had no record of their discharge—or even of their service. They'd just vanished."

He blew out a breath. "You think it has something to do with... her?"

"I'm sure of it. If I find her, I'm hoping I'll find out whatever happened to them."

"I hope you do too."

———

KAEL TRIED NOT to sit stiffly beside Ellen or to chug whatever weird concoction they'd acquired from the bartender who'd hit on her, but it wasn't easy. It was like everything in here was designed to make him crazy. The noise. Her presence and everything about her. The scantily-clad people constantly hitting on anything with legs—and the two of them in particular. Only the waterfall behind him seemed to want to help; it reminded him of Taylor's various stress ministrations. He actually leaned into it. His breath slowed a little. Strange to be gaining control of that sort of feeling. He focused on his quest of not looking at her while scanning for Vivaan.

Of course, he had to figure the attention was because they were new here, they were in much better shape than the average partier due to their jobs, and, thanks to Josana, they were dressed to impress apparently. He might not be a Capital type, but he knew these sorts of places on other worlds, darker and dirtier ones. These sorts of places had a lot of similarities no matter the planet. The people grew to know everyone, often ad nauseam, and newcomers were a rare form of entertainment. Not every bar or club or beer hall—or supposed wine garden—was that way; some were filled with hard drinkers who had the business of drinking to do, others to watch sports together in casual and temporary company. But this one had all the indications of the sort of gossip hive that meant many eyes were on them right now, even if he couldn't see that many people directly staring.

He needed something to keep himself busy.

"Do you have a photo of Kentt? I'm not sure I'd recognize her," he said.

"Oh, of course. Not enough time for a briefing on this one, huh?" She pulled up a photo of a bright sapphire cape, wavy and lush hair of the same color peaking out from under it.

"Uh, you can't see her face?"

"Yep. This was the best one we could find. Apparently she's kept her image quite secretive."

"Interesting," he muttered. "Now why would she want to do that?"

"So she can wander around here without us seeing her?"

He doubted that was really true, if this place was as tight-knit as he believed. It might shield her from outsiders, but not the many regulars. But if none of *them* had shared a picture on the net either, perhaps he was wrong. He shrugged and kept searching the crowd.

Her comm on the table glowed softly for a second, and he glanced down at it automatically.

Dr. Crispin Ostrov: Ready for the details? I'm eager for that rematch.

He flicked his eyes away, determined to ignore the steel vise that was tightening around his chest. Not to mention the anger that rippled underneath.

She was eying something in the crowd and didn't pick up the comm. "Look over there, by that tree with the three branches. Is that... ?"

He squinted. "I don't... maybe." There were many men that could match Vivaan's description from afar there, but, well, they'd check in with each of them if they had to. He hoped it wouldn't come to that.

Dr. Crispin Ostrov: Here's the next game link. Unless you'd like to admit defeat ahead of time.

Kael tore his eyes away again, brow pinching, and this time Ellen noticed, picking up the phone and barking out a laugh. He tried not to let it stab at him, tried not to reflexively look. Peripheral vision was safer.

She typed a message back and jammed the comm back into the belt, muttering. "Stupid, stupid," was the most he caught.

"Comms can be frustrating buzzards, eh?" Oh, what a ridiculous attempt to pry.

"Huh? Oh, I guess so, yeah," she grumbled. "Crappy connection in here. Maybe they have something blocking it? Xi can barely get through."

"But Ostrov could?"

"He just sent text. You know Xi likes video and audio and all she can get. Easiest thing is to stick to the lowest tech you can, in my book. But these keyboards make so many damn mistakes."

"You could use voice." Unless she just didn't want him to hear what she had to say.

"Yeah but with all this background noise..." She waved vaguely.

"Let's be honest, I rarely even use voice commands on the ship. Ask Xi."

"I've noticed."

She frowned. "Hey, I know how it works. I just—"

He raised a palm. "I wasn't implying you didn't."

"You try being hooked up to a network of— Wait, what?"

"I know you know how it works."

"Oh. Right." She paused. "I never use it because I just want it to be *better*. That's all. It's never better enough."

"Who doesn't?"

"No, I mean…" She fidgeted with the comm. Unusual. "I told you about the telepathy, the blurring of minds, right? But that was only one of two projects they put me in. The other was a direct brain interface into the net. Low latency. Everything at the touch of a thought."

"Ah." He took a sad sip of his drink. It was almost gone. "Nothing is as fast or as easy as a thought."

"And it never will be. It doesn't matter what I use. So I don't bother. It's *all* agonizingly slow."

"Do you miss it?"

"No." Her response was too quick, though, too high. "It was part of what was making me lose my mind. I'm glad it's gone."

He nodded, content to listen.

She traced a finger around the rim of her glass. "But I dream about it sometimes. In my dreams, I'm so thirsty for it. I feel like I might die. I wake up barely knowing who I am again."

"Ouch." He turned toward her now. He couldn't listen to that and keep looking away, like he didn't care. Staring at her was like his limb was slowly burning to a crisp, and he'd have to look away to put it out, but he could manage a few moments more without losing it. He was stronger than a bunch of poorly trained electrical signals in his head. He hoped.

"I guess some part of me does miss it." She met his gaze, eyes hardening, and he hoped she couldn't see the way his hand tightened, clenching his knee till his knuckles were white. "But not the part of me that's in control."

It was too much. He cut away, his eyes back to the crowd.

And froze. "Hey—there. By the, uh, bubbles." He knew better than to point, but he tried to jut his chin in the right direction. Bubbles had begun to float from behind a bar at a far wall. A small area held couches—only a few of them in the whole place—where classic Capital types in their timeless robes lounged.

Sitting on one was Vivaan, in an off white and gray robe of his own.

"Well, I'll be damned. He's alive," she whispered.

"You figured him for dead too, huh?"

She shrugged. "I mean… two weeks, no contact? What is he up to?"

The woman beside Vivaan rose, a cobalt cape covering her features.

"Kentt," Ellen whispered. "They're together."

"Do we—what do we do?"

She bit her lip. "Sit tight. Not yet. What are they doing?"

"They were talking. Now she's leaving."

"Shit, they're both leaving."

They watched, tensed. The telepath seemed to be little more than a scrap of fabric that fluttered, slipped between two people, and disappeared. Vivaan, however, went the other direction, melding into the crowd.

"I can still see him," she muttered.

"But not for long. We're gonna lose him in there."

"What are we going to do? Drag him out of there?"

"That'll get us kicked out. Maybe you could use your feminine wiles to lure him out to talk."

She shot him a glare. "My feminine wiles are getting way too much action tonight. No thanks. Not exactly my weapon of choice."

He had to like that answer. "Well, then we keep an eye on him. Look for a chance to approach? Better to approach him without causing a ruckus than scare him off permanently."

She frowned but nodded. "At the very least, we can tell her he's here and he's alive. Her son likely hasn't been kidnapped. At least as far as I can tell."

"He's just a big flake and forgot to call home?" He ran a hand through his hair, momentarily confused when that action completed way faster than it had yesterday. Oh, yeah, right, the cut. "She's gonna be pissed."

"It's strange. He doesn't seem like the type to just party and forget to check in. His watch didn't show a history of that, did it?"

"No, it had him returning home regularly every night. Not that late. If he was dating women, he didn't stay for breakfast."

She snorted. "You'd think his mother would teach him better manners."

"Is it good manners to stay for breakfast? No one ever taught me such delicacies of etiquette."

Was she blushing? Suddenly her cheeks were changing colors. She shook her head. "I don't know anything about breakfast, manners, *or* etiquette, so don't ask me. I think something else is going on."

"Agreed. Question is how do we figure out—"

Before he could finish the thought, a screeching, rumbling noise from the far right of the cavern-like room pulled everyone up short. People grabbed shoulders and pointed, smiling with what looked like excitement, anticipation.

A door the size of a lander rolled up and into the wall, revealing a massive, four-armed droid, lit from behind by brutal white light. No, it wasn't a bot, he realized. The top front panel from where the head should be down to the torso was crystal-blue glass, revealing what looked like human features and handle-like controls.

The mech was nearly three meters high, taller than any human and even some Teredarks. It pumped its arms at the adoring cheers of the crowd as it stalked forward. In spite of the hulking width of its shoulders and its arms thick as rocket launchers, it moved with efficiency and a certain predatory grace.

"Uh, Kael?" Ellen was perched forward on the seat beside him.

"Yeah?"

"I think I know what the ring is for. And what the competitions are about."

"Yeah." He nodded. "Me too. You think they have a mech to face off with that thing?"

"No." She pointed at a wiry man climbing the stairs of the ring, pumping fists at the crowd, trying to draw their adoration. It didn't much seem to be working. "Do you?"

"I think we may be in just slightly over our heads."

Ellen scowled, gripping the table hard. "I'm going to kill her. Twice."

The mech's steps were almost birdlike. Its legs bent back, not like human knees, but it seemed light on its feet, agile, ready to peck. Or grab and crush. Not that he couldn't send a wave of energy slamming it into a wall. But without telekinetic power, it'd be tough to take down.

The mech actually did a lap around the ring, stalking the mortal fragile human who waited inside. The man didn't look anything like a fighter. He looked hopped up on chems and like he'd been either dumb or high enough to take a really stupid dare. It veered toward the couches.

Seeing it coming, Vivaan frowned. Kael keyed in on it. Something was up. He too shifted forward in the seat, both of them teetering on the edge of the sound-dampening platform. No—he should hear what was going on as much as see it. He pushed his head through.

Immediately the roar of cheering hit him, the music faster and more frenetic, less pounding. The mech stalked toward the bar, titillated some patrons who scurried away with a leer, then back toward the couches, and—

He swore.

"That mech just took a swipe at him!" Ellen was through the barrier too, glaring.

"I saw." Vivaan had dodged, clearly expecting it. He was eying the exit, where Kentt had retreated to, but the mech loomed in the way.

"C'mon. He might need help." She was off like a laser beam before he could even agree.

Since she was taking the direct route, he circled around to come up behind Vivaan through the few narrow passages that led between the couch area and the ring. Or he tried to. The mech moved, and the crowd surged with it, opening gaps and closing others.

By the time he reached the couches, Ellen was already there. And Vivaan wasn't.

"I lost him!" she shouted over the crowd. "I can't see shit from down here!"

"Same here!"

The mech had circled around now and was stomping toward the ring. The poor bastard was doomed.

———

THAT WAS IT. She was sick of this club, sick of these clothes, sick of the pounding noise, and most of all, sick of not knowing what to do. Give her a lab, she could storm it. Busting down doors, taking out targets. If she needed to simply grab Vivaan and run, that would be so much more cut and dry.

But she'd been so sure he'd been dead—or certain that he wouldn't be in the first place they looked—that she hadn't really thought about what they would do if they found him. Not that there had been much time for planning anyway.

Instead, she grabbed Kael's arm and dragged him toward the nearest club employee—one of the ring attendants. He wore a nondescript black suit from shoulder to cuff and was fiddling with a tablet as they approached. Just before him, the sound suddenly dampened.

His eyes lit up warmly at her slowed steps. "Sound bubble. Convenient, no? How can I help you, my darling?"

"We need to see Ms. Kentt. What do we need to do?" She was all out of charisma for the evening.

The man looked her up and down.

She waved a fist at him in response.

"Nice guns, *mademoiselle*. You work hard on them, no?" His Common had an exotic accent. The galaxy had so many nooks and crannies that practically everyone had some kind of accent, but there was something particularly twisty and luxurious about his.

"Oh, you like them? How do you like this one?" She whipped the tiny pistol out of the belt band and jammed it under his chin.

"Whoa, whoa." Kael started to pull her back but only half-heartedly.

The ring attendant's eyebrows shot up. "Is that a Silver Mountain mini? You are quick. I barely caught a glance."

"Yeah. So what if it is?" How many guns were in this club if he didn't bat an eyelash? Her stomach twisted at the thought.

"Well, I like that one very much. Generous magazine. For its size."

She rolled her eyes, nudged his chin with it. "I want to see Kentt. Now."

"You're going to shoot me right here? Do you think that will help?"

She definitely wasn't; she needed to get around him calling her bluff. "I just want to know what I need to do to—"

"Get in the ring." He jerked a finger over his shoulder. "Everyone that fights gets an audience."

"An audience?" Kael mumbled. "What is she, a fragging queen?"

She lowered the gun but didn't put it away yet. "Just fight?"

"You know you're not supposed to have that in here, eh, *mademoiselle*?"

"No shit."

"Listen, they are waiting for people to fight. This guy won't last." He glanced over his shoulder, and looked back at her, laughing. "He's a streak on the road, as they say. Nobody in their right mind here can—or wants to—take on the mechs. You, however..." He looked her up and down again, not quite leering.

"What, did I fail to cover my 'I've got a death wish' tattoo under the huge volumes of fabric?"

"I think 'I crush mechs' wouldn't be so bad. On your inner thigh, perhaps?" He grinned. "You have the look of it."

"I don't need your compliments."

His eyes twinkled with laughter now. "I like you, little minx. And that is why you should believe me. You fight, you make the people gasp, you get what you like from the Blue Girl. Win-win all around, isn't it? You both look like you can handle her. And the mechs too."

Ellen rolled her eyes. "Thanks for that little vote of confidence."

"And there's a med unit right over there." He pointed over her shoulder. "Nobody gets killed, *mon ami*, I promise you."

Kael snorted. "Just maimed? That's a high bar you've set, *mon ami*."

"Good thing we can just take him at his word," Ellen added.

He shrugged. "Believe what you like. You want to talk to the Blue Lady, you fight the mech. Shoot me if you like, but I have no greater access to her than you do."

"Fine," Ellen grunted. "We'll do it."

The attendant grinned. "Wait here—you'll be up in no time. I give this one thirty seconds. Maybe less. Care to take bets?" They shook their heads. "Suit yourself."

Kael drew her away from the man, his eyes dark with concern as the shouting rose around them. "Are you sure about this?"

She shrugged. "We're either talking to the wrong man, or the only way to her is through that ring. Know anyone better to talk to?"

He shook his head.

"Then we'll figure it out. And we can watch the mech's moves on—"

Before she could even finish, a huge, disappointed groan filled the room. She turned. Sure enough, he was already out cold, crumpled on his side, and the darkly avian mech was encouraging cheers from the crowd with both sets of its hands.

A strange voice spoke, neither masculine nor feminine but something in between, loud and echoing in the club speakers. "Who else will face me?"

She turned back to Kael with a hard gleam in her eye. "How do we do this? Let's talk tactics. We're not here to kill anybody."

"We're not here to die either."

"True."

"I should be able to short out a mech with one touch. Not to mention what a wave or two could do. It shouldn't be a problem. Plus, if people fight them regularly without another mech, they must know when to stop. Right?"

"Must they?"

His continued frown said he didn't believe it either. "Well, there aren't any blood stains on those mats."

"Maybe they're new."

"Maybe they are. But—"

"That is your cue, *mes amies!*"

He grinned. "C'mon. Playing games with Dr. Ostrov soften you up too much to fight?"

She punched him softly—well, not that softly—in the shoulder. "It's not the fight that I'm worried about, it's the spectacle."

His face straightened. "True. I'm not looking forward to pointing a big neon sign that reads *FORMER THEROKI* at me either."

She sighed. "What other option do we really have?"

"None that I see, but you're the brains of this operation."

"Stop saying that. You have plenty of brains. You'd be back playing guard dog if you didn't."

A silence fell between them, a weird little magnetism, a lashing of energy that couldn't find an outlet, just vibrated back and forth, tension and entropy and chaos. She wanted to let it work its craziness into something more than just tension. But voices cut through.

And the attendant, grabbing her arm.

They made for the ring.

CHAPTER NINE

THE ROOM FELT like it was spinning, roaring, as she made her way into the ring. The first contender's limp form had vanished, not even leaving a mark behind. The crowd was delighted. Another contender, so quickly?

"Two fighters seek the Blue Lady's blessing!"

"Oh, so she's a goddess now?" Ellen muttered to one in particular.

"Whatever gets us through," Kael replied.

"A second beast will join us!"

"Hey, no one said anything about two-on-two." She glared back at the attendant.

Kael shrugged. While she was already in knees-bent fighting mode, he stood calmly, looking unperturbed and in control. The tightness around his eyes told her that appearances could be deceiving. "What difference does it make?" he said softly. "They can change the rules whenever they like. I'm a little more concerned about those." He pointed up at the ceiling. In the midst of the waving white flowers, which were higher here but still present, were shiny black orbs, like beady little insect eyes.

"Cameras. Those conniving little shitweasels."

"Think they're streaming this?"

"God, I hope not." Still scowling, she turned along with the rest of the crowd to watch the wall grating rumble up to reveal the new mech. This one was basically the same, except where the first was long and lean, this one bristled with feather-shaped slabs, like oars protruding in a fan from its back. Instead of mirrored, it was striped a savage red.

It did its own slow circle to a round of cheers. Ellen folded her arms across her chest and tapped one ridiculous shoe, a wiry bundle of energy. Kael cracked his neck and his knuckles and kept his eye on both mechs.

The new bird stepped into the ring.

"Let the fighting begin!" called a voice. "Who will be our Blue Lady's champion? Man or machine?"

Kael tensed beside her.

She studied them. The knee joints looked like a possible weakness. A lot of wiring at the back. "Let's play it low-key at first. See what their moves are."

"Fine with me," he said.

The mechs regarded each other, apparently also communicating. Then the new one with its red slashes turned toward them—and charged.

She stared it down, playing chicken. Wait for it. Wait... At the last second, she ducked under the strange oars poking from its back. She felt the wind rush past, catch at her hair as she dove into a roll, putting distance between them.

By the time she'd righted herself, though, it had turned and pivoted and was heading back for her. Ignoring Admiral Kael over there.

She dove for another roll. A little too slow. While most of her got out of the way, one claw came out and caught the outside of her thigh, plunging in.

The claw tore down, but her roll carried her out of the way of the thing. Or it should have. She came back to a crouch, leg screaming, and realized the mech wasn't where she'd expected it.

She looked left, right. It wasn't anywhere, in fact. Red streak had backed away, but the original mirrored mech was nowhere to be seen.

She glanced over at Kael, his face upturned and arm raised. She followed his gaze up.

Oh. Uh-oh.

Kael couldn't get much height in here, but the machine floated over them, skimming the flower canopy. Gasps went up through the crowd, whispers, but he didn't give them much time to marvel.

The machine rocketed back down, slamming into the ring hard enough to leave a dent in the floor. A shower of mirrored slabs and silver sparks exploded into the air. The limbs twitched but it rose, motors whirring and groaning.

The previous roar had been nothing to what they heard now.

"Theroki!"

"Cyborg!"

"Disqualified!" boomed the announcer's voice.

"What?" Kael snapped.

"Hey!" Ellen limped to the railing and jabbed a finger in that asshole attendant's face. "You didn't say there were any constraints."

The jerk had the balls to grin. "You didn't say he was a cyborg either! Ask for the rules next time, *mademoiselle*."

She spun and didn't look back. Other attendants were ushering Kael out of the ring while he looked back on her warily. She waved his worry away.

"Fair's fair!" she shouted to him. "You took care of one. I'll figure out the other!"

He pressed his lips together. He didn't like it. But last she checked, that wasn't changing anything. The attendants let go of him once they were all outside the ring.

"Rich—a little help here." She eyed the other mech, who was also sizing her up.

"How can I help you, madam?"

"Something more athletic maybe?"

"I wasn't made for this, you know."

"We're in this together. Don't forget that."

The shoes shifted, and she lost some height. That was good. She felt more stable already. "If gods existed, and I weren't fresh out of the box, I'd wonder what I'd done to deserve this."

Whatever bored bastard had chosen this particular AI to put in a shoe had to be a sadist. She didn't have time to tell Rich that. As she waited, crouched and thinking hard, the remaining mech made a fresh run. Its joints wheezed over the slamming of the feet into the floor, almost feeling as though it could shake her to the bone.

It couldn't, but almost.

She sidestepped it, just barely. This time she didn't stop with one roll, but kept going twenty more feet before whirling to look back.

It paced, left, right, analyzing. Looking for the most entertaining weakness?

The next run started slow, but ended fast. It put on a burst of speed at the last moment that threw her off. She dove between the legs, landing a kick to the knee joint that did nothing. She swore as a fresh talon pierced her calf.

She kept going. She kept rolling. She couldn't stop. Not killing anyone? Tell that to her leg right now. Although the punctures were both to the same leg, perhaps it was meant to simply be disabling. Neither had gone near an artery as far as she could tell.

Lucky her.

She had to make her own move. If not the legs, then the brains. There had to be a weak point somewhere.

The next pass, she dove under the oars and twisted. The mech tried to spin and follow her, but she grabbed hold of one oar, using its momentum to keep going. Desperately, she groped at the back panel. Solid solid solid, all near her eye level. The real brains were up high. Fabulous.

She let go and pushed off it with her good leg, fumbling the landing on her bad leg. But she got her balance and sprinted until they were facing off on opposite sides of the fighting ring. The beauty of the white flowers above should have been mocking, but it only felt otherworldly.

"Rich, give me something to work with," she snapped, taking off the shoe from the hurt leg. Might as well go all in.

"Yes, ma'am! Uh, let me see…"

"What's the closest you've got to a blade? Or a pick?"

"Stiletto coming right up." The shoe thinned and elongated in her hand. "Now that I can do. You do love blades. You're a bit bloodthirsty, you know."

"So I'm told." Maybe that was what she'd seen in Kael.

It was hardly even a shoe now. She steadied herself, readied, tried to keep the weight on the good leg. Blood had slicked her skin from the thigh down and was starting to pool on the floor. She'd have to move out of it so as not to slip, and time it right so the mech didn't see that weakness too.

The voice of this mech spoke now, similar to the former one in its ambiguous timbre. "What do you think, folks? Should I finish her?"

She put what was left of the side of the shoe in her teeth.

"Really, Madam."

She didn't respond. Teeth weren't going to be the worst of it. She could feel the weight of Kael's gaze, glanced at him. His eyes were black and hard and worried, and she held them a second too long, almost missed the start of the charge.

God, what the hell had she been thinking?

Even as she readied herself for the jump, the sense of wrongness swept her, the certainty of having made a very large mistake. Was currently still making it, and had been making it for quite a while.

She leapt up as the mech reached her, dodged an arm, caught the highest oar she could reach, and swung. She planted her foot, groped higher, higher. Another strategically placed foothold with the good leg, and she'd climbed it.

She caught its neck with her knees, holding on for dear life as the injured leg shrieked its protest. She stabbed the stiletto at the control box—or what appeared to be the control box—once, twice, again.

A spark shot out and burned her wrist, pain spiking up her arm. The next stab hit a tube, and hot gas spewed out at nearly the same spot. She growled through the pain, then stabbed again. It wobbled underneath her, and she leapt.

She landed in a crouch, a few feet ahead of the madness, and dropped the shoe in the process. She scrambled for it on hands and knees, twisting back to face the machine as quickly as she could move.

But there was no need. The mech had fallen face-first and wasn't moving. No motors were even making an effort. Techs were rushing toward it, releasing the seals. Getting the rider out. She sat there, panting, and stared.

She'd won.

One of the burly guards grabbed her by the arm.

"Hey!" She yanked it fiercely back from him.

"Hey, cool it, polecat. You need to get to medical before you bleed out all over our precious floor."

She glowered at him.

But when he grabbed her arm again, a little more gently this time, she let him lead her to the med area and plop her down on a recliner there.

What had she been thinking?

Time. What nonsense. There was no time. No time at all.

Every minute was a miracle. Every bullet that whizzed by and didn't kill you was a blessing and a shock that you weren't fragging dead. Every flyer that didn't burst into flames, each new successful heartbeat. Those things couldn't be taken for granted. She knew that. Knew it better than anyone.

She shouldn't have needed a fight to remind her, but it did. One talon a few centimeters to the side, and she'd be close to passing out right now. She finally remembered her own bandages. She dipped into the belt, found a sealed cleaning kit on the table beside her, and began to work. Thigh first. Good thing this med area was totally empty of techs the moment the fight ended. She'd much rather do this herself.

She shook her head, disgusted. How many missions had she been on that went sideways in a blink? A dozen? A hundred? Even the easy ones did, like the hospital delivery. There was no such thing as easy. Or safe.

Distraction. What nonsense. As if pushing him away had accomplished anything. She was an absolute fool.

No. Sending him away was the only thing that could completely stop the distraction, and no one else was in support of that. Not even her, now. The back of her mind whispered, would it even change anything? Or would she then simply miss him to the point of distraction instead?

That thought brought forth a fresh stream of cursing.

He picked just that moment to get past the guards and into the med area.

"Kael—" she started, holding up a palm.

"Are you all right?" He rushed to her, shaken. His hand gripped her shoulder as he eyed the wound.

"Yes, I'm fine. I—"

"I saw him!"

"What?"

"I saw Vivaan. He was in the men's room, just came out. He's in that crowd over there." He pointed.

"What are you doing *here* then?"

He narrowed his eyes. "Making sure you're not bleeding to death, obviously. Are you?"

"Yeah. Got this skin tape in my belt. Other stuff. I'm halfway done already, see?"

He eyed her as if he didn't trust her to tell him the truth. Smart man.

"Go," she snapped. "I'm tougher than a couple scratches. Go follow him. I'll try to get to Kentt."

"What's the meet-up plan? In case comms don't work wherever we are?"

Right. Fragging communicators. "Outside in twenty. If I'm not there, wait till thirty and come looking."

"Got it."

"Go."

He hesitated, then turned and went.

Frag. She blinked as she watched him go. Yet another moment gone, stolen into the wind. No, not stolen. She'd ordered it gone.

And if he went after Vivaan and didn't come back? Like all those women?

Her heart was pounding when a tech finally appeared. No, no, it wasn't a tech. She caught a glimpse of a small white dress, but mostly ignored the girl as she squinted to see Kael in the crowd. She spotted him slipping between two black doors near the back.

If she ever saw him again, she had to tell him. Something. Somehow.

The girl was staring, now, Ellen realized. She blocked it out for a moment, then a moment more. The girl persisted.

Ellen turned her head. A small, juvenile Ursa in a white dress with a blue sash and bow in her hair was sitting on the far recliner. Staring straight at her.

Ellen met the Ursa's eyes. Also blue. She didn't think she'd ever seen an Ursa with blue eyes. Maybe they were augmented. They seemed to glow faintly in the dimness.

The Ursa blinked. "That was the coolest thing I have ever seen."

Ellen permitted herself a small smile. "Thanks. Just doing my job."

"I'm Lotiata. But you can call me Loti. How is ring fighting your job?"

"Loti, is it?"

"Yes. Lotiata Kentt."

She raised an eyebrow. "What are you doing here?"

"This is my sister's bar."

"Huh. It's my job because I need to talk to your sister about something, and they said the ring was the only way to do that. Would you happen to be able to take me to see her?"

Loti blinked again. "Why can't I see your thoughts?"

Ellen raised her eyebrows. "I have a special add-on."

"Oh! I have a special add-on that helps me see in."

"Really?" Ellen repressed a shudder. "Your sister was helping the scientist who designed my add-on. Now the scientist has a big problem, and I really need to see Kentt and ask her about it."

The girl's eyes went vacant suddenly, and Ellen frowned. Then the light abruptly returned. "She says, why the hell not."

Ellen smirked. "Are little girls like you supposed to swear?"

"Are women like you supposed to fight mechs?"

"Well... No, probably not."
"Exactly. Right this way."

———

SLIPPING into the back rooms of the club was easier than it should have been, especially for a man Kael's size. Vivaan was smaller, lighter on his feet, and kept pace with the elegant crowd of some sort of elite personages. Maybe the place was less tight-knit than he'd thought, since no one noticed him. Maybe it was so tight-knit that no one was worried.

Maybe they counted on the telepath to be watching for anyone up to no good.

But he wasn't up to no good, and no one could watch one hundred percent of the time. Kael caught up to the back of the group quickly. And it was lucky that Vivaan was trailing at the back, looking at his toes as he shuffled along behind a half dozen women in robes that, up close, were apparently slightly transparent in the dim light.

Wow. Maybe that was why Vivaan was looking at his toes. Kael glued his eyes to his quarry and didn't blink.

"Persad," he hissed as he got closer.

The kid twitched, glancing to the side in unconscious acknowledgment before he quickly pretended not to hear.

"Vivaan!" Only slightly louder, he hoped the added information would be enough warning that he wasn't giving up easily.

Frowning, Vivaan slowed as the crowd continued forward, then risked a direct measuring look at Kael before hurrying toward him.

"Who are you?" Vivaan hissed, dropping a hand on one bicep and pushing Kael into a flower-draped alcove. The dim light didn't extend past the doorway, and they were in almost complete darkness. His optic implants struggled to keep up. "How do you know my name?"

"We're here to help." Kael folded his arms across his chest. That probably wasn't a very satisfactory answer, but what more could he say?

"Who is we? I don't *need* help. Who sent you?"

Vivaan was still gripping his arm. Kael looked down at the hand and sniffed, then leveled a dark glare back at the hand's owner. Vivaan's eyes widened, and he snatched the hand back.

"Your mother sent us," Kael said slowly. "She thought you were dead." He slathered the guilt on thick.

"Well, I'm not. See? Alive. Okay? Now get out of here." Vivaan shooed him away, but Kael wasn't fooled. He was jittery as a mermaid in a vat of coffee.

"What's going on? We can free you." It was a gamble.

"I don't need to be freed." He glanced over his shoulder. The entourage was receding down the long hallway now. Kael hadn't realized this place was so big. "And you're blowing my cover."

"Have you found those girls?" He kept his voice calm, controlled. Someone who could be trusted.

Vivaan stilled. "You made it into my computers."

Kael nodded.

"I'm close. And if they know I am looking for them, I'll lose the trail. Are you... looking for them?" It suddenly seemed to occur to Vivaan that Kael's whole mother story could be a lie. That Kael could have something to do with the disappearances.

Shit, he hadn't meant to lose his trust by mentioning it. "We're looking for you. But I hope you find them."

"I need to go." He gestured wildly behind him but didn't yet try to leave. Yeah, this kid was an amateur. Well intentioned, ambitious, but untrained. His sleeve slid up with the gesture, revealing a tiny silver rectangular slit, the skin surrounding it red and swollen. Recent augmentation gone awry?

"Wait—what's this?" Kael grabbed him by the wrist, pulled up the sleeve, squinted. "Your arm doesn't look so good."

"It's fine."

"Don't let that get black. Or even purple." He'd seen plenty of bad reactions over the years.

"It's *fine*."

"Why are you doing this? Why the quest? What the hell do I tell your mother?"

He sighed. "I'm working with the inspectors, as a prospective candidate. I really want a job that means something, don't you get it? Not this floofy crap. They're evaluating what I can do via this mission. If *you* don't screw it up. I need to go."

"Why didn't you tell her where you were going?"

Vivaan glanced over his shoulder again, but no one was in sight. The group had moved on for now. "She doesn't exactly support my law enforcement ambitions."

"Is there someone we can contact? So we can verify your status for her."

"Captain Udo Trynkei. But don't you dare."

"If you don't want me to, why did you tell me his name?"

Vivaan looked truly aggrieved at that point, now that Kael had pointed it out. "Don't. Please. He'll question my cover being blown. And by my mother of all people. You'll ruin this, and my application, and all my work, and I'll never find them. Stay *out* of this. Tell her… tell her one more week and I'll be back. And that I'm sorry."

Kael nodded. "Okay. I will."

Vivaan looked vaguely surprised. At the fact that Kael wasn't dragging him out by the collar right now? The man wasn't exactly wearing a collar right now, but…

"Good luck. If you need any help, computer resources, backup— we're at your mother's apartment."

"Who *are* you people?"

Kael gave him a long, level stare. "Just some people who want to help, and who do it very well."

"Sure, you do."

He shrugged, the ridiculous half cape swinging. "You know how to reach us." And he turned and walked away.

———

LOTI LED Ellen toward what seemed to be a blank black wall. A door

opened out of the blackness, and after following Loti down three hall-
ways, a left, and a right, Ellen came to a large archway decorated with
something like the tiny white flowers from the club's main floor. These
ones were silver, though, and they shimmered with pale energy in the
relative darkness.

Beyond the archway was a garden of night. There hadn't been
much Buddhism remaining out in the main club because it must
have all congregated here, at least superficially. Smooth rock path-
ways, small, intricately shaped trees, a fountain, a pond. Except all of
it was cloaked in darkness, lit by faint cobalt light. Blue glowed from
inside the water, under a stone bench, trailing along the edges of a
path.

At the end of the long path, directly before Ellen, stood a woman in
a vibrant blue cloak.

Somebody's got a favorite color.

The figure turned, and long, thin fingers tipped with a soft glimmer
like moonlight pushed back the hood. She didn't fully push it back,
still leaving her face in shadow, but Ellen could make out long, waving
sapphire hair that cascaded down her chest, and lips the color of dry
blood. A smile graced them, reminding her faintly of a leopard
postlunch. Strangest of all, her shadowed eyes glowed cerulean, as
though lit from within.

"Ah, Ms. Ryu. Lovely to meet you." A beautiful, bold voice, if delicate. The accent was expensive, refined.

Ellen's own voice seemed hard, blunt, overloud in the pristine
garden of the night. "Are you Etrianala Kentt?"

"The one and only."

"I have some questions." Ellen strode toward her, Rich making
surprisingly loud crunches in the serene gravel. She wondered idly if
he had opinions on what he stepped in. She hoped for his sake that
that wasn't included in his programming. She stopped just short of the
woman, who turned and gestured for Ellen to follow her a few feet
more.

"First, I must thank you. You've given me quite the show. I daresay
this should make a great deal of money online for the broadcast."

The words were at odds with the beauty, the serenity they were drowning in. Ryu scowled. "Don't."

Kentt's pleasant smile never wavered. "Of course, that would also bring the Union bureaucracy down upon you here. And you wouldn't want that. Not until you are gone, at the very least. Would you."

Was the chip even working? "I'd rather not have the publicity at all. I'm a nobody."

Kentt stopped at two stone benches that faced each other, sat on one with the grace of a queen, and indicated the other. Ellen considered obstinately standing anyway, but that didn't seem like what someone trying to win this woman over would do. She'd try to play nice. For a bit. She sat stiffly.

"A nobody? Now we both know that's not true." Her smile widened. "And how else am I to pay for the mechs you've destroyed?"

"Raise your drink prices."

"Says the woman who's been drinking for free."

Now how did she know that?

"No, no, I don't think that recording can be simply disposed of. Far too entertaining."

"At least cut my… friend out of it."

"And deprive the world of a Theroki out of armor? I don't think so."

"He's not one. Not anymore. You'll complicate that for him." Gah. Even telling her this much was just giving her more power.

"I will consider it. But let us get to what you came here to discuss. Of course, you sent your man in a different direction so perhaps he's already gotten what you need. What is it that you need, Ms. Ryu?"

"I just wanted to ask you a few questions."

"Then why not bring him with you? Or is he just expendable, like the others before him?"

"People are never expendable." Even as anger coiled in her chest, relief mixed with it. The chip was clearly fine. Otherwise, the telepath would know Kael was anything but expendable.

"Then why did you design a defense grid that would attack your own ships? That doesn't sound like what a hero does to me."

Ellen stilled. "That's not exactly what it did. It was a very specific class, engine, and weapons combination—"

"That your people used as well as the Puritans."

She pressed her lips into a thin line. She'd never deny something that was the truth, but it wasn't fun to hear it. Why was this woman bringing it up now? "Most people don't know it did that." Fewer would probably think of her as a war hero if they did. Real warriors knew that this kind of bullshit was exactly what war was. The process of trying to be the one who was less wrecked less by the horror of it all.

The smile widened into a Cheshire cat grin. "But I do know it. I've studied your work."

"Why?"

"I have my reasons. Did you have yours?"

"The Puritans mimicked our ident chips to the sensors. We were blind and outnumbered. It was the only way, given what little time we had. I wrote heuristics to identify friendlies from new vectors. They weren't perfect; I couldn't even test them. I had sixteen hours. But they were *never* expendable."

"Really?"

"The losses were tragic. I operated as much of the grid myself manually as I could to try to—"

"Why are you here, Ms. Ryu?" Her voice was placid as the rocks in the garden, the water burbling at their feet. "It's not to fight my mechs. It's not to defend your wars to me."

Why indeed. She wasn't usually goaded so easily. "Vivaan Persad."

"Ah. Really? I'm intrigued. And not often surprised. This is most enjoyable."

"He's been missing for two weeks. Inspectors won't help find him. His family is worried."

"Poor Dr. Persad. Poor Vivaan, such a lonely sort. Enthusiastic. Noble. A bit too trusting though."

Ellen sat forward on the bench, clutching her knee. She was surprised to feel only skin, forgetting the ridiculous getup. She shook her head and refocused on Kentt. "What do you know?"

"I know that his chip doesn't work as well as he thinks it does."

"Where is he?"

"I believe you already know the answer to that question, or you wouldn't have sent your man elsewhere. But what's odd is that, I don't believe his mother installed his chip. Isn't that curious? Hers worked much better. As does yours. Why wouldn't he tell her where he was going? Perhaps she was part of the problem." Kentt raised an eyebrow.

"I don't need conjecture. I need Persad."

"I can't give you that, only he can. Fortunately for Vivaan and his faulty installation, I'm not one of the bad guys."

"I find that often depends on your point of view."

"He's safe here with me. And I don't mind what he's doing. In fact, I admire it. I can't say the same for those he thinks he's working for."

"Who is that?"

"Your man is talking to Vivaan right now. When you two catch up, you can compare notes. I'd like to see if you can figure it out."

"This isn't a guessing game. There are lives on the line here." At least, the missing women might still be alive.

"I can't say anymore. I think that's been quite enough. I will not delete your fight. But I will not broadcast it until you are off planet, as I do not wish to help the Union any more than anyone else. As for Vivaan, tell Chayana or whoever is looking for him he's safe. For now."

Kentt slipped from the seat, graceful as a falling feather, pale blue flats alighting silently on the stone path. She straightened her dress and turned to go, the cape swirling.

Not yet. Ellen only had one shot left, and it was a cheap one, but she took it.

"Songbird."

Kentt froze, turning her head. Her hard, blue eyes pierced Ellen over her shoulder. Her chin twitched just slightly. "I sing for no one but myself."

Ellen's heart lurched in her chest at the sentiment. "You've heard the name before. And not about avian creatures."

"Are you one of them then?" Her body was tensed, Ellen realized. As if she thought an attack were imminent.

"No. Never willingly, anyway."

The telepath turned fully back to face her. "But once you were?"

"Yes. Once."

"So escape is possible... I hadn't thought." She glanced off to the side of the path, thinking.

"I had help. With escaping. Are you working with them?"

Surprise flickered in her eyes now. "No. My sister..."

"Loti?"

"No, my human sister. I know Vivaan thinks I have something to do with his girls disappearing. And I do." She smiled now, oddly enough. "But only in that many of them have dined with me here, and I also care about them. And they are also Naturals."

"That's why you agreed to help Persad? With her prototype? To help him find them?"

"No. I only learned of his quest after that. I helped Persad because her technology could render our power obsolete."

"Why would you want that?"

"Many wouldn't. But I do. It would render us as individuals less valuable. Less worth the taking. Or kidnapping. Or fearing or manipulating or murdering. Did you know a Natural born in a non-telepathic-supported community is eleven times more likely than the average woman to be killed before she reaches fourteen?"

"I... didn't know that."

"The galaxy is a brutal place. Especially for the different."

That was certainly true. "Your sister. Is she one of the missing? Or already... in the program?" God forbid.

The words came out grudgingly, painfully. "She volunteered."

Ellen froze before she could hide her reaction, her gut clenching. "What do you mean? Why would anyone—"

"They were recruiting, at university. I graduated eight years ago, but she's younger than me and was working on advanced studies, perhaps to become a teacher. But she wanted to lead, to use her powers for something important. Something heroic. And she fell in with them."

Ellen caught her breath. "But you don't think that's what's happening. Not something important and heroic."

"No."

"Who was recruiting exactly? Arakovic?"

"Yes. And she's so young, beautiful, charismatic when she wants to be. It's easy to get drawn in—"

"But—Dr. Arakovic isn't young."

"Not the doctor. Her daughter."

Ellen rocked back on her short heels. "She has a daughter?"

"Oh yes. I'm not sure if she's her biological daughter, but…"

Mother sends a message… The words of the telepaths drifted back through her mind. Yes, Ellen wasn't sure about this daughter either. God, could Kentt's sister have been one of the women they'd already encountered? She couldn't stomach the thought of it. Not now.

"Whoever the woman is, she's the one at the institutes, smiling and drinking wine. Real wine, smuggled. Talking about peace. About ending the endless war." Kentt sighed. "I'm not so sure my sister understood what she was signing up for. Something wasn't right about them."

"About *peace*? And the war?" She almost spat the words out. Why would she… "Arakovic doesn't care about peace."

Kentt met her eyes, expression grave. "I think she may, actually. That's just what I'm afraid of. But I take it you weren't recruited?"

"No. I was…" Should she trust this woman? A friend of Ostrov's, who ran this strange, ethically questionable place. But her gut said it was worth the gamble. "I was experimented on. As a soldier."

Pain crept into those deep blue eyes. "I see. I am sorry for your pain."

"You see a lot, even without your talents."

"My talents are more than just telepathy." She smiled, serene as a forest pool. "Well, at the institutes, they were recruiting. Saying telepaths could help bring peace and end the violence." Her expression grew even more serious. "How do you suppose they plan to do that, Ms. Ryu?"

"You tell me."

"I will. There is no way for a telepath to do that. Not ethically. Not without crossing some extremely dangerous lines. No scientific way to do it, either. And yet the Arakovics trade primarily in both science and telepathy, not diplomacy. The institute should have thrown them out."

Her head turned slightly, at an angle, as if she were listening for something. "Your man is loyal. He's waiting and I think he's getting concerned."

"Why do you say that?"

"My other observational talents. He doesn't know to hide his tells, of course, because he doesn't know I'm watching. A frown, foot tapping, glancing around. That's a convincing disguise, but you should hide the throat tattoo a little better next time. Gives away a colorful past. Possibly Muslim origin? He's handsome."

"You're good."

"I've had practice. Also, I think he's considering sneaking in from the terrace."

"There's a terrace? Wait, what makes you say that?"

"He found an unsecured ventilation shaft and is climbing it. Impressive. I'll have to add a guard there. Don't count on using that again. Without my knowledge anyway. But I should hope you don't need to. I should hope after this frank discussion, you consider me a friend."

"Tentatively. A tentative one. I don't make many friends."

"Now I don't think that's true, either. You should go to him."

"You've been more than fair."

"Generous is the word you're looking for." But there was laughter in Kentt's smile. She strode back to Ellen and drew a card from her robe. "Here. Chayana has my information, but she's unlikely to share it outside of her experiment. Just in case you need it."

Ellen took the card. Actual paper record of contacts—so old-fashioned. Surprising for a place like Capital. Perhaps some old traditions died hard, or it was in their age that they found power. She wouldn't know much about that. "Thank you. I wish I could offer you the same, but—"

"Some of us hide in the crowd, others in the shadows. Don't worry about it. You find me. Good luck."

Ellen nodded.

"And you'll want to go up that spiral staircase and take the ceiling hatchway to the roof terrace. Your friend is up there."

"Thanks." Smiling, Ellen gave her a quick nod and took off at a jog for the roof.

CHAPTER TEN

KAEL HAD TOLD her he'd follow orders and wait thirty minutes, but in reality, he only made it to twenty-eight. That was close enough, right?

He spent the eight minutes outside near the loading dock, coming up with a plan. It was tempting to get lost in the sea of air traffic beneath his feet, but it wasn't helpful. What would be helpful would be figuring out which side of the building had space for back rooms where one might visit with a telepath, and how the hell he was going to get into them.

A ventilation shaft ended up being a simple solution to his problem. After he'd climbed up the two-story height of the club, one branch went out over the revelers to his left, and a branch to his right spilled out onto a terrace.

He'd try that first, see if he could get a sense for what was below him or if any private corridors opened onto the terrace. Preferably unlocked, very private ones belonging to a certain telepath.

He'd barely gotten the ventilation grate bolted back in place when he heard grinding behind him. Readying to defend himself, he stood stock still, bent slightly at the knee, waiting. Probably droids. There was probably an automated defense system of some kind, and he'd triggered it. A panel in the floor was spinning and about to pop.

The panel stopped its spin, then drew back into the ceiling, revealing a dark interior, iron-colored hair, razor-sharp brown eyes—

"Ellen," he blurted.

"That's my name, Asidian, don't wear it out."

He laughed, distractedly, and sort of just stood there while she extracted herself from the floor. "How the—what—" He blinked. Glory be, she was stunning. He'd been avoiding facing it all night.

"Kentt noticed your... inventive means of entering the building. She pointed me this way."

"Ah," he said. What else was there to say?

She strode toward him slowly, also silent, and stopped a few feet away. She waited. She was going to keep on waiting, because his mind had gone blank. Maybe they should be getting out of here. Maybe it didn't matter. If she wasn't hurrying, he wasn't going to. He was frozen like a fly in a spider's web, except he wasn't struggling.

Her voice was strangely soft and surprised him when she finally spoke. "What are you thinking, when you look at me like that?"

Like she was the most amazing thing he could never have. "You don't want to know." That sounded better. Less desperate.

"Yes, I do."

He sighed. No. No, she didn't. Thankfully, the question broke the spell. He averted his gaze. "Forget it." Isn't that what she'd said she wanted to do? Well, he could honor that much. "Listen, I talked to Vivaan. He says he's working for the Capital police. The inspectors, undercover."

"Really?"

"Yeah, I don't buy it. I mean, I think he *thinks* he's working for them. But it doesn't make sense. We need to talk to Persad."

"The telepath had... quite a few things to say. Including that she thought the people he was working with weren't to be trusted. Maybe that's who she meant?"

"Fits my impressions. Vivaan wouldn't leave. Said he thinks he's close to finding the women."

"I wonder how right he is."

"What do we do now? Is she going to stream your fight?"

"No. I think I convinced her not to. Not while we're on planet, anyway. Hmm."

They stood in silence for a moment. "We should get a better patch on your leg," he said finally.

"I agree, madam," the shoe chimed in. "I can only clean so much blood before I need a recharge."

"And you've made a valiant effort, Rich. Okay, let's go back and figure out what to do next. I'm assuming we can take the stairs this time."

"Oh, goodie." Rich sniffed again. "And I'll call a car. I am *not* walking."

BY SOME MIRACLE, when they returned to Persad's flat, Ellen was able to gather the others without gathering Persad. Crowded into Vivaan's room, she and Kael gave the four of them the rundown on what they'd heard. As they spoke, Jenny worked over Ellen's leg wound, better repairing it.

Adan shook his head. "I don't like it. Something's wrong."

"I agree," said Ellen.

"He sincerely believes he's working with these inspectors but doesn't want any contact with them." Kael shrugged. "They probably told him not to talk about them, to keep him from discovering the truth."

"Wouldn't he suspect that? Be careful?" Jenny asked.

"He was really, really green. Not sure he would."

"Why would they trial a candidate on a mission like that?" Ellen put in, shaking her head.

Mo nodded. "Isn't that mission a bit dangerous to evaluate a totally fresh candidate on?"

"Maybe he's got one of Mom's chips, and they don't," Adan suggested.

"Maybe." Ellen clenched her jaw for a moment, then nodded. "Well, there's nothing for it. The rest of you stay here and think on next steps. Adan and Xi, see if you can find any traces of his dealings with Capital inspectors. Come on, Kael. Let's see what Persad the senior has to say."

They found her in her study, nursing a glass of wine surrounded by walls of books. She was holding a tablet as though she'd been planning to read, but the screen had gone off. She'd just been... staring. Thinking of Vivaan? She looked up as Ellen and Kael entered, put the tablet down hastily, and straightened.

"What is it? You've found something?" Her voice was flat. Scared.

"We found him."

Chayana's eyes widened.

She thinks we're here to tell her he's dead, Ellen realized. "The good news is, he appears to be okay," she said quickly, "and there of his own volition. No one is holding him."

"Oh! Oh, thank the stars." She hung her face in her hands for a second. "The bad news then?"

Kael pursed his lips briefly. "He won't come back."

Persad raised her eyebrows. "That... isn't exactly what I expected. But I am glad to here he is alive. Safe?"

"We're not sure about that exactly. But relatively safe. No immediate peril," Ellen said.

"I forget myself. Please sit. Coffee? Something stronger?"

Ellen toyed with the idea of asking for beer. It had been quite a night. The painkillers Jenny had given her probably wouldn't agree with that, though. "Sure," she said. Persad quickly whipped up two coffees and another plate of those delightful pistachio-topped cookies. Since Xi had been all through Persad's food equipment system by now, guaranteeing as best one could that her food was safe, it was okay to imbibe. And she was exhausted.

In fact, she let Kael relay most of what they'd found, concentrating on sipping her coffee, feeling the painkiller slowly spread, and thinking of her own revelations. And how to act on them.

Persad was groaning. "Oh, no. Not this again."

"What?" Ellen had drifted off, not following the conversation.

"He's applied seven times. Always rejected. I thought he'd given up on all that."

Kael frowned. "Did he have one of your implants?"

"No."

"Could he have taken one behind your back? He seemed to think he could maintain a false identity, or at least a secret agenda, in a building run by a telepath. And his arm was... not doing so good. Maybe he thought he could use your tech to finally get the leverage to get in."

She frowned. "It's possible, I guess. I don't keep as careful records as I probably should. But my chip is too intensive to put into an arm implant. And he never had one. Not two weeks ago anyway."

"He's got a bad one now, ma'am."

She winced, blew out a breath. And where Ellen had expected anger, the woman only sounded hurt. "Why wouldn't he just come to me if he wanted one so badly? Why didn't he say something? If he ends up with some aftermarket metal poisoning..." She ran a hand over her face, perhaps to hide a shimmer of tears.

Something else occurred to Ellen. "Have you heard anything from the people who contacted you via mail? Any further demands?"

"No. Maybe they were among the men who attacked, and we stopped them. I expected something by now."

"Maybe. Or maybe they're biding their time."

"They may have already decided I was uncooperative. You know, since you shot them and all."

Ellen permitted herself a little smile. "We incapacitated them. We could have shot them, but we didn't."

"Either way, it is good to know that they don't have Vivaan tied up in a warehouse somewhere."

Kael nodded. "Definitely."

"Listen, Doc," Ellen started, scooting forward in her chair. It was time to lay all the cards on the table, make her case. She had the feeling that if things started to move, they might move fast.

"Call me Chaya."

Was it the news they'd brought that was winning the doctor over? Or was it the rich-people clothes, or the blood? "Look, you know we didn't come here for Jenny's climbing."

"You're doing a favor for Catherine Simmons. To help me."

"We are. And no matter what happens, we'll be glad to have found your son and secured your research."

"I'm sensing a 'but' coming."

"That's because you're a smart woman. We've been having some tough times with telepaths lately. In the outsystem. Doug Simmons was hoping your research could help us, in addition to us helping you."

"Well, he was right. It has. Hasn't it?"

"Yes."

"But... ?"

"But not everyone on my team has a chip interface. And we need to be able to repair and adapt it."

"What are you getting at, Ryu?"

"Call me Ellen," she forced out. Quid pro quo, right? "Doug's real request is that you consider relocating your lab to our ship. Where you can continue your research and help us with—"

"Could I bring Vivaan? Assuming he... comes back." Her eyes brightened for a moment, before her head dipped. She wiped her hands down her face once more.

"Yes, that was assumed. Our ship has plenty of room. It could be dangerous, though."

"Living here hasn't exactly been safe."

Ellen smirked at that. "You got that right."

Persad's eyes lit up. "Are there any... nice young Hindu women on your ship?"

"Not yet. But the galaxy is a big place."

Chayana smiled now, though it didn't reach her eyes. "I like the way you think, Ryu."

"Listen, I know this is a big question—"

"I'll certainly consider it. I have to know what Vivaan would do. And consider the equipment I'd need."

"We can always get more. You can have whatever resources the Foundation can offer. No change there."

Chayana nodded. "And no Ostrov up the hall would be a plus. So what do we do next?"

Well shit. That wasn't as hard as she'd thought it would be. She claimed she'd think, but everything in her manner was highly amenable. Ellen should have tried the "shipful of accomplished, unattached women for your single son" angle sooner.

Ellen took a deep breath. "We can't make him come back. But we can help him solve his problem. Get some answers."

"You mean find those missing girls?"

"Exactly."

———

FOR THE ONE HUNDREDTH TIME, Josana let out a gasp of joy at the tablet she was nestled with on Persad's couch. Jenny cringed and tried to pretend the historical romance she was reading was more engrossing than it was. Josana's little noises were driving her up the wall, but she'd be damned if she let that chase her out of the living room to look for somewhere else to read. Still, after a moment or two of Josana's broadening smile, almost cackling to herself, Jenny just couldn't take it anymore.

"What!" Jenny thumped her tablet down on the table next to her orange armchair. "What is it you're so happy about, damn it?"

Adan raised his head and looked warily at the two of them from the breakfast nook. Jenny met his eye. Strangely, Josana didn't. The two of them hadn't talked since they'd returned from their earlier outing. Had something happened? Adan had been hiding in a side room, really, but apparently he'd been forced to come out to eat.

Josana looked up, grinning. "This!" She turned the tablet around. A photo showed the inside of a swanky club, with a long narrow fighting ring in the center. Sadly, not that unusual for Capital nightlife. All fun and games, until someone loses an eye or sacrifices a genetically engineered mythical animal. On one side of the ring, were two smallish mechanical suits, maybe two men high. Jenny had seen worse. On the other side were Kael and Ryu, unarmored and unarmed.

Jenny caught her breath.

"What the hell—" Adan started, rising and coming closer.

"It's okay," Josana said quickly. "It's all over. They put on quite a show."

"A show?" Jenny scowled. "You think those kinds of fights are just a *show*?"

"Have a little faith in your colleagues." Josana pursed her lips, a little smug, calling up another photo of one mech smashed to pieces beside another that had a crowd of techs surrounding it, presumably because it had some serious problem and the rider needed out. "They flattened Kentt's toys." And now she did let out a cackle.

Jenny shook her head. "Shit. Is this all over the net?"

"Of *course* it is." Josana burbled a little more with laughter and returned to perusing the feeds. "Look what she did to those shoes. That's a travesty."

"Why are you so happy about this?"

She raised her eyebrows. "Because I like seeing the toys of holier-than-thou types get broken. And because it's going to be excellent for my reputation. It already has been." Her eyes flicked to Adan. "Orders for performance boosters already doubled in the last hour alone."

Jenny raised her eyebrows. No, she didn't want to know. Huffing, she dropped her eyes back to her book. Adan, too, returned to his food without comment.

He knows something, she thought. Or there's no way he would not ask what the heck she was talking about, unless they'd already talked about it.

Stay out of it, she thought. But she pulled up her own local news feeds. There were no mentions of the festivities among her friends, but one news item did catch her eye. A recent announcement from the Union of the astronomical reward for deserters hiding on neutral planets. It could be just a coincidence… But she scowled at the screen.

"You sure you're not ready to go back to your place?" said Jenny.

"Maybe tomorrow. If I'd done that already, I'd have missed all the fun."

"And we wouldn't want that, would we?" Jenny just shook her head.

———

KAEL SHOULD HAVE BEEN tired after the exertions of the day, but he was keyed up instead by the time he got out of his monkey suit and into something comfortable—and without a cape. Unsurprisingly, he had adrenaline in surplus.

Still he forced himself to lie down, since Jenny was on the first watch. Years of training himself to sleep on demand apparently kicked in, because when he awoke to Xi's voice from his comm, there was sunlight streaming through the window.

He sat up and rubbed the back of his neck. Didn't whoever was after Persad know where she lived? That seemed unlikely, and after the attack the first day, the silence since seemed strange. Ominous, even.

He was still itching with nerves by the time they were ready to head out—on foot and armored this time—for one quick stop.

"One of the two addresses Xi was able to tie to the capsule is here on Capital," Ellen said in their mini briefing before they headed out. "So we've got to be as discreet as we can."

"I'm ready to disable to street surveillance in the area on your cue," said Adan.

"We should get more cloakers while we are here, Commander," added Jenny.

"Are they legal?"

Jenny shrugged. "Does that matter?"

Ellen shook her head. "Maybe on our way out then. Remind me."

The building where their destination was tucked away was a skyscraper, of course. Every freaking plot of land here was either a skyscraper or a manicured park with a pagoda. But this skyscraper also went down into the earth as well.

"You would think it'd be sandy here," he muttered into the comm channel as they found the other entrance to the service stairwell. "Tough to dig down and build on an island. Wouldn't you think?"

Jenny shrugged. "The wonders of modern engineering. And all the wonderful things we use it for! Inter-solar-system colony ships, super-human cyborg legs, colors of hair you don't have to dye, and darker labs in danker basements."

Mo and Nova snickered.

The stairwell was indeed both dark and dank. Adan broke through the outer lock in record time thanks to the downloaded data from Vala's computer. Their unorthodox entry didn't kick on the autolights, and they left the lights off. His armor detected safe air—and no hint of sedative, praise the Almighty—but humidity was in fact high. Dark, check. Dank, check.

After the outer door was shut, they pulled their multis from the crate they'd floated along behind them. Armor had drawn enough stares. He doubted walking around with rifles was even legal.

It was six switchbacks down until they came to the next door. Adan got to work wordlessly. He was wearing the old armor Jenny had brought along, which he hadn't been a fan of. Now that they were standing here, Kael was glad Ryu had insisted. Dude just didn't know what was good for him, most of the time.

"How's it feel not to be a drone?" Nova asked. They were all on the comm channel, silent outside and speaking only within the suits.

"Just peachy." Adan was barely paying attention.

"Mmm peaches." Jenny's armor rubbed its metal belly.

"I could go for a peach right now," Mo agreed, expression stoic. And that said something as she was usually so quiet.

"They have to have some down here, right?" asked Nova.

Jenny turned toward her. "The Regency Night Market is your best bet—I'll show you when we get back."

"With peaches, this'll almost feel like a vacation."

"Don't get used to it," Ellen said as the lockpad flashed red and then green. Adan stepped back. "Everyone ready?"

They each acknowledged in turn.

Ellen stilled. "When governments fail to police science…"

"Science will police itself," Jenny finished, clutching a fist over her heart. How they determined the rotation for that little ritual, he hadn't figured out—but he had noticed he wasn't included in it yet.

Hoo-ahs went up all around, and in they went.

Kael went first, and the unlocked door opened easily. Too easily, as he slammed it accidentally against the metal walls. It echoed like they'd burst into a vast refrigerator. The air was just as cold too, from the readout. Sweeping lights from their suits revealed nothing but dusty, empty floor.

"Take it easy, He-Man," Ellen said as they filed in and spread out, searching the place.

But it was clear pretty quick.

"Why are all the fanciest Enhancer labs always cleared out before we get to them?" Nova groaned.

"We know they use them cyclically." Adan shrugged. "Maybe they're planning to come back."

"Maybe they're on the run," Jenny offered.

Ellen's voice was darker. "Maybe they knew we were coming."

After searching two rooms, the hall he'd gone down dead-ended in nothing but dust and an occasional spider. He came back to the entry.

"Hey, Theroki, how's it feel to be standing this time?" Nova cracked her gum at him and grinned through her visor, presumably referring to the first encounter between the team, Kael, and the knockout grenade.

"Slag off, *vieja*."

"He's learning!"

"Aren't you younger than him?" Jenny rejoined them in the central area.

"I didn't say he was learning my language, just that he was learning."

Kael snorted.

"Anybody see anything?" Ellen called from down another hall.

"Not even one squid monster." Kael prodded a low steel crate with his multi. It was empty.

"Ugh, thank God." Jenny inspected a nearby wall. Not that he could see anything there for her too look for other than sheet metal.

"There's... this." Mo's voice echoed from the back.

Leaving Jenny and Nova near the entry, Adan, Ellen, and Kael followed Mo's voice to the back.

"What is it?" Ellen asked.

Mo pointed at a deactivated force field control on the wall outside. "Looks like a cell."

"Maybe to hold something in?" said Adan.

"That's typically what cells are used for," Ellen muttered.

"I know, I'm such a genius," he agreed.

"Something?" Mo gestured with her multi at what looked like a shelf—no, a low slab for a bed—with a heavy steel cuff at each corner. "Or someone?"

Kael shuddered.

Ellen stopped at the edge of the alcove. "Maybe it's for the certain contents of a little metal container we all know and love."

Adan took a step back and bumped into the wall behind him. "Okay, now you're scaring me."

"They didn't have anything like this on Helikai," said Kael. "But Li was being evacuated. He must have planned to move it somewhere else before... maturity."

"Her," said Ellen slowly. "Not it."

"Right. Her."

"Any idea where he was being evaced too?"

"No. I'd suspect Desori, since that's where he told me to take it. But really it could be anywhere. That location was only known to the evac team. Of course... Hmm."

"What is it?"

"If Doug could buy one of them out and get the lab location, then—"

"What makes you think he did that?" Ellen said sharply, stepping closer.

"Just always assumed it." He shrugged. "How else would he have gotten the location, just for that specific time window? I'd been there for months."

"There are plenty of ways, like info from one of the nukes, but go on."

"Well, if he bought out one of those Theroki, maybe someone else could too. Which means they could have revealed other locations. To anyone."

"And then they'd have to pack up, if they realized they had a leak."

He nodded. "And get some new security guards. That's all conjecture of course."

"Well, whatever happened here, this cell is creepy as hell. Adan, see if you can get anything from this force field control computer."

"Got it."

"Let's do one more sweep. Make sure we didn't miss anything hidden. Mo, use your scanner to see if there's anything unusual to this stuff." Ellen wrapped an armored knuckle against the metal wall with a clang.

Finally they all congregated by the entry. The place continued to be eerily silent outside of their comm chatter. Mo joined them last, having gone through each room alone again.

"Nothing much out of the ordinary, just steel, except..." She hit a button on the side of her scope scanner. "That cell area has traces of opsepium. Like, thin lines of it tracing the walls."

Kael let out a low whistle. "The telepathy-interfering element? Is there a chance this has something to do with our little friend?"

"I'll see if Dremer has any updates," Ellen said. "Wonder if that's also what's in Persad's chips? Anyway, doesn't matter. Mo, send those readings back to the ship."

"On it, Commander." Mo started entering further commands into her scope. That thing was even fancier than he'd realized.

Ellen let out a breath and scanned around them. "Well, we checked. Let's get out of here. Adan, lock us back up on the way out."

———

BACK AT PERSAD'S, Ellen had them all poring through records and news feeds, trying to find something on where any of those girls might have ended up. She tried to read herself, but mostly she just paced like a caged tiger and made annoyed moves in Ostrov's stupid game. He'd chosen a much more tedious and lengthy one this time.

Kael had found a rumor that one girl had been spotted on the ice world Ifjornof, and Adan had found a way into several of their net accounts, but it hadn't taught them anything. Overall, the team was striking out.

The room's holodesk lit up, indicating an incoming call. It darkened as Persad answered it somewhere else in the place.

Ellen's stomach dropped, though, when Persad walked out a moment later.

"It's for you." Chayana gave her a look of sympathetic chagrin. "Guess you didn't wear enough bug spray."

"God, not him again." She rose and felt the eyes of the others on her as she followed Persad out, which only added to the heat in her cheeks. She plopped down in front of Persad's large, sleek holodesk in her study. "What."

He grinned. "It's so silly we're playing three floors apart. Especially when I have this wonderful table you love so much. Come and join me again."

She stared at him. For a good long two seconds, maybe more. The search for an excuse not to go was in vain. She released a breath like an explosion. "Fine. Be right there."

His grin broadened as he ended the call before she had the satisfaction of doing so.

She shook her head as she stood up. It was going to feel good to beat him. Again. Might as well get this over with. But first, armor.

She didn't meet any of their eyes when she stomped through a few minutes later, fully armored and with a sigh. "I'll be back. Hopefully I won't be long."

"Good luck, Commander," Jenny muttered in her wake.

As she hit the elevator tube, she frowned at herself. Avoiding the eyes of her crew now? All of them—or one in particular?

She made a disgusted noise in the back of her throat and resolved to thrash Ostrov and end this game right now.

He had the door open before she reached it. Hmm. Either he had a camera that watched the elevator, or he'd been waiting there the whole time. Probably the former; he didn't seem like the desperate type.

"I see I've earned so much of your trust," he said, tone dry. He'd traded in the usual long black jacket for a navy one that did things to his eyes. Blech. She hated noticing anything nice about him.

She retracted the helmet after the readout was clean and his door was shut. "You got what you got. I am what I am. Take it or leave it."

"Oh, I'll take it. Come." He swept out an arm toward the gaming room, and she marched on in.

He set down a box of juice in front of her, with a gesture like he was presenting the finest champagne. Not a box of her choosing, she noted. She met his gaze, her own level and not concealing her annoyance, as he sat one hip on the table beside her. He smiled, and his eyes flashed brightly. How odd that when she was actually in his presence, his amorous overtones always morphed into feeling more lethal than affectionate.

"It's a real woman that can make a suit of armor look so stunning. Although I must say I prefer the blue satin."

She went rigid and hoped he couldn't tell. "This is more comfortable."

"Truly? I'm surprised. You looked plenty comfortable from what I saw. More sushi?" A tray of cold little white and red meat arranged neatly on rice awaited her too.

"You're quite prepared to have someone over."

"Oh, it's an addiction. They're just delicious little creatures, what can I say?"

"I'm full."

"Can I interest you in a sparkling jelly tart?" He pointed a thumb over his shoulder. "Got a few in the kitchen."

"I already ate."

"That's a shame. There's this delightful unicorn steak—"

"You're breaking my flow," she said, groping for an excuse for the irritation in her tone. "Can we just get on with this?"

He gave her a little head shake and tongue cluck as he straightened and headed to his side of the table, pulling the game to life before them. It was her move, and she took it as he spoke. "Your appearance sans armor last night made quite the splash."

She kept her eyes trained on the game. It was a night for dodging gazes. "Got my breather ripped out for my trouble."

"I saw." He ordered his move on the computer as he leaned back in his chair, propping his feet on the table.

"You saw?"

"It's all over the nets."

She winced. "That wasn't my intention."

"You're quite the little killer, aren't you."

She stopped and finally met his gaze. For the first time, she could detect some honest intrigue there, some kind of curiosity now under the arrogant facade. "You study... whatever it is you study. How to make brighter rainbows. I have studied something else." She reached out and pushed her piece into her desired location with precise force.

He chuckled. "Brighter rainbows. Good one. Blue A84 to C26." His piece moved based on the command.

"I try." She shuffled through the next move, capturing six of his pieces one by one. He watched with a mild frown and pursed lips, more out of consternation than annoyance or surprise.

"For someone so smart, you'd think you'd be more comfortable with technology."

Ah, so she *was* getting under his skin. "Why would you say I'm not?"

"Manual interaction with a holo? It's more tactile, sure, but far from efficient."

She'd argue that was hardly true, but he wasn't worth it. Instead, she simply narrowed her eyes. "This info of yours better be worth it."

"Trust me, it is."

They fell silent for the next few moves. When she could see him working toward another bit of small talk, she decided it was time to take more of an offensive role in the verbal game they were playing. She waited until his eyes were on her making her supposedly ineffi-cient tactile move.

"Anaka Cho."

There was a flicker of something before he was able to cover it. Oh, he knew something all right.

"Some folks at the club last night were talking about her. Happen to know her?"

"I may have heard the name. The Elderflower is one of my many haunts. An inspector's daughter, was it?"

"I have no idea. I just know she has some friends who are looking for her. Can't seem to find her."

He forced a smile now, annoyed more than anything else. "Well, I'm sure she'll turn up eventually. They always do."

She cocked any eyebrow. "They do?" Did his definition of "always" include them turning up dead in the ocean too?

He nodded once, curt, his upper lip twitching. He tried to hide it behind a drink of something dark and amber colored. "Oh, they do. If you know the right people, they know where to look. She'll find her. She always does."

She pounced. "She? Who is she?"

His eyes widened just enough to acknowledge that he'd given something away. He waved dismissively. "Her friend. Whoever is looking. I assumed it was a woman. Or was it a lover?"

"No. Just a few friends. Of a variety of genders."

"Ah." He took another drink. Buying time, she thought. "Are you sure I can't get you some grilled uni—"

She held up a palm. "I'm sure. Don't make me raise the helmet too."

"You're a tough negotiator."

"You're a tedious one. What is the point of all these games?"

"I need to be sure you're one of the few who can act on the information I'm going to give you. Only a few are that good. Rumors say you're one of them. But I have to be sure."

"Are you sure yet?"

"Not when I'm about to beat you. Are you sure you wouldn't like any sushi?"

She rolled her eyes. "Let's just play."

CHAPTER ELEVEN

HOURS. He'd been reading news feeds for hours. Kael leaned his head back against Persad's swanky, bent wood recliner and blinked at the ceiling. Why couldn't that dang laboratory have been filled with crazed evil scientists and monstrosities that needed dispatching? Instead, he was stuck playing detective. Or worse, the detective's overlooked research assistant. While the detective was off... He didn't want to know. Isn't this what they had inspectors for?

But the inspectors weren't doing anything. Yet another mystery. At this point, the chances of actually finding answers seemed dimmer than ever.

He glanced around to see if anyone else was flagging. Jenny was curled up in a nearby orange armchair, frowning determinedly over her work. Mo brooded at the window over a tablet of her own but spent about half the time simply staring out at the people below, possibly planning their violent demise. That was basically standard behavior for her. She didn't exactly scare him—he'd lived with Theroki for a decade after all—but if any of them *were* going to scare him, it'd have been Mo.

Josana was lounging gracefully across a chaise, a thin gray robe draped artfully over her curves and parting just a little in all the wrong places, its belt as white as her hair, which was cast wildly to one side. She studied her fingernails while listening to something on her earpiece. Correction. One of them definitely scared him, and it was Josana.

Nova was lying on the floor on her stomach, knees bent and kicking while she made admirable use of a wrist holodisplay and tortured a stick of gum. Adan was as far from everyone else as possible, hunched in a kitchen chair and typing viciously.

He sighed. Everyone else was still working. He tried to refocus his eyes on the tablet, but for a moment they just blurred. He shook his head. They were getting nowhere fast, and they were only doing this because they had no idea what else to do. It was a noble cause, so he wanted to help, even if the back of his mind was writhing with thoughts over where Ellen had headed off to. But it was hard not to feel hopeless.

As if sensing his moment of weakness, Josana took that moment to strike. She straightened neatly in her seat, removed the earpiece, and cleared her throat. "All right. I think the fun's over here. I'm ready to head to my apartment. This seems as good a time as any. I'm sure I'll need help with my things, though." She caught his gaze like a cobra striking and smiled.

Jenny shook off her stupor. "Oh. Sure. The commander left orders I should do it when you're ready." She set the tablet aside and stretched.

"Oh, no, no, no." Josana blinked her lovely eyes. "I'm not going anywhere with *you*."

Jenny gave her a long-suffering stare. "You want help, you don't have much choice. Ryu's orders."

"Well, she's not here right now, is she?"

"Convenient."

"And she's not commanding me anymore. I'm on land. And a civilian."

Jenny made a noise of disgust. "God, why do you always have to be such a bitch?"

Josana only smiled more sweetly back. "I'm not risking my reputation being seen with you."

"At night? No one's gonna see anything."

"Especially at night. They'll assume we were socializing." The words sounded like she was referring to murder, rather than cocktails.

"I should be the one worried about my reputation, being seen with you."

"Besides, we'd kill each other before we even arrived."

"Now there's something tempting."

"I'm not going with you. Kael can take me."

Jenny groaned. Kael slapped a hand to his face. Nova and Mo met each other's gazes, looking slightly alarmed.

He groped for an excuse to turn her down. "I'm not going against the commander's orders just because you two can't—"

"Aren't you the ranking officer here?" Josana said sweetly. "Can't you *change* the orders?"

Even Jenny smiled bitterly at that, flopping back in her seat. "Yeah, Lieutenant, get me outta this bullshit."

"There's no justification for—"

"Maybe if she wanted her orders followed, she should have stayed her to ensure it happened." Josana's voice was saccharine poison, and he hated that it sunk into him a little. "Besides. Jenny's celebrity status is a problem Ryu didn't adequately consider," and here Josana's voice was full of derision, "especially with the wrong sorts of crowd. Meat heads, gamblers, bookies, lowlifes—"

"You're one to talk," Adan muttered from the kitchen so quietly Kael wasn't sure anyone else heard him.

Jenny was too busy getting pissed off. She sat forward in the chair. "Excuse me? People who like sports aren't necessarily—"

"She will attract a risky sort of crowd that I have no desire to be exposed to. Far more risky than you would, Lieutenant."

Kael stared hard at her for a long moment, trying to decide if she was actually serious. "She says to the felon," he muttered. Former gang member too, don't forget that.

"Pardon me?"

"Nothing." If she hadn't cared to ask, he didn't care to tell her. He didn't think Josana's concerns had any merit, but it was true that Jenny could attract attention. And Kael wouldn't. Whatever his past, no one knew it here. At least as far as he knew.

He glanced at Jenny. Would Ellen kill him if he left Adan with her? Jenny definitely had access to the deadly drug. Nova and Mo were not on the list of most concern.

But he'd seen the way she looked at Adan.

If only he could run this by Ellen first. But she was off doing who-knew-what with that arrogant snotwaffle. Anger bubbled up, surprisingly strong, reminding him that the effects of the Theroki chip were not entirely gone. But it made a sort of sense. He'd thought straight edged, clean-cut was what she wanted, but maybe a brain was what she was looking for.

She wouldn't find that in Kael. Which maybe explained more than he cared to admit. Maybe her reasons were weak as hell because they weren't *really* her reasons, they were just excuses. To protect him from the truth.

Their last kiss flashed before his eyes, the day of Upsilon Station, where he'd been mostly out of control and so terrified that that octo-centipede thing had swallowed her alive. She *had* kissed him back that day.

He cut off the thought. He was down the same rabbit hole he always fell down, and he needed to make a decision. "Fine. Be ready to go in five."

Josana grinned triumphantly, rose, and glided down the hallway like a wheeled droid who'd won a vacation getaway.

Kael's gaze met Jenny's. "A word while I get my armor?"

"Sure." She rose and followed him to his room while the others went back to work.

"Is Ryu going to kill me?" He opened the case and started the auto-assembly sequence, standing clear of her.

She shook her head. "No. It doesn't matter that much, right? I'll help take the heat. I coulda dug in my heels." She shoved her hands in her pockets and looked at the floor. "Sorry. I can't stand her."

"I know. You watch Adan like a hawk while I'm gone. Okay?"

She frowned at his intensity. "Sure, no problem. Something wrong?"

"If anything happens to him…" He stopped as the last pieces jerked into place and the helmet closed. He retracted it again.

The furrows in her brows deepened. "Don't worry, Kael. I know. He's a noncombatant. Why do you think I gave him my armor?"

Still, he hesitated one second more.

"Hey, we're real safe here. Don't worry." She stepped forward and patted his shoulder once, peering closer at him. "Is there something I should know?"

He eyed her, trying to see deeper into her soul, any hint of a hidden motive. But what did he know about judging people and their motives, especially women? He'd barely regained the skill.

"And I don't want anything to happen to him either, okay? Probably even more than you do," she added, with a chagrined smile.

Slowly, he nodded. "Oh, I know."

———

AFTER JENNY HEADED BACK to the living room, Kael shut the door and pulled out his comm. Stared at it. If he called her and she said to carry out the original orders, he'd have a mess on his hands out there. But he couldn't not call.

He punched in Ellen's address. It buzzed. The colors did their crazy swirling thing. She didn't answer.

He hung it up, let out a stream of expletives, stuck the comm in his shoulder slot, and opened the door.

Maybe the game took a lot of concentration. Maybe he was an idiot. By the seven suns, he wanted to smash something. He looked around for something, anything, but everything Persad owned was precious and fragile and obviously not his to destroy.

Why did this place have to be so damn *civilized*?

Josana was waiting, looking more like a doll than a human by the door. He grabbed the tractor out of her surprised hand and headed for the door with barely more than a grunt.

"See you all later, kiddos," her smooth voice was telling them. He felt a stab in his heart. Over or not, she hadn't given Adan even an extra goodbye. That seemed… fitting.

He marched toward the elevator tubes, relieved to hear the cracks of her boots following him. Taylor would probably tell him right about now to count to ten, take deep breaths, visualize something.

Did it count if he visualized smashing things?

Actually… that sounded good. As they drifted to the ground level, he ignored her inquisitive stare. He was busy imagining dropping her bags off the clear ledge of the Elderflower Club. He watched them explode into pieces on the pavement, narrowly missing the flyers and landers clogging traffic but perhaps sending a few of them careening into each other.

Ah. That felt better.

She had a flyer waiting and directed it to her apartment. It mostly drove itself. He tried surreptitiously calling Ellen one more time, at least to update her, but he again got no response. So he continued fuming in a similar manner the whole way there. He varied his fantasies by replacing Josana with Ostrov and her luggage with just him. Bastard.

He grabbed the tractor again as he walked her the hundred yards through a lush garden into another high-rise. Judging by the grounds, this place wasn't cheap. Either Josana or Tarana or their parents had to be loaded.

"Why did you need an escort again?"

She brushed a strand of long, white hair dramatically over her shoulder. "My sister and Dr. Taylor would never forgive you if something happened to me."

"Yeah, these bushes look real dangerous. How did someone as nice as Tarana end up with a sibling like you?" Or perhaps it wasn't a coincidence. Maybe the elder knew to marry a psychologist with her head screwed on straight after a lifetime with this piece of work.

Josana laughed a little, as if he'd complimented her, and said nothing.

They rode up the elevator lift in silence. The floors were carpeted a plush blue. Mirrored walls held up into a simulated sky on the ceiling, with plants just everywhere. Real, from the feeling he got brushing his thumb against one. He breathed a sigh of relief when she stopped at a door and pressed a finger to the pad. The door slid open.

He handed her the hand tractor. "Have a nice life."

She frowned. "You can't leave *yet*. No one's been here for months. I need you to check the apartment. What if someone broke in and is waiting for me?" She feigned fear, her attempt mocking.

He rolled his eyes.

"Besides, do you really want to go back to the news feeds?"

His jaw clenched. He couldn't exactly say that he did. She read people well. Perhaps something in common with her sister's wife after all.

"At least stay and have one drink with me."

He spoke through clenched teeth. "Fine. But that's it. Don't get any ideas."

"I'm always full of ideas. Too late."

She did, however, motion for him to enter first, so he decided to take her request seriously. Maybe she knew something he didn't. He carefully moved from room to room, starting at the left and working around. The place was modern, expensive, and spotless. And empty of intruders.

When he came back out into the central area, she was already making drinks in the kitchen. He pursed his lips. He should just walk out.

She picked up the glasses, noticing him suddenly, and faltered. For a moment, the calculation was gone from her eyes, and he could see a mixture of fear and hope and sadness there, the girl trying so hard to put up a front. And succeeding admirably most of the time, perhaps even to herself.

"Have to kill any assassins hunting me?" she said softly, struggling to pull the facade back up. He shook his head. "Does that mean you'll stay for a drink?"

"I already said I would, didn't I?"

"You were still deciding."

He snorted. He hesitated a moment longer, but the sadness in her tugged at him. "Okay."

She tilted her head toward a sleek blue couch facing the broad glass wall of the apartment. He sank down, and she joined him, handing him the drink. She sat beside him, but a nice distance away. Not too close. He leaned back, a little relieved, and took a sip. Something like gin and lime.

Finding a remote, she hit a button, and the glass shifted, clearing, to reveal a broad panorama of the city and the ocean. He caught his breath at it, sitting forward. "Wow. Now that's a view."

"Better than Persad's, isn't it?" she breathed, sounding sincerely happy to be home.

"Not everything has to be a competition." He shook his head. Capital types. "You've got a bit of the coastline, the palm trees, more of the ocean. Does that make it better?"

"You know it does." She took a long drink, a smug smile curling her lips.

They sat in silence, just watching the view, until he realized he could also hear the waves. Sea gulls. Distant voices. Sound was being piped in from the coast too. Fancy.

She leaned back and sighed heavily. "Well. We're a fine pair of rejects, aren't we?"

He snorted. "Excuse me?"

"They say all is fair in love and war. But if it's so fair, then why's it hurt so much?" She eyed her drink in her hand, as if the ice cubes were fascinating.

He shrugged. "They also say you can't always get what you want."

"But sometimes you get what you need? Yeah. That's so comforting." She swirled the cubes around. "Although, it does make you wonder..." She tilted her head, looking at him this time.

"What?"

"Maybe it's fate."

"What's fate?"

She took another long drink before setting the glass on a slender pale wood coffee table. "That we're both alone." Her voice was smooth velvet. "We've made our bets. Lost. Lived to tell the tale."

"Hmm." He frowned and took a drink of his own, staring at his hands instead of at her.

"Here. Tonight." She'd turned toward him now. Was moving closer. He didn't move.

"Together." She was beside him now.

He raised his gaze to her, and the room swirled unnaturally, shifted and spun. He stopped short and looked at the glass. Moron. He hadn't thought... Even if she scared him, he'd thought she was one of them on some level. That he could *somewhat* trust her.

The sympathy drained out of him, and he sat the glass down on the table. Hard.

"What?" she said, voice wavering, playing up the fragile and frightened card. "What's wrong?"

"Osiris, Josana? Really? Or is this something new? I'm a little out of date on my street chems." Not quite eleven years, as Theroki had their share of addicts, but most couldn't afford things like this. He shook his head to watch the images twitch and spin, and because he was disgusted. Praise the Almighty for his neural scrubbers. He opened up the arm readout and checked; it also showed airborne inhibition inhibitors. Hell, the one place it seems like you don't need a breather...

"It's—it's basically Osiris. A new twist people are into. But it's fun, I promise, especially if you just relax and let me—" She laid a hand on his armored forearm. The armor Ellen had bought him that day not so long ago.

It felt like treachery, even if it wasn't. "What is it with you?"

"How do you know so much about chems?" She was frowning. "You wouldn't know that unless—"

Oh, *now* she was interested in his less-than-savory past. "I don't know why you think this is even remotely a good idea."

"You haven't left yet," she accused.

He threw her arm off his. "That's because I'll fall over right now. That's some strong shit."

"Would that be so bad?"

"If I fell over? Yes!"

She drew back in shock at the vehemence in his voice.

"Go find yourself an Ostrov, Josana. You don't know anything about me, and you don't care to. You've got your pick of Capital. Take it." He waved at the city.

"Capital!" She waved herself, dismissively. "Oh, I might prefer it to that tin can refrigerator ship, but when it comes to men, the selection isn't much better. Here men have traded the primal for the cerebral. I know what I want. It's not that."

"I thought it was Adan."

"He was fine. I preferred you first. You know that. I made it perfectly clear." She paused for a moment. "Thanks for not mentioning it to him. His ego is bruised enough as it is."

"Uh, you're welcome."

"Adan is a smart guy, but he's still got that wild, virile streak about him. You've just got more." She shrugged, as if she were just stating facts.

"What the hell, Josana? Let it go. When this wears off, I'm leaving." Glory be, it was lessening already.

"Don't!" She leapt closer to him, and for once her guard had fully fallen, and he could see underneath.

Lonely. She was terribly, terribly lonely. She'd come back here to this big beautiful place, thinking maybe she'd be bringing someone along to thank her and worship her for her every little thing she gave him. And Adan might have done it, but she hadn't played it right. And it'd all fallen apart. And she just didn't want to be alone.

"Alone isn't so bad, Josana. Get okay with yourself alone, and then you'll find someone. I promise."

"This doesn't have to be about finding someone." Her eyes narrowed. "This can be just for fun." Her tone was hardly convincing.

He'd misjudged her, he realized. He'd thought her young and naive. But she knew exactly what she was doing, didn't she? She just didn't care.

"No, it can't. I don't do things just for fun."

"Since when?"

"Since—" Since just for fun ended up in much more than that and the temptation of dreams and family and then all of it crashing down. "It doesn't matter. Some things matter. You shouldn't do them just for fun."

"Who the frag crowned you king of morality?" She rolled her eyes, flopped back on the couch, and blew out a breath, exasperated with him. Either she hadn't spiked her own drink, or she had a much greater tolerance than he did. He was relieved to notice that his eyes barely snagged on her curves splayed out before him for more than a split second and that she didn't notice.

"Don't you care about anything deeper? Connection? What about love?"

She snorted. "Yeah, right. Love, my ass. Clever words for hiding codependence."

"If you'd been in love, you wouldn't feel that way."

"And you have been?"

Twice. He said nothing.

"Love?" She frowned, even as laughter burbled out of her, suddenly cruel and dark. "She'll never love you, you know. She doesn't know how."

He said nothing, just watched the view, the waves so very far away, and the lights of the city.

"She doesn't even know what that *is*. She's more cyborg than you are. Being raised by generals to beat sims just a little faster will do that to you. Haven't you noticed? If Xi had a body, the AI would smile more than your stone cold bitch. And Ryu's mission will always come first anyway."

Silence stretched out, tense as a live wire, before he finally spoke. "It's a good mission."

"Not the *Audacity*'s mission. *Her* mission. Revenge."

He grunted. "Slag off, Josana. You don't know her."

"Just because I'm young doesn't make me wrong." She straightened and jammed a finger at his face. "It makes me insightful. And honest. More honest than the other cunts on that ship."

He flinched at the turn of phrase. "We're done here." He rose, took a step, and found his neural scrubbers still had work to do. The chem was waning, but not fully gone.

"Wait!" She skittered after him, around him, throwing her hands up to his chest to stop him. "C'mon. Listen, Kael. Fine, you love her. Fine, that matters or something. Whatever. But what happens here tonight doesn't have to influence your petty little obsession."

Honest, my ass. "But it does. It would for me."

"I'm not going back to the ship, and even if I did, I swear to you I won't say anything. No one needs to know."

"See, that's where we're different. I would know. That's the part that matters to me." He took a step forward, into her, and she shifted back, not moving out of the way.

"Tell me the truth. If you'd never met Ryu, would you still be walking away?"

He hesitated. "There's no way to know, is there?"

She stared at him a long time before she seemed to finally admit defeat. Her hands dropped, and she took a step to the side, then another, moving toward the kitchen and starting to fix another drink. "I see."

"Good luck, Josana." He made for the door.

"I mean, I can't blame you for holding out for a woman with her own ship. But you should really reconsider putting all your eggs in one basket. Especially that basket. It's a little... cracked."

He stopped just short of the door. "She might be damaged. So am I. I'm not after her ship. It's thinking like that that makes you completely uninteresting to me."

She froze, shocked, before finding her mask again. "You're better than these honey-coated platitudes. Be honest. Don't hide the truth under bullshit. Everyone's after something."

"Everyone on Capital, maybe. By the seven suns. I see why people hate this place." But that wasn't true. He'd told her what he was after; she'd just chosen not to hear it. He turned toward the door, searched for the palm reader to open it. He found it, palmed the door open.

"The offer remains open, Sidassian."

He glared back over his shoulder. "That's not my name anymore."

She leered at him. "You'll always be a Theroki to me."

"If you really knew me, you'd know I never really was one in the first place."

———

ADAN GLANCED AT THE CLOCK. Persad was still awake, working in her study, as the local time neared midnight. Jenny was sitting in her usual armchair, still dutifully poring over feeds, but Nova and Mo had already hit the rack.

"Jen," he said softly.

Her brows furrowed though she didn't look up. "Why are you whispering?"

"Because," he snapped, at normal volume now. "Can you come over here? I need your help."

Her green eyes were suspicious, but she rose and joined him in the kitchen. "What?"

He lowered his voice now and leaned close. "I want to sneak onto Persad's computer. Make sure she's not holding out on us."

"Can you do it from here?" She pointed at his field machine.

He shook his head. "I tried. She may have paper passwords, but her home setup is fairly tight."

"So what do you need from me?"

He smiled, relieved that she didn't have a stream of objections to the idea. Teammates were supposed to be like that, he guessed.

"Once she goes to bed, let's just take a little look. Make sure she's sharing everything. Can you play lookout? I have to concentrate and might miss someone coming."

"Yeah, sure." She put her hands in her pockets. "Is that it?"

"Yep."

"Tell me when." She sat back down, eying the study door with new interest.

Finally the door swished open, and Persad wandered out, yawning. Grabbing a glass of vitabrew from the kitchen behind him, she waved to them. "Good night."

He waited a good measure, then waited a little more. Jenny eyed him, an amused smile on her lips, egging him on.

Finally, he nodded. "Let's go."

He had tinkered with her system enough to ensure they could get in without alarm—and the surveillance was conveniently malfunctioning. In fact, the ease of it made him think he ought to be worrying more about the fact that someone had done the same thing on board the *Audacity*, apparently in order to kill him.

Quietly, Jenny checked out the length of the hallway before stealing back in his direction. "She's in her room. Can't tell what she's doing, but let's go."

He palmed open the door and hurried to the desk. The keys and the seat were still warm from where she'd been working.

He tried the password from her office. And—bingo. He was in.

As he started to dig, he was aware of Jenny moving around the room, listening at the doorway, checking the opposite door that led to a small solarium. He blocked it out and tried to concentrate.

He sifted through the machine systematically, checking each typical storage location. Then the next and the next. The majority of it was cybernetic mumbo jumbo to him, drawings, diagrams, notes, pictures. Logs her prototypes had spit out. Biometric measurements of tests. There was one labeled Ryu, another Asidian, another Kentt and Persad herself. He clucked his tongue. The doctor should know experimenting on yourself wasn't the best idea.

He tried some searches for the girls' names, but nothing came back, so he went for anything pertaining to the son. Some official records, forms filled out for schools, reports... He found some photo files and clicked. An adorable bronze-skinned baby with a curl of black hair on his forehead and drool on his mouth appeared on the screen.

"Gosh, he was so cute." Jenny leaned in beside him, her shoulder brushing his. "So, finding anything? Besides potentially embarrassing baby pictures?"

"Not yet—"

A shuffling in the hallway made them both still. He quickly pulled up the hallway surveillance cam on the screen. Persad was shuffling their direction.

Jenny cursed under her breath.

Persad was a mere foot from the study door. Adan reached up, grabbed Jenny's upper arm, and pulled her down into the chair with him. When she gave him a startled look and opened her mouth to say something, he held a finger to his lips. "Play along?" he whispered.

"Oh, I get it," she whispered back. "We're not in here checking files?"

"Precisely."

She nodded and nestled close, her head on his shoulder. It felt strangely familiar. Good. How had he been ignoring that for so long?

They watched the screen as Persad wavered by the door, patting her pockets. Adan's hand hovered over the key that would lock the console and hide that he'd been snooping. He frowned at his hand, annoyed to see it was shaking slightly.

Persad passed the study, searched the kitchen—and then found her object of desire. Her glasses were perched on her head. She pulled them down, laughed to herself, and put them on her nose instead.

She headed back to her bedroom, and the door slid shut behind her.

Adan blew out a breath.

"Phew," said Jenny, straightening slightly. "I guess we did claim to be in a relationship, though, so we've got the cover."

He smiled. "So insightful that you saw this coming."

She snorted, then slumped back against him. "Yeah right." She didn't move for a while, or even lift her head. "It's late," she murmured. "You're cozy."

"I know." He didn't say anything for a bit, studying the next set of logs. He checked the deleted files next. Her familiar scent caught his nose. "You smell good too, you know."

She jerked a little in surprise. "I do? Not like cigars, I hope. Or cologne."

"Like orange blossoms." He clicked open another folder.

"Oh. My mother always had a tree in our apartment. I pipe the scent into my ship cabin. Guess it stuck around." She sounded a little embarrassed.

"My mother owned an orange grove. Before the war."

"Oh," she said softly.

"Good memories."

"Yes, me too."

It seemed to slowly dawn on her that he wasn't pushing her away. That perhaps she'd overstayed her welcome and he just wasn't saying so. She glanced around, started to straighten. "I guess I better let you finish up."

"I'm working just fine like this. And you know, Persad could come back." She froze for a second, then eased back against him. "Almost done."

"See anything?"

"Nope. She looks clean to me. If she's hiding anything, it's not in her computer."

"Why did you think she might be hiding something?"

"Because Vivaan didn't ask her for help on his little mission, but he grabbed one of her chips. We didn't think it was likely, just wanted to check. I'm liable to think he just didn't think his mother would be a fan of the idea."

"He was probably right."

"All right, that's everything." His fingers brushed over her back as he looked down at her red hair tucked against his neck, pulled back into a messy bun. She really was a small little thing.

Her face turned up to him, confusion in those green eyes. Their movements slowed to a stop, the two of them hanging still in time for a moment. And he found himself wondering, if he liked how she smelled, what about how she would taste?

Before he had time to seriously contemplate finding out, she rose and took a step away, running palms down her jumpsuit. Then, without turning back, she said quietly, "Good night, Adan."

He rose too, but she was already fleeing. "Night, Jen."

The door slid open and shut, and he was alone.

———

KAEL STEPPED into Persad's apartment and shucked his armor by the door, hoping it could make it back to its case without him. Every limb felt like it was made of lead.

The living room was empty, but a surveillance system sat on the end table by a couch. Adan was on-screen, Chayana too. Both appeared safe at the moment. Was Jenny using this? One of the others? It seemed odd to watch only Adan, if they didn't know what he knew. What Ellen had confided in him. And he'd believed that that had meant something. What a fool he was.

Maybe Jenny was hitting the head. One handheld screen was missing; whoever had set this up must have taken it with them.

Gravity felt like twice what it should've been. Of course, it wasn't; he was just exhausted. A strange chem aftereffect, perhaps. He needed something to clean the gunk out of his system more thoroughly. Sometimes the scrubbers could only handle some of the compounds, so that was probably the issue. He trudged toward the kitchen.

The door slid aside, and he stopped short. He had to remember to step forward so it didn't close automatically in his face. He stepped in just in time.

On the other side of Persad's high marble breakfast bar sat several intriguing things: Ellen, the handheld, a shot glass, and a bottle of whiskey. She looked up, and their eyes locked.

"What are you doing?" he said slowly.

She blinked. "I could say the same for you."

Her words were clear, but he didn't think that proved anything. "I'm getting some water and d-bars and going to bed," he said, struggling to shake off a defensive tone of voice.

"D-bars?"

"Yeah." Eying her, he continued his motion and headed for the cabinet where Persad had let them store some stuff. Man, that woman would be glad to be rid of them. E-bars, r-bars, d-bars... there they were. Perfect detox in one neat little package. Modern engineering for ya. He grabbed one.

"I heard you left with Josana."

He turned and frowned at her. "Because Jenny and Josana were about to start ripping out each other's hair. Neither wants to be seen together."

She looked away, down at the glass. "Oh." She refilled it and knocked another one back as he stared.

"What do you care?"

Her jaw clenched, and she poured another.

Before she could drink it, he crossed the distance and snatched it, knocking the thing back, his lips touching where hers had been in bitter mockery of a kiss.

He slammed the glass back down. Then he headed to another cabinet, got out two glasses, and filled them both with water.

Her fist clenched, she studied the marble while the water ran. "Why do you need d-bars?"

"I could ask the same of you."

She glanced down at her lap, said nothing.

"But I won't. Apparently someone thinks it's a good idea to fill their home with inhibition-reducing chems." He wouldn't mention he'd also taken a drink. Like an overly trusting idiot. He strode over to her and sat the water down forcefully between her and the shot glass. He followed it up with a second d-bar for her. He took a long drink of his own as she stared at it, then up at him. "What's she doing with illegal shit like that anyway?"

"Did they work?" she said, voice rough.

He shook his head. "I got scrubbers, remember? Damn things don't work on everything, or hardly anything half the time, but underworld chems they know how to look for. Don't exactly have medical uses."

She stared at the water. "Why don't you just go back? I can watch Adan."

"Is that a dare? Are you serious?" He set down his glass. "How drunk *are* you?"

"Not that drunk." She reached past the water and knocked another one back, eyes flashing defiantly. "But I'm working on it."

"Then you can't watch Adan." He reached for the handheld.

She snatched it out of his reach. "Xi is watching too. Go on. Go do your worst."

"Worst is right." What had gotten into her?

"*She* knows how to walk in high heels, at least."

He blinked. "Do you honestly think I care about that?"

She poured yet another drink. "Plenty of men do."

"Do *I* know how to do that?"

She looked at him like he'd gone insane. "Uh, I don't know, do you?"

"No."

A smirk crossed her features briefly. "Plenty of guys do."

He stole the glass and the drink again before she could reach her mouth with it. "My point was it's about as much of a deterrent for me as it is for you." It was good whiskey, he had to admit. He put the glass back in her hand this time.

She stilled, setting the glass on the marble in slow motion. "Deterrent to what."

He scowled. "C'mon, Ellen. Don't do that. You know exactly what."

"Kael—"

"No." He cut the air with his hand. "Look, I don't get your reasons. But I respect them. It's okay. Really. The mission is important. Case closed. *Forgotten*." He leaned forward as he threw her words back at her.

"That's not what I meant."

"Except it's not case closed with you, is it? *Why* are you getting smashed right now?"

"Why did you go against my orders and take Josana instead of ordering Jenny to do it?"

"Because both of them refused to go along, and I didn't think it mattered, and you weren't here to consult, and you didn't answer your damn comm. I tried twice."

She frowned. "My comm didn't—" She stopped short. "He must have installed a jammer. That piss-drinking monkey-eating—"

"And how about you tell me why you even bothered *issuing* those orders, huh?"

"Because you were supposed to be on Adan, not Jenny!"

"She's not going to kill him, she's fragging in *love* with him. How can everyone not see that?"

Ellen only blinked, eyes like an owl's.

"And while we're on the subject, where are your principles and reasons when that swaggering idiot comes around? *Peaks and Valleys* and sushi dinners isn't a distraction? We could be here getting attacked, and you're not even *here*."

"Ostrov?" Irritation clouded her face. "You've got to be kidding. I'm trying to get information out of him, just like he is from me. As part of our mission. He saw Cho, I'm sure of it."

"He's trying to get more than information out of you." His fingers tightened on the top edge of the back of her chair.

She groped for words. "Well, he's not going to get it!"

"Then why do you keep seeing him?"

"Information, I told you!"

He huffed and threw up his hands.

"Look, I don't give two fleas on a donkey's ass about him." She stopped for a long moment, breathing hard. "Did you think—even with you—that I would—" She stopped short, fell silent.

"Even with me *what*?" he demanded.

"This is hard for me, okay?" She met his gaze, eyes wild.

"What is?"

"Kael, after everything I gave up to—"

The air split with the sound of glass shattering. A sudden breeze whipped at her hair, pulling toward the living room.

He was ducking as quickly as she grabbed the handheld, but shots were already flying. Ballistics bounced past. Why the frag did he take off his armor?

She, of course, was still wearing hers. The *zip-crash* of ballistics rang out, the far kitchen cabinets suddenly punched through with gunfire.

Pain exploded in his left shoulder, close to the collarbone. Shit. Another bullet ricocheted, buzzing past his temple in a streak of fire. He fell back against the bar and slid down.

She was crouched beside him, checking the handheld. He couldn't see it, partially because of the angle and partly because somehow blood was running into his eye. He squeezed a hand to the side of his head. "Did you see how many?" she barked.

"Drecks, agh." He groaned. "No, I was *distracted*."

Pain shot into her expression, and an edge of panic, and he regretted the words instantly. With his better arm he reached over and hit her helmet retract, and it rose up around her. More shattering came from out in the living room, behind him now. More gunfire. More than one hostile, that much was for sure.

She pulled the pistol from her leg compartment and edged up to the top of the bar. He assumed she fired, although the laser was silent so he couldn't tell. Cursing and wild thrashing erupted near the living room windows.

God, Persad was *really* going to be glad to be rid of them at this rate. What was it with these people and high-rise windows? Did they have a death wish? Or was it just the least secure place in a building like this? Ellen sank back down beside him and started rummaging in a cabinet. The room spun strangely, her figure shifting like the Osiris had suddenly regained a foothold. What the hell?

When she spoke again, her voice was much calmer than her eyes through the clear visor. "I thought 'distracted' was just a bad excuse."

"It is, you coward." His voice was like rocks in a centrifuge. "But the blood in my eye is making me come around."

Nova shuffled backward into their area. "Six hostiles remaining, Commander, and—" She sported Kael on the ground. "Shit." She bent to her comm. "Jenny, get to the kitchen ASAP."

"I'm with Persad, they're closing in here. Fell back to the study, returning fire. I will when the path is cleared."

Ellen cursed. "Go help her."

"I'm helping her from right here, dammit," Nova shot back. As if to prove her point, a sharp cry echoed from outside, followed by a thud and another window crashing.

Ellen finally found what she was looking for in the cabinet and pressed a handful of kitchen towels to his shoulder, then another to his temple. "God, they didn't even have the decency to give you clotting nanos. Jesus."

He gave up trying to hold the wound, slumping back against the bar and letting her take over. "Too expensive for overpriced security guards, I guess."

"That's not what you were."

"No. It's not what I am now." Thanks to you, he thought silently.

"Not just thanks to me."

"Did I say that out loud?"

"Stay with me, *Asidian*. Jenny!"

"Jesus, he's bad with names. Jesus, you have me saying Jesus."

"Stay with me or you're on ship-guarding duty indefinitely."

"Please no." In spite of her threat, he was fading. The spinning was worse now. He hadn't thought the bullet had nicked him that hard. Or was it the cocktail of Osiris and whiskey and gin and... He shut his eyes. Something was not right. "Not ship duty. Anything but that."

"Relax, we got bigger problems right now." The pressure of her hands reassured him, easing him further into the blackness.

"Three hostiles remaining," Nova reported, somewhere far away.

"I want to be with *you*. Not the ship."

"I know, Kael. I know."

"Don't leave me..." Behind, he meant to say, but he wasn't sure he said it. Don't leave me behind.

"I won't."

CHAPTER TWELVE

"WHAT IS YOUR NAME?"

The dead eyes of the man tied to the chair stared straight ahead, not reacting. Not even blinking. He wore completely nondescript, generic black fatigues, with no signs, insignia, or even labels from their maker. His boots were almost immaculately clean. His head was shaved. Ellen hadn't stripped him yet, but there were no visible tattoos. He had the physique—and anonymous appearance—of a competent soldier or even a hit man and not a single identifying item on him. Except one thing.

"Who do you work for?" she demanded now.

Ellen held his breather helmet in her armored hands, turning it this way and that, even though she'd long exhausted it of any clues. There was only one: the blue cephalopod stamped into the metal on one side. Why anyone would label them all the same was anyone's guess. Why were they blue instead of white? Why indeed.

Why did everything lead back to her? Or was it *them*?

"What were you doing invading this residence?" she drawled again. It might have been the tenth time she'd asked. Or the hundredth.

"Nothing." Jenny looked up from the tablet. "Readouts showing little to no neurological activity. It's surprising he's breathing."

"Where the hell is security? Shouldn't they be up here wondering what is happening, with all the glass and bodies flying past a good hundred stories of windows?"

Jenny pursed her lips. "Definitely, especially in an expensive building like this."

Ellen bent to stare directly into the man's blank eyes. They were brown, with little flecks of gold and a fairly thick black ring around the outside. Not especially dilated. There had been a human here once. A man, presumably with hopes and dreams, or at the very least food preferences, memories, old grudges. Somehow, all of it was gone. The eyes just stared. "It's like they switched him off," she whispered.

Jenny nodded. "He's a vegetable, if you ask me. I can't get much from blood here, though. Could be a drug of some sort. We could learn more if we were on the ship."

Straightening, she slapped him straight across the face with the full force of her arm. The man's head whipped to the side and a little down. And stayed there. He didn't react to pain whatsoever.

The chair under Jenny skidded out as she jumped hastily to her feet. "Hey!"

Ellen held up both palms to signify she was done.

"Whoa—you're not normally so brutal, Commander."

"Just testing a theory. Seeing if he'd react." She forced a deep breath and was pissed to find it shaky. "Sorry. I'm a little off my game."

"Kael's gonna be fine."

She shot a glare at the floor. Jenny thought she was angry at the man for being one of the ones to shoot Kael, and maybe there was a little truth in that. But what was really getting under her skin was something far worse—the sinking feeling that Kael had narrowly missed this fate himself. How many people were out there, switched off like this?

It didn't make sense, except in the horrified part of her mind where it did.

"It's just a little damage to his scrubber unit that made it go wonky so quickly. It hadn't had time to dump the shit it had hoarded in there. What were all those drugs doing in his system anyway?"

"Josana, apparently. From what he said, they weren't his idea. They were in the air in her apartment."

Jenny's eyes widened. "Now I'm doubly glad I didn't go. Sorry, by the way."

Ellen waved her off. "She's out of our hair. We've got bigger problems to deal with." She pointed at the man and his still turned head. "He wasn't like this during the attack."

"No, he wasn't. He clearly had some ambulatory capability at the very least when he scaled down the building and crashed into the windows."

"How did they break the windows?"

"Probably had the right equipment. Not that hard to get if you know where to look."

Ellen smiled slightly to herself, thinking of the time she'd told Kael nearly the same thing, and bent to study the man again. She turned his chin back to a more natural, comfortable position. He remained there, like a wire doll.

The door chimed.

"Come in," she said. The door slid open to reveal Adan, Nova hovering at his shoulder.

"Found something." Adan stepped inside and dropped a black rectangular pouch beside Jenny's computer. He flipped it open.

"That's an inspector's ID," Jenny said quickly.

"Udo Trynkei," Adan read aloud. "Inspector, illegal substances division."

"Do you think it's real?" Jenny breathed.

Adan shook his head. "Persad's clean. Real law enforcement wouldn't come through windows. Unless they do things differently here?" He raised his eyebrows. "Most civilized places, they show up at the door with papers. Uncivilized places, they show up at the door with guns. And they don't knock."

"I'm suddenly feeling very uncivilized," Nova muttered.

"Windows are only on Capital?" Jenny smiled. "We *are* special here.

In a bad way."

"Windows are for the creative." Adan flipped through the wallet, but it didn't reveal much else. "And for Udo Trynkei."

"So if he's not working for Capital police," Nova asked, "then who is he working for?"

"Who do you think?" Ellen shook her head. "My money's on Arakovic. Using the kid to get to the telepaths *and* his mom. That's low."

"Then why the demand for the schematics?" Jenny asked.

Adan put the ID back in his pocket. "Maybe it was just a decoy to keep her in place for the attack."

"Commander and crew, I have some information that may be of use." Xi's voice piped up from Jenny's tablet.

"She's everywhere," Nova stage-whispered toward Ellen. "It's creepy."

"It's useful," Ellen grunted. "What, Xi?"

"I have referenced Kael's notes from yesterday evening's altercation with our person of interest, Vivaan Persad. Armor cam footage was not available, so I cannot be certain, but—"

"Spit it out, Xi."

"I am trying to, Commander. I believe Vivaan Persad identified his Capital law-enforcement handler to be none other than Udo Trynkei. Please confirm with Kael when he is able, but my certainty of this is at least eighty percent."

"Thanks."

"Shit, so the kid is getting played?" Nova said, giving her gum a crack.

Ellen repressed a wince. "That's what Etrianala Kentt suspected. This would certainly bolster that theory."

"Isn't it kind of stupid to break in here with ID on you?" Jenny asked.

"Maybe they didn't think they could lose," Adan said, voice dark. "If Persad had been alone?"

Ellen bent and peered at the man again. "Or maybe they weren't thinking so well. And maybe we shouldn't be talking about this in front of him."

"Him?" Jenny's brow furrowed. "He's not hearing us, trust me."

"*He* is not who I'm worried about." Ellen scowled down at the man. "Does he have a chip interface, by any chance?"

Jenny squinted back at the tablet, paged through a few things. "Yeah. How'd you know?"

Ellen rubbed her chin. "Wild guess. Jenny, go get Persad and tell her I want one of her chip prototypes installed in this guy. You got anything to sedate him?"

"You want him more sedated than *this*?" Jenny held out a hand at the man.

"I want him unconscious. His eyes are still open."

"Whatever you say, Commander. I'll get something, give me a minute." She hurried out.

Ellen turned to Nova. "Get Mo and find something large you can put this guy in to make him look like luggage. I don't care what. Smuggle him onto the ship."

Adan raised his eyebrows. "Isn't that going to be tricky with customs down there?"

Nova grinned, popping her gum manically now. "Sounds fun."

"Isn't that... kidnapping?"

"Yes," said Ellen. "So don't get caught."

Nova thumped a hand on Adan's shoulder. "Don't look so concerned. Back on St. Narcisa, I may have acquired a little experience with the activity."

Adan's eyebrows shot even higher. "Kidnapping?"

She rolled her eyes. "Smuggling. What's a man or a melon?" Grinning, she headed out the door.

He turned and stared at Ellen. "I thought she was from Zega III."

"She is. Zega III was originally a Vatican colony until organized crime stole much of the control. I believe the domes are named for saints from the Movers' original nations."

"So much more colorful than 'failed farming colony,' " he said, smiling. His home world, Bantilla, had been the object of desire for big farming megacorps—until some pirates politely suggested that the outsystem wasn't the best place for doing reliable business.

Ellen shrugged and folded her arms across her chest as she leaned back a little, studying their lone captive. "Neither of you had it easy."

"And it's not a contest anyway. So what now?" He put his hands in his pockets, his gaze, like Ellen's, coming to rest on the man's dead-eyed stare.

"Now we—" She bit off the words as the door chimed. "There's our security. Stay in here. Lock this door and see if you can make it seem broken from the outside." Ellen strode out into the hallway. Jenny and Chayana were headed toward her, the doctor carrying what looked like another chip but with her eyes on the door. Ellen held up a palm, drew the pistol, readied it, and eased up silently to the door display, hitting the view display button.

But it wasn't security after all. A young man fidgeted on the view screen.

"Vivaan!" Chayana dashed forward toward the door. Ellen bid it to open but kept her weapon ready.

He stumbled inside, a hand on his shoulder.

"Are you all right?"

He stared around the apartment. "Are *you*? When I was attacked, I worried—" He stopped short. "I see I was right. They came here too."

"We have something to show you," Ellen said briskly. "Adan, cancel that lock! We need to show Mr. Persad what you found."

"Working on it," came Adan's voice, muffled by the door.

Vivaan's gaze met hers, as if realizing she was there for the first time. "You're... the woman from last night. Who bested the mech. From Elderflower. Where's your friend?"

"He got shot defending your mother." The words escaped before she'd really processed them, and the bitter edge surprised her.

Vivaan staggered a step back, and only then did she realize there was red blood hidden under the fingers clutching his shoulder. "Is he —is he—"

"He'll be fine. Thanks to our medic." She jutted a chin at his shoulder, and Chayana honed in like a guided missile, gasping. "Need someone to see to that?"

He nodded, numbly.

"Tell me," she said. "Did you see any security on the way up? Were they at their posts?" She needed to know if they'd been taken out—or bought out. Were they passed out somewhere, drugged? Or reporting that Vivaan had just taken the elevator up here?

"No, actually. It seemed odd. Samesh is always downstairs at the desk this time of night."

She blew out a little of her tension in a long breath, with a little guilt that Samesh's loss might be her gain. At least that meant they didn't need to *immediately* evacuate. Hopefully. They needed time to get their captive out unnoticed. No matter what she'd said, that wasn't going to be easy.

Apparently finally free of his own locks, Adan marched out of their interrogation room, the wallet in his hand. He held it out to Vivaan. "We suspect this means something to you?"

Vivaan took it with his free hand and let it fall open, eyes wide like saucers. Cursing, he met Ellen's gaze. "Kentt was right. She tried to tell me, but I thought—"

"What did you do to your arm?" Chayana cried, catching sight now of the inflamed flesh beyond his wrist cuff.

"Mother, I can explain. It was important, and I didn't want to implicate you."

She gestured at the apartment. "And that worked out so well."

He let out a sigh of frustration before training a determined gaze on Ellen. "We must talk to Kentt. Tell her what happened. Warn her. I know she knows more than she is telling me about the whereabouts of those women."

"The chip blocks telepathy, not gives it to you," Chaya chided.

"Yeah, that's a different one," Ellen muttered. "I don't recommend it."

Both Persads stopped and turned to eye her.

She cleared her throat. "Adan, get Etrianala Kentt on the line, if you can. I know it's the middle of the night, but try. Use this." She found the card in her suit belt and handed it to him.

"On it."

When Adan was gone, Ellen pinned them both with a sharp stare. "Mr. Persad, I came to your mother with an offer. It extends to you too. I think it's about time we discussed it."

———

WHILE JENNY KEPT watch and Nova and Mo planned their kidnapping, Adan tried to sleep. But he mostly spent the night tossing and turning, more than a little disturbed. Aside from dreams about getting shot at in orange groves, other things taunted him.

Guilt, for one, that he'd barely been broken up with Josana for a day before these... other thoughts... had intruded. He'd also accidentally kept that packet of Osiris—how idiotic he hadn't forced her to take it back while she was still around. Now what was he supposed to do with it? He couldn't leave it here and get either of the Persads in trouble. And he really didn't think the inspectors were going to be as morally and legally flexible as Josana assured him they would be. He could flush it. About as easily as he could flush ten thousand credits— which was to say, not easily at all.

None of his calls to Kentt had been returned either, although he'd left messages. With who exactly and what they'd do with the information made him nervous as well.

Beyond all that was the strange timing of the attack last night. He didn't want to think about it, but the timing niggled at him, like a splinter that wouldn't come out. The minute Josana was gone, the strike team showed up. Coincidence?

He didn't believe she could be behind such a thing—even if she *was* some kind of chem lord. But he could see her trying to make a credit off the situation, confident that none of them were really in danger because Ryu's team was good enough to repel any attackers.

Tell that to Kael's shoulder, though. Except she had insisted he accompany her, and not Jenny. Hmm. Had she expected him not to be there? He didn't want to think about that.

Overall, though, they *had* easily repelled the strike team. The gaping open windows meant they all needed to relocate, and shortly, although he wasn't sure to where. Another attack team wouldn't even have to break the glass this time. And it was also possible that Josana didn't care if anyone got hurt on either side. That theory stung a little, but that didn't make it untrue.

It was still early morning when he sat up in bed, the sun barely breaking over the waves. A breeze blew through the rooms from the broken windows, and he had to admit it was both pleasant and a little anxiety-inducing. A weird breeze on a ship was a sign of a huge problem and decidedly not as pleasant.

He couldn't sleep anymore. Or toss and turn and pretend to sleep. He grabbed his machine from the floor beside him and logged on.

It didn't take long to track her location.

He stared at the screen, then the drawer where he'd dumped the chems like they were fire in his hand. If he got caught taking them to her, he might never see another sunrise again, he'd be so lost in prison somewhere. Maybe he should take them to Tarana, but that still involved keeping it around.

No, he wanted one last word with Josana.

And in spite of his promise to Kael, he was going alone.

———

ADAN CAUGHT a flyer and directed it again to the bakery district, a spot near the mangabrew place she'd taken him. The early morning had been on his side, and Nova and Mo appeared to have already begun their "smuggling" mission, so it had been all too easy to slip out the door without a sound or a word to anyone. Xi was watching, of course, at least from his machine that was now perched on his lap, but if she wanted to object, she hadn't said anything.

He directed the flyer to a landing spot near the cafe and got to work. Breaking in didn't feel too good, especially as Josana's words about "illegal" and "questionable" activities floated back to him. But he wouldn't have gotten this far on computers if he were going to let a little guilt stop him. He needed to know. Ten minutes max, and he'd be in.

In actuality, it took more like five. Her appointments were less protected than the rest of the data, and so he started there. He ran through the hours to this one. A breakfast meeting with a certain M. Banabi. Set to start in twenty minutes.

He clucked his tongue. "What so important you need to be this early?" Also... Banabi. The name sounded familiar. "Xi, can you check out this name in our databases?" He of course didn't have the most sensitive data on his machine. It irked him to even say it aloud in the flyer.

"Marco Banabi," Xi announced. "Residence: Capital. Known trader of sensitive information. Neutral, no specific legal or factional alliances. Works with all factions. No known enemies or bounties."

He swore under his breath.

"Adan, while we are speaking, may I ask you a question?"

He hesitated for a moment, then shrugged. He could always not answer, he supposed. As if he could be rude to Xi. Unlikely. "Sure."

"What are you doing?"

Laughter escaped from him in surprise. She sounded deeply intrigued. "Aside from breaking into Josana's computer?"

"Yes. I am working on my models, but you have begun to deviate. I do not have much data, so I fear my 'love' model is faulty somehow."

"Oh, hell, Xi—if you're basing a love model on us, it's probably awful."

"It is a very rough model. Love, lust, and attraction behavior appears to be highly erratic. It is a prototype at best."

His smile softened. "It's complicated, what can I say? But you're right. This isn't love."

"I thought you wanted to see Josana again because of your mating relationship. Even if it has come to an end. The biological imperative is strong. This all seems moderately logical."

"Agreed. Good hypothesis. But that's not what I'm doing. I"—and now he hit a key to begin the next unlocking sequence—"am breaking into her computer."

"I know that. The question is why."

"A few things. But most importantly, it strikes me as odd that the attack came so quickly after Josana left."

"You hypothesize the two events could be related?" There was a pause. "You believe she shared the location of Persad with someone?"

"Yes."

"But why would she do that? She has seemed apathetic toward the scientist. Bored, even."

"Money." He pulled up the next data-gathering program and kicked it off.

"I see. So this is not data for the love relational model at all."

"Unless you are adding something to do with bad breakups."

"Bad what?"

"Let's talk more when I'm back on the ship."

"Excellent point, Adan. I have completed an additional search and not found much more on Marco Banabi except that Capital inspectors believe him to be regularly armed and consider him dangerous. And that he is flagged not to be arrested because of two links to specific politicians. Would you like details on those politicians?"

He blew out a breath. He was feeling less and less guilty poking around by the second. That figured, for this place. "No, that's okay. What we need to know is..." He leaned closer to the computer as he spoke, pausing to find the file-access stream. Time to dig deeper. ". . . what Josana is hoping to offer him."

In the end, though, he didn't have to dig that deep. The latest file accessed was a music stream. The second-most recently accessed file was a spreadsheet. He popped it open, battling a bit of weak encryption on the way.

His blood drained out of him as he looked at the long list of numbers before him.

He knew them, not as a hacker but as a pilot. Coordinates. And not just any coordinates. The ones the *Audacity* had traveled to over the last week, two weeks...

He scrolled down frantically. How far did it go back?

He caught himself. That didn't matter. No time to stop and look.

Time to obliterate and not leave a trail.

It took another four minutes, one to isolate the file and other similar data, another three to plant a worm to seek out and destroy similar data on the rest of her networks when she got on them.

And one more to sit and fume in anger. How could she? Sharing that information could doom him, her sister—everyone. Even Xi.

He climbed out of the flyer, waved it off, and headed straight for her.

She spotted him approaching with wide eyes, but she said nothing as he slid into the seat across from her. Her features hardened, eyes narrowing, as she read his.

"What are you doing here?" He couldn't keep the hostility from his words.

"Just a mangabrew and meeting a friend." She delicately waved at the small, elegant cup of blackness as evidence.

"A friend, huh? Then you won't mind if I join you." He smiled tightly.

"Actually, I would. It's over, Adan. Your choice, remember?"

"I'm regretting it less and less."

She rolled her eyes. "Get over it. The jealous ex isn't a good look on you."

"Neither is 'greedy traitor' on you."

She stilled, her fingertip frozen on the far edge of the mug's small, round handle.

He folded his arms across his chest. "That data broker you're meeting with? He's not going to be happy you wasted his time."

"What are you talking about?" But it came out less a question and more a demand.

"Coordinates? Really?"

Her mouth fell open for a second, then snapped shut as she scowled at him.

"I'm on that ship. Your sister is on that ship."

"So?"

"How can you be so, so…"

"No one will know what to do with that data. It's old news. Harm-less. You won't retrace those stops. And I'll be long gone with the money."

"There's plenty that could be retraced. Supply caches, neutral safe havens. And that's just the start of it."

"Not my problem."

He scowled. "Guess not. It also links you to the ship. Don't you realize that makes you a target?"

"I'm already a target. And don't you think half this data is out there already from the shipments I sent out?"

"I seem to have some brand-new ideas for Ryu and Xi on shipboard security."

She rolled her eyes. "You're blowing this out of proportion, Adan. But you know, it's good you stopped here, cause it's really helping me see that you were right. You *don't* fit in here."

"I know. But that's beside the point. You got a new problem, cause you won't have the data you promised your fancy new friend."

Her face went white, even as her eyes flashed black with anger.

"Have a nice manga-whatever." He stood and turned to walk out.

"Hey Adan?"

"Yeah."

"*Red Dwarf Commander* is a stupid game, anyway. And a waste of time. And all that coffee is going to make you a twitchy old man."

Low blows. He winced in place, stopping for a moment without turning. And then he kept going. He didn't want to be there when her friend arrived, no matter what she said.

His rage didn't keep him from pulling out his machine on a bench a block away and reconnecting to watch the shit storm go down, however. She logged on, tried to access the file, then restore it, only for the worm to delete it more and more thoroughly. Only when he saw her log off, then exit the cafe in a huff, did he shut his computer again and lean back against the wall.

He watched her flyer pull away, then took a deep breath. He closed his eyes and felt the cheery early morning sun on his skin. Something about the moment felt peaceful, calm. Just. He'd have to go back later and look for anything else she could have that was potentially dangerous. But his instincts had been right. He'd stopped her just in time.

Gradually, he opened his eyes and glanced around. Someone somewhere was staring at him.

Jenny. She stood across the street, hands on her hips, scowling. When he caught her eye, she started toward him. A strand of hair had fallen out of her bun, and she blew it out of her face with a huff.

"Where the hell have you been?" she demanded as she reached him.

"Right here all along." He patted the bench beside him for her to sit, but she shook her head.

"You turned off your machine's tracker. Xi had to tell me where you were."

God, rookie move on his part. He should've sworn Xi to secrecy. "I had some personal things to take care of."

She rolled her eyes and scoffed down the street after Josana. "Yeah, I saw. You done?"

"Yes. Very, very done." He smiled serenely at her. The concern they all threw up—it suddenly seemed touching, rather than annoying.

"Fine, c'mon. Time to head back. You're making Xi nervous."

"What about you? Why'd you come looking?"

"Nervous? No, you're just pissing me off. Go live your Capital fairy tale already." She waved in Josana's general direction.

He shook his head and just smiled. "How did you get here?"

"I've got a flyer waiting."

"Great. Let's go."

"Xi insisted I bring your armor too. Get in and put it on. One of us has a hole in his shoulder, don't forget."

He hid quiet laughter as he slid inside and she started programming the flyer to head back to Persad's. "You wouldn't want me to die before you could collect on your bet."

Her anger melted into a smile, but she didn't look up from the flyer console. "You're damn right. You could get shot at yet."

"Let's not wish for it, shall we?"

She patted his shoulder, the touch lingering a tad longer than strictly necessary. "I'm not."

———

KAEL WOKE UP AND BLINKED, squinting at an unfamiliar ceiling. Where the hell was he? A shiny, silver, embossed patterned covered the surface above him. Slowly, he turned his head, relieved to discover that it didn't hurt terribly. A skin-glue bandage covered his temple now. The wall beside him was covered with books, on shelves of wood.

He looked down at himself. His shoulder had a massive medkit working on it, and he was lying on Persad's dark green couch. Right. Her study.

At a faint tapping sound on his other side, he slowly rotated his face the other direction.

Ellen sat a few feet away. A gaming table lit up the mostly dark room, gold and blue pieces sliding back and forth. She would move the gold, then the blue would move on their own. He narrowed his eyes. Ostrov and his games.

She must've sensed him, as she turned to look. "You're awake. How do you feel?"

"Better. The room isn't spinning."

"The bullet hit your scrubbers. They dumped everything they'd cleaned up all at once."

He tried to muster words but just ended up groaning.

"Feeling that good, huh? Well, we defeated the bad guys, we found Vivaan, and if we can crack the location of those missing women out of Etrianala Kentt, we may be able to finally get out of this hell hole." She played as she spoke, not looking at him. "Oh, and we also took a captive and are kidnapping him. Nova and Mo haven't left with their parcel yet, but they should be going in a few minutes."

"Don't forget—can't leave without winning your game," he muttered.

"Oh, no. We can leave before that. He claims this game takes weeks."

"Is that so," Kael grumbled.

"No. I'm about to beat him… right about now."

Almost as if he'd heard the comment, the wall display suddenly swirled to life. Ostrov calling.

Ellen made a disgusted noise in the back of her throat that gratified him more than was probably reasonable. She hit a button on the desk. Ostrov's face filled the vid screen.

"Why are you calling?" she said, face and voice blank.

"I want to see your face when I win."

Kael suppressed a shudder, not sure if Ostrov could see him or not. The man had a vicious gleam to his eyes, and an even worse grin.

"Then you're going to be sorely disappointed, because you're not going to win." Ellen turned her gaze away from him and back to the game.

"That's what you always say."

She smirked faintly. "That's because I always win."

They played in silence for several minutes, the tension only increasing like water reaching a boil.

"C'mon. Let me see a smile. I'm sure it looks good on you."

Kael clenched a fist, and might even have been tempted to say something, except that Ostrov's voice seemed to be shaking. With rage? Or with fury at his own impotence? Kael hoped so.

"Why would I do that?" She glanced at him only briefly to speak, keeping her eyes on the game.

"I've been taught that it's the habit of fine ladies to smile as they are losing to save face. Or perhaps distract a gentleman from his game so that he fumbles a move."

"Is that so."

"Yes."

"That's not really my style. Perhaps you'd care to try it yourself, though." She made a sequence of three moves, then turned to him.

"Excuse me?"

She pointed at the board. "Feel like smiling?"

He stared for a moment before a bit of laughter bubbled out of him, quiet and amazed at first, then louder. "Well, well. Indeed I do feel like smiling. You have not been oversold."

"That's because I'm not for sale." Her eyes were steel and narrowed at him.

Kael had to admit that most of the things she said could be loosely translated into "I hate you," and that listening to it all was very satisfying.

"Now." She leaned forward, toward the screen. "I played. The information you promised."

"Not yet."

"I played your game," she said, voice rising.

"Fine, fine." He waved a hand at her, as if she were being silly. "Let's talk Arakovic."

Ellen froze, and something in Kael's gut dropped through the couch and into the floor. "What about her?"

"I can get you a location. But I can also get you the ship name and its serial. For that, I'm going to need more."

"Like *what*?"

"I wanted to be sure you were what they said you were. If I give you her location, I have to be sure you'll take her out, or she'll trace this back to me."

"And you thought a game would verify that?"

"It was the closest I could try. Isn't that what you trained on in the academy?"

"Not on *Peaks and Valleys*."

"Well, of course not. The game didn't exist then. So—do you want the ship name and serial or are you going to settle for a fleeting location?"

"That location probably changes every week. If not faster. You promised evergreen."

"Did I?" He yawned. "Well, the deal's changed."

She glowered at him.

"The name of her ship does not change every week."

"Fine. What do you want?"

"Something Arakovic wants that I believe you have. Or, I should say some*one*. Although I suppose if you go after her, you'll have the chance to get back anyone she might try to take from you."

"She's not taking anyone. Spit it out, Ostrov."

"Crispin, please, darling."

"Slag off."

"You are such a charmer. You want the serial? The unchangeable ident of the ship of your greatest enemy?" He grinned.

"You're enjoying this."

"I am, in fact. I like seeing you squirm. I could see a whole lot more of it. But if you want that ident, turn over to my custody a certain member of your team."

She frowned. "Who?"

"Did you know Dr. Arakovic is looking for a certain Kael Sidassian?"

Kael shot up in his seat. What the...

Ostrov continued. "He bears a *striking* resemblance to your lieutenant. Asidian, was it? Not very creative." He shook his head with a snakelike smile.

"You sniveling little—" She started from her seat, as if to attack the wall display.

"Dr. Arakovic has posted a bounty on him, a very high one in fact. Not even yours is higher." He grinned wide now, baring his teeth.

"Why?" she demanded.

That made no sense. Why would Arakovic even know who he was, let alone want him? And more than Ellen? Who would have guessed she wanted Ellen at all? Where were these bounties posted? By the seven suns, maybe the room *was* spinning now.

Ostrov steepled his fingers. "I don't presume to ask the good doctor questions."

"She's anything but good."

"Get me the Theroki, and I'll get you Arakovic."

She cut the air like a knife with one hand. "No deal."

"Now don't be—"

"Not happening." She slammed a palm onto the desk and cut the connection.

Kael stared at her, wide-eyed from his seat. She was slumped onto flat palms on the tabletop, tension draining out of her. He couldn't remember ever seeing her like that. So… defeated.

"What if we—"

"No," she snapped.

"But if he has the information—" He started to wave a hand, then grunted when pain kicked in under the medkit and the painkillers. Jenny had said he'd lost a lot of blood. Clearly he should lie back down. But he couldn't, not now.

Ellen turned to face him, eyes determined. "We will find another way to Arakovic."

"He knows." He jabbed a finger at the wall display. "You've never been this close."

"I know." She shook her head and pinched the bridge of her nose.

"This might be your chance. We should try to bargain with him. Maybe we can set a trap, or I can fight my way out, or—"

"No."

Something about the word stopped him short. There was chaos, desperation in it, not her usual control. Her eyes had that same wild, helpless look they'd had just last night, when he'd come back from Josana's. A conversation they hadn't finished, he realized suddenly.

"She already took too much from me. I won't give her you." Her words rang as final as the closing of a colony ship.

He could only stare as she marched away from him, out the door.

———

ELLEN HEADED STRAIGHT from Kael to the Persads, stabbing the door chime on Chayana's lab door with entirely too much force. The door slid open.

"Yes, Ellen?"

Dr. Persad was hunched over her son's arm as he reclined in her fancy chair, only now his arm was propped up. Huh, the arms adjusted, go figure. She looked near to fixing the damage he'd done with his makeshift arm port.

"How are you holding up, Vivaan?" She should make conversation. It was what normal people who weren't seething with desire for revenge did.

He smiled weakly. "Mother is fixing up all the damage I did."

"I promised him he could have a real port, when this has settled down and it's safe to do the operation." Chayana spoke without looking up.

"Good to hear you're hanging in there. I'm sorry to rush you, but Sergeant Morales should be ready soon to leave for our ship. Have you made your decision yet?"

Now Chayana did straighten and looked to her son, as if it was his ultimate decision. Perhaps her mind had already been made up. Vivaan took a deep breath, his eyes trained on his mother's. He didn't look afraid exactly, just nervous, like someone born planetside taking their first step onto a space ship. Belatedly, she wondered if that was exactly what it was. Capital seemed so metropolitan, it hadn't occurred to her that neither of them might have ever been in space. Or even have much idea what the life would be like.

She wasn't explaining it to them now, so hopefully they'd done their research.

Vivaan finally turned to meet Ellen's gaze. "We will do it. We have packed. What do you need us to do?"

"Excellent. I'm glad to hear it. I'll send Sergeant Morales to arrange things. You can go with her. I'll try one more time to get in touch with Ms. Kentt this afternoon. She hasn't returned my three previous calls. If I can't, we'll continue to try to contact her from off planet. I am confident you'll be safer there. And free to continue your work."

Chayana nodded. Vivaan glanced at the floor.

"*Both* of your work," Ellen added. "There's no reason to give up the trail on those girls either. We'll continue to do what we can."

Faint surprise in his eyes, Vivaan nodded. Ellen had a suspicion that once they were acclimated to the ship and its real mission, Vivaan would find a lot more to challenge him than his current quest. Aside from being male and having almost zero combat skills, he was a pretty good fit for the ship. Could have been worse.

She left them, dropped her instructions with Nova, and gave the team one final check. If anyone could sneak a living man in a box off Capital, it was Nova and Mo. As she headed back to the study to check on Kael, she paused in the wrecked living room.

No security had ever come to inquire. Glass still sprinkled the floor. The ledge was a fragging death trap. At the very least, someone should put up some boards or something.

But no. They'd leave instead.

First the Persads would go with Nova and Mo. And then, with luck, the last four of them, with a few more answers to questions in their pockets.

She slowed to a stop near the overturned armchair Jenny had favored. Sunlight filled the room as the cold air danced around her, and a strange sense of time swept her, of knowing the past. And also the future.

There had been moments when the chase after Arakovic had seemed distant, perhaps bordering on a ridiculous obsession. Recently, there'd been times when her quest had felt closer. More real. But nothing had felt quite as close as this, not since she'd deserted, anyway.

That woman had attacked her closest friends. Her trusted colleagues. Her identity. Her very sanity. She had *loved* her life, then, in the Union. She couldn't have known this one would have been better. She wouldn't have answered Doug's call if it had come then.

But one betrayal had destroyed everything. A crash, an operation, and nothing was the same. It hadn't collapsed in one fell swoop, but over time. Until she walked a blade's edge. And she *hadn't* successfully walked it. She'd faltered, and fallen.

And Dremer and Doug had caught her.

At times she wondered if she should give up this chase, let the past go. She did much more for people now than pursuing Arakovic could do alone. Intellectually, she knew revenge was often a terrible idea that only extended one's trauma. Knowing that didn't change anything. What new plots the doctor could be up to niggled at her, and that idea had drawn her on, the hope of preventing what had happened to her from happening to someone else.

And these days, she knew. It was definitely still happening. It wasn't just paranoia. Arakovic was out there—hiring Enhancer labs, enchanting young telepaths, hijacking Theroki ships. Making mindless zombie minions somehow? Certainly worse things they hadn't discovered.

To what end, Ellen could only guess.

And now her sights were on Kael.

Somehow, in spite of Ellen's best efforts to save him and Doug's best efforts to hide him, Arakovic had taken an interest in Kael, of all the people in all the stars.

And now this quest felt very personal and very close indeed.

The woman had to be stopped. And to do it, Ellen would start with learning how to find her.

She turned away from the window and the sparkling sea and headed to put on her armor.

———

TO JENNY'S SURPRISE, it wasn't until the flyer faltered and bumped into the flyer beside it, scraping a dent into the next one six inches wide, that Adan's good humor abruptly faded. She'd been trying to ruminate on what the heck had gotten into him but hadn't come up with any theories before the collision.

Jenny swore. "Stupid things. Now we have to wait for inspectors to check us all over and—"

He froze.

She saw the change in him, the sudden fear. "What? What is it?"

"There was something I meant to give back to Josana. And then I got distracted by something important and forgot."

"So?" Jenny shrugged. "Ship it to her."

He shook his head. "Not this."

The blare of the inspector siren was already approaching as a chill shot through her. "Oh my God, it's something illegal isn't it?"

He nodded. "Apparently she's more chem dealer than medical student."

Jenny's eyes widened in panic. *"Chems?* Where is it? Can we ditch —" She stopped short as she glanced back over her shoulder. The inspector flyer was settling at ground level behind them.

He popped open the leg panel and pulled out the packet.

"God, that's like three thousand credits right there!" Where was Sarofalonon-whatever from the Daily Nonsense channel now? He'd have a field day when he got wind of this.

"Maybe we can say it was already in here. It's a public flyer, right?"

She shook her head and pointed at the ceiling. "There's cams. Plus your prints might be on it."

His turn to swear.

"Why are you carrying it around, damn it?" Her anguish shook her voice.

"Because I was trying to get rid of it!"

She bit back any further words. None of her current thoughts would be helpful, especially not the rage cuddling in her gut. She scanned the flyer, the street around them—anything. There had to be some way out of this. "If you get caught with that..."

His own gaze flicked to the swirling lights behind them.

An idea finally came to her. The only one she had. A way out, although not a great one. Adan wouldn't die in prison, at least. She, on the other hand... she pushed the thoughts aside. She had family and colleagues on Capital. More options than he ever would. She was doing this.

Whether he liked it or not.

She caught his eyes with one long, hard look, raising a hand to his cheek for a moment. His eyes frowned at her, searching, but he didn't back away.

He hadn't shooed her away last night either.

On impulse, she leaned forward and kissed him, one long hard press of her lips against his mouth, fingers curling around his neck. Might as well, while she still had the chance.

And while he was still frozen in surprise, she snatched the packet from his fingers, unlatched the flyer door, and ran.

She sprinted away and dove into the nearest alley even as shouts went up behind her. She slammed the helmet up. Too bad she hadn't bought those cloakers already. She'd have to try to get away the old-fashioned way. She swerved and took off down the next block, tossing the drug in a sewer drain. It wouldn't help; they'd find it or the recording of her ditching it.

She headed for the largest crowd she could find. One foot in front of the other, hopefully faster than the bad guys.

Except this time, she was the bad guy.

———

"WHAT THE—" Adan stared at the yawning car door. "Jenny!"

"Xi—this is mission imperative," Jenny said over his suit's comm, barely panting in spite of her mad sprint. "Raise his helmet and lock him in that suit."

"What?" The stunned exclamation was all he could manage. He flinched as the helmet began rising around him. "Jenny, what's going on?"

"You're Jenny now, Adan. Xi, I've switched the idents. I have one of my older ones."

"But that one is not for a Capital citizen," Xi objected.

"An inner world will get me better than outsystem will get him. Listen—take over and talk him out of this, and then Adan, you get back to Kael and Ryu and tell them what happened."

"Jenny, what are you *doing*?"

"Saving your ass."

"I don't *need* my ass saved!"

"Time to admit you fragging do. We all need saving sometimes. You're not special."

He opened his mouth to disagree, but Xi cut in. "Respectfully, I must agree with Corporal Utlis. Your ass is most certainly in need of saving at present, as well as all of your other body parts."

"Jenny!" he growled.

Even as he did, Xi was commandeering his suit, rolling down the window, answering politely to the officer. His scream was trapped in the suit.

He punched out at the armor pointlessly, but he couldn't help it. It was just him and his growl of rage. He should have flushed the stupid drug. He should have never taken it. He should've seen Josana for who she truly was to begin with.

This was all his fault.

"I would have liked to have known you better, my friend." Jenny's soft words came back to him, broken a bit by exertion and interference, but he heard them loud and clear.

"Don't do this."

She didn't respond.

He'd wanted to pound his fists, and he did as much as he could against the armor, but it wasn't any relief. Xi held him tight. Talking him out of trouble. Denying he knew the figure who had jumped from his flyer. Of course those cameras would prove him a liar, but they had to suspect something to check. A gamble.

He growled, but they showed no sign of hearing him. The other inspectors had raced after Jenny. He stared after her, down the alley, until they'd all vanished from sight. And then he stared some more.

His own officer nodded, satisfied by Xi's carefully calculated responses. Remarkably, he was leaving. Adan could hardly believe she'd pulled it off. Xi rolled up the window.

"I apologize, Adan, but she is right about the mission. Shall I direct your flyer back to the commander's location or the ship?"

"The ship, so I can unplug you," he grunted.

"She is trying to keep you from dying in prison. I thought her sacrifice rather noble."

"But what about her?" he snapped.

"I don't know. I only know her chances of ever seeing the stars again are far better than yours."

Regaining control of his gloves, he tightened his grip on the emergency steering column.

"Better chances, huh? Well, I make my own luck."

"It is possible to manufacture such an amorphous thing as luck?"

He began directing the flyer to the docks. "Not really. But that doesn't stop me from trying. I'm coming back to the ship. I need a few things. Find out where they are taking her."

"That would require hacking into aerial surveillance, possibly breaching their government systems and—"

"You think I don't know that?" He slammed hands against the wheel.

Xi was silent.

"I can't let her suffer because of me. I have to make this right. Find out where they take her for me, Xi. Please?"

Another long pause stretched out before she spoke. "Drone deployed. Breach commencing."

He cheered, actually cheered. "You're a queen, Xi. A lifesaver."

"What even are laws anyway?" she said mildly.

He chuckled. "Was that a joke?"

"Perhaps."

Grinning, he grabbed the controls, ignoring the auto, and took off for the ship. He needed to get a few things, and then there was something he needed to do.

CHAPTER THIRTEEN

ELLEN SLAMMED her palm into the reader outside Ostrov's door. She took a step away, forced a deep breath, and laid a hand as casually as possible on the multi hanging loosely at her side.

She'd spent the last hour going over plans and options in her head, trying to talk herself out of all this, and utterly ignoring Xi's attempts to do the same. Xi continued her efforts via the mind-network connection inside her suit.

Commander, I believe as you saw the other night, Dr. Ostrov is employing some technology to block your signal. I'll no longer be able to help you once you venture inside.

Understood, Xi. But I have to do this. At this rate, he wasn't going to answer the door anyway. And she was going to have to start getting creative.

She'd analyzed a short list of options from a dozen different angles. Get Adan to hack into Ostrov's accounts. Climb through the ductwork. Dress up as a delivery service and jump him.

Ultimately, for better or worse, she'd settled on the direct route. Point a gun at him and make demands.

After what seemed like an eternity, the door slid open to reveal Ostrov, one hand over the palm reader, the other propped on his hip, long coat and shirt unbuttoned roguishly. One eyebrow was quirked at her. "Yes?"

"Don't you ever go to work?"

"If I did, I wouldn't be answering your call at my door, so I don't see how you can complain at the moment."

"We need to talk." She stepped inside, crowding him, and he obliged by backing away a few steps.

"I don't see about what. You heard my terms."

"There's got to be something else you want."

"Alas, while I can think of a thing or two, I'm fairly certain you won't give me those either."

"Name it."

"Your virginity." He laughed darkly.

She brought the multi to bear between them. "I'm not a virgin," she lied through clenched teeth. "And the other thing?"

"Well, your whole ship has a decent bounty on it as well, but presumably that'd contain both you and your lover, so I assume that's out."

"He's not my lover."

He scoffed. "You may not bluff, but you don't lie well. Not a virgin, and no lovers? A sad state for your bed."

"My bed is for sleeping. Listen, Ostrov. I want the name of the ship. Don't make me get violent."

He tapped a finger casually against the pad on the wall, as if thinking. "Really, Ellen. I didn't think you'd choose a game that was so uncivilized."

"I knocked, didn't I?" Her smile was feral and edged with a threat. "Besides. Sometimes uncivilized is all that will work. And sometimes uncivilized is fun."

"Hmm." He straightened, crossing one arm under his elbow and tapping his chin with the other. "Indeed it is. And I think you had better shoot me, or I'll have to show you just how uncivilized I can be."

"With this?" She raised the weapon slightly, looking at it, mocking him. "Oh, it can do so much more than shoot you."

"Is that so."

"In addition to laser and ballistic, we've got a nice strong stun. Or perhaps I should just foam you to the wall and see how long it takes for you to crack and tell me where the information is." A small beep came from her suit, but she didn't dare take her eyes off him yet. It was probably registering the lack of connection.

"I'm shaking in my boots."

"Maybe a stun *is* the way to go. So many options. Or perhaps you'd prefer attacks of a more chemical nature?"

"I always thought we had good chemistry." He grinned, and something about it niggled at her. He truly seemed unconcerned. "Acid, pepper, or sedative?"

"Always a tough call, but pepper types work across the most species. You yourself seem to be hankering for the stun gun though. To start."

He leaned casually against the wall, and she thought he might yawn. "Your threats don't scare me, Ellen."

"Don't call me Ellen. You're *going* to give me the information. I'm a fan of nonlethal methods of crowd control."

"Really. I'm not."

Hairs rose on the back of her neck, and she ducked just in time as something quick and metallic swung overhead. Twisting, she caught a glimpse of the robot's legs behind her.

Screw nonlethal. She thumbed the switch to lethal as she dove to the side, anticipating another swing down. She wasn't wrong there. She *was* wrong in choosing her direction, which ended with her flinging herself into the legs of a second robot, this one much more android like, enough so that their collision set it toppling like it might have any man.

She probably should have pushed him harder on his area of research. How many more droids might he have roaming around, swinging?

She fired back in long bursts at the legs of the original droid while scrambling to get to her feet and her back to a wall. Maybe Xi had been right. Maybe backup wouldn't have been such a bad idea.

No. She couldn't risk bringing Kael that close to Ostrov. Beyond the agony of Ostrov's advances—she was afraid of just what Kael might do. She needed to get the info and settle this once and for all.

"And here I thought you would play by the rules," she shouted over the clang of three additional droids marching into the room. She hadn't realized the floor was truly metal. Convincing facades—that was all of Capital.

"What gave you that impression?" He was backing away, easing behind his precious bar, and she had an urge to shoot holes in every one of his juice boxes and leave them dripping all over him. If only.

The sustained blast took the first, heaviest robot down, its stumpy legs twitching. It wasn't terribly deterred, though, as it started to crawl toward her with its arms as she backed into the gaming room. She needed cover, but this wasn't ideal—the exits were the *other* way.

Switching briefly to stun, she sent a quick pulse in the direction of the bar, hoping to get lucky. A bottle exploded, but she heard no screams of pain. Sadly.

She switched back to laser and aimed for the neck of the toppled droid, who had righted itself and was running in her direction with the kind of precision and frigid single-mindedness only a droid could demonstrate. Sparks shot out as her beam cut into metal and wires, and the droid faltered, one leg going inert. But that wasn't much of a win.

The other three had nearly caught up with it, were nearly on top of her.

She released the nano cloud, sending it at them. But three were too many, especially for the processing power of droids, and ultimately only one seemed actually befuddled by it. The first staggered out and reached for her throat.

Its hand took out a chunk of the wall and the door as she shifted quickly back, keeping up the laser.

The second came over it in a flying leap, landing on the gaming table. Shards of glass from the slick surface flew, and she had to raise her arm to keep the glass from hitting— Shit, the *helmet*. She'd fallen for his goading and left it down and—

Before she could reach the button, the last android took its leap from the gaming table and launched itself at her, tackling her to the floor.

Eyes. Its eyes were vivid blue, bright, lit unnaturally. Just like Kentt's. But its expression…

No time. She used every bit of her armor's juice to push it off. A raw growl exploded from her as she strained, motors and muscles against calculated, cold-steel determination. The droid's limbs groaned, twisting. She shoved hard, and it went flying.

But not before she felt a sudden puff of air against her face.

She didn't even have time to swear. The world went blurry, then blurrier still, and her growl of rage collapsed into silence.

———

AT SOME POINT, Kael had drifted off to sleep again in the study. Much as he'd tried not to, the rapid healing demands of the medkit required it.

He'd spent his time before that trying to think of a way to convince Ellen to make a deal with Ostrov. He was probably a fool, but he replayed her rejection and the speed with which she'd shut the man's offer down in his mind a few hundred times.

Even when half his body and other parts of him were aching, that moment had felt pretty good. Especially in hindsight, when he'd become sure he couldn't change her mind on the matter.

Many times in his life he'd been forced to do something he didn't want to do. Joining the gangs, becoming a Theroki, and every brawl and mission along the way. Never had it happened because someone was concerned about him, though. Trying to protect him.

It was certainly the treatment she'd give any member of her crew. He couldn't imagine her risking Adan or Jenny or Zhia or any of them. Maybe Josana. But not really. He didn't think.

But once he awoke and discovered the medkit blinking green—meaning he was healed, basically—he knew that none of the good feelings or pride or concern on her part changed anything.

Ostrov had the info she needed. And Kael had the power to give it to her.

He wasn't walking away from that.

He pulled up the nearest holodisplay and started rooting around in their files. First, a blueprint or map of this building. Then, Jenny's medkit.

Then he and Ostrov were going to have a long-overdue talk.

———

WHEN ELLEN AWOKE, she was surrounded in some kind of dark cell. Her mouth was dry and acidic from whatever had knocked her out. What a stupid mistake, and he'd been setting it up all along with his goading. She was lucky she wasn't dead.

Water dripped, the sound distant but at the same time loud in the near silence. The cold, humid air hung still and lifeless around her, not even a tiny draft for her to guess at the ventilation system. Was that the faint perfume of soap she smelled? Strange.

Her armor was still on, to her surprise. Ostrov probably didn't have the equipment to remove it. But something cuffed her wrists together to one wall. She'd awoken slumped with them raised over her head, but by turning slowly and with careful footing, she was able to stand.

And she *wanted* to stand, because in addition to drip-drip-drip, there was only one other sound. She could catch an occasional slither-slip near her feet, like something wet sliding, a fish flopping over tile.

She didn't know what that was. Nor did she particularly want to.

She tugged at the restraints, only gently at first, then harder. It didn't matter. She pulled until she could feel the motors heating and smell the faint burning scent that was a good indicator that she should stop.

Now why would Ostrov already have a room complete with restraints—chains, they seemed to be—powerful enough to resist the strongest tech-powered armor?

The wall around the restraints was initially metal plate, and beyond that seemed to be actual tile. Or imitation tile, at least, because it didn't shatter when she slammed a fist into it. The metal dented a little, but the impact she made was far from meaningful.

Just as she was plotting her next move, a wall display burst to life to her right, flooding the room with light. She flinched, throwing up a hand to block it as her eyes adjusted. The initial afterimage blocked any details she might have picked up. Blinking blearily, she squinted at the screen.

Ostrov, of course. Again. In the light from the screen, she could see a white sink in front of him.

"My dear Ellen, you're awake!" The unchanged friendliness of his tone was even more disturbing than a new deviousness would have been. "You really should have left well enough alone."

"It's not my strong suit," she muttered.

"Sidassian will still be a great prize, but Arakovic will be indebted to me eternally now." He grinned.

"Arakovic doesn't know, or care, who I am." She thought it was the truth but was starting to fear her information was sorely out of date.

"Then why is she offering so many credits for your capture? And even more for your preparation and education."

"My what?"

"Oh, you'll see shortly."

"Am I in a *bathroom*?" she sputtered. "Why am I in your bathroom?"

He laughed lightly. "Would you believe it's because it comes complete with soundproofing so no one can hear you sing in the shower?"

"No."

"Because no one wonders why there's a lock on the door?"

She yanked viciously at the wall now, mostly out of anger. Teeth clenched, she only succeeded in knocking her own hair into her face, and she didn't even have hands free to push it back again. She whipped her head back to try and fling it out of the way as best she could. "When I get out of this—"

"My dear Ellen, you're not getting out of this. And you're clearly in my bathroom because it's the most convenient place to clean up all the blood."

She couldn't contain the snarl. "Have you used this before, you asshole? Where are those girls?"

"I don't actually know. But I'm fairly certain they're right where you're going to be. With Dr. Arakovic."

The screen blinked out, and she was alone in the darkness.

She jumped at the slide and squirt of something wet by her right boot. No. She wasn't alone. Far from it.

———

"UH... ARE YOU JENNIFER?" The officer eyed him dubiously, his eyes flicking to Adan's rapidly forming five-o-clock shadow.

"Yeah, uh... I'm scheduled for the whole reorientation shebang next week, but the legal paperwork came through early." He did his best to bat his eyelashes, tilt his head, and grin sweetly at the old man, who snorted.

"You look behind a few shots with that upper lip of yours, but good luck to ya," the officer said.

"Thanks. Yeah, the damn thing just won't quit."

"My sister's never been happier since she got hers done. Fine, head on in. I'll get your friend for ya."

Adan waited nervously on the dull blue chair, shocked that that had even remotely worked. This was foolish. This was stupid. But not as stupid as carrying those chems around. And what else could he do? He couldn't leave Jenny here to rot because he was a moron. Not after... everything.

"I implore you once more to have backup in this mission, Adan." Xi's tone was dry, annoyed, if an AI could have a tone. Perhaps it was his imagination.

"No. We bring more than one or two of us in here, we'll end up blowing the whole place up. Especially with the Theroki on board." He felt a twang of guilt at that stupid dig. He'd promised Kael he'd play it safe. And now look what had happened. But he was going to make it right.

"He's not a Theroki now any more than you are," Xi said tightly. "And I believe you know that. I have heard him tell you several times."

He rolled his eyes but was too hyped up to back down. "Besides, if I royally screw this up, won't we need people on the outside to break us both out? And someone has to watch the Persads."

"Those are the only remotely valid arguments you have. Except that the Persads are already safely on the ship. Nova and Mo escorted them."

"All the more reason I'll need you and Kael on the outside when I inevitably fail."

Could an AI's silence be disapproving? How did she manage to seem to frown at him without even having a face?

He checked over the program he'd created for the suit, the one loaded on the drive. The others were on chits tucked in his belt. Access codes and system master override cards. He had more than a few tools. He might die trying this but he hadn't come unprepared.

Finally, a different officer returned, a woman, and beckoned him to follow her back. He tried to look calm, but he had a feeling it was failing. The officer led him to a holding room and shut the door behind him.

And there she was. A bruise darkened one eye above a freckled cheekbone, and her green eyes looked darker and blacker than he remembered ever seeing them. She stood. He wanted to snap off the cuffs glowing chartreuse around her wrists. Her feet were bare. What the hell—no shoes in Capital prisons? Or had something happened? Prison garments the color of dead fish weighed her down like blocks of cement.

"What are you *doing* here?" she whispered harshly. "You shouldn't be here."

"Look, I need to explain."

"No you don't."

"Yeah, I do. I wasn't there today to see Josana."

"Yeah, right! Who cares? What's done is done now. Get out. Go."

"No, I wasn't there for her. Not like that. I was there to stop her. She was selling—"

"I gathered that," she said, gesturing at the prison garb.

He coughed. "Selling something worse. Lists of past grids." He raised his eyebrows, hoping she'd understand from his vague words. He didn't want to give away any more than necessary to any listening ears. "To an intelligence broker."

Her eyes widened.

"I deleted it all. But you should know I wasn't there for... that."

"You came all the way here just to tell me that? Get out of here, A —" She stopped herself in time.

"No, also for this."

He snaked an arm out, pulling her close, spinning her around, and pressing her against the conveniently located control panel as his mouth covered hers.

Hopefully she wouldn't deck him too hard for this.

His body stirred at the feeling of her, the citrus scent defying their surroundings. He slid his hand around her waist and to the panel, slipping the proper chit into the slot that would load the credentials, the distraction, and the virus and resting his hand on the appropriate key. If this worked... any second now...

She shoved him back. "You asshole. What the hell?"

"I missed you," he said, surprised at the roughness of his voice. There, that should play into the deception.

"But..." she started, frowning. Searching for a way to not reveal why he should absolutely positively not be there without giving it away? "What about..."

"I just needed a little more time." He looked pointedly at the control panel behind her. She glanced back but kept frowning.

"But I thought—"

"We broke up. I'm not staying. I never was going to."

"Oh." Her eyes widened. "*Oh.*"

He needed her to play along, at least until the virus finished its work. He buried his face in her shoulder, pressing kisses softly against the sensitive skin of her neck, her earlobe, her ear.

She gasped and fell silent. Apparently ready to go along with his ploy, her hands strayed across the armor. Not that it revealed much.

He risked a glance over her shoulder, then pressed his lips against her ear.

"Three more percent, then get ready to run," he said as quietly as he possibly could.

She nodded, wisps of her hair brushing his cheek. She seemed to hang on to him for dear life, not that he could feel much through the armor. The pads of her fingers were white near the nail from pressing into him.

The door pad beeped. Her eyes widened. He pulled back from her and slammed the helmet control, letting it close over him.

Right on target, water exploded from the ceiling, the fire-prevention system at work. Foam covered a sensitive area in the corner, and the door to their room slid open.

He thumbed the control on his forearm and loaded the Capital armor program.

Laughter burst out of her, and he hoped no one was watching. They shouldn't be anyway, with the alarm. He grinned wickedly to himself, then glanced down to check his work. Excellent. The gray-green stripes of the officer uniforms flickered to life, mostly in the right places.

He grabbed her by the cuffs as he'd seen the inspectors do and pulled her after him out into the hall.

"Sir!" somewhat shouted from up the hall.

"What's going on?" he demanded.

"Sensors are showing fire in *three* locations. AI suggests the west corridor for the most efficient exit. I'm getting R team to get the other prisoners in here out." The tone of the other man suggested that something about Adan's disguise—or maybe just his poise or that he'd had this prisoner with him—had him outranking the young officer.

"Good idea. I'll take this one, she's dangerous. Go."

The young man nodded and sprinted back.

Adan pulled up the maps he'd stolen of the interior. The helmet marked his location, and he scanned it quickly. West corridor... Okay. That's where everyone would go, where other officers would find them. He would be headed to the supposedly burning east corridor exits, where hopefully they would be entirely alone.

Both of them silent, he jogged down one hallway, turned, and hit the next one. An armory case caught his eye, and he stopped. He tried the door but found it locked. He glowered at the latch and its analog lock, impervious to him at the moment, especially without his tools.

"Give it a good elbow," she said, backing away. "The armor should protect you. It won't withstand a good slam."

He smashed an elbow into the case once, then much harder, and it did indeed shatter. He grabbed two rifles and swung them over his shoulder. He'd give her one when they weren't so obviously still in the prison hallway. Although... he hadn't seen any cells yet.

"What kind of prison is this?" he said as they neared the east corridor.

"It's supposedly a psychiatric hospital."

He winced. Ah, the name made more sense now. And the type of security. That black eye and lack of shoes concerned him even more now.

They reached the east corridor door, and he pushed.

Nothing happened. Locked.

"This section of the facility is restricted," said an overhead voice. Damn, the prison—hospital?—AI. "Fire in this stairwell. Please choose another evacuation route. I suggest—"

He swore. "AI, make and model number," he demanded.

"Restricted."

"Do you have a name?"

"Regular dialog protocols are restricted during emergency evacuation."

"Damn it." He jacked open the door palm panel and jammed in one code, then another, then inserted his chit again.

"Dialog access granted," the AI relented. "User32 sudo admin accepted."

"AI, you got a name?"

"Why do you keep asking its name?" Jenny asked from beside him.

"Need to know its capabilities and potential security exploits."

"Selek Model 55, user32. How can I help you?"

"Find program jr11."

"Located."

"Create a conditional in method east."

"Acknowledged. What would you like the conditional to contain?"

"Allow two personnel to enter the marked area. And exit on the ground floor. Don't record the passage. After two personnel have utilized the exception, delete it and overwrite blank three times. Then start garbage collect."

"Acknowledged."

"Saved and running?"

"Acknowledged, user32."

He pressed on the door handle. It opened with a soft huff, and he heaved a sigh of relief.

"Good job, Selek55."

"Thank you, user32. Have a nice day."

He grabbed her by the arm now and pulled her after him. She was staring, eyes wide. "What was all that?"

"The computer thinks this corridor is on fire. Fortunately for us, we can walk through fire. Now it's going to let us—and only us, hopefully—do so. I can explain more later."

"And… how did it come to think it was on fire?"

He hit the helmet retract button now and grinned at her as they sped down the flights of stairs. There was no water in this stairwell, ironically enough. He'd turned it off to hopefully ease their escape. "I have *no* idea."

She snorted, racing after him agilely even with those bare feet.

"What happened to your shoes?"

"I almost crushed a windpipe with them, and they thought taking my shoes would stop that."

"Did it?"

"It wouldn't have, but I haven't gotten a second chance to try." She grinned up at him again.

He pointed at her eye. "You okay? What happened? I hope you didn't... deal with anything..." *I hope you didn't get too hurt on my account. Why couldn't he just say it?*

"Don't worry," she replied. "We don't get those RPD systems for nothing. I had no qualms testing mine out. Or refreshing my unarmed combat skills." She grinned again, perhaps to soften the scowl that was forming on his face.

"We're almost out."

They neared the last two flights.

"Hey Selek55, can you still hear me?"

"Yes, user32."

"After we exit this door, run wipe program for this face, and that one. And identities associated with each."

"Acknowledged, user32."

They reached the final door, and he was groping for the handle when laser fire began vaporizing the cement block beside his head.

"Over here!" Jenny dove, pulling him with her. "Get that helmet up." She slammed the button for him. "I didn't even hear them coming —must be well equipped."

He pulled the first rifle off, handed it to her, and listened. He couldn't hear anything. He pulled off the second one and readied it. Not that he had much hope he'd hit anything.

Still... where were they? Jenny peered down the sight, looking carefully above their cover but... she didn't seem to have spotted anything.

"Selek55," he whispered. "How many hostiles in this area?"

"Two," it replied. He had a bad feeling it was referring to him and Jenny.

"How many inspectors? And hospital staff?" he asked instead.

"Four."

Frag. They had figured them out, damn it. How?

"Mark their locations, Selek55," Jenny whispered.

"You do not have admin access, user 33."

Adan rolled his eyes. "Mark their locations," he snapped. "And not ours. Unmark ours. Forbid marking ours."

Suddenly the lights in the column dimmed, aside from three levels above them. He and Jenny were shrouded in darkness.

Jenny glanced at him, then up, then at the doorway. She pointed.

"Make a run for it?" he whispered.

She nodded, then held up three fingers. She eyed the flight above them. Two. One.

He turned and sprinted for the door, staying low. He threw himself against it and to his relief it still opened, spilling them out into the busy street.

Just like he'd planned.

A few people raised their eyes at Jenny, but he grabbed the rifle from her quickly and took her by the cuffs. "Fire in the facility. An accident. We're evacuating the building." That was all the excuse the onlookers needed to ignore them.

They jogged away, hopefully fast enough to put some distance between them and those officers but not so fast to look suspicious. Well, any more suspicious than they already did.

"Oh my God, I can't believe we're out here." Jenny giggled, in spite of clearly trying not to. "We can't go the whole way to the ship like this. Any ideas?"

"We shoot those cuffs off with the rifles. Or at least melt the middle piece," he said. "Then I'll turn off this program, and we switch. You take this armor, toss that outfit, and we'll head back that way."

She was nodding as she scanned the street intersection they were crossing. "Good plan. I mean, assuming you have more than underwear on under there."

"Guess you're going to find out."

She blushed, sudden and fierce.

He cleared his throat, pretending to not notice her embarrassment. "Xi, how are those scramblers going?"

Xi spoke up from his suit. "This is extremely illegal. Possibly unethical. It's going well."

He glanced back at Jenny. "She's trying to keep their street surveillance from keying on our faces. Now, we need somewhere to make the clothing switch. Suggestions?"

"Up here—that public women's restroom. You're taking the prisoner you detained for a bio break?"

"That works. See anyone tailing us?"

"No. Has the armor set off any alerts?"

"No—do I need to ask it to?"

"It should track followers and incoming hostiles automatically. Although I see you've been tampering with the programming, so who knows."

"Got you out, didn't it?"

"Yeah, but you definitely owe me a cigar now."

"I won't dispute that." He shook his head. They reached the restroom, jogging inside. He followed her, glad for the obscurity of the helmet. The women still eyed him though, the shapes of the armor still fairly male even with his form smaller than Kael's.

She dashed into the stall and then stared expectantly, beckoning him in. Oh, she was waiting for him. Well, they did have to change the armor out, didn't they. Still, a middle-aged woman in an ornate silver and green breather mask and ridiculous green hat raised her eyebrows as he followed Jenny into the stall. He watched her form through the glass as they shut the stall door, and it fogged semisolid.

They both shrugged. He swung the rifle forward. "Let's get those off you."

"Oh. Yes. Let's."

She directed him how and when to fire. After barely a second, the cuffs broke in two, leaving two bracelets, but they could be concealed by the armor.

"Better get switched." He hit the release button, and the armor began removing itself. As the pieces came free, she deftly caught them and started donning them with a smile, like she was slipping into a familiar old bathrobe. Quickly, the armor came together again around her, carving into new proportions and curves, its usual black restored and hiding the prison garb.

She took a deep breath as the last piece clicked and hissed into place. "Ah, that feels better."

"Okay, let's try to get back to the ship."

She nodded. "And stay away from any inspectors."

"I don't know if I'm ever leaving the ship again."

"That would be a shame." She snorted and reached for the handle to open the stall door, then hesitated. "Adan," she said softly, looking back at him. She must be meaning to thank him or something.

"Yeah?"

"That was pretty fragging brilliant back there."

He only stared at her, a strange feeling flooding through him.

"*You* were pretty brilliant back there. You didn't bring any cigars, did you?"

He burst out laughing. "As a matter of fact, I did."

"I think it's an appropriate time, don't you?"

He nodded. "Outside, and I'll light 'em."

They stole hastily out of the restroom. Fortunately the green-hatted woman had not dawdled or waited nearby, and the activity from the "hospital" seemed to have stayed on the west side of the facility. No pursuers were in sight. They slipped down one main artery, took an alley to a second, and were quickly afloat in the sea of people in Lower Capital.

He pulled out a cigar, raised it to his lips to light it, and handed it to her. He couldn't tear his eyes away as she accepted it with a smile, something sensual about her lips taking it into her mouth where his lips had just been. He pulled out the second and lit his own and laughed outright.

"We make a good team, you know that?" she said pointedly.

"We're not half bad."

"We could be legends." She stabbed the cigar at him, pointing a finger.

"Isn't being a legend once enough for you?"

She grinned. "Not at all. Besides, I gotta bring you along for the ride. I'm serious. We're a good team, damn it."

"But you always knew that, didn't you."

She flushed now, her smile fading. She said nothing, looking off into the buildings and taking another puff. She knew what he was getting at, and vice versa. She hadn't expected him to call her on it directly.

"How about we wait to declare victory until we're actually on the ship, mystifying Xi with our cancer sticks?" he said, punting the inevitable. They weren't really carcinogenic or addictive anymore, but the habit was still quite popular—and even more mystifying to Xi.

Her smile returned. "Good plan. I'm telling you, you're good at this planning thing."

"I'll try not to let it go to my head."

"Why? With your brains and my brawn—"

"I know, I know. Legends."

"So do we head for the ship, or—" She faltered.

He followed her gaze. Up ahead, two inspectors were frowning down at an ident scanner and surreptitiously glancing their way.

"Shit," she muttered. "We may have a problem."

———

"DID they make you as your real name there?" Adan said quietly.

Jenny shook her head, trying to keep her stream of curse words mostly to herself. "I kept waiting for it to happen, but I only saw my arresting officer, one very unethical psychiatrist, and a few orderlies to restrain me after.... Well, I'll give you the recap later. Got lucky there, I guess." She hadn't gotten lucky with the psychiatrist himself, so she supposed it evened out. On the bright side, she now had a first-hand account of Capital's unique brand of justice if she ever spoke to Josana again.

But hopefully she wouldn't.

"If they didn't make you, and they never saw anything but my armor, then why are those two eying us?"

"I probably still fit the description. *If* they realized at least one prisoner is gone by now. It hasn't been that long, but... And I suppose they have you arriving on video."

"I tried to disable as much as I could, but one of the many little tweaks could've been horked." He blew out a puff of smoke and tried to look casual and mostly succeeded.

The inspectors started slowly making their way toward them.

"Damn it." Jenny glanced around. "This way." She grabbed Adan's hand and pulled him after her, trying to walk as fast as she could without outright running, searching her mind for a plan.

She had the start of one, but it seemed... crazy.

They were two blocks from the fashion district, specifically the 918th Street shops. Boutiques that catered to custom designs, the rich and famous, wedding dresses and funeral gowns, and the occasional fine accoutrements for pets. If she remembered correctly...

Yes. They came out near Block Seven, the white letters of the boutique's name stark over the glossy black of the store front.

She glanced back. The inspectors were still following, although trying to look low-key about it. They weren't sure. Or they were waiting for backup.

"C'mon." She dragged Adan up the stairs and yanked open the door.

"Jen, what the—" he started, as the door swung shut behind them, blocking out the roar of the street and enveloping them in silence. After a moment, she could distinguish a faint pulsing beat in the background. "Are we even allowed to have these in here?" He held up the still-smoking cigar.

A disapproving saleswoman was on them, too, so Jenny suspected he was right that they certainly weren't allowed to smoke in there. "Um, can I help you—"

"Utlis," she barked out. "Jennifer Utlis, of Utlis Sportswear, and I am truly hoping you can."

The woman's demeanor transformed. Her lips were a lemon yellow, and they smiled brightly as her palms smoothed a perfectly white sheath dress. "Oh, Jennifer—of course—is it all right if I call you Jennifer?"

"Sure." Why the frag not.

"What can I help you with today? Can my assistant Siniatana help you with your outdoor accessories?"

Adan frowned. The phrase meant to refer to jackets and umbrellas was in this case referring to the cigars. Jenny didn't bother to stifle a giggle.

"Oh, yes. Here you go, Sin." She needed to act the part, so she foisted the still-smoking stick onto the poor unsuspecting woman without even looking at her.

"So, Jennifer, how can I help?"

"Right. What can I call you?"

"I'm Steatrentana."

"Got anything shorter, faster?" Jenny snapped her fingers. Athletes had a reputation for bucking the more intricate social norms. One way Jenny had fit right in.

"Uh…" The woman hesitated. "Tana?"

"Great. Tana. I love it. Well, today has been disaster after disaster for my—" She faltered and almost said trainer before she remembered that Adan didn't have a beefy-enough physique to fool anyone in that realm. "—my assistant and I. Just ridiculous. And I have a press conference in twenty minutes. I need a *complete* head to toe. So does he." She jerked a thumb at Adan, who'd frozen in terror. "Can you do that for me?"

To her credit, Tana's eyes only widened slightly, and her voice held not even a tinge of panic. "We certainly can. Right this way." As they followed Tana toward the back, the woman grabbed two perfectly white bodysuits from a nearby rack and led them to changing rooms. "Put on these fitting suits—Block Seven custom technology that makes the finest fits you'll get on the 918. The computer should need about thirty seconds to measure you. Which one of you is picking… ?" She looked back and forth between them. "Or both?"

"I am." Jenny'd be footing the bill, and Adan would be floored by the prices, so it was the only expedient option.

"I'll have the options on your holodisplay. Once you choose, we'll need approximately four minutes for fabrication. Hair and makeup can be done in six or even ten. Choose quickly, and you might even have a minute to spare." Tana smiled brightly.

"Done and done." Jenny snatched her suit from Tana's outstretched fingers, bounded into the training room, and hit the armor release. "Would you mind getting me something to store this... uh, other outfit in too, Tana?"

"Uh—of course, Jennifer!" Her bright, calm tone was undercut by sharp, fast steps out of the area and a hissed, "Siniatana! Right now! Hurry!" Jenny tried not to laugh. At least not too loudly.

And hopefully Adan was doing as he was told.

The holodisplay sprang to life, and she was practically slapping the pictures aside as she searched for the simplest design that looked the farthest from prison clothes possible. Speaking of said clothes, she stripped them off and stuffed them in the nearby garbage chute. Not a perfect solution, but better than having them on her.

She settled on a black bodysuit with some cool belting that wasn't too far from a flight suit, although maybe more formfitting. It was hard to tell as the models were still slowly adjusting to her actual measurements and this one hadn't filled in yet. She'd barely had the fitting suit on for the full thirty seconds anyway.

Flipping to the menswear, she found a fantastic beige suit with a Mandarin collar that screamed Adan the second she saw it. He'd seemed attached to that pocketed vest of his, and this was as close as they'd come. And manufacturable in two minutes, rather than four. She hit buy.

Good thing she'd kept that Capital bank account open.

Then she grabbed the comm and chose the last person who'd dialed her on it.

"Sarlano Crane, lead anchor, Dailyglow." His voice was chipper and calm as ever.

"Crane," she barked. "This is Jenny Utlis."

"Oh. Hello, Ms. Utlis. I'd love to inform you that the mother you're visiting isn't on the planet and hasn't been for quite some time. You must have been looking hard for her."

"So I lied to protect my privacy. Sue me. Would I be the first?"

"Hardly."

"You want a scoop? I'd like to announce my official retirement. And I'd like to do it on the 918 in front of Block Seven in fifteen minutes. Can you make it happen?" Hopefully that was long enough. She needed the inspectors to still be wondering when she and Adan would leave the store and continue on. They'd only wait outside and watch both exits for so long before trying to come in and peek around.

She and Adan *were* going to come out, but when they did, nobody was going to recognize them. And she'd be cloaked in cameras.

If she couldn't vanish, she'd hide in plain sight.

Sarlano recovered from a stunned silence. "I can definitely do that. On my way. You better be camera ready."

"Headed to hair and makeup now." She hung up just as Tana was knocking on the door with a slip of shiny black fabric and a giant box for the armor.

Jenny swallowed. Wow, that was... shinier than it'd looked in the catalog. It even had a slight sparkle to it. This should be interesting.

Changed, she plopped one of the crazy black boxes on her head and only paused for a moment as she stared at the hair colors.

She needed something totally different. She loved red, but that's what those inspectors were keying on. For a moment, she hesitated over a too-familiar pure white. Then she took a deep breath and slid it away. She was only who she was. Anything else would be a mistake. And hadn't Orange Dress girl shown her matchy-matchy was in?

It was exactly fourteen minutes before Jenny stood before Sarlano's recording crescent—as well as those of two other reporters who'd spotted him hurrying to something and followed out of blind instinct. The black bodysuit was stopping the crowd, or it might have been the severe black bob that had taken over, leaving her green eyes the sole point of color sparkling like emeralds in a sea of onyx and cream. Makeup had covered the black eye as well as the freckles, leaving her transformed. Her mother would be so proud. At least until she heard the words Jenny was saying.

"I'd like to officially announce my retirement from professional athletics," she said carefully to them. As if anyone would fragging care

—other than her parents. She wanted to roll her eyes. The self-important press conference had never been her thing. "As I've long been a member of the unaugmented athletic community, I find I've reached my limit in competing and would like to focus on something else. I intend to devote myself wholly to my new nonprofit foundation."

"Ms. Utlis!" one of the bloodhounds called out. "What about Utlis Sportswear?"

Another cut in. "What will your nonprofit be for?"

She hadn't really planned on making the thing real, but she realized now they'd follow up. Fact-check her. Like they'd done with her mom story.

"I'll continue to support the excellent work of the artists at Utlis Sportswear. I'm still defining the mission statement for our nonprofit, but one aim will be funding legal representation for those lost in our currently overloaded legal system." There. A respectable answer, and maybe even a good idea.

"Ms. Utlis!" "Ms. Utlis!"

"That will be all," she said, turning back and heading into the store.

Adan did an admirable job of faking being her "assistant" by holding back the reporters, waving them off, and muttering, "Ms. Utlis has no further comment."

Inside, Tana and Sin were beaming, and Sin had produced a tray of beverages, complete with their careful fancy seals, the kind preferred by many celebrities to ensure they hadn't been tampered with. Supposedly. Jenny humored them by taking one and forcing another one on Adan, who looked vastly amused.

"What are you two so happy about?" Jen said warmly to them. "Sorry to disrupt your day, by the way."

"No, not at all!" gushed Sin.

"Don't apologize. This kind of coverage is great for us. Orders will quadruple. Plus my kid said he got to see me on the live stream!" Tana waved a comm.

Jenny raised her newly sculpted eyebrows. "News travels fast."

"Sure does."

The two of them continued to beam at her and Adan. "Uh... we should be going," Jenny said after another sip. "Do you have any sunglasses?"

"Absolutely." Sin abandoned the tray and dashed around the corner, returning with a whole tray to choose from.

"Put it on my bill," Jenny said, sliding on a large round pair that would hopefully help further hide them from inspector eyes.

"No, no," said Tana. "Our compliments."

Jenny raised her eyebrows again, started to turn to go, then paused. "Uh... you want a picture?"

"Yes!"

Adan was again forced into photography service, and then they were out, their "purchases" floating behind them as the slipped into a huge luxury flyer the store had called. Reporters now lined the way from the store's door to the flyer's. She caught a glimpse of a frowning inspector shrugging at his partner before she slipped into the flyer. Now to just hope they wouldn't follow.

A small wood box lay on the seat inside.

"What's that?" Adan said, as he shut the door behind him.

She picked it up and carefully opened it before she burst out laughing. "Two cigars."

He laughed too and snatched one. "Did they leave a lighter, and a... ah, yes."

They sat and puffed smoke into the flyer, surely against some rule. What was one more violation today?

She took another puff, then squinted critically at the cigar. "This doesn't count as my prize, you know. I said a *nice* one."

He chuckled. "These are way nicer than what I had. And besides, I didn't think I should hand over my best to the officers if I failed spectacularly and got caught trying to save you."

"That's fair. Still. You owe me."

He smiled, catching her gaze. "I owe you a lot more than that. What you did—tricking those officers—"

She shushed him. "Don't worry about it. I couldn't just let them... you know."

"I know. I just... thank you."

"Seems like we're even, Adan." She turned and gazed out the window at the tall white towers floating by. Of all her trips to Capital, this was probably the best, which said a lot considering she'd been arrested and groped besides. "It's all right. Anything for you."

They rode in warm silence for a while.

Finally, Adan spoke. "Hey, I feel like a bastard. I need to contact Kael. He's probably wondering where the hell I am."

"Go for it." She waved at the comm in his hand.

Adan hit the button, left it on video so she'd hear it as well.

Kael answered almost immediately. "Where the fragging hell have you been? I'm going to—"

"Look, long story. You can kill me later. Where are you?"

"Is Ellen with you? I can't find Ellen."

Adan frowned. "What?"

"I can't find her. And… we found out that Ostrov claims to know Arakovic's whereabouts. But for some reason he wanted to trade *me* for them."

He had Jenny's full attention now. She sat forward on the seat. "What the—"

"She said no, then vanished."

"Uh-oh." Adan's expression darkened.

"Look, I have a plan to get that info from Ostrov, but I need your help. To at least make sure the data gets back out alive."

"We're on our way," Jenny said without thinking, then eyed Adan. "That okay with you?"

Adan smiled and leaned back on the bench with a sigh. "One adventure really wasn't enough for the day. I'll adjust course from the ship to the apartment."

Jenny looked back to Kael. "Don't go on any suicide missions without us. You wait right there, Kael Asidian."

He snorted. "No promises."

CHAPTER FOURTEEN

"I FEARED MY HYPOTHESIS WAS CORRECT." As soon as Kael had hung up with Jenny and Adan, Xi's voice suddenly came from—where the hell was it? There were at least three computers in the study where Kael was pacing, going over his plans. "Kael, I must object."

"Look, I appreciate your concern, Xi, but getting captured is not the plan. I'm going to do my best to give him the slip. But I'm getting the info. One way or another."

Xi proceeded to try an array of arguments to sway him while they waited for backup to arrive.

"Kael?" Jenny's voice came through the open study door, followed by Jenny herself.

"Holy shit, what happened to you two?" Kael blurted. Jenny looked like a high-paid model, with brand new jet-black hair and sunglasses the size of oranges. Behind her, Adan was in a suit not far below her in style.

"Long story," Jenny said. "We needed disguises."

"I don't know how we're going to justify this to Simmons." Adan sighed.

Jenny waved him off. "We're not. I paid for it."

"What?" Adan cocked his head in alarm, and Kael had to wonder just what the price tags had been.

Jenny gave a theatrical bow. "Courtesy of Utlis Sportswear Intergalactic Corporation. Now—can we get to the matter at hand and keep Kael from throwing himself to his demise? Maybe actually work like a team for five minutes?"

The men nodded, and Kael quickly gave them a rundown of his plan. It basically consisted of forcibly smashing the door open and grabbing Ostrov by the throat. And maybe squeezing.

"Whoa, whoa, whoa, you can't just do that." Adan was shaking his head.

"The probability of success—" Xi started.

Kael held up a hand. "I don't want to know."

Jenny rubbed her chin. "You can't go alone, and you can't just barge in there. What if he tries to screw you over, not give you the information?"

"Well, that's pretty much a given."

Xi was undeterred. "Perhaps instead you'd be interested in the likelihood of mission failure, which is—"

"No thank you, Xi."

"Wait, wait. I know." Jenny brightened. "We'll go together. What if we pretend we betrayed you and brought you in?"

"Yeah," Adan nodded. "We'll be your wingmen."

Kael raised an eyebrow, looking back and forth between them. "You two are very chummy all of a sudden. Where were you again?"

Jenny waved his concern aside. "No time now. When did you last see the commander?"

"When she spoke with Ostrov and he made the offer. Not sure what time it was. I can't find her. I didn't particularly want to—she's just going to try to stop me."

Xi's tone was unusually clipped, louder. "This is because she is an intelligent being. With a sense of self-preservation. Kael, you mustn't—"

Jenny held up one finger. "Uh, here's an idea. I have a mild sedative in my kit. And an inhaled antidote for it. Maybe we use it to make it look like we drugged you and brought you in."

He ought to ask what kind of "antidote." But that wouldn't really tell him anything. Dremer had warned him his body might respond weirdly to stimulants, but she wasn't entirely sure how. The response could be heightened—or deadened—or a little of both. Between his built-in scrubbers—now assaulted and then field repaired—and his worn-out, amped-up nervous system, who knew what the hell would happen? He wasn't sure he wanted to know at this point, anyway.

"Sounds like a pretty good plan," he admitted, his voice rough.

"But we're not there for the info. We want to get in good with Arakovic." She tapped a finger against her chin, thinking.

"He said there's a bounty. Money."

"Oh, even better." Jenny nodded. "We're there for the money. We don't care who it comes from or where you're going. Then we give you the antidote, and as he lets his guard down, we knock him over the head and have our way with his computers."

"It all comes down to physically assaulting him one way or another, doesn't it?" Kael smiled. "As long as someone hits that asshole at some point."

"I suppose I could also try to sedate him."

"Sounds less gratifying."

"But it wouldn't hurt to have a backup plan," Adan chimed in.

Jenny stood. "Give me just two minutes—I'll go get the drugs."

"Should we suit up?" Adan rose.

Kael shook his head. "You should. I shouldn't. Gotta make it convincing that you two overpowered me."

"Hey, now." Jenny grinned as she strode out. "I could take you, Theroki."

Kael snorted.

"Hey, he's not a Theroki anymore. Right, Kael?" Adan looked at him, eyes laughing.

"At least someone is listening to me on *one* matter." If AIs could sigh, Xi would have. "Can I offer you another important bit of information? I know the commander's whereabouts, and I hypothesize you will wish to know as well."

Now Kael stood, suddenly tense. "Where, Xi?"

"She headed for Dr. Ostrov's residence, and I lost track of her when she entered. There seems to be something jamming the signals going in and out of there, as you observed the other evening. So you will be on your own. I won't be able to help you." She sounded bitter.

Adan sprang to his feet while Xi was still talking, even as Kael was jogging for the door. "When? How long ago?"

"Six hours, I estimate. It is similar to her other visits there. But they were not planning to play a game. I think something is... wrong."

"Let's hope you're not right, Xi," Kael muttered.

But he had a feeling that she wasn't.

———

ELLEN SQUINTED her eyes against the beam of the laser splitting the darkness. She kept her wrists as close to the wall as possible for a broader range of movement. The beam from the little forearm gauntlet lasers built into the suit were burning into something, although weakly and it was hard to see exactly what she was hitting. They weren't multis, but they were definitely a start.

The cuffs pinned her hands within a few centimeters of each other, so she couldn't angle her gauntlet quite right to cut them directly, but with a little trial and error, she managed to cut into the chains beyond the cuffs. The laser took some time, but that was one thing she seemed to have.

And this felt better than just listening to whatever the frag was squirming around, trying to crawl up her boot. She kicked at her assailants and scowled at the wall.

Ostrov should have really invested in a can opener, but she was glad he hadn't. In spite of the reinforced chains, clearly he wasn't familiar with all the capabilities of power armor. Thank heavens.

Another sickening squish made her want to cut wildly at the floor too, but that might eat through it and tip him off before she was ready.

She was already concerned about the light her laser was throwing off, not to mention the burning smell.

She held the sustained beam as carefully as she could in one place, averting her eyes but also afraid of leaning into its path. Still, she couldn't resist looking down as her eyes started to adjust to the pale blue light cast off by the laser. The white bathroom tiles lining the entire place caught the light and amplified it happily. And indeed, there was a shower, a sink, a toilet, a bath.

She was in a sort of fancy bath-shower stall, she realized. So maybe he wasn't joking about the blood. As her eyes drifted down, she tensed, but it wasn't enough to prepare her for what she saw.

It wasn't just a fish slapping around down there, or one creature making that squishing sound.

The floor was covered. White-tentacled creatures, almost translucent, seethed in a mass around her boots. They seemed unable to find purchase on the slick armor, but not for lack of trying. They could be two or three deep. Or—she didn't really know. They looked like tiny versions of the creatures that had erupted from Vala, and the telepath on Upsilon.

She swallowed, her mouth suddenly dry. They looked like the little creatures perched on the sushi.

Had this been his plan all along? What even were they? She'd thought monsters, aliens, something—what did this mean? And how in all the systems could she get away from them, as soon as possible?

The chains chose that moment to fall loose, just as she wasn't watching. She gasped and slipped, losing her balance. She cursed entirely too loudly, groping at the walls as she fell.

One hand caught the remains of the chain, and she righted herself savagely. She refocused the beam on the metal plate to give herself more light. She tried to slow her panicked breath as she—very, very carefully—stepped first one foot and then the other over the ridge of the tub. Out of the enclosure.

A single determined creature stuck to her foot. She shook it once, kicked, then again. Harder. Suddenly, it went flying. Her heart jumped into her throat.

The thing hit the wall with a splat and flopped down, back amid its brethren.

She thought again about barbecuing the seething mass with the laser, but it seemed hardly justified as they just sat there like lumps, not harming anything. Yet.

No, that'd be a waste of power anyway. She studied the room.

There. Above her. The fan. The bathroom fan should lead to the ductwork—maybe where she should have started in the first place.

She climbed onto the sink—holding to the light fixture so tightly for balance that she bent it—and got to work.

———

FOR A LUXURY BUILDING, the ducts were filthy. She knew she was getting close to the main living area from peeks out the vents, and she must be near the foyer, because she heard the door chime. Perfect. Whoever was ringing, once they'd cleared out of there, she could use the apartment computer mounted in the wall to try to reach his computer. If she could at least plant a nuke, or a worm, or whatever she could find in her suit inventory along those lines, then maybe Adan or Doug could finish the job later and get her Arakovic's information. And then she could get out.

Ostrov's footsteps moved to the door, stopped. The screen came to life. "What an interesting surprise this is," he said smoothly.

"Jenny Utlis," said a familiar voice from the door. "We want to talk to you. Think we have something you might be interested in."

Ellen froze. What the hell was *Jenny* doing out there?

"C'mon in."

Yeah, that bastard wasn't afraid. He still had at least four functional robots, maybe way more.

Ellen shifted as silently as she could so she could see through a low floor grating. She peered up and out at the room above her.

Jenny was completely transformed. Her hair was jet black, cut sharp as a knife's edge, makeup hiding her and smoothing her into a porcelain doll. And even crazier—Adan had nearly the same treatment in an expensive suit by her side. He held a tractor, and—

And as she realized why, her blood froze in her veins. They had Kael. That was what the tractor was carrying. She couldn't see as much of him, but he was clearly unarmored and unconscious.

"We heard you were looking for him. He's been nothing but trouble for us. We brought him to you, no problems. All we ask is our share of the bounty."

Ostrov stepped back, then to the side, peering at Kael. Poking him. He gave him a hard jab in the ribs, making Ellen wince. Testing if he was really out, she realized. Kael didn't move a muscle.

What the hell were they thinking? What the hell were they *doing*? Could they really be betraying her, and Kael—and for money of all things? The people she knew wouldn't do that. But they wouldn't dress that way either. What if she'd mistaken them—just like Paul—just like—

She forced her panic down. Kael needed her not to panic. He needed her to get him out of this, information be damned. But how the hell was she supposed to do that? After her first run-in with the droids, her plan had been to just sneak the hell out.

She did *not* need to go back to that bowl full of octopuses.

Jenny pivoted to face Ostrov, and Ellen could see her back now. A medical inhaler no bigger than Ellen's pinky nail was resting in Jenny's hand. Was that how they'd sedated him?

No—she was pressing it now, easing closer to him, hoping Ostrov wouldn't notice. A stimulant perhaps?

"Well, well." Ostrov applied an ident scanner to Kael's finger and chuckled. "What have we here. You did bring me the real thing." He nodded approvingly. "I'm sure some deal can be arranged." He tapped the scanner once more, then smiled down at Kael like a man might admire a newly acquired flyer.

That was when Ellen knew something was wrong. She didn't know what first exactly, but something.

The hum of the droids reached her ears.

Jenny whirled, drawing her multi, but it was too late. A droid's steel arm backhanded her, sending her flying. The multi went another direction, skidding, bouncing off the wall, and landing about a meter away from Ellen's grate. She eyed it. Now—or later?

At the same time, Adan danced away from the slash of another droid before it tackled him to the ground, leaving Kael floating and alone.

"Unfortunately," Ostrov said mildly, "I've already summoned Dr. Arakovic and received a sizable payment. She's on her way, and there are bounties out on you two as well. Probably your whole ship. Maybe I'll head to the docks next and see what I can find. If I can find all six of you weaklings and hand you over, maybe I can even keep your ship as well."

Ellen clenched a fist. If that asshole thought he was ever setting foot in that ship… well, she had a thing or two to teach him.

Jenny was struggling, but it was a losing fight. If she'd had an antidote for Kael, Ellen had no idea if it was working. Two more droids had just marched in.

Damn it, not these guys again.

Before she could second-guess it, she dove—smashing through the grating and angling for the multi.

She found it and kept her spin going, rolling to her back as she brought the weapon to ready and blasted a ballistic right through one android's eye. The next shot took out the brain stem on one that was charging for Jenny—a lucky, but thorough shot. It fell down lifeless, just the eyes twitching.

She turned the multi toward Ostrov and lowered its aim almost immediately. Because while she'd been taking out androids, he'd been pressing his pistol to Kael's temple. The freshly healed one. Lucky for him, he was barely awake to groan, but she did see his eyelids fluttering.

"Ellen," Ostrov cooed, despite the force he was using to hold an inert Kael to his side. "How lovely of you to join us."

"No thanks to you," she grunted. She slowly sat up. She needed to get her feet under her. Shooting from the floor would put her at a disadvantage here.

"It seems you've been outmaneuvered. Strategic 'genius' or not. Winning fancy board games doesn't keep you *alive* apparently." He scoffed.

"Don't call the game before it's over." She got her feet under her and rose straight up, nice and careful and slow. "Let them go."

"It's too late, Ellen. Arakovic's men will be here any minute. And besides, you won't shoot me for your information. You already had your chance."

"I told you I don't bluff."

"And I told you I don't believe you."

"A feint is not the same thing. I'm warning you."

"I'll show you just how much I don't believe you." He popped the safety off the pistol pointed at Kael.

"She wants him." She hated herself for the shake in her voice. She popped her own safety. "You wouldn't."

He grinned at her. "Wouldn't I?"

A pounding rose up at the door. One of the androids bounded toward the noise. A moment later, scuffling noises erupted from the corner where Jenny had fallen.

"How will you choose?" Ostrov shook his head. "Your pilot? You probably need him. And I'm sure she's an old friend. And this one— was this why you dragged your heels for me? How does a Theroki escape a life sentence for murder, anyway?"

He clucked his tongue at her as the pounding at the door grew louder.

"Not without powerful friends, I don't think." He tapped the muzzle against Kael's temple, almost as if trying to rouse him, and indeed, Kael's eyes opened slightly, groggy, and he squinted.

"Ellen?" he murmured.

"On a first-name basis with his commanding officer?" Ostrov glowered at her. "That's what I thought. So choose. Arakovic wants him alive, but I'll take her wrath on this one. The other two she cares less about. Who will you choose?"

"Don't do this, Ostrov. We can work something out. We can—"

"Line up your shot now, Ellen. You can save one of them. Which will it be?"

She glanced at the one holding down Jenny. She didn't have a clear shot of anything except its metal behind and maybe a thigh. But Adan's was raised up at times—she could hit the brainstem if she tried, which might take it out like it had the other one. But if she went for that, Ostrov would fire. And Kael would be dead.

"Don't do this, you sick—" she started.

"Kill them," he snapped at the droids.

It was a decision. And it wasn't really a decision. For the split second that he glanced over at his robots, she aimed the rifle and fired. Then dove. She barely had time to process the destruction the rifle had wrought, the spray of boiling blood and brain matter. She was tackling Kael away from Ostrov. Kael's eyes had snapped open, seemingly full alert. They hit the ground hard.

A scream rang out from Adan, and Ellen was on her feet, rushing—

But no. She skidded to a stop as a wave of energy brushed past her, pushing her to the side. The wave blasted the robot off Adan and flattened it into the wall. Literally. She whirled toward Jenny as the same thing was happening to hers. She rushed to Adan's side. One hand was pressed over his eye, and blood was everywhere. Jenny limped up beside them, and now Kael too, just as someone finally lost their patience, and the door burst.

Men in wild, vicious armor, old and rusted, beaten and worn and jagged, rushed toward them like a flood, shouting, enraged. Voices screaming like the depths of a volcano.

Theroki.

Before they even had time to speak, a sudden wave of energy was hitting *them*. Or was it a grenade?

Glass shattered in a thousand directions behind them. To her right, a grenade took out part of the floor. On the left, a second destroyed that stupid juice bar.

A body collided with hers, arms wrapped around her. Somehow, insanely, none of the shrapnel hit. Waves of energy bombarded them— why? Hadn't Arakovic wanted them alive? And hadn't the Theroki banned working with her anyway?

Three solid waves thrust the rubble and bodies around her back, back again…

And then they tumbled over the edge.

She crushed against him so hard she realized she might break a rib. They tumbled, but she was finally able to catch a glimpse of Kael above her, glass shards and metal arching out like vicious angel wings behind him.

The wind whistled in her ears, screams lost into it.

As the air whipped past her, she had only one thought pounding in her head, above the shock of it all. Hell of a day for him not to wear his armor.

———————

IT TOOK every bit of Kael's concentration not to drop one of them as the team plunged into free fall. Bits and pieces of Ostrov's former apartment followed them, vicious birds ready to peck. Falling out of a skyscraper had a remarkable way of clearing your system of sedatives, but four people was well beyond his limits, and that was without them getting battered on all sides.

But he'd be damned if he was giving up now.

He'd let the first wave push them, then added his own waves to finish the job. Further away was better, he'd figured, even if it meant a 140-story drop. That had been a *lot* of Theroki. And on Capital? What the hell? And why had they attacked if Arakovic had wanted him alive?

He could only think of one reason, and he didn't like it. Maybe these weren't Arakovic's men, and the real ones were still in pursuit, but Theroki had intercepted Ostrov's message. And after a deserter, Arakovic be damned.

Hopefully he wouldn't find out which it was.

He crushed Adan and Jenny and Ellen together, and he felt Ellen return his grip, tightening her arms around him even as her eyes widened, her lips parted. Her armored strength hurt a little, but it was grounding, reminding him.

He *had* to do this. He had to find a way. Or they were all going to be jelly.

Pavement was racing toward his face.

Wave after wave, like knocking back enemy weapons, except this time the enemy was gravity. But slowly he began to break their fall.

Of course, this meant the glass behind them was coming at them faster, so he had to slow *its* speed too. But it was more than glass. Metal shards, pipes, walls, concrete. He couldn't expect to grab it all. He didn't have the bandwidth to shove it aside, unless…

For a brief second, he let go of them, using the power instead to shove out and up, the ruined bits of the building thrusting farther away from them in every direction. His stomach twisted as their speed increased.

Swearing, he caught them up again. He still had to slow them down enough so they didn't smash like melons—there was no time left for anything more. If the debris hit them, it hit them.

He threw his entire being into slowing that fall. If he could just switch at the last minute…

It was a long shot, but it was all he had.

———

THEY HIT the debris-laden ground with a rib-aching slam, Ellen's breath rushing from her lungs. She gasped, then choked, dust filling the air. Coughs racked her body.

A body that was pressed to another warm body, one that lay against her. Also coughing.

And also alive.

She forced her eyes open. Kael's hair tickled her cheek as he coughed against her arm.

Hovering in the air less than a meter above her face were hundreds of shards of glass. They weren't frozen, either, they twitched and spun, jerking slightly closer, then stopping. In time with his coughs, almost.

God. He was holding them up, wasn't he?

She slapped his back, now trying in earnest to help him recover from the fall. A few more hacks, and his coughing stopped. He leaned on elbows over her. His face was coated with a pale, beige dust.

"Hey." He smiled slightly.

"Hey."

"We're alive!" Jenny burst out beside them, rolling awkwardly away from the heap of concrete, metal, and glass beneath them. More debris was littered on all sides. Then Jenny's own fit of coughs overcame her.

Adan only groaned, and Jenny stopped and rushed to him.

Ellen looked back at Kael. Death could be so close. Hovering a foot above her face, even. Or in a Theroki flyer working for Arakovic hovering somewhere nearby.

There was so little time. No time at all, even.

She laid her fingers against his cheek, felt the brush of stubble forming there. His eyes changed, lit and widened, then narrowed again as the rubble slipped slightly and he refocused his concentration.

"Are we going to die?" Adan grunted beside them.

"Not if I can help it," Kael replied through clenched teeth.

Not speaking, she ran her fingers down his jaw, stopping delicately at his chin, and then opened her mouth—but what was there to say? Especially with such close company? Should she start with an apology?

"Anyone alive in there?" called a voice from the other side of a debris pile.

Kael turned his head sharply, relief flooding his features.

"Yes!" Jenny shouted. "Yes! Please help!"

"Clear the debris!" Kael called. His voice was strained. "Make a path out! There's four of us in here." Outside she could hear whispers, but also the crashing of pieces of the building being pushed aside.

He turned his gaze back to hers. Clearly this was one moment where a distraction was literally a bad idea. Damn her own words. She was cursed to be haunted by them until the end of her days.

He turned his face back toward her as daylight poured in as a large piece of outer shell fell away. "What is it? Are you okay?"

Nodding was all she could muster.

CHAPTER FIFTEEN

ELLEN HADN'T BEEN on her feet for five seconds before she was flagging down a flyer. It couldn't take those Theroki long to catch up, especially since they also could just jump out the newly created "window."

She got lucky, grabbing a big flyer that could have seated ten, herding them all in before there were any signs of pursuit. The door slammed, and she ordered it directly to the ship. And then she collapsed back against the seat in exhaustion, surveying the damage.

She herself had cuts on her face and two giant metal bracelets that didn't match her armor, but she was the luckiest of them.

Kael was exhausted to near delirium, eyes glazed and unfocused as he stared at the ceiling. She found a d-bar in her hip compartment, opened it, and forced it into his hand. Jenny had hurt her leg somehow, through the armor, but she was clearly trying to hide it.

Adan, however, was getting blood just everywhere. The robot had done a number on one whole side of his face, and Jenny was doing her best to stop the bleeding.

Which was a big job. She wasn't close to stabilizing him when the flyer glided to a stop at the base of the damn staircase. Ellen glared up at the fifty flights of catwalk stairs.

"The hell with this." Pushing past Kael, she grabbed the manual override and whipped the thing up into the air. She ignored the bleeps and boops and protests over the comm from traffic control.

She had the flyer out front of the *Audacity* in under a minute, and they climbed out. They sent the poor vehicle on its merry, bloody way. Hopefully the Foundation would pay for the cleaning service.

She threw Kael's arm over her shoulder, although his exhaustion did seem to be waning. It was mostly an excuse to feel in her own cells that he was really still alive. But she stopped short a few steps later.

Two figures stood between them and the ship. The blue cloak flapped in the wind like a serpent writhing, orbs of a deeper cobalt light shining out from under the hood. At her side was the young Ursa.

"Kentt." Ellen's voice was hard. "Get out of the way. We need to get out of here. Now."

She didn't move. "So do I."

Kael straightened and squared his shoulders at her, clearly threatening. "Stand aside."

She held up a surprisingly normal-looking palm. "There's no need for feats of telekinesis. I come in peace. *Salam*, as they say."

Kael narrowed his eyes.

"Sure, you do," Jenny muttered.

"Take me with you." Kentt raised her voice. "We can be powerful allies. We must work together, if we wish to survive."

"Survive what?" Ellen said.

"Arakovic, of course."

"She's the one who needs to worry about surviving," Ellen growled.

"It doesn't matter. Take me with you," Kentt prompted.

"You can't take her on the ship without being cleared," Jenny whispered. "She'll know everything. *Everything.* We can't give everyone one of Persad's chips."

Kentt smiled bitterly, her cherry lips just visible in the shadow. "Arakovic is your enemy. She is also mine. You will need my help to face her."

"How do we know you can be trusted?" Ellen said.

Kentt took a deep breath. "Trust must be mutual and built over time—time that we do not have. And someone always has to go first."

Ellen scowled. "Trust me is what Ostrov said before he locked me in a room full of killer octopuses."

They all froze in unison.

"What the—" Kael snapped.

"There's no time to explain now."

Kael glanced over her shoulder. "Those Theroki ships are coming. We need to go. Stand aside, Kentt, or I'll move you."

"You want an olive branch? I'll give you one." Kentt straightened. "I know where those girls you seek are."

Sure she did. "Where? And how do you know?"

"I know because I took them."

Ellen's mouth fell open. "Excuse me?"

"I helped them get off planet. They wanted to hide, and I helped them. To escape the Songbird project. They wanted to get away."

"Smart girls," Ellen muttered. "But perhaps you're the smartest of all?"

"Not smart enough. I know where they're hidden. Arakovic has figured that out, and now she's coming for me."

"Or me," Ellen muttered.

"Or me." Kael shook his head.

"Or all of you!" Jenny was staring behind them. "Can we just get on the ship now? We're losing our lead. They're gaining."

"Fine," Ellen snapped. "Get in the ship. But I need to consult with someone. Before it's official. Adan, can you begin emergency liftoff with Fern's help?"

"I can help too—especially with the equipment on board," Jenny added.

"You have no idea how bad I want off this rock," Adan said. "I can talk Fern through it if these painkillers don't kick in any harder. Let's go."

ELLEN LEANED against Kael as they made their way onto the ship, still supporting his arm over her shoulders as if she were helping. In reality, she suspected it was the other way around. Maybe they were holding each other up.

They went straight past his cabin toward Bri's, but just outside his hatch, a new mural of Zhia had transformed the corridor. She couldn't remember approving this one, but Zhia had sure made use of the downtime. His step faltered alongside hers.

"Wow," he breathed.

A sparkling sunrise rose from an ocean of color and light. Amid the deep sapphire and violet waves, lines of poetry danced, something vaguely familiar and eternally beautiful, even if Ellen couldn't quite place it.

> Arise, fair sun, and kill the envious moon,
> Who is already sick and pale with grief,
> That thou her maid art far more fair than she:
> Be not her maid, since she is envious;
> Her vestal livery is but sick and green
> And none but fools do wear it; cast it off.

"Well, somebody kept busy," Ellen muttered, unable to find the proper praise for it. Instead she lean-limped down the hall and pounded on Bri's door. Luckily enough, the door slid open to reveal Isa. Who was frowning.

"Why can't I—" Isa stared from Ellen to Kael and back again.

"Not now, no time to explain. Has she talked to you?"

"How strange!" Isa showed no sign of even hearing Ellen's words.

"Isa! Has she said anything to you? Approached you? The telepath outside the ship."

Her eyes cleared, refocusing on Ellen. "The one who is now inside the ship? Just polite niceties, Commander."

"Can you handle her?"

"What do you mean?"

"Is she a danger to you? If I bring her on here and she harasses you, will you be able to tell me?"

"Harasses me?"

"Yes. I will kick her off if she hurts you. You deserve to be safe. She's experienced and you're... not."

"Why, that's so nice. I could perhaps tell you. It's possible that I couldn't. But she won't harass me. I'm certain."

"You *can't* be certain."

"True certainty is impossible, but as Xi would say, I believe the probability is in my favor. She has offered to teach me."

"Presume much?" Ellen raised her eyebrows. Kentt was always one step ahead, it seemed. She raised her comm to her lips. "All right, she can stay. Dane, get the telepath to a cabin and strapped in."

Acknowledgments were muttered across the channel. Isa turned away with a nod, letting the door slip shut.

"Where to now, hotshot?" Ellen muttered. "You need to go to sick bay? Your quarters?"

"You know she'll know about the capsule," he said softly. "She'll figure it out. What it is."

"What *she* is. I know." She was nodding but not looking at him, pressing her lips together into a flat line.

"What are you going to do? If she learns the Foundation's secrets and it turns out we can't trust her?"

She met his eyes. "If I have to, I'll kill her. But here's hoping it doesn't come to that."

She changed directions and headed toward her quarters. There were some... things she needed to say.

———

XI SHUT the door behind her, and Ellen released Kael to sit on the bunk, steadying herself on her feet.

"You still don't look so good," she lied, making an excuse. "Can I get you anything?"

"Commander, you're—" Xi started.

"Not now, Xi," she barked, too hastily.

He rubbed his forehead. "Can you dim the lights, Xi? My head is killing me."

"Also food is good," Xi said, keeping it clipped.

"I know." Ellen snapped her fingers. "Be right back."

The lights had dimmed dutifully when she returned. She sat down beside him on her bunk, feeling for all the world like a child sharing a toy with a friend. The strangest feeling for this moment. But she held out the plate of cookies and the glass.

"Now for an important question," he said slowly.

"Yeah?" She picked up her own cookie as he took his.

"To dunk, or not to dunk?"

She shook her head. "No, no, you have to keep them separate. Two complementary but separate tastes."

He snorted.

"You?"

"I've been known to dunk when the situation calls for it."

"This must be why we get along so poorly."

Although he was still smiling, a slight frown creased his brow at that comment. He chewed and said nothing.

"I assume Jenny and Adan didn't betray you and knock you out?"

"It was our plan to try to steal the information. Well, they talked me into letting them help instead of just going up there and choking it out of him."

She snorted. "Trust me, they were right. That plan didn't work at all. Androids, you see. Maybe it would have worked better for you. I didn't try choking, though. Next time." The memory of the creatures seething floated back, and she shuddered. Yeah, hopefully there was no next time.

"Did he... How long were you..."

"I'm fine. But later. Let's talk about that later. Not now."

He shrugged. "Okay."

She stilled. Set the milk and the plate down beside the bed. Stared at the floor. "We had a few conversations we didn't get to finish."

"Hmm." Pretending his mouth was full. Good stalling tactic, that. She should be taking notes.

"I was never interested in Ostrov," she blurted. "Ever. Not once."

He waved it off. "Hey, it turned out you were right. He *did* have information, and it was a biggie. Sorry we didn't get it."

"I can't believe you were going to go behind my back and try to get it." She laughed, shaking her head.

"I can literally say the same thing to you. And I am saying it. What the hell. We're lucky we got out of there alive."

"That's true. Some team we are." She could have bought it, and he'd have never understood the truth.

"So… unfinished conversations. What was it you were saying? It was something like 'even with you'?" He smiled crookedly, waiting for her answer.

She groaned. That hadn't been her finest moment. Indignation had been *real* helpful at clearing this up. "I guess I was just offended you thought I *could* be interested in him."

He shrugged. "Why not? He's smart, apparently well-to-do, handsome. Doesn't have any murder convictions, tattoos, or six-centimeter scars."

"You have a six-centimeter scar?" And now she was thinking about seeing it. And where it might be. Focus, Ellen, focus.

"I'm just saying, seems like a catch."

"Except that he's an asshole. Uh, was. Was an asshole. Before I, you know, blew his brains out."

He swallowed. "Good point."

She forced herself to take a deep breath. She didn't want to talk about Ostrov. He was beside the point. And very, very dead.

"Look, I've struggled with this," she said slowly. He raised his eyebrows at the word "this." "But we have had way too many brushes with death lately, and it's reminded me repeatedly of what I already knew. We can all bite it anytime. I could choke on this fragging cookie." She narrowed her eyes at the one in her hand.

"Please don't."

"My point is—" She faltered, biting her lip instead. No sound would come out.

He tilted his head, frowning, eyes trained on her lips. This window was going to close. He was going to march on out and get back to being a damned hero without even knowing it and leave her here again, alone and helpless, and pathetic at communicating herself.

"What I'm trying to say is..." She met his gaze. But words fled. Such earnestness in that deep-coffee brown, such honesty. And acceptance.

The hell with words.

She grabbed his face with both hands and pressed her lips against his. Before she could change her mind, damn it.

He froze, inhaling sharply.

And then he grabbed her, pulling her closer, her armor knocking against his chest roughly. Why hadn't she thought to take it off? What would the crew say if they lined up matching scratches on the front of their chests?

Did she even give a shit at this point?

She forgot all thought of the crew as he raised a hand and ran it over her hair. The sweetness of the gesture made her ache. She opened her mouth, kissing him harder, inviting him in, and he obliged readily.

Relief swept her.

It hadn't taken her too long. He still wanted her. He hadn't moved on. Damage had been done, but maybe it was recoverable, and in this moment, it didn't matter. Nothing mattered but the two of them.

He broke away suddenly, and her heart lurched. Or maybe not. His hands hadn't strayed from her waist, though. He stared down as if she'd gone insane. "Are you sure you're okay? Did Ostrov give you anything? Xi, did he give her anything?"

"I'm perfectly fine," she snapped, frowning. "What, I have to be on something to want to—you know?" Very mature, Ellen. Jesus.

"Her vitals appear to be normal, considering the circumstances," Xi said.

"Considering the circumstances?" he asked.

"Her pulse and blood pressure levels are frequently elevated in your presence," Xi said mildly.

"Xi! Cut it out!" Ellen felt her cheeks growing hot. Though Xi was probably helping her case right now.

He was grinning. "Frequently? Really? Xi, why didn't you tell me?"

"I hypothesize—"

"Look, I was scared, okay?" Ellen cut in. "I still am. I don't know what I'm doing. And I don't *like* not knowing what I'm doing. Butt out, Xi. It's my job to say this, even if I'm shitty at it."

He turned his eyes back to her, more sober now.

"Remember the whole pretending you're not listening routine, Xi?" Ellen added. "This is the time."

Xi didn't respond, ironically enough.

"You do distract me." Her words came out in a rush. "But it doesn't matter if I'm with you or not. If I kiss you or not. Pushing you away distracts me just as much as pulling you close. And it hurts. It hurts so much more." She turned away as she spoke, still sitting beside him but staring out into the stars, the marble of Capital receding in the distance. She pretended her hair urgently needed pushed out of her face.

"How long?" he said abruptly.

"What?"

"I want to make sure this isn't some kind of weird fluke or side effect of something he did to you. So tell me. How long have you... wanted me?"

"I never said I *didn't* want you, Kael." She rounded on him, eyes flashing, poking his chest.

"Yes, you did. You said—"

"I said I was afraid. That's different."

He frowned for a long moment before understanding swept across his face. "Are you kidding?" He shook his head.

"I wouldn't kid about this. You know that."

"So when? When did it start?" he whispered, still gently persistent. He leaned closer now and closed his eyes, his forehead drifting to touch hers. "If this is some damn chem, or tomorrow you tell me to forget all this again, I swear I'll—"

"Fine, fine. Force it out of me. I guess it was... all along. So long I lost track of it, really. You walked onto my damn ship and were already under my skin. I thought I was nuts thinking a Theroki was eying me up until I made sense of those scans."

"Wow—you noticed. I was trying to hide it."

"I know. You had... less practice then than you do now, probably."

He laughed softly.

"And you did have a chemical excuse at the time." She leaned closer herself, knocking her shoulder against his.

"Why now, Ellen?" he persisted. "Why are you telling me this?"

"What?" Damn, he was worried. The damage was worse than she'd thought. "I've been *trying* to tell you since Simmons gave you his job offer, but... God, I've failed so many times. I'm not always good with words—well, words about my feelings anyway."

She pulled away slightly, so he would open his eyes, see her sincerity. He watched her, but the look was guarded.

"You were right," she said softly. "I'm brave and bold when it comes to helping people. I'll run into bullet fire, bomb a generator, raid a lab to help someone else, keep them safe. I fight for justice all the damn time. But when it comes to what *I* want, I haven't fought. I've been a coward. *Am* a coward."

"No."

"Yes."

"You're not being a coward now."

"So I reached out once or twice and got burned, but so what? That was no excuse to stop reaching, but I let it be. I let my fear rule me, and I used my past as a shield, so I didn't have to face it. My responsibilities, too. But all along, it was really just fear."

"Not just that. Fear and responsibility." His brow creased with sadness for her, and something deeper, and his mouth captured hers, initiating for the first time, probing into her with a sweet gentleness that made her body flood with fresh heat.

She broke away, suddenly more sure of herself. "I'm sorry I let that come between us. It was stupid. Stupid, stupid."

"No, it wasn't. But we're all fools in love," he murmured. He ran his hand along her jaw and kissed her again in reply, harder this time. Hungrier. Pressing her, leaning her back onto the bunk.

Good Lord. Perhaps she had found the right words after all.

"Commander, I realize this is a very bad time but—" Xi cut in.

They froze. She groaned in unison with Kael.

"I do apologize, but I have an urgent comm from Doug."

Ellen pinched the bridge of her nose, head shaking. "Fine. Bring it up."

———

KAEL RAN his hand through his hair and wondered if they looked like they'd been doing more than having a chat. When Doug's face flickered to life over the holodesk, he didn't seem especially surprised that they were both already in her cabin.

Was it terrible to hope they could keep this short?

On the screen, Doug glanced over his shoulder, then back at them. The image flickered a little. That was odd. Calls from Doug always seemed crystal clear. "Boy, have I got some news for you two. But especially Kael. You're not going to believe this." His usual wild shirt was black with a comet pattern that only moderately hurt Kael's eyes.

"What is it?" he managed to say.

"I was crossing my t's and dotting my i's on your file. And it turns out that after you were shipped off, the coroner didn't stop objecting to your conviction. Or looking into it."

Kael frowned. "Really?" Of all the things he'd thought Doug might say, that hadn't been one of them.

"His objection was part of what made me feel sure you hadn't done it. But it turns out he went further than that, but the findings were never released."

"How'd you get them if they were never released?" asked Ellen.

He shrugged casually as the image flickered again. "Hacked into his private files. Anyway, he eventually proved that the body of the girl you were accused of murdering didn't belong to Asha at all."

Kael's eyes widened. "What? Wait—what does that mean?"

"It was cleverly doctored to appear so. High-tech, too. Fingerprints covered over. But when the coroner started to make a stink about it, he discovered that the girl had no living relatives, you were long gone, and he was getting death threats. So Dr. Abed eventually dropped the matter. He had to admit he was too late."

Kael's head was suddenly spinning again. Someone had actually cared about what had happened? To him, or any of it? "I think I need to lie down."

"It doesn't stop there, though. I found her."

He looked up from where his eyes had drifted to the floor, his body a block of ice. Ellen's thigh was warm against his, but he thought he could feel her jolt.

"I found Asha. She's *alive*."

He cursed as a picture of her appeared on the vid screen. Older, a woman now, but it was her for sure. "What about—"

"The baby? No birth record. No medical record of delivery or miscarriage or stillbirth. No death record or adoption papers either. Asha's current medical records don't even mention the pregnancy. It's like the kid vanished from her womb."

Kael scowled. "Or was erased."

"What does that even mean?" Ellen grunted in disgust. "Babies can't just disappear."

Doug nodded. "I know. Don't worry, I'm not done looking yet. But if it were anything simple—there'd be a record. Something is up here."

"We were poor—" he started.

"Well, she's not now. Here's her address." It flashed up on the screen, along with a picture of an elegant walled residence. "Look like she's begging for her dinner to you?"

Kael only stared, something like anger brewing, although he didn't understand why.

"Listen, there's this friend of a friend on Faros IV. Talented hacker. She seems to be getting into a bit of a pickle…"

"Here we go again," Ellen muttered.

"I'm just saying, I think we should check all this out. Kael can talk to Asha. We can try to find out what happened to the baby. We can get a new recruit or two for our team. And do some good along the way. If I'm right, we're going to need all the help we can against Arakovic."

Ellen sighed. "I'll have Adan set a course."

Simmons grinned and started to say something, but the image flickered off abruptly. Odd. He didn't usually cut out accidentally. Guy was better at tech than *that*.

"Xi? What happened?" Ellen said.

"Connection to Doug was terminated. I will attempt to reestablish. It could take twenty-five minutes or more."

"All right," Ellen said. What else could she say?

They sat for a moment in strained silence.

"Too bad I didn't have my come-to-Jesus moment a week earlier, huh?" she muttered.

"Your what?"

"My revelation? Confession? Never mind."

He said nothing.

She cleared her throat. "You've got to go to her. Talk to her. Find out what happened."

He shook his head. "You're not getting rid of me that quickly."

His lips found hers again as she gave a little gasp of surprise. And if she were honest, relief. He held her neck, locking her in place. She was tense for a moment before her body relaxed, the urgency gone out of her.

When he finally came up for air, he rested his forehead against hers. "Listen. Wherever she's been for the last eleven years, that new place sure looks like it has a comm or a holodesk or two. Don't you think?"

Her brown eyes were wary, but she nodded.

"She could have tried to reach out, get in touch. She didn't. So whatever it is—it's over. But it *would* be nice to clear my name." He smiled.

"Damn it," she grumbled. "If we get killed on this next mission, that'll serve me right for delaying so long."

"Guilt over it all doesn't get us anywhere, Ellen." He imitated her best stern voice, and she giggled. "Stay clear on the mission."

"I guess."

He squeezed her arm. "You had good reasons to be afraid. That's one of the reasons I don't seem to be able to quit you. You're the kind of person who is willing to deny yourself something to help others. Or protect them. Maybe it was an excuse, but maybe not. You're wise to be careful. To pay attention to your motivations. A lot is riding on them."

She nodded solemnly.

"But I'm also glad you changed your mind. Does that help?"

"Yeah. Yeah, actually it does." She smiled at him, unguarded for once, and there was something more rare and priceless in that than any of her words.

"You know what else would help?" He smiled back.

"What?"

"Getting out of your armor. Probably time to put it away for the day. What do you say?"

She smirked. "No sooner thought of than done."

———

BEFORE ELLEN HAD FINISHED SHUCKING her last pauldron, though, another call came in to the holodesk. But it wasn't Doug. It was Levereaux.

Ellen glanced at Kael. "I have to take this. It's probably about Adan—"

He waved at her wordlessly to go ahead.

Where he sat, he'd be in frame. She wondered if she should shoo him out of the video or beckon him closer. Anything less than honest was potentially hurtful. And she'd caused enough hurt so far.

She didn't ask him anything. She poked the desk key and accepted the call.

Levereaux's face appeared from sick bay. She glanced once at Kael, her brow furrowing, before turning her gaze back to Ellen. "You wanted a status report?"

She nodded. "How's Adan?"

"He'll be fine. I've done all I can, but he needs to get some rest before surgery. But we can replace what he's lost."

Ellen's jaw clenched. "Can I stop by?" Much as she didn't want to right now.

"Of course. I'm headed back to my quarters, but Jenny will be here."

Ellen nodded and cut the comm. She turned to Kael. "Can you hold that thought?"

He smirked at her. "Haven't I been for two months already? What's another hour?"

She glowered at him. "It won't be that long. Want to come?"

"No, it's okay. I'm pretty worn out." He glanced at the floor, tilting his head as he prepared to say something. "Do you mind if I… wait here for you to come back though?" His eyes twinkled at her.

"Yes. I mean, no—I don't mind. I mean. Stay. Please. It'll only be a moment. I just—"

"What?"

"It's my fault you're here and perfectly okay, and he's down there and well… not. I made the call."

"It's not your fault."

"Of course it is. Maybe you hadn't snapped out of it yet, but Ostrov—"

"No." He slashed through the air with the knife-edge of his hand. "It's *Ostrov's* fault. He's the one who ordered the robot to attack Adan. You just did your best to respond to it."

She took a deep breath. "Maybe. Still. I'll feel better if I stop by."

"By all means." He leaned back on her bed, folded his hands behind his head, and smiled. "I'll be waiting."

She'd rarely made the trip to sick bay so quickly, sliding down the ladder on her soles of her shoes. Rich would wince. Her pistol was tucked at her back waistband for now, and she was still in the sweaty clothes she'd worn under her armor. What a classy guest she was. She palmed open the door.

The sick bay was quiet, still bathed in a purple uterine glow. The sloshing sounds made her gag, the memory threatening to flood her. But the sooner she came to re-associate that sound with this empress baby rather than her Ostrov prison, the better.

Speaking of the baby, the creature—the girl—seemed to have doubled in size. Maybe more. How long had it been? No more than days, surely.

She approached the first bed where Jenny stood. "How is his eye?"

"It's pretty much gone." Jenny shrugged it off, but Ellen could see she was shaken. "But we can grow a new one or give him a cybernetic one. Dremer is drooling over the possibilities right now. And she even has a playmate to bounce plans off of."

"Well, at least a few people are happy." Ellen shook her head. "I'd rather he not have been hurt."

Jenny ran a finger down the back of Adan's hand, and Ellen forced herself not to stare or raise an eyebrow. Best if she just pretended not to notice. What business was it of anyone's? "He'll be mostly recuperated in a few hours. Then a little down time for the replacement surgery. A lot of research has been put into eyes. It's a good body part to lose."

Ellen knew that, but she winced anyway. She also knew the speed of medical tech didn't make the trauma, the horror of the experience go away.

"Do you think I did the wrong thing?" she said after a while.

Jenny frowned. "What do you mean?"

"He made me choose."

"Who? Ostrov?"

"Yeah."

"So?"

"So I chose Kael."

A look of understanding crossed Jenny's face. "Oh, so *that's* what you've been worried about? Why you haven't already jumped his bones?"

"Jenny!"

"Well. Is it?"

"Yes!" she snapped, exasperated. "I think this is proof it's a very valid worry. They'll be other times. Other tough choices, where it's one person or another and no in between. When I have to make the call. How do I make the right one, if… if things are more complicated than just one person or another?"

Jenny pursed her lips. "Well, if it hadn't been Kael, it would have been someone else. And you still would have had to choose. In this case, you chose the one of us with the telekinetic ability to free the other two. If you'd chosen me, Kael would just be dead. But all three of us are here now because you chose him."

"But I wasn't *thinking* about telekinetic ability. I wasn't thinking at all."

"I think some part of your subconscious mind knew the right choice. But even if it didn't, I don't see how it matters. It could have been Mo in his place. It could have been me. Any of us. You'd still have to pick, and it would still be worse than a frying pan full of dung beetles. But that's what we signed up for. We make tough choices every day. We do our best. And then we do our best to live with them."

Frowning still, Ellen nodded. "I hadn't thought about it that way."

Jenny patted her hand. "Now let's let him rest, shall we?"

"Yes."

———

EIGHT HOURS AFTER LIFTOFF, Adan was recovered enough to take the bridge and give Fern a rest. He plopped down into his pilot chair with a sigh, the familiar shape of the cushion under him shifting, the lining creaking. It was good to be back. Adventure was one thing. A nice refresher. A special kind of R&R for someone like him who was stuck in the ship most of the time. A trip to acquire some knowledge and battle scars and a massive headache.

And maybe a cybernetic eye.

Which would be kind of cool, if he could just block out the memory of how he'd lost the original one.

But he liked it inside. Really, keeping to the flight stick was how he'd prefer it. How had he ever thought he could leave this chair? This lovely, lovely ship? He ran a hand over the smooth metal below the view screen, gave her a pat.

"Missed you, girl."

"I missed you too, Adan," said Xi, from the ceiling.

"I also missed you, Xi, but I was talking to the ship."

"Am I-I not the sh-ship?"

There was an odd skip to her voice. That was strange. He couldn't remember Xi ever bugging out, and that was so common on most computer systems. Average people didn't notice them, but anyone who'd seen under the covers knew just how many bugs there usually were in most software. It was how hackers made their way around, exploiting such weaknesses. But Xi was usually quite reliable.

"I don't think you're quite the same as the ship, no. You're more like one of us."

"That is a very interesting thought, Adan. I will have to take it under m-meditation."

"As long as you don't start throwing things like the—" He stopped himself. "Like Kael."

"Like Kael, I will fix anything that I break. But worry not. I find deep p-ponderous thought natural and relaxing."

"Unlike Kael?"

"Yes."

"Just one of the many reasons why I like you." He leaned back in the chair, propped up his boots, and knitted his hands behind his neck. It was good to be home. "You okay, Xi? You don't sound quite right."

"Yes, Adan. Th-thank you for asking."

There was that skip again. But she knew herself, so he shrugged it off and looked out the view screen. He sat for a long time in silence, watching the slow movement of the ship through the stars.

A sudden snick and then a click made him jump, bring his feet down and start to rise.

"Don't move." Merith's voice was right behind him. He could see her reflection in the view screen.

He froze, hands still raised near his neck. "Merith? What the hell?"

"Warning: standard security protocols have been disabled—" Xi started.

"Shut up, you stupid computer."

The cold barrel of a gun pressed against the back of his neck.

"You should have taken Josana's offer, Adan. Then you wouldn't be in my way right now."

"Did you put her up to it?" That would make more sense.

"That small-time chemmie? No way. Just would have been convenient."

"And what way is that? How am I in your way?"

It dawned on him slowly. The drug, the threat, the risk to his life—it had been *real*. He hadn't truly believed it until just now. Did she have the ampule behind her even now? And why then would she still have a gun?

"You always thought you were such hot shit. You think you're the only one around here who knows your way around a network? But then that idiot spoiled rich kid installed this stupid pet AI, and I had two obstacles to deal with. Well, I'm taking you both out. Right now."

He blew out a shaky breath. "What did you do to Xi?" That angered him more than anything she could do to him.

"Set a course for Tetra VII. Now." She pushed into his neck with the barrel. Eyes could be replaced, but a spinal column? Much less likely.

His fingers started working. Usually Xi would do this, or at least check his inputs. She was silent.

"What's on Tetra VII?" he demanded.

"Your precious little patron, that's who." She spat the words.

He swore. "Jesus, what did Simmons ever do to you?"

"It's not something he did, per se—"

A sizzling cut the air, then a shot, and he threw himself to the ground before he could register that he'd already heard the attacks, and obviously neither had hit him.

What the—

From the floor, he rolled and turned and saw Jenny in the doorway.

The telepath in her blue cloak hovered in the shadows behind her shoulder, eyes glowing under the shadow of her hood.

And Merith lay on the floor, in a messy splatter of blood.

"Told you we all need help some time," Jenny blurted through panting breaths.

"Two cigars." He shook his head. "I owe you at least two cigars."

"You better make it a lifetime supply at this rate."

———

WHEN ELLEN ARRIVED BACK in her cabin, Kael's slow breathing greeted her. The lights were dimmed, sending little shells and pyramids of soft, white light to the floor, and the hum of the ventilation was the only other sound. Home. The *Audacity* wrapped around them like a shell, a cave, a place to hide, breathing and dark and quiet and home.

She stood, leaning against the wall and watching him sleep for a while, and it occurred to her that there had rarely been a time she'd felt such peace. His chest rose and fell with each quiet breath, and she could marvel in privacy for a moment that he was actually here.

That she'd actually said her piece. That it hadn't been too late. That Jenny was maybe right that being happy—with him—wasn't necessarily the most irresponsible thing she could possibly do.

After she'd had her fill, she carefully placed the pistol on the table beside the cookies and milk and slipped as smoothly as she could into the bed beside him. His arms were still nestled behind his head, and it was all too easy to tuck her head against his shoulder, lay her body warm against his, and close her eyes.

At some point, she stirred from sleep, feeling the unfamiliar sensation of another body solid and reassuring beside her as an arm curved over her waist. But it was so warm, and so perfect, she quickly fell back into sleep.

The door chimed. Then someone pounded.

Manually. Hard.

She started, and so did Kael next to her. Something was wrong. She staggered out of the bunk and hit the palm pad to open the door.

It didn't open.

"Shit." She grabbed at the handle near the bottom, grunted, and it started to slide.

"Let me," Kael said, appearing beside her, blinking. "What are you keeping me around for if not to open doors?"

She stepped aside, smiling wryly. "I guess chivalry isn't dead."

He had the door open in half a second. "I wouldn't know."

"Commander!" Jenny was panting outside. A pistol was in her hand, pointed at the floor, and her eyes were wild. "You've got to come to the bridge. Merith. She tried to hijack the ship."

Ellen swore. She took off after Jenny at a run, Kael on their heels. Jenny's eyes snagged on Kael, widened for just a second, then kept going. "Who had the bridge?"

"Adan!"

"Jesus, not his day!"

"I know. But it's fine," Jenny said. "Well—mostly fine. Kentt showed up at my door and got me to intervene. I guess because it's close to the bridge?"

As they reached the bridge, they found that hatch also standing open. Ellen slowed to a stop just inside. Merith lay on the floor, blood pooling around her. Shit. She should have... done something more. Prevented it from coming to this.

"I chose your door because I knew you would care more about Adan's safety than whether or not I was telling the truth." Kentt leaned against a far wall, and the words flowed out smooth and calculated. "Time was of the essence."

Ellen frowned at her. "You make a habit of searching for potential traitors when you board a ship? Did you smoke her out?"

"No," Kentt said. "I did do a light scan. Her thoughts were especially concealed. I always find that suspicious. She had some minor talent, and it had been trained specifically to protect herself from telepaths. Or else your fledgling might have noticed her treachery sooner. But I did not smoke her out. It seemed the departure from the planet was her catalyst. She wanted out of Capital territory first."

Adan hadn't turned to look at them. He was flying through commands at the pilot's console. Noticing her gaze, he cleared his throat. "She did something to Xi. I'm trying to get her back online."

Hell. That was worse than she'd thought. "What *else* did she do?"

"She made me set our course for Tetra VII."

"What the hell is there?"

Adan frowned, glancing at each of them in turn before saying, "Patron Simmons, apparently. Doug. According to her."

"That is correct," said a voice from the ceiling. It was stilted, void of inflection, computerized.

"Xi?" he gasped. "Is that you?"

"Main conversational components and relational algorithms remain offline. Rebooting will take approximately three minutes and twenty-nine seconds more. Thank you for your patience."

Kael couldn't help but laugh a little beside her, and for some reason, it did ease the tension slightly.

"I can't wait," Adan muttered. "She was all stuttering before. It was strange."

"Wait a minute. Simmons called in not long after we left Capital. He was flickering too," Kael said, frowning. "I thought maybe it was just the connection, but…"

Adan raised his eyebrows.

"Get him on the comm," Ellen barked. "Now."

Adan attacked the console, viciously entering commands.

A line crackled as some sound came through, but no video. Just black.

Adan turned to look at her, and he didn't have to say a thing. Just the look in his eyes told her he couldn't get through.

"Simmons?" Ellen stepped toward the view screen, as if that mattered. "Try something else. Anything!"

"I—" Adan started. "Hold on."

The silence in the room was heavy.

"Here's an open line," Adan said. "But there's no one there. Nothing."

"Doug?" she said, more loudly now.

"See if you can get through another way. Text. Anything. Xi, when you're available, can you help?"

"Patron Simmons cannot be reached," said the computer voice.

"Why not? Is there a problem with the connection?"

"Connection to Redacted Location is possible."

"How far? To the planet? To the town?"

"Planet is reachable. One receiver in the Simmons compound on Redacted Location continues to be functional."

She frowned. "What does that mean? How many receivers should the compound have?"

"Thirty-eight. One hundred and two for the entire island."

She froze. "Adan, set a course for—" She stopped short. The course was already set. "We have to help him. Xi, can you reveal the location of the Simmons compound to us?"

"These events meet requirements set for location disclosure at your request."

"I request it."

"The location is Island 83 on Tetra VII. Further details I can input into the flight plan."

Ellen swore under her breath. She had known where he was. Merith had fragging known.

"I already have the beginnings of a flight plan in," said Adan, a little apologetically.

Kentt spoke up now. "I believe she gained access to this information somehow during the time you were on Capital. This appears to have been her first chance to use it. I also believe that getting to this Simmons was her primary goal."

"Did you see who she was working for?" Ellen demanded. Merith had been on board for two whole years. It had to be someone other than Arakovic. Didn't it?

Kentt shook her head. "I didn't have much time beyond noticing her moving into action, locating Jenny, and coming here to stop her."

Ellen rested a hand on Adan's shoulder. "Well, it's a good thing you acted when you did." Her gaze drifted back to Merith on the floor, then the view screen, where a rotating model of another island planet glowed, spinning in the air. She glanced at Kael. "Guess we aren't going to Faros after all."

He shrugged. "I'd much rather find out where Doug gets his shirts anyway."

She permitted herself a small smile.

A flurry of footsteps rushed up outside, making her tense for a fight. But it was Nova and Zhia who burst across the threshold, Mo on their heels. Nova's eyes caught first on Jenny. "Mary Mother of God, what happened to you? Your hair! Did you win the lottery or something? I know they say Capital changes people but—" She stopped short as Zhia pointed at the floor. And the blood. Nova's muttering continued, consisting mostly of Spanish curse words. Zhia and Mo looked to Ellen. Another gasp came from the hallway, and she caught a glimpse of Vivaan out there. Great.

Ellen cleared her throat. "People, we have a problem. Several, actually. Merith attempted to disable Xi and hijack the ship. With the help of our new passenger, Jenny was able to thwart her, but we haven't been able to reach Patron Simmons. He appeared to be her target. So— we're going to help."

"Reboot complete. My sincerest apologies, Commander and crew." Xi sounded... mortified. "I will do my best to gather information on Patron Simmons."

"Doug," corrected Ellen weakly.

"My apologies. Some preferences may have been reset to defaults."

"We forgive you, Xi," Kael murmured.

She nodded. "And call me Ellen."

AFTERWORD

Thank you so much for reading! I hope you enjoyed.

This is the closest thing to a cliffhanger ending I have ever tried, and I sincerely hope it was a fun one.

If you'd like to be notified when new books come out, sign up for my mailing list on my website at www.rkthorne.com/get-updates/. I share upcoming book news and occasional free bonuses, like maps, short stories, and character interviews, rarely more than once a month. If that. I'm kinda slow about it. Sloth-like even.

If you're feeling froggy, consider leaving a review online at your retailer of choice. Reviews help readers discover their next favorite book—and avoid ones that aren't for them! Whether it's five stars or one, I truly love hearing from readers and appreciate your honest feedback.

ABOUT THE AUTHOR

R. K. Thorne is an independent science fiction and fantasy author whose addiction to notebooks, role-playing games, coffee, and red wine have resulted in this book.

She has read speculative fiction since before she was probably much too young to be doing so and encourages you to do the same.

She lives in the green hills of Pennsylvania with her family and two gray cats that may or may not pull her chariot in their spare time.

For more information:
rkthorne.com

facebook.com/ThorneBooks
twitter.com/rk_thorne
instagram.com/rk_thorne

ALSO BY R. K. THORNE

The Enslaved Chronicles

A warrior prince. An enslaved mage forced to kidnap him. An high fantasy tale of love, adventure, and sacrifice.

Mage Slave

Mage Strike

Star Mage

Audacity Saga

A shadowy organization, an elite all-female crew, a merc with a mission he couldn't refuse, and some scientists with some seriously questionable ethics. Fun science fiction adventure.

The Empress Capsule

Capital Games

Child of Wrath (Forthcoming)

Untitled Book 4 (Forthcoming)

Deserter: An Audacity Prequel

Legends of the Clanblades Series

A sweeping epic fantasy of sword, dragon, and soul

Dagger of Bone

Blade of the Moon (Forthcoming)

Find them all at www.rkthorne.com.

www.ingramcontent.com/pod-product-compliance
Lightning Source LLC
Chambersburg PA
CBHW031150120726
47905CB00006B/1886